PB

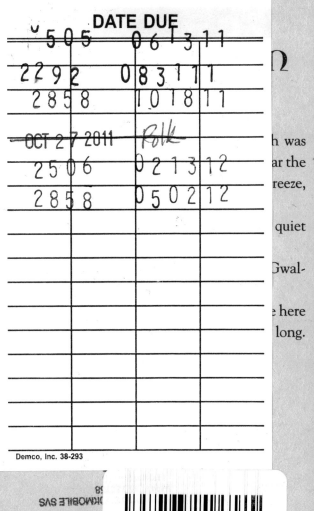

Ω

h was
ar the
reeze,

quiet

Gwal-

e here
long.

Also from Robert Doherty

AVAILABLE FROM DELL

AREA 51

LEGEND

Robert Doherty

A DELL BOOK

AREA 51: LEGEND
A Dell Book / April 2004

Published by
Bantam Dell
A Division of Random House, Inc.
New York, New York

Dell is a registered trademark of Random House, Inc., and the colophon
is a trademark of Random House, Inc.

ISBN 978-0-440-23725-9

Manufactured in the United States of America
Published simultaneously in Canada

OPM   10   9   8   7   6   5   4   3

AREA 51

LEGEND

I

The king was dying, and with him the promise of a new age. That was clear to the few surviving knights who huddled around his bloodied body in the middle of the dismal swamp in which they had been fighting Mordred's forces. They had all known much battle over the past years and they knew a fatal wound when they saw it. They all also knew that no one other than Arthur was capable of leading England out of the darkness it had known for as long as any could remember. The brief hope of peace and prosperity for the land was leaking into the swamp with the king's blood.

Percival stood astride Arthur's body, bloody sword gripped in hand, glaring wildly about. Percival was the most faithful of those who had sat at the Round Table, and he had sworn to give his life for his king. Both the oath and his sword were useless now. They needed help of another kind altogether.

"Where is Merlin?" he cried out.

If anyone could save the king, it would be the sorcerer, but none had seen him today. Indeed, searching for the sorcerer—and the wondrous Grail he was rumored to have—was the reason the king's army was here. As it was also the reason the usurper Mordred's forces were here. The battle had begun this morning and the fighting had been brutal and fierce throughout the grim day.

It was a dark day, hung with dank clouds that rumbled with thunder, muting the moans and screams of the wounded. Shortly after the battle had been joined, a mist had begun to creep through the swamp that encompassed the battlefield. Arthur's men could still hear the sporadic sound of metal on metal all around as the battle sputtered on.

They were safe for the moment, although none knew how the battle was going. Immediately after the king was wounded, they had pulled Arthur back from the front line, through the knee-deep swamp, to this small, dry rise. The growth in the swamp, combined with the mist, was too thick to see more than twenty feet in any direction. For all they knew, their side was losing, although Gawain had struck Mordred a grievous blow before going down.

A cloaked figure loomed out the mist.

"Hold, witch," Percival ordered, lifting his weary sword arm.

The woman grew as still as the dead trees around them. She pulled back the hood of her long black cloak, revealing a pale face, hollowed by fatigue. Her hair was dark and cropped short, shot with a streak of gray that ran from above her right eye straight back. She held her hands up in a gesture of peace, but Percival did not lower the sword.

"Let me help him," the woman said.

"Morgana." Percival said the name as a curse. "You are not to be trusted."

Morgana looked about. "Where is Sir Gawain?"

"Mordred slew him when he tried to rescue the king."

Morgana took a step back as if the words were a blow to her chest. "Where does he lie?"

Percival nodded toward the sound of battle. "Out there, somewhere. Among the others. Many have died today because of you and Merlin."

"You don't know what you're talking about," Morgana said as she moved toward the king.

"Stay, witch."

"He will die if you do not let me help him," Morgana said.

Percival glanced down. Arthur's eyes were open and he nodded ever so slightly. Percival yielded to the command, stepping back.

Morgana strode up onto the hillock and knelt next to the stricken king. Her hands went to the rips in his armor, where blood trickled forth. She ripped strips from the bottom of her cloak and stuffed them in the holes, a crude but relatively effective stopgap measure.

"Why do you help me?" Arthur whispered in a voice only she could hear.

"I want you to live until your knights take you to Avalon. There you will give the sword to the Watcher who is there now. Restore the balance."

Arthur weakly shook his head. "I cannot do that."

"If you don't, I will let you die here and take the sword myself. You came here to restore the truce. Let the Watchers take the sword back. They will restore the balance for you."

"Who are you?" Arthur demanded. "You have worked both sides of this conflict, betraying me and also betraying Mordred. Whom do you serve?"

"Humans."

Arthur said nothing for several seconds, digesting the implications of that answer. "You're a Watcher?"

"I'm more than a Watcher," Morgana replied. "Give the sword to the Watcher of Avalon."

Arthur's eyelids fluttered, his mind on the edge of unconsciousness. "Who are you?" he asked again weakly.

Morgana didn't answer and the eyes slid shut. She shoved the last piece of cloth into the final wound, staunching the seepage of blood. "This will help," she said. She looked up at Percival. "Take him to Avalon."

Percival's eyes widened. "The island is said to be haunted."

"Take him there," Morgana said. "It is your only hope for him." She turned in the direction that Gawain had been said to lie.

"Where do you go?" Percival demanded.

"To make sure Mordred is finished."

As soon as Morgana was gone into the dark mist, Percival issued orders for four other knights to lift the stricken king. As they did so, Percival took the beautiful sword that had lain across the king's chest. Excalibur. The thing that had started all this just a few years earlier. Despite battle, its edges were unmarked and keen. The pommel was un-adorned, unlike many other great swords, but there was no doubting the sense of power and strength emanating from the weapon. Percival wrapped it in his cloak and held it tight as they moved off to the north, heading toward the legendary island of Avalon.

Morgana felt the pull of duty warring with the draw of love as she moved toward the diminishing sound of the fighting. If what Percival said was true—and there was no reason to disbelieve him, as Percival was the noblest and most honest of the knights who had sat at the Round Table—then there was no rush to get to Gawain. Still, her eyes darted about in the mist, looking for his body as she walked toward the clash of metal and men locked in mortal combat.

A figure staggered out of the mist. A knight, his hands to his visor, blood spewing through the metal gap. He had taken a blow through the visor slit, and was now wandering blindly, moaning in pain. He would shortly be food for carrion. Soon she passed other wounded men limping and crawling their way back the way they had come. None she passed were unmarked, a testament to the ferocity of the fighting. Here and there she recognized a knight. Once, to her left, she saw a handful of peasants ripping armor off a prone figure, vultures stripping the dead of anything valuable.

Soon she began to find more bodies. They were grouped in clusters, indicating spots where the lines had met. Some had died arm in arm with their foes, the last embrace of combat.

Morgana paused and took a deep breath. Something was different. She cocked her head and listened. There was no longer any sound of fighting. The battle was over, though who had won, she suspected not even the survivors knew yet. She heard muffled voices somewhere ahead and set off in that direction. The land began to rise and the swamp gave way to grassland. She passed a few tents and knew she was entering Mordred's camp. He had set up on the west side of the swamp, Arthur's army on the east. And somewhere in that swamp, among the dead trees and rotting vegetation, was Merlin's lair, which both armies had been seeking in their quest to find the Grail.

Morgana spotted several standing knights, blue sashes tied around their upper right arms, indicating they were part of Mordred's army. Encased inside armor suits, many made by the same metalsmiths who worked for pay, not loyalty, it was hard in combat to tell friend and foe apart, so each army had taken to wearing their leader's colors: Mordred's blue and Arthur's royal red. She noted that two of them had eagle plumes on the top of their helmets indicating they were part of Mordred's elite guard—Guides. She would have to watch those two in particular. The knights were hovering over a prone figure in a once-shining suit of armor. Etched into the

metal on the chest was an intricate design of flying dragons
that no armorer in England was capable of doing.

Mordred.

Morgana knew that armor well. She walked into the camp
as if she belonged. Without a word the knights gave way, allowing her to approach the usurper.

"Move back," she ordered.

They did as she commanded, except for the two Guides,
who could not move away from the man they were programmed to defend. They had no free will, their minds suborned by the machinery of the creature who lay at their feet.

Morgana knelt next to Mordred. The Guides had swords
raised, ready to strike her down if she made any threatening
move. Like Arthur, Mordred had serious wounds. She lifted
his visor and stared into dark eyes that glittered with malice.

"Mordred."

He nodded. "Morgana."

"Where is the Grail?"

His eyes shifted toward his tent, a place she also knew. "It
is mine. You don't know what it is."

"I do know what it is," Morgana said.

"You know legends and myth."

"I know the reality."

Despite his pain, a frown creased Mordred's face. "How
could that be?"

Morgana did not reply.

"Without the stones—the urim and thummin," Mordred
continued, "the Grail is worthless."

"I think not," Morgana said. "Or else why would you be
here?"

To that Mordred had no answer.

"Morgana is not my real name."

Mordred frowned once more.

She leaned closer, until her face was just above his. "My

real name is Donnchadh. I was born on a world far from here. A world where those whom you serve ruled just like they rule here. But we—humans—defeated them. I came here to help these humans defeat you and those you serve also." She glared at him. "Mordred, better known as Aspasia's Shadow."

With that, she slid the dagger she had hidden up the sleeve of her cloak into the opening of his visor, jerking the blade across his neck. A spout of arterial blood covered her arm, but she was already moving, swinging the blade around to block the blow from one of the Guides, while her other hand searched for something around Mordred's neck. Her fingers, wet with blood, could not grasp it, then she was forced to stand and defend herself against one of the Guides as the other futilely tried to stem the loss of blood from its master.

Morgana had been trained by experts in the martial arts. She stepped inside the Guide's next thrust and slammed the point of her dagger into his armpit, where there was only leather, no armor. The blade went deep and she levered up on the handle, ripping through muscle until the tip punctured its heart. The Guide collapsed at her feet.

She stepped toward Mordred's body to finish the job and take the small metal figure, the *ka*, which hung around Mordred's neck, but the second Guide was on his feet, weapon ready, shouting for help. The other knights, humans who had been fooled into following what they thought was a man, came rushing in.

Morgana knew there was no hope of getting to the body and retrieving the *ka*. Not with Gawain dead. If she was killed here, it would be over. She had to find her lover's body. But first she had to get the Grail. She darted past one of the cumbersome knights, into Mordred's tent. An object covered by a white cloth sat on a rough field table. As soon as she grabbed it she knew it was the Grail. Tucking it under one arm, she slashed at the back of the tent with her dagger even as knights poured in the front. Slipping through the opening she had created, she ran off into the swamp, easily outdistancing the knights in their cumbersome armor.

The rays of the setting sun tried to penetrate the mist covering the swamp, creating an ethereal glow that illuminated Morgana as she walked, her cloak muddy and torn from her long afternoon of wandering. She held the Grail, still covered with the white cloth, in one hand, her dagger at the ready in the other.

The place smelled of decay and death. She had already stumbled across hundreds of bodies, but not Gawain's. She'd also discovered wounded from both sides. Unable to help them, she'd shown them the mercy of the blade. Anything was better than dying slowly in this forsaken place.

She heard splashing to her left front and turned in that direction. Someone—more than one—was moving. As she got closer to the sound she could discern three figures dressed in long black cloaks slowly making their way through the swamp.

"Merlin," Morgana called out.

The figures froze, and one, the man in the lead, turned to her. "Walking among the dead, Morgana?"

"The dead you are responsible for," Morgana said as she came closer to the wizard. He had a long white beard and his face was lined with worry.

"I tried to do the right—" Merlin began, but Morgana held up her hand. There was such power in the gesture that he fell silent.

"You know so little, supposed wizard. Ignorant people should not act."

To that Merlin had no reply.

"Have you seen Gawain?" Morgana asked.

Merlin pointed to his left. "There are numerous bodies in a group about fifty meters that way. Many of Arthur's court and of Mordred's followers. It must have been where the center of the two armies met. Gawain and many other knights lie there. But where is Arthur? And Mordred? We did not find them among the bodies."

Morgana looked past Merlin at the two men with him. They all had an emblem around their necks, a medallion with an open eye inside a pyramid. Watchers. Who had broken their vow and done more than watch.

"Are you just concerned with them?" Morgana asked.

"The Grail and the sword," Merlin acknowledged with a glance at the cloth-covered object in her hand. "Where are they?"

"Arthur had Excalibur. Percival takes him to Avalon."

"And the Grail?"

Morgana lifted the cloth from the object in her right hand. She held a golden hourglass figure, eighteen inches high by eight wide at each end. The center, where she had her hand, was an inch wide.

For millennia it had been an object of legend and myth among humans around the world. One could see how it might be confused with a cup, but both ends were solid. The surface was translucent, emitting a slight golden glow. The Watchers with Merlin went to one knee, heads bowed, awed by the object.

"I feared it was lost to Mordred," Merlin said. "Guides attacked us last night and took it."

"It almost was lost." Morgana held her other hand over one of the flat tops. Her skin tingled. She touched the flat golden surface and held it there. The surface irised open, revealing a six-inch-wide opening. Merlin came forward while the others remained in place.

"I feared to do that," he said. "I do not know how it works."

"It does not work by itself," Morgana said. Four inches inside was a small, round depression, an inch and a half in diameter. "A stone is placed in each of these. One on each side."

"And then?" Merlin was mesmerized.

"And then it does as promised," Morgana said. "Eternal life."

"And the stones that make it complete?"

"They are far from here." She removed her hand and the top shut. "I had them once. Long ago and a long way from here." She was lost in memories for a moment before returning abruptly to the present. "You cannot get to the stones. And the Grail is dangerous. As is the sword. As you should finally know by now. They are beyond you and all other humans right now. You must take them and hide them far away."

"They are powerful—" Merlin began, but she cut him off.

"Look around. This is what happens when you meddle in things you are not prepared to handle. Death." She stared at Merlin, her dark eyes boring into his. "You have violated your oath as a Watcher. The oath that was made during the First Gathering on Avalon and has been passed down through the generations."

"What do you know of Watcher oaths?" Merlin demanded.

Morgana lowered her voice so only he could hear. "I know more than you or any other Watcher. I was there for the First Gathering. I wrote the oath."

"That cannot be," Merlin protested. "That was thousands of—"

"Over ten thousand years ago," Morgana finished for him. "I have walked this planet longer than that. I stood in the shadow of the great spire of the temple of Atlantis. I saw Atlantis destroyed during the Great Civil War among the Airlia Gods. I came here to England and organized the rebellious high priests who became the first Watchers. I was there when the first stone was raised at Stonehenge. I have seen things of which you have no concept. I have fought these creatures, the Airlia, and their minions for all that time. And Gawain, whom you know, was there with me through all that.

"So I tell you, Merlin the Watcher, you must do as I order. You will take the Grail and Excalibur. You will travel to the roof of the world and hide them there. So that someday men can go there and claim them, but only when the time is right. When we are prepared to do battle with those who rule us from the shadows."

"When will that be?" Merlin asked.

Morgana sighed. "A long, very long, time, I fear. Beyond the scope of your mortal life surely." She reached inside her cloak and pulled out a chain. On it were two things. One was a small figure looking like two arms raised in prayer. The other was a medallion similar to the ones Merlin and the others wore, except hers was golden, like the Grail. "Do you recognize this?"

"I have read of it," Merlin whispered, still trying to accept what she had told him. "It is the symbol of the head of our order. It is written that it disappeared a long time ago."

"It did not disappear," Morgana said. "I disappeared with it."

"I do not understand this," Merlin whispered.

"That is why you must do as I order. I founded the Watchers long ago and I still rule. I have the symbol."

"Why do you not keep the Grail then?" Merlin asked.

"Because it is too tempting to me also," Morgana said.

Merlin lowered his head and stood silent for a long time.

"You have only to look around you to see what happens when you meddle with things," Morgana said. "Arthur is not who you think he is. Neither is Mordred. They are not men."

"Arthur—" Merlin began, but fell silent, as the many strange things he had seen in the past decade fell into place.

"It is not time," Morgana said. "You failed and many have died because of it. The burden is on you now to make things right. Or as right as they can be now."

Merlin slowly nodded. "I will do as you say."

Morgana held out the Grail. "Take it. Then go to Avalon and recover Excalibur. It will be in the possession of the Watcher who lives there, Brynn." She reached into her cloak and pulled out a sheet of leather on which a map had been drawn. "This is where you must go." She pointed.

Merlin tried to grasp the scale.

Morgana helped him by pointing to an island in the upper left hand corner. "This is England." The destination she had indicated was far to the right and down.

"No one has ever gone that far," Merlin protested.

"I have. And you will. It will be a noble quest, worthy of Arthur's wizard." Morgana handed the parchment to him and walked away, heading in the direction he had pointed to earlier.

She finally found the center of the battle. The corpses were piled three deep in places along a sandbar that rose out of the swamp. The sand was bleached red from blood. The smell of death was strong. The bodies had not had time to begin to decay but the odor of fresh blood and voided bowels was almost overwhelming. Morgana had seen—and dealt—much death in her long life but it had not hardened her heart.

She carefully stepped among the bodies, searching with both hope and trepidation.

She found Gawain where she had suspected he would be. In the very middle of what must have been a terrible fight.

He was floating lifeless in the shallow water. Morgana grabbed one of his arms and with great effort pulled him clear of the other bodies. She could see he had been wounded at least a dozen times. His eyes were blank, staring with a dead gaze past her shoulder at nothing. Her hand began to tremble as she unbuckled his breastplate. An edged weapon had obviously hit Gawain horizontally just above the sternum, cutting through the metal, into the flesh beneath.

She lifted the front half of the upper body armor off Gawain and cried out in anguish as she saw that his *ka* had taken the blow as well. The front part of the arms had been sliced cleanly off. It was destroyed.

After so long, to have it end like this. In a stinking swamp, among bloody bodies. In a war that resolved nothing, a war caused by a fool who had not known what he was doing. After over ten thousand years. She could not believe it. Could not accept it. Morgana lifted her head up to the darkening sky as if she could see through the clouds and into space, across the light-years, to the very beginning, to the day when it should have ended, but had actually begun for both of them. She howled out her anguish like a stricken animal.

II

It was the fourth planet from the star, nestled in that narrow orbit that allowed human life to flourish. It had been chosen for that reason. Once its land surface had been green and vibrant but now most of the ground had been blasted by the weapons of war. Blackened and broken terrain covered most of the four continents and once-proud cities were battered graveyards. Even the oceans had not escaped unscathed—large areas of the blue seas were tainted black and lifeless sea creatures floated on the surface. Where once a large island had held the Gods' temple and city, there was only black water, floating debris, and bodies.

The war—actually a revolt—was all but over. In only one place was there still fighting. A walled compound, a mile and a half long by half a mile wide, surrounded a totally flat space. Inside the twenty-foot-high wall, set on a cradle of black metal, was the Airlia mothership, a cigar-shaped craft over a mile long and a quarter mile wide in the center. Its outer hull was also of black metal, but the skin was scarred and blistered from heavy weapons fire and blasts that had struck it.

Outside of the wall came the people. Hundreds of thousands of humans, the survivors of a worldwide army that had once numbered in the billions, surged forward. In the lead were the select few, teams of God-killers armed with the only weapons that could permanently kill their Airlia enemy.

Donnchadh was just behind the front wave of God-killers as they blew holes in the tall black wall that surrounded the landing field. She was a scientist, not a God-killer, but knew she needed to be near the front. They would need to move swiftly if they were to grasp success from the jaws of victory.

The first man through the nearest breach was hit with a golden bolt and knocked backward, dead. As was the second man. The third edged the muzzle of his weapon into the breach and fired blindly for several seconds on full automatic. The God-killers worked in teams of two—one man with an automatic weapon, the other with a sword. A strange, but necessary, combination in order to fight the Airlia.

Her name—Donnchadh—meant eldest daughter of Donn, who had been one of the first rebel leaders. He'd died at the hands of the human high priests who served their alien overlords, crucified on the wooden X, pinned to it by straps of wet leather that dried and squeezed the life out of him over the course of many hours. She'd watched him die over two years ago, as had thousands of other herded by the high priests and Guides who served the Airlia into the open plain in front of the very wall they had just blasted a hole in. The high priests and Guides were all dead now. There was just this last pocket of Airlia to kill and they would be free of the alien influence.

The next pair of God-killers threw themselves through the breach. The firing must have worked as there were no more golden bolts. Donnchadh scrambled after them. The man with the rifle was shooting as he leapt over the body of the alien who had been firing the golden bolts from a long spear clutched in its hands.

The creature was taller than a human, almost seven feet from the top of its head to the soles of its feet. Red hair framed a thin face with ears that had long lobes that stretched almost to its shoulders. The eyes were not human, but catlike and red. The hands that gripped the spear had six long, pale fingers.

Blood was still seeping out of the wounds in the alien's chest and, from experience, Donnchadh knew they had about five minutes before the creature came back to life and the wounds healed. The second God-killer with the sword was there to ensure that didn't happen. He swung the weapon with an experienced hand and sliced through the alien's neck, severing head from body. It was not simply that the head had been removed that prevented the creature from coming back to life. There was something on the edge of the sword, stolen from an Airlia armory, that cauterized the wound and prevented the cells from regenerating as they would from the wound caused by a human-made weapon.

Looking left and right, Donnchadh could see that there were other holes blown in the wall, and more God-killer teams were pouring through them. The prize of the mothership was directly ahead.

The man with the rifle was hit by a golden bolt from an Airlia standing near one of the cradle's legs. He was knocked backward and went down hard. Donnchadh darted forward and scooped up the rifle. She put the stock to her shoulder and fired as she'd been trained. The recoil of the gun felt satisfying, almost as much as watching the Airlia stagger as the rounds tore into its flesh.

The aliens were trapped. The mothership could not take off because the humans had already taken over the Master Guardian and isolated the ship's controls. They had destroyed the mothership's warships, the Talons, one by one over the course of the Revolution. It had cost billions of lives to get to this point. The planet was ravaged, the environment destroyed. Better that than slavery. But Donnchadh believed they had once last chance to make things right, to save her people.

Donnchadh reached the cradle leg and pressed her body tight against the metal. The arc was ten feet wide and deep, towering overhead to the bottom of the starship. The God-killer with the sword met her there, pausing to finish off the alien she had shot. He was a large man, solidly built, with long black hair that hung down almost to his shoulders. His face was like a block of granite, marred only by the fracture of a scar that ran from the corner of his right eye down to his chin.

"Gwalcmai," he said, introducing himself as he searched the metal with his free hand.

She was doing the same. "Donnchadh." She found an indentation. "Here." She grabbed the medallion around her neck and pressed it against the spot. The outline of a door appeared, eight feet high by four wide. It slid open and an elevator beckoned.

"Wait for help," Gwalcmai advised.

Donnchadh shook her head. "We cannot wait. They may destroy the ship. If it explodes, it will take the continent with it. We have to find out the truth. And the Grail should be inside." She went into the elevator. Gwalcmai followed without hesitation. The door slid shut and they began to move up the massive strut.

"Too slow," Donnchadh muttered.

"Be ready." Gwalcmai nodded toward the door.

They came to a halt. Gwalcmai cursed as the wall behind them opened, catching them by surprise. Both whirled about to face an empty corridor. They edged forward cautiously. The corridor curved slightly to the left and they could only see about fifty feet.

Donnchadh kept the stock of the rifle tight against her shoulder as they moved ahead. The corridor straightened out and they both paused. The corridor extended as far as they could see, apparently running the entire length of the mothership. There was nothing moving. They could also see cross corridors intersecting at regular intervals.

Having been at the lead of a massive army, the two suddenly felt quite isolated. Donnchadh reached into her shirt and pulled out a rolled-up piece of paper. Gwalcmai watched the move, then hurriedly shifted his gaze when she noted him watching. To her surprise, after so much battling and death, she found herself blushing. She brushed away the feeling quickly.

"One of your kind died getting this information," she said as she unrolled it.

"Many of my kind have died," Gwalcmai said as he knelt next to her. There were not many God-killers left, so many having been killed in the line of duty. Fighting at the forefront of every attack, as they did, most God-Killers did not expect to live long lives. Either Gwalcmai was very good at what he did or very lucky; most likely both, in order to be alive.

"The engines are centrally located and below," Donnchadh said as she ran her finger along the map they had captured from an Airlia outpost. "The control room forward."

Both knew that any surviving Airlia would set some sort of self-destruct, taking out not only the ship but all the humans around it.

"Since we cut off the control room," Gwalcmai said, "any destruct would have to be done manually."

Donnchadh stood. "The engine room."

They ran forward, both slightly hunched over, expecting to be ambushed from one of the side corridors that in their haste they could not take the time to clear. Donnchadh was counting the passageways, trying to stay oriented.

She skidded to a halt and pointed right. "Here." A short corridor came to a dead end.

"Where—" Gwalcmai began as they moved forward, but he cut off whatever else he was going to say as the section of floor beneath them suddenly began to descend.

Unlike their trip up the strut, this elevator moved swiftly, straight down into the bowels of the ship. Black walls on all four sides sped past. Without a word the two went back-to-back in the center of the platform. Through her sweat-soaked combat uniform Donnchadh could feel the heat of Gwalcmai's body. A drop of sweat from a strand of his long hair dripped onto her neck.

Their knees flexed as the platform suddenly decelerated. The surrounding walls disappeared as they entered a large open area. The curving bottom of the ship was below them. The chamber was almost a half mile long by a third wide, the bottom slice of the ship. All along the inner edge of the hull running the length of the chamber were long machines—the engines, they had to assume. The surfaces of the machines were striated, composed of long metal strings that had been twisted together.

"There." Even as she said it, Donnchadh aimed the rifle.

About a hundred meters in front of her, an Airlia stood atop one of the strands, a hatch open in front of it. Donnchadh fired a burst, but her aim was low, the rounds ricocheting off the metal. The creature acted as if nothing had happened, continuing to do whatever it was focused on. Donnchadh pulled the trigger again, but the weapon was empty. In her haste she had forgotten to take extra ammunition from the body.

Gwalcmai didn't hesitate, rushing past her toward the Airlia. Donnchadh followed, tossing aside the useless weapon and drawing the short black dagger with which she had originally been armed. A ladder was built into the side of the engine strand about halfway between them and the creature and Gwalcmai bounded up it, Donnchadh right behind. Once on top, they had to leap from strand to strand.

The Airlia glanced up and saw them coming. It was not dressed like one of the Airlia soldiers. It wore a white linen robe over which there was a sleeveless shirt of blue and on top of that a long cloak of many colors. The shoulders of the cloak were fastened with what appeared to be glittering stones. Over it was a breastplate covered with more precious stones. On the creature's head was a crown consisting of three bands.

A gasp escaped Donnchadh's lips as the Airlia lifted up a chalice-shaped golden object. "The Grail," she cried out.

Gwalcmai needed no further urging. Every human on the planet knew it was their only hope. The Airlia's lips were moving as if it were saying some sort of prayer. It set the Grail down on the metal in front of it and reached into the shoulders of the breastplate, removing two glowing stones.

Donnchadh and Gwalcmai were now within twenty meters of the creature. They could clearly see one end of the Grail iris open and the creature place a stone inside. It then flipped the Grail over and did the same on the other side.

Gwalcmai lifted his sword high as he leapt from the last strand to the one on which the Airlia stood. The alien was now holding the Grail out over the open hatch. Gwalcmai swung the sword even as he was still airborne, the blade horizontal, slicing through the Airlia's neck. As the head toppled from the body, Donnchadh dived low from the last strand, hands outstretched, reaching for the Grail.

Even in the moment of final death, the Airlia's body did its duty. Its fingers separated, letting go of the Grail. Donnchadh was a fraction of a second too late as the golden object tumbled down into the open hatch. She landed hard, almost falling into the opening herself.

She looked down. There was a pulsing stream of golden power about five meters below. She watched with wide eyes as the Grail hit the stream. There was a flash and the entire ship shook for several moments.

The Grail was gone.

The skin on Donnchadh's face was red and blistered from the surge in power she had witnessed when the Grail was destroyed. She was in the control room of the mothership, the room filled with other God-killers and scientists. The sense of victory in killing the last of the Airlia was muted by the loss of the Grail, and many a glance was directed at her, accompanied by muttered words.

"It was my fault," Gwalcmai said, loud enough to be heard not only by Donnchadh but by most in the control room. "I should not have struck as quickly."

"If you had not, it would have dropped it anyway," Donnchadh said. "I was too late in—"

A new voice cut him off. "It was no one's fault."

A wheelchair-bound woman in a black robe tinged with silver was wheeled into the control room. Everyone inclined their heads toward her as a sign of respect. Her name was Enan and she was the leader of the humans. Her legs and arms were gone, amputated many years ago. She had survived the X-cross and leather bands long enough to be rescued after the Airlia who had put her there thought she was dead and left her body to be picked apart by scavenger birds. Rebels had sneaked up to the cross just after dark and cut her loose. Her limbs, broken and dead from lack of blood, had been removed by a surgeon, and she'd been nursed back to health.

Enan looked slowly back and forth, taking in everyone in the room. "We have done what we did not think we could do—we've defeated the Airlia. We are free." With the slightest inclination of her head she indicated for the young woman who pushed her wheelchair to move her to the front of the room. "I have just come from science headquarters. They've finally managed to access the history banks of the Master Guardian."

The room went silent as they waited to hear the truth. Donnchadh felt both fear and anticipation. No one knew when the Airlia had come to this planet and taken over—that was lost in the fog beyond recorded human history. Some said the Airlia had always been here, but Donnchadh and the other scientists did not believe that—the small numbers, the single mothership, and other factors pointed to an occupying force, although *why* the Airlia had occupied their planet was also a mystery.

Enan closed her eyes and her head drooped slightly as if bearing some terrible weight. With great effort she opened her eyes and lifted her head. "We are not native to this planet as we always thought we were, and the Airlia are not alien invaders who conquered our species long ago in the past."

A long silence followed this statement, which Enan broke with another startling piece of information. "The Airlia brought us here with them."

Without even thinking about it, Donnchadh found her hand reaching out and taking Gwalcmai's as they listened. She was stunned, having never considered the possibility that humans were not native to this planet.

"We always knew that we had certain genetic similarities to the Airlia, given that we breathe the same air and can eat the same food and even appear to be very similar. We thought that was what brought them to this planet and to us. But it is not so. We are similar because we are genetic cousins to them, developed by them. The first humans were grown by the Airlia through manipulation of their own genetic mapping."

"Why?" the word escaped someone's lips.

Enan nodded. "That is the key question and the answer is not a good one. The Airlia have been engaged in an interstellar war against another alien species officially called the Swarm and unofficially the Ancient Enemy. This war has been going on for such a long time that those of our scientists who accessed these data from the Master Guardian could not quantify it. Spread over galaxies, this war seems to have been going on forever as far as we are concerned. At the very least beyond the scope of what we can imagine.

"We are part of a long-range Airlia plan to take part in this war. We were designed to be what we became, rather ironic in a way—soldiers. Except we were supposed to be used against the Swarm, not revolt against the Airlia. When the time came that they needed us, they would have given that generation access to the Grail so we could be better soldiers. Until that time, they kept us mortal, with short life spans. They taught us to worship them as Gods while they bred us like cattle."

Enan smile grimly. "Except as everyone in this room knows it did not work as they planned. We became more than cannon fodder to be used by them."

She fell silent, allowing everyone to assimilate this startling and unexpected information.

"That is not all," Enan finally said. One of the scientists who had entered the room with her went over to the large curving control console for the mothership. He seemed to know what he was doing and Donnchadh had to assume he'd been in physical contact with the Master Guardian and directly learned information about the mothership from the alien computer. How he had done that without being taken over by the alien computer she didn't know, but Enan had in-dicated it had been done safely.

They'd captured the Master Guardian two days ago, an assault on a massive underground Airlia outpost that had cost the humans over two hundred thousand casu-alties. Donnchadh, along with a large force of God-killers and scientists, had immediately been sent to this location to secure the mothership. Donnchadh had been glad to be de-tached as she had no desire to come into physical contact, which led to mind-to-computer interface, with the alien machine.

The scientist ran his hands over the panel of glowing hexagonal images. They were marked with the Airlia High Runes. The lights in the control room dimmed and the curv-ing display on the front wall flickered, then came alive with images of a star field.

"We are here," the scientist announced. A star glowed red. "According to the Master Guardian we were not the only planet seeded by the Airlia." He touched a control. A dozen stars, spread out across the star map also glowed red. "By the time they came here, they had already seeded twelve other worlds. And we don't know how many were seeded with humans after us."

Donnchadh had assumed that the Airlia Empire stretched over vast reaches of space, but the spectrum displayed before them was staggering.

"We have won the war," Enan continued. "But in doing so we have lost much. We may have lost our planet. I will not lie to you. Our initial environmental assessments are not promising. We do have access to the Master Guardian and the knowledge it holds. The hope is that we will find in there the scientific means to reverse what has happened. How-ever"—Enan let the word float through the control room—"we cannot count on that. And we cannot allow our cousins on these other worlds"—she nodded toward the display—"to suffer our fate or the even worse fate of staying under Airlia control."

Donnchadh's fingers intertwined with Gwalcmai's and squeezed tight.

"Therefore," Enan said, "I propose that we get this mothership in operational condition. We bring in the ruby sphere power source that we captured over a year ago. We select and train as many God-killers and scientists as this ship can hold. Since we destroyed the Talons, we will develop our own spaceships to launch from this mothership to these worlds, with teams on board to help them defeat the Airlia in a safer manner."

FOUR YEARS LATER

It was time.

The battle for the environment had not gone well. Since the end of the Revolution, the amount of arable land had shrunk to an acreage that could not even sustain a population severely reduced by war. Despite this, scarce resources had been allocated to developing spacecraft to be launched from the mothership.

It had not been easy. The design finally settled upon was much smaller than desired, capable of carrying only two people with their supplies, and having a maximum velocity well short of light speed. They built fifteen of the ships before the deteriorating economy could no longer support the project. The ships were loaded into one of the mothership's holds.

Other changes had occurred.

Armed guards patrolled the rebuilt wall around the mothership. On the inside were the chosen. On the outside the rest of the survivors. Donnchadh and Gwalcmai were on the inside, paired together by Enan's council and by their own choice. The result of their personal union was their son, who was on the outside.

They had both seen so much death that despite the condition of the planet the decision to bring forth a life had been mutual. They had held on to the hope that the scientists would find a way to reverse the damage; or that their son would be allowed to come with them when they departed on their mission. Both hopes were now as dry and fruitless as the ash that covered most of the planet.

The parting had been brutal. They left their son in the care of Gwalcmai's sister, having said their final farewells the previous evening, all knowing they would never see each other again.

As the final countdown for liftoff began, the troops were needed to encircle the launch site to keep out protestors who wanted to stop the launch and those not chosen in the last selection, who desperately fought to be on the ship.

Donnchadh and Gwalcmai were in one of the holds, which were full of others like them and supplies.

"Ten years," Donnchadh said.

Gwalcmai knew what she was referring to—the best estimate by the scientists for how much longer the planet they were leaving could sustain life.

"At least it will be ten free years," Gwalcmai said.

Both had argued long and hard with Enan to have their son allowed on board, but the leader had denied them every time. Where they were going and the mission they had been assigned was not amenable to having a child along. Once they deployed from the mothership, there was no room in the smaller spacecraft for a third person. It had been their choice to have a child, knowing their ultimate fate, and Enan had declared they must accept the consequences of that choice.

The cargo door slowly began to close, cutting off their view of the distant crowd held at bay by the soldiers. Tears streamed down Donnchadh's face. She knew no matter what her destiny, she would never see her child again.

She had had many discussions with her husband about the future of both the mission and their planet. He had been blunt and honest, as was his nature, hiding any emotions with a focus on preparing for the upcoming mission and the practical matters that had to be dealt with in doing so. But she noted his chest moving rapidly as the cargo door shut and their world disappeared from sight. He kept his face averted from hers as he reached out and put his arm around her shoulders. All on board had left loved ones behind; they were merely an island of misery amid a sea of pain. Large as the ship was, the five thousand chosen were tightly packed on board along with their supplies. Although only thirty would be deployed in teams of two on the fifteen spacecraft, the rest were put on board to populate any unoccupied planet amenable to human life that the craft found on its journey. In this way the line of their people could go on. If such a planet could be found quickly, perhaps the ship could be sent back to get more.

At the appointed moment, the ship lifted out of its cradle without a sound. It moved upward, accelerating through the planet's polluted atmosphere until it was in the vacuum of space and out of sight of the millions of eyes on the planet's surface who watched it with mixed emotions. It continued to accelerate conventionally away from the planet and the system star's gravitational field.

After two years of travel, the star's field was negligible and the mothership was moving at three-quarters of the speed of light. It was also far enough away that those on board hoped any sign of its passage would not be linked back to their home world and bring the Swarm.

At that point the mothership's interstellar drive was engaged. With a massive surge of power as great as that of a brief supernova, the ship shifted into faster-than-light travel and snapped into warp speed.

III

The scientists had been wrong in one respect. Human life still existed on Donnchadh and Gwalcmai's home planet sixty years after the mothership departed. Not much life, granted, and the existence was miserable, but man still walked the face of the planet. The people left behind had adapted as best they could, tilling the land by hand after the last of the machines had broken down and could not be repaired. They ate plants and animals their ancestors would not have even considered as food. It was the human way to cling to life and the survivors were the hardiest of the race.

Unfortunately, the scientists had been right about something else. The mothership's warp shift had been picked up by a Swarm scout ship on patrol over twenty light-years away from the star system. While the scout ship had immediately turned in the direction of the shift, it also sent out an alert to the nearest Swarm Battle Core.

It took the Swarm some time to find the planet the mothership had come from and for the Battle Core to arrive, but the Swarm were a patient race, who had little concept of time except as an operational variable. On the planet's surface, there were few still alive who had witnessed the mothership's departure. Their descendants cared more about gathering their meager crops than stories of spaceships and aliens. There were fewer than twenty million humans left, down from the peak of over five billion prior to the Revolution. They were crowded into the few places on the planet's surface where food could be grown and the land didn't emit radiation that killed all who walked upon it.

According to the Master Guardian, the Swarm was a strange race, one whose origins were unknown even to the Airlia. There were some scientists among the races who encountered them who speculated that the Swarm was an invented species, designed as weapons, as it showed only a capacity to destroy and no inclination to create. Whatever alien race had invented the Swarm, if this was true, had long since disappeared from the universe, perhaps consumed by its own invention, the inherent danger in any form of bioweapon. And most species that encountered the Swarm no longer existed either. Only the Airlia, so far, had been powerful enough to resist the Swarm.

One of the Swarm consisted of a gray orb, four feet in diameter, with numerous eyes spaced evenly around the body. Anywhere from one to a dozen gray tentacles extended from bulbous knobs on the orb, placed next to the eyes. At maturity a tentacle was over six feet long. The orb had a massive four-hemisphere brain. Each of the tentacles had a rudimentary brain stem and could detach from the orb and operate on their own. The tentacles could infiltrate the bodies of other species and take over the cognitive functioning of intelligent creatures, a most effective means of reconnaissance. The tentacle could gather information hidden inside an alien's body, then exit the body, reattach to the orb, and relay the information learned to the main brain. If a tentacle was lost, the orb could grow a new one from a knob.

It was speculated that the Swarm had some sort of basic telepathic capability among members of its own species when in close proximity to each other. Certainly no other species had ever been able to communicate with it and no Swarm member had ever been taken alive. No prisoner taken by the Swarm had ever been recovered alive, and those who had fought the Swarm learned quickly to kill any of their own that had contact with the Swarm because of the possibility of tentacle infiltration. There was no negotiating with the Swarm—once contact was made, it was war, and a war that could only end in extinction for one side or the other. So far, except for the Airlia, the Swarm had wiped out every race it had encountered.

The Swarm scout landed on the planet and detached tentacles. They learned that this was indeed the place the mothership had departed from. Surprisingly, though, the Swarm also found no trace of the Airlia, its longtime enemy, who it knew had built the mothership. The assumption was made that the Airlia had, for some reason, fled the planet, abandoning these lesser, somewhat intelligent, creatures.

The race that still existed on the planet posed no threat to the Swarm. Indeed, it appeared that none would be left alive in another generation or two. That meant nothing to the Swarm. Over the millennia the Swarm had already wiped out numerous intelligent species in the universe.

Sixty years after the mothership's departure, Donnchadh and Gwalcmai's son was still alive and a grandparent. He had vague memories of his parents and their departure. For years he tried to tell the generations after him the story of the mothership lifting off, but the story became more myth than real as the years went by, and even he began to wonder at his own memories. If it were not for the ruins of a nearby city, he would not believe his own stories. People who could have built such a magnificent place must have been capable of great things.

Once, his grandson, after hearing the story for the umpteenth time, asked a few questions that kept him from telling it again: Why had his parents abandoned him? What was there out there in the stars more important than family?

By the time the Swarm Battle Core arrived in the planet's system, the son was now confined to a chair and daily contemplated taking his own life rather than being a burden to his family. He ate little and his body was emaciated.

As the Core appeared in orbit overhead, it was visible to the naked eye, and for several wild moments, the son wondered if the mothership had returned. Then he realized that whatever was in orbit was far larger than even the massive mothership. In fact, though the humans had no way of knowing it, the eclipse caused by the Core cut off sunlight from half the surface of the planet.

As his family huddled around him in fright at the strange apparition, he remembered vague stories of an Ancient Enemy and a sensation of dread replaced the brief feeling of hope he had had.

The Battle Core in orbit was essentially a self-sustaining mechanical planet and starship; the Swarm had no known home world. There were hundreds of these Battle Cores spread out in the Galaxy. Each was over two thousand miles long, by a thousand wide, and two hundred in depth. Its mass was so great that it generated a discernible gravity field that affected the tides of the planet below. During the war with the Airlia several dozen of these Cores had been destroyed, but each at great cost, and their loss was offset by the annihilation of dozens of Airlia-colonized planets along the frontier.

The Swarm scout ship took off from its hide site on the planet and rendezvoused with the Core to render its report. The intelligent species on the planet below was dying out and offered no military threat. There was only one thing of value on the planet's surface: the people themselves. Report done, the scout was dispatched to the point where the warp drive had been initiated with orders to try to track the path of the mothership.

Smaller capital warships deployed from the Battle Core, moving to equidistant positions around the planet. Each of these "smaller" ships was still twice as large as an Airlia mothership. They were large orbs with eight protruding arms bristling with weapons and launch portals. The capital warships descended into the planet's atmosphere above populated areas until they were at an altitude of ten miles and clearly visible to the frightened humans below.

At this point, the arms on the capital ships spewed out smaller versions of themselves. Over two million drop ships descended on the planet's surface like black rain. They all touched down at the exact same moment. Portals in the craft opened and the Swarm emerged.

Donnchadh and Gwalcmai's son watched as one of the craft landed in the field in front of his house. When he saw what emerged, the shock stilled his heart and he died relatively peacefully. He was one of the fortunate ones.

The Swarm began their harvest and in less than six hours there was no human life left on the planet.

10,800 B.C.: THE SOL SYSTEM

Donnchadh and Gwalcmai, along with the other fourteen teams selected for planet infiltration, had been put into deep sleep shortly after liftoff from their planet. Placed inside the black tubes the Airlia had used for the same purpose, they spent most of the interstellar journey unaware of not only what was happening on their home world but events on board the ship. Members of the crew died, children were born, and new generations grew up in the unique environment of the alien spaceship. The only planets they found capable of supporting human life were ones that the Airlia had seeded and were still occupied by their enemy, so each time they swooped in close to the star system—but not close enough to be detected by Airlia surveillance—and dispatched one of the system craft with a crew of two to infiltrate the planet.

For those inside the mothership it seemed as if only eighty years had passed, but the relative physics of warp speed was such that much more time passed in the universe around them. Still, when Donnchadh and Gwalcmai were brought out of the deep sleep, they awoke to mostly strangers.

Brought to the control room, they learned that the mothership was looping near the edge of a nine-planet system at sub–light speed. It had come out of light speed over four years earlier, decelerating ever since. Prior to this, four teams had already been deployed in other systems. After each deployment, the mothership took four years at sub–light speed to move in and four years to move far enough out before triggering the warp drive, accounting for a great chunk of the relative time lost.

As Donnchadh and Gwalcmai stood in the control room and studied the solar system, unspoken between them was the acceptance that their son had long ago turned to dust. They did not know his fate, but hoped he had lived a relatively happy life. They also learned that Enan had died over thirty years ago and there was a new ruler on board the ship. They felt distant from the younger generation around them, a generation that had not gone through the Revolution and did not even know what it was to walk on the surface of a planet. They had only each other and the interior of the mothership.

They were relieved when they were sealed into their spacecraft, inside one of the mothership's holds, as it approached the edge of the solar system. The interior of the ship, which they had named *Fynbar* after their son, was crowded with weapons, explosives, and technology, most of it appropriated from the Airlia. There was also a considerable amount of food and water crammed into the craft.

The cargo bay door opened and Gwalcmai took the controls. The spacecraft was saucer-shaped, with a bulge in the forward center rising up and two large pods in the rear providing power. The forward bulge was where the two seats for Gwalcmai and Donnchadh were located. The craft's surface was gray. As soon as the *Fynbar* was clear of the mothership, the larger craft turned away from the solar system, heading back toward deep space.

The goal was the third planet, the only one in the system capable of supporting human life. It was a long way from where they had been left off to the planet. The two made most of the journey toward the third planet in silence, each lost in his or her own thoughts. From the Master Guardian they had learned how to cloak their ship from Airlia detection and Gwalcmai turned on the shield as soon as they were inside the orbit of the ninth and outermost planet.

They did not electronically probe the planet as they came in because, while they could passively avoid the Airlia scans, any active scanning on their part would bring them to the attention of the Airlia. They did, however, use passive scanning, which boiled down to using the strongest magnification on their forward imagers to study the planet. They detected seven continents, if one included an icebound mass on the southern pole. As they closed on the planet, they spotted the main Airlia outpost on what appeared to be an artificially constructed series of concentric islands in the middle of one of the oceans. On the very center island, surrounded by six strands of alternating land and water, was a massive golden palace stretching up into the sky—exactly the same as the Airlia command center had been on their own planet. As they closed on the third planet, they passed the fourth, a mostly red one with no apparent water, noting an Airlia outpost on that planet, including an interstellar transmitter array.

As they got closer to the third planet, Donnchadh got up from her seat and began preparing for their arrival. She took two backpacks and filled them with supplies for an initial foray, including a brace of a dozen black daggers that could kill Airlia, small earpieces that would allow them to communicate with each other at distances if separated, and a half dozen explosive charges that she could detonate with a remote the size of a small ball. She also opened a metal case and took out a golden scepter, a foot long and two inches thick. On one end was the head of a lion with ruby red eyes. She slid it into an outside pocket of one of the packs.

Donnchadh took two chains made of fine silver and looped one over her neck, then one over Gwalcmai's. Two items hung from hers: a golden medallion emblazoned with an eye inside a triangle; and a *ka*, a device in the shape of two arms held out in supplication. There was only a *ka* on Gwalcmai's chain.

"Do you have time to update your *ka* before we land?" she asked Gwalcmai. "Or do you want to do it after we land?"

Gwalcmai checked the control console. "Let's do it now. We have a while before we get into orbit."

To the rear of the two command chairs, crammed among the supplies, were two black tubes, Airlia in design. They were the same as deep sleep tubes, with console extensions on one end. A body lay inside each—clones of Donnchadh and Gwalcmai. Set into the rear wall was a vat of green fluid in which another clone of either one of them was already gestating.

On each of the bodies in the tubes was a skullcap from which several dozen wires ran to a main line that fed to a command console between the two tubes. The eyes on each body were open, but betrayed no hint of intelligence or awareness. Donnchadh opened the top of each tube and removed the skullcaps and leads. She took the *ka* from around her neck and slid it into two small holes on the right side of the console. A light glowed orange, indicating it was in place. She then set one of the skullcaps onto Gwalcmai's head as he sat in the pilot's seat, she then tapped out a sequence on the hexagonal display.

Nanoprobes slid out of the skullcap into Gwalcmai's brain. They were so thin, barely five molecules in width, they caused no pain as they pierced flesh and bone. His memories and experiences were quickly uploaded and transferred to the *ka*. It took all of ten seconds, then the nanoprobes withdrew. The skullcap was taken off and put back on the body in the tube. Gwalcmai performed the same procedure on Donnchadh. Both *kas* were now updated to the present.

"Once we land—" Donnchadh began, but halted.

"Yes?" Gwalcmai was unconsciously rubbing his head. Even though he'd felt nothing when the probes went in, there was still a part of him that sensed the violation.

"We will have to keep power settings on the ship at a minimum," Donnchadh said. "The bodies will be maintained, but to keep the memories viable in the main console will require an unacceptable level of power consumption." This was an issue she had thought long and hard about during their flight into the star system.

Gwalcmai digested this, then realized what she was getting at. "So our memories, our selves, will only be in the *kas*?"

"Yes."

"And if we both are killed?" The machine had a fail-safe system. It could be set to inject the memories and personalities of a person into the clone after a certain amount of time. This was the pinnacle of Airlia technology—not only did they have a virus in their blood that allowed them almost immortal life spans and could regenerate their flesh, they also had the ability to regenerate their personality via the machinery. But Donnchadh had just told him that they couldn't afford the power to maintain the fail-safe.

"Then it is over."

"Then let us not both be killed," Gwalcmai said as he took the pilot's seat once more.

Donnchadh took the seat next to him as they closed on the third planet.

"They will have a Grail here," Donnchadh said after a long silence.

"Most likely," Gwalcmai agreed.

"We could do what we failed to do on our planet," she continued. "There will most likely also be a mothership somewhere on the planet."

"That is not our mandate," Gwalcmai reminded her. "Our mission is to try to work to subvert the Airlia so that these humans can eventually defeat them without suffering the losses and damage to the planet our world did."

"Still—" Donnchadh said no more, leaving the issue open.

They came into orbit around the third planet and circled it several times, studying the surface. There was no mistaking the main Airlia base on the planet now—set on an island in the center of an ocean between two continents. The concentric rings of land and water surrounded a magnificent city. On the large hill in the exact center was a golden palace over a mile wide at the base and stretching three thousand feet into the sky. The land in the surrounding rings boasted bountiful crops and many villages. They had seen the exact same type of building on their own planet.

On the other continents there was abundant life—and humans. Their technological level was depressingly low—

some places did not even have the wheel. Of major concern to Gwalcmai was the fact that the most sophisticated weaponry was swords, spears, and bows. While, as a highly trained God-killer, he was an expert with the sword, he still preferred the range of projectile weapons.

"It will be a very long time before they have the weapons necessary to fight the Airlia," Gwalcmai noted as they circled the planet another time.

"We can help accelerate that process as much as possible," Donnchadh said.

Gwalcmai directed the spacecraft to a large island to the northeast of the Airlia-controlled capital. They flew over the southern shore and inland until they were over a large plain of tall grass. The sky above was gray and rainy. A river ran across the plain, cutting deep into the ground.

Gwalcmai brought the spacecraft down, the skin of the craft glowing red from its entry through the atmosphere. He flew back and forth across the plain, searching for just the right spot. Once he found it, he flew north to a mountainous area, halting above a jumble of boulders on the side of a mountain. He activated a cutting beam, shaping three of the boulders into large rectangular shapes. Then he used a tractor beam to lift them off the ground. He flew back to the plain, the three large stones in tow.

Gwalcmai flew back to the river and laid the stones down on the plain about sixty feet away before moving back to the river. He dropped altitude until the *Fynbar* was just above the water, the heat emanating from the spacecraft's skin causing steam to rise from the river. The forward edge of the craft touched the riverbank and the two pod engines whined with exertion as the narrow forward edge of the craft dug into the ground. Ever so slowly, Gwalcmai dug the craft into the dirt and rock, angling down and burying it until only the engine pod and the rear edge of the craft were visible. He rocked it back and forth, widening the cavity it had dug in the earth. As the ship moved, the heat from the spacecraft's surface fused the limestone, creating a cavern. He then backed the spaceship out of the large hole he had created and landed on the plain above.

For several moments, Gwalcmai and Donnchadh sat still in their command chairs. They wore black jumpsuits, marked only by the insignia of their respective units from the Revolution sewn onto the left chest.

"Shall we?" Gwalcmai asked.

Donnchadh nodded. They unstrapped from their chairs and moved to the ladder leading to the top forward hatch. Gwalcmai led the way, unsealing the hatch. With a hiss of slight pressure equalization, it opened. He was greeted by drops of rain splashing onto his face. He paused, breathing in the fresh, moist air. Sensing Donnchadh's impatience, he climbed up, his partner following. They stood on top of the ship, faces turned up, letting the water course over their skin, soaking their suits. It was the first time they'd breathed anything but regenerated ship's air since departing their home world.

For a moment all their sorrow was forgotten. Donnchadh raised her arms and danced, twirling about. Gwalcmai watched her with a rare smile on his face. He spent precious moments soaking up her joy along with the rain, then duty called. He went to a hatch on the hull and opened the door. He pulled out a bundle of red web netting, which he carried to the rear and draped over one of the engine pods. He did the same to the other engine, connecting the two nets. Donnchadh finally joined him and they completely covered the craft with the antidetection netting they had appropriated from the Airlia.

Once done, Donnchadh climbed off the craft onto the plain. She took off her boots, savoring the feel of grass and dirt beneath her feet. Gwalcmai went back inside the craft. He used the *Fynbar* to lift the stones, positioning them on the plain above the cavern he had gouged out. Two stones went upright, while the third was placed across the top as a lintel piece.

Once the stones were in place, Gwalcmai piloted the *Fynbar* into the cavern, setting it at rest inside. He sealed the opening to the cavern with explosives, isolating the ship. He then used more Airlia technology they had brought from their world to partially hollow out the left stone above the ship, cutting a door in the stone that could only be opened with a special medallion and emplacing a small lift to give access from the ship to the stone.

Once this was done, Gwalcmai took his leave of the ship, carrying a large pack on his back and another in his arms. He exited the stone, the door sealing behind him. He gave one of the packs to Donnchadh. They stared at the stones for several moments, then Gwalcmai pointed, and they set off across the plain.

They were on Earth and their mission had begun.

IV

10,500 B.C.: EARTH

Donnchadh and Gwalcmai had regenerated eight times via the *ka* and black tubes since their arrival on Earth. They had walked the entire large island on which they had landed, from the south shore to the wild and bitterly cold north where men with blue faces fought amongst themselves. They'd even taken voyage on a boat across the sea to the smaller, neighboring isle. They also spent the multiple lifetimes meeting the local people and learning the languages of those they encountered. They'd discovered that envoys from Atlantis visited every decade collecting tribute in the form of metals and children, a pattern that matched the ancient history of their own planet. It had never been clearly determined whether the Airlia did this because they needed what they collected or merely as a means of making sure their control was exerted beyond the colony.

The humans outside of Atlantis were like cattle allowed to range free. They were wild and knew little of the Airlia, just vague legends and myths, and the tributes paid. They warred among themselves, tribe against tribe, something which Donnchadh realized probably fit well into the Airlia's ultimate plan for the humans. Her own planet had had a history of warfare among nations until the greater cause of the Revolution had united mankind. She knew it would be a long hard road to accomplish the same here.

Satisfied that they could fit into the population, Donnchadh and Gwalcmai took passage on a trading vessel that was one of the few willing to venture out into open water beyond the sight of land. The crew was from the mainland to the east of the island where they had landed their craft—large men with long blonde hair who armed themselves with axes and swords. These men prided themselves on both their sailing ability and martial skills. Their language was different, but like all they had encountered so far, rooted in the Airlia tongue to some extent.

Gwalcmai won their respect by sparring with their leader and fighting him to a draw. Donnchadh knew her partner had held back and was easily capable of beating the leader. With the martial arts training he had received on their home world, his combat experience, and the numerous lifetimes he had had to hone his craft, his skills far exceeded what any human could achieve in a single lifetime. She also knew that the leader could see he was outmatched and respected and appreciated Gwalcmai's discretion and restraint.

It was a cold and rainy day when they left the southern shore of their island with the men whose distant ancestors would one day be known as Vikings and sailed west along the coast, until they came to the sea that separated the larger island from its smaller partner to the west. The trip to what would be called Ireland took three days. For Donnchadh it was a strange and humbling journey. Having crossed light-years in the mothership and across a solar system in the *Fynbar*, to move on top of the water at the whim of the winds made her realize the gap that these people had to bridge even to attempt to battle the Airlia. This world must have been seeded long after her own. There would be no possibility of freedom here anytime soon.

It was three weeks before they saw land again. Actually, it was not land they first sighted, but the golden tower of

Atlantis poking above the horizon to the west. As they drew closer, its scale became clearer as land appeared beneath it. Only the Airlia and their high priests were allowed in the palace, while humans tilled the land around it. Donnchadh asked the sailors on her ship to heave to and wait until nightfall before approaching the outer ring. They did as she requested and made landfall several hours after darkness had fallen along an empty stretch of coastline.

Donnchadh paid the sailors a bonus of gold. She and Gwalcmai watched as the long-prowed ship disappeared into the darkness, heading for home. They were at the heart of the Airlia's power on this planet, armed only with swords and daggers. And knowledge of the true nature of the Airlia.

T hey took their time. They spent a full year on the outermost ring of land. It was over six miles wide and covered with farms. The people who worked the land worshipped the Airlia but had little interaction with the Gods. Every so often a golden saucer-shaped craft would fly overhead, heading toward some faraway destination. Donnchadh knew these were the flying machines that the Airlia used in the atmosphere, powered by engines that used the magnetic field of the planet.

They discovered that all was not bliss and harmony in Atlantis. The farther one went from the Airlia palace, the less the benefits of the Gods extended. And the less the control of the Gods held sway. There were those on the outer ring who worked both sides, dealing in the black market. It was this group that Donnchadh and her partner slowly infiltrated. Gwalcmai was quickly accepted for his martial prowess. For Donnchadh it was a different matter. She had to fight off the uncouth advances in the seedy drinking houses along the waterfront, with Gwalcmai lurking in the background, frustrated, but knowing she had to earn her own way. Her fighting skills, inferior to Gwalcmai's, were still far beyond what these humans knew, and she was able to hold her own and more.

She became the deal maker. After several years she came to know all who plied their occupations in the dark and she put together those who could benefit each other. Doing so allowed her and Gwalcmai to accumulate what passed for wealth among these humans, but more important, she gathered people. She learned who could be trusted and who could not. Who was content with the rule of the Airlia and who seethed against it for varying reasons. And her reach grew longer, not only outward to the traders who came from faraway lands, but inward, toward those who served the Gods on the inner island.

Gwalcmai, meanwhile, worked with blacksmiths and other craftsmen, slowly improving the quality of the weapons and armor among the humans. It was an exceedingly slow and often frustrating process, but he and Donnchadh had accepted the need for a very, very long view of the war they were fighting.

Donnchadh knew it was impossible to corrupt a high priest or Guide. Those humans who had made direct contact with an Airlia guardian computer were now just like programmed machines, their free will suborned to do as they had been directed. They had had to kill many of these Guides—either priest or warrior—on their own planet. But the Airlia took only so many humans into their inner sanctum to be so corrupted. There were many—lesser priests; the rank-and-file soldiers; the laborers who maintained the inner city—who served out of faith or for money or, mostly, from fear and ignorance. It was they whom Donnchadh went after, searching for just the right person. After six years of questing, she found her man.

His name was Jobb. He was a level-four supplicant, meaning he was one of the next to be taken into the temple, put against a guardian, and made a high priest. As such he initially seemed to be a waste of time, as he would shortly be brainwashed by the Airlia. But Jobb had a daughter whom he worshipped as much as he gave allegiance to the Airlia Gods. Supplicants were not supposed to have families, but Jobb had had an illicit lover years previously. Knowing her fate for committing this sin, the woman had run away after giving birth, taking passage on one of the black market ships—how Donnchadh had first learned of this—but Jobb had kept the baby, hiring nannies to care for the girl.

Only four days before he was to be brought into the ranks of the high priests, his daughter became ill. He tried to bring her to the palace to be placed in the high priest's infirmary, claiming she was his brother's daughter. But rules were rules and his daughter was denied treatment. The infirmary was only for the priests. She died three days later, on the eve of Jobb's induction.

All this Donnchadh heard from a trader who plied the inland seas in a small, skin-covered ship, which he could carry over the rings of land between. It was just before dawn and Donnchadh was in a traders' tavern. The man had just returned from a journey to the palace island, where he had been directed to Jobb, who was desperately searching for any possible cure for his daughter's sickness, even something from the outer lands, where, he had heard, people used roots and other strange concoctions for medicine.

The trader had been unable to help Jobb. He told Donnchadh that the girl had died in her father's arms just before he headed back.

Donnchadh wasted no time. With Gwalcmai at her side, she made her way into Atlantis, toward the inner island that held the great city and tower. They arrived just before noon, when the elevation ceremony for high priests was to occur. Thousands of people crowded the open plaza inside the city's wall. Wearing dark, travel-stained cloaks, Donnchadh and Gwalcmai stood in the shadow of the wall, looking up at a balcony on the tower on which stood a pair of Airlia, regally garbed as befitted their status as Gods, and flanked by high priests.

At the base of the tower were two dozen red-robed level-four supplicants. One of the high priests began to call names, and one by one the supplicants entered a door at the base of the tower.

When Jobb's name was called there was no response. That was the sign that Donnchadh was looking for. With her partner she took back streets to the place where the trader said Jobb's daughter had lived. They found him inside, the cold body of his daughter still in his arms. His skin was pale, his eyes red from countless tears.

"You do not have much time," Donnchadh said as they stepped through the doorway.

Jobb did not reply or even look up.

"They will come for you," she continued. She went to him and knelt at his side. He finally reacted when she placed a hand on his shoulder, slowly turning his head to look at her, gazing at her with uncomprehending eyes.

"You must tell them that this is indeed your brother's daughter. And that you were too grief-stricken to make the induction ceremony. And that you are now ready to serve."

Jobb tried to speak, but his voice cracked. Gwalcmai gave him a flask of water and Jobb drank for several seconds before giving it back. "I will never serve them. They did not help me in my time of need. What kind of Gods are they? They say they are here to help us, but when I asked, there was no help."

Donnchadh glanced up at Gwalcmai, who met her gaze and nodded very slightly. She took a deep breath, then spoke, knowing she had to lie in order to achieve a higher goal. "It is worse than you imagine. Do you think it was just coincidence that she grew ill four days before you were to be inducted into the ranks of the high priests?"

"What are you saying?" Jobb demanded.

"The Airlia Gods do not care about humans except that we serve them. You have spent many years in preparation to serve. Your daughter would have stood in the way of that. That is why there is the rule against high priests or Guides having family. They are to serve only the Airlia, with no distractions."

The Airlia did not pick stupid humans to become high priests. Jobb connected what she had said within seconds.

"You are saying they killed her?"

"Not the Airlia directly, but the high priests who serve them. They killed her twice," Donnchadh said. "First by making her ill. Second by refusing to treat her."

Gwalcmai reached down and slid his hands under the dead girl's body. "I will take her and make sure she is buried."

Jobb blinked. "Why?"

"So you may have vengeance," Donnchadh said. She went to the wall and retrieved the red robe of the level-four supplicant. "When they come, you must have this on and tell them you are ready to fulfill your duty. Any other action and they will kill you."

"But"—Jobb tried to think it through—"once they take me into the palace and I touch the golden pyramid, I will be theirs."

Donnchadh reached into her pack and pulled out a thin silver chain. She slipped it around the top of Jobb's head, hiding it under his hair. "This will stop the golden pyramid from affecting your brain."

"Where did you get it?"

"From the Airlia," Donnchadh said.

"How can that be? Everything is guarded tightly in the temple. Only the high priests have access."

"And soon you will have access," Donnchadh said.

"But how did you get this?" Jobb asked.

"You would not understand if I told you," Donnchadh said.

"Who are you?" Jobb demanded,

"I am like you," Donnchadh said. "I am the enemy of the Airlia. I can help you get vengeance for your daughter. I too lost a child to them."

"They are not Gods, are they?" Jobb asked, staring at the body that Gwalcmai gently held.

"No."

"I always feared that. Even in training. Even in the temple. It is what none of us would speak of, even when we thought we were alone and could not be overheard. It was easier to believe. And we feared the high priests and Guides. Any word of dissent or heresy would be dealt with on the X-cross. I saw one of my fellows suffer that fate for asking too many questions of a high priest."

"It was easier in the short run to believe," Donnchadh said. "But we are concerned about the long-term outcome of all of this. We need your help."

Jobb got to his feet and walked over to the wall. He took the robe and slipped it over his head. Then he went to Gwalcmai and leaned forward, kissing the cold child in the warrior's arms on the forehead. "They should have saved her," he whispered. "They will pay for that."

Three weeks later Jobb came back to the house. He wore the white robe with silver fringe that indicated he was a high priest. Around his neck was a silver medallion with the image of the eye within the triangle, the access key that allowed him into most places inside the temple and palace.

Donnchadh had spent the three weeks anxiously awaiting his return. The silver chain was a device her people had discovered inside the mothership on their planet, in a tray near the Master Guardian. Her fellow scientists said it was used by technicians who serviced the alien computer, allowing them to be in contact with it without having the mental field affect them. It had never been tried by a human, so they did not know if Jobb was still free or a Guide as he came through the door. Would he be alone, or would he bring a platoon of Guides? As a precaution, she and Gwalcmai had split up. He had taken her *ka* and gone to another place, a backup in case Jobb had been corrupted.

Jobb closed the door behind him and faced her alone, his hands inside the sleeves of his robe, arms crossed on his chest. "It is as you said. The Airlia just use us."

Donnchadh felt a surge of relief and took her hand off the dagger strapped to her side. She knew no Guide would be able to speak against the Airlia. Jobb reached up and removed the silver chain from underneath his hair. "I do not need that anymore. They only give access to the Master Guardian once. That is all that is needed."

"Where have they assigned you?" Donnchadh asked as she took the chain.

"I work in the temple, overseeing the processing of tribute brought by the traders."

"How much contact do you have with the Airlia?" Donnchadh asked.

"Very little. It takes many years to gain the rank to be close to them."

"We have time. We'll come back."

* * *

Thirty years. A trip back to England. A regeneration. A return trip to Atlantis.

If Jobb was surprised at their youthful appearance when they met again, he didn't indicate it when he entered his humble home and found them waiting for him. The years had not been kind to him. His hair was gone. His face was hard. His body was stooped with the weight of time. He moved slowly, his body riddled with arthritis. He had been used by the Airlia, and Donnchadh had no doubt his replacement was already in training.

The small room where his daughter had lived was still the same. Just a simple bed and bare walls. His garments were slightly different. Still a black robe with silver trim, but there was a series of red loops around his right sleeve, indicating higher rank.

"You have done well," Donnchadh said as she mentally counted the loops.

"I have done as you told me to," Jobb replied as he wearily sat on his bed after greeting them.

"You are the Director of Temple Operations for the high priests," Donnchadh said. "A position of great trust and responsibility. With great access."

"For a human," Jobb said. "For a human who is supposed to be corrupted."

"And the Airlia?" Gwalcmai asked. "How do they fare?"

Jobb looked at him. "Do you know of the black tubes?"

"Sleep and regeneration tubes?" Gwalcmai said. "The Airlia use—"

"No." Jobb cut him off. "Do you know of the half-breeds they put in the black tubes and what they use them for?"

"'Half-breeds'?" Donnchadh repeated. Her face had gone even paler, if that were possible.

"Half-human, half-Airlia," Jobb said. "There are royal consorts. Something no one other than the highest ranking of the corrupted know about. Human women who are taken as part of the tribute. Taken deep below the temple, where the Airlia live in their tunnels. And they are never seen again."

"I know of such," Donnchadh said sharply, earning her a surprised look from Gwalcmai.

"They are raised down there," Jobb said. "By a special cadre of high priests. Men whose tongues have been cut out so they can never speak of the dark things they are a part of." He fell silent, reluctant to speak further.

"Tell us what else you have learned," Donnchadh said, changing the subject.

"As you told me so many years ago, they are not Gods," Jobb finally said. "They are demons. They take their own offspring from the human consorts and put them in the black tubes. Then, once a month, they go down there and open the tubes. And drink the blood of these half-breeds. For pleasure." He tapped his chest. "The high priests lie. They are programmed to lie. I wish sometimes I had been programmed. So I could deny the truth of what I have seen and heard, to myself, never mind the people we preach to and control for these creatures." Jobb laughed, the bitter edge indicating no humor. "Even the Airlia are beginning to believe their own lies."

Donnchadh leaned forward. "What do you mean?"

"They believe they are Gods. Why shouldn't they? They've been doing it for long enough. Who has challenged them? Who *can* challenge them?"

A long silence followed.

"Other Gods," Donnchadh finally whispered, her body stiffening as a surge of excitement coursed through it.

"What?" Gwalcmai turned toward her.

"Other Gods can challenge them," Donnchadh said with more confidence in her voice.

"What other Gods?" Jobb demanded.

"The Airlia here are just a few of a larger group," Donn-chadh said. "They are an outpost. Outposts have to report in, right?" she asked of Gwalcmai, the military expert.

Gwalcmai shrugged. "One would assume so. It would be normal operating procedure."

"And if an outpost doesn't report?" Donnchadh pressed.

"You send someone to find out why," Gwalcmai said.

"And we know how they communicate," Donnchadh said.

"That's your area of expertise," Gwalcmai said.

"We saw the deep-space transmitter array coming here," Donnchadh said. "But that's only the transmitter. The mes-sage has to originate from here. This planet. From the Master Guardian." She turned to Jobb, who had been following their brief conversation without comprehension. "You were taken to the red pyramid—the Master Guardian—to be condi-tioned to be a high priest, correct?"

Jobb nodded.

"Where is it?" she asked.

"Inside the holiest place in the temple," Jobb said. "The inner sanctum, high up in the holy spire."

"And the sword that controls it?" Donnchadh pressed.

"Excalibur?" Jobb asked.

"Is that what it is called here?" Donnchadh asked. "Yes, Excalibur."

"It is set in the crystal stone in front of the red pyramid," Jobb said.

"They are very confident," Donnchadh murmured. "Can you get us there?"

"When do you wish to go?" Jobb asked.

"Tonight."

*   *   *

Donnchadh gave a silver chain to Gwalcmai as Jobb led them into the temple. "Wear this just in case," she whispered to him. He took it from her and strapped it around his head. She took another from out of her cloak and put it around her own head.

They wore the yellow robes of the favored—those who contributed greatly to the upkeep of the temple. This, and being guided by a high-ranking priest, allowed them to pass the Guides who manned all the entryways into the temple. After all, high priests were above suspicion, just as the Guides were.

Donnchadh had to admit to herself that she was impressed as they made their way into the temple. The one on her home world had been destroyed during the first year of the Revolution, leveled by multiple nuclear explosions that had also eventually devastated half the surface of the planet with radioactive fallout. The weapons had been sneaked in underneath the Airlia shield that protected the island via an undersea tunnel that took over twelve years to build. Their detonation had been the first act of outright rebellion.

Donnchadh and Gwalcmai knew this world was far away from any outright attempt to use force against the Airlia, so they had decided on a different course of action. Tonight would bring the initiation of that plan.

They made their way up into the temple tower. It was almost deserted so late at night. The Airlia, Donnchadh knew, had a fondness for living underground. Whether that was something inherent in their species or a defensive measure, she didn't know. Jobb had confirmed that the Airlia lived in tunnels deep under the palace and rarely came to the surface or to the temple anymore. They were so confident in the imprinting of the Master Guardian on the high priests and Guides that they felt the temple was most secure.

The three walked up a long spiral ramp that wound along

the interior wall of the tower. It took over an hour to get near the top, where the Master Guardian computer was secreted. The entire journey was made in silence, and after getting past the guards at the bottom of the ramp, they saw no one. Jobb was able to use the medallion around his neck to open a large set of doors that blocked the ramp at the top. The doors swung wide, revealing a large, cone-shaped room. On a black platform in the center was a red pyramid, fifteen feet high. Its surface glowed, pulsing with power.

Gwalcmai put out an arm, abruptly stopping Donnchadh from stepping forward. She then immediately saw what she had missed in her excitement over seeing the Master Guardian. The black platform was attached to the three-foot-high ledge that ran around the interior of the space by only a single walkway on the far side. If she had taken that extra step, she would have fallen into an opening that went down the tower as far as the eye could see.

Donnchadh led the way around the ledge. When she reached the walkway, she paused. Halfway across the ledge was a crystal, three feet high. Set in it was a sword, its pommel extending up. From what they had learned on their own planet, she knew that the sword was the power control for the Master Guardian. Donnchadh walked forward and put her hand on the pommel of the sword, fingers curling around the metal.

"What are you doing?" Gwalcmai hissed as he came to her side, clamping his own hand over hers.

Donnchadh didn't respond, her eyes glued to the glowing surface of the computer. With one hand she checked the silver chain around her head that would keep the alien computer from overwhelming her mind.

"If you turn it off, they will come," Gwalcmai said. "We cannot defeat them. They will kill us and turn it back on."

Donnchadh knew the truth of his words, but still did not

let go. The sword was the key. She knew that. The key to the Master Guardian, which was the heart of the Airlia's power. She allowed Gwalcmai to lift her hand off the sword. "I don't see the sheath," she said. "Putting the sword in the sheath turns off the master."

Gwalcmai kept his hand on hers, watching her carefully.

"I'm all right," she reassured him. She moved around the crystal. As she got closer to the Master Guardian, she slowed. The air felt as if it were changing from gas to liquid, pressing against her, absorbing her. Her hand reached out for the pulsing red surface, even as her upper body leaned away, her head going back, instinctively avoiding the alien device. She knew she had no choice. She was the lone scientist on this planet and it was her responsibility.

Like a solar flare, a glow came out of the computer and encompassed her hand. She tried to draw it back but was unable to do so. The glow enveloped her body. Donnchadh went rigid, a series of "visions" flashing through her brain. Planets. Great space battles between Airlia mothership/Talon fleets and Swarm Battle Cores. Other alien species, some of them warring with the Airlia, some as allies and trading partners. Things she couldn't comprehend in the millisecond she "saw" them.

Even with the chain, it took all her willpower to gain a measure of control over the link. She had studied the data on the guardians prior to departing her planet, although she had never made contact with one before. She had a good understanding of how they functioned but the reality was almost overwhelming.

Almost.

Donnchadh felt Gwalcmai's hand on her back, his presence giving her the strength to stop the runaway visions. Since he too had the silver chain around his head and wasn't directly touching the alien computer, he wasn't affected by the guardian. Donnchadh focused on communications. She "saw" the array on Mars that they had passed on their way to Earth. A green crystal was in the center of the massive dish. That was the transmitter.

But the messages originated here and were sent to a guardian computer on Mars to be transmitted. The same exact message each time. Just a code, which indicated this particular outpost. No details. And all that came back from the Airlia Empire was a simple acknowledgment. Donnchadh searched the logs. The same acknowledgment time after time. No new orders. No updates. Ever since this outpost had been established.

Donnchadh thought about that, then realized that the Airlia were afraid of the messages being intercepted. The message system was simple and functional. And Donnchadh knew enough about computers to set up a self-sustaining loop by which the messages were sent to the guardian on Mars and returned with an indication they had been sent—and acknowledged—when in fact they had not been.

Then she checked on something—how long it took a message to reach the Airlia command center and how long it would take a ship to travel to Earth from wherever that was located.

She then looked in a direction that scientists from her own planets had gone—examining the master plan for the development of the humans on the planet. There was a set schedule depending on population spread and Empire need. The humans away from Atlantis were to be allowed to breed and at the same time given the rudiments of civilization to allow more and more to be sustained by less and less land.

At the same time, two things were to be insinuated into society: a common bond and divisiveness. The first was to be done through the concept of God and religion. The second through national and ethnic differences.

For the first, the Airlia would use the promise of eternal

life. A real promise, given the potential of the Grail, but one they would shroud in the concept of various Gods and dogma surrounding each.

For the latter, the Airlia introduced slight ethnic differences into the human gene pool—skin color, facial characteristics, and other overall minor aberrations. Warfare among the various human segments was to be encouraged. Population was to be allowed to grow up to certain levels, at which time the herd would be culled via disease and warfare.

Right now, this outpost was at Level One—the human population had been thinly spread over the arable land and was growing in numbers. Strong control was maintained at the Airlia headquarters on Atlantis, but outside of there, little influence was being exerted.

Level Two was estimated to be implemented sometime in the next several hundred years upon authorization from the Airlia Empire.

When she was done, Donnchadh had difficulty breaking her contact with the Master Guardian. She tried to pull her hand back, but the field kept her in place. She was able to shift her eyes enough to catch Gwalcmai's attention. With one hard tug, he pulled her away from the alien computer.

"Finished?"

Donnchadh could only nod. They quickly retraced their steps, heading down the winding ramp. Donnchadh half expected an alarm to be raised, fearful that somehow the Master Guardian had alerted the Airlia, but nothing happened. They made it out of the temple and back to Jobb's small house.

"And what now?" Jobb asked as soon as they were inside.

"Now we wait," Donnchadh said.

"How long?" Jobb asked.

Donnchadh exchanged a knowing glance with Gwalcmai. They knew how long it had taken them to journey to this planet on board the mothership. They both knew it would probably be many, many years before the Airlia reacted to the lack of contact from Earth. More than Jobb's lifetime, that was certain.

"I don't know how long," Donnchadh said.

"You are going back to wherever it is you came from?" Jobb sat down on his bed.

"Yes," Donnchadh said.

"What do you want me to do?"

"Watch. Write down what you learn. We will come back here someday."

Jobb stared at the two of them. "I will not see the end of the Airlia, will I?"

Donnchadh sighed. "No. You won't. It will be a long time."

"But I have helped?"

"Greatly," Donnchadh acknowledged.

"Then I am done," Jobb said. He gestured toward Gwalcmai. "Finish me."

Gwalcmai shook his head. "It is not our way."

"I can't live like this anymore," Jobb said. Without another word he drew the ceremonial dagger from the belt around his robe and slashed the blade along his forearm from wrist to elbow. Such was his determination that he was then able to switch the dagger to the hand with the cut arm and do the same to his other arm. Donnchadh belatedly tried to stem the bleeding, but Gwalcmai put an arm out, stopping her.

"It's his choice." Gwalcmai pushed her toward the door as Jobb slumped down on his cot, blood soaking the blankets and dripping onto the floor, his eyes closed. "There are worse things than death," Gwalcmai said.

V

Darkness. Donnchadh woke to absolute darkness. She lifted her right arm and found that the movement was restricted by bands wrapped around it. She managed to get it in front of her face, the back of it lightly striking against something above her, and saw nothing. She pushed upward with both hands and realized she was in a tight, enclosed space.

Her heart rate accelerated along with her breathing. She reached out to the sides and hit cold metal. She blinked in the darkness, not even sure her eyelids were working, as she perceived no difference with them open or shut. Her mind wasn't working right. She tried to recall where she was, when she had lain down to sleep, but couldn't.

Where was Gwalcmai? Why wasn't he by her side?

She slammed the palms of her hand against the metal above, hearing a slight thud, but experiencing no give in her prison top.

"Gwalcmai," she cried out in a weak voice that only bounced back to her.

She screwed her eyelids shut and tried to concentrate. Where was she? What had happened?

A heavy weight suddenly hit her chest. Her son. Fynbar. She knew he was dead.

But the name drew another thread of memory out of the confusion and she grasped onto it. A gray spaceship. Leaving a massive mothership. An Airlia mothership. Her mission. Gwalcmai's and her mission. Earth. Atlantis. The high priest Jobb.

He had killed himself. That oriented her.

Time. That was why she was here. She was in the Airlia tube in the *Fynbar*. Coming out of the deep sleep.

Donnchadh fought to get her breathing under control.

She knew Gwalcmai was close by. In the other tube. He should also be coming out of the deep sleep. They had set the controls for five hundred revolutions of the planet around the sun. It had been just short of the number she had gleaned from the Master Guardian for the lack of messages from Earth to be noticed and a ship dispatched and travel the distance to the planet.

There was a latch. Donnchadh's heart rate decelerated to normal as she remembered the latch on the inside of the tube. She felt to her right and her fingers curled around a small lever. She pulled it and, with a hiss, the top of the tube unsealed and slowly swung upward. At first it was just as dark, then faint red light invaded the tube and hit her eyes.

She had to close them for several minutes to adjust. This was the absolute minimum emergency lighting setting, activated by the movement of the tube's lid as they had programmed, but it took a while for her eyes to be able to take even that much light after so many years of darkness. She used the time to remove the muscle stimulator bands from around her upper body.

Then Donnchadh sat up and opened her eyes once more. The familiar interior of the *Fynbar* was all around. She looked to her right, at Gwalcmai's tube. The top had not opened yet. She smiled. He always was slow to rise after the deep sleep. She removed the muscle stimulators from her lower body, then carefully lifted herself over the edge of the tube and set her feet on the floor.

It was cold. And damp. Donnchadh shivered and grabbed a robe that was hung near the tube, sliding it over her head and shoulders and pulling tight a cinch at the waist. Then she slipped on a pair of leather sandals. They reminded her of the old lady in the south of this island who had made them and Donnchadh smiled once more, until she remembered that all the humans who had been alive when she entered this spacecraft were now dust.

She shivered and turned to Gwalcmai's tube, impatient. There was the hiss of the lid unsealing. As the top swung open she went over. As Gwalcmai sat up, a slightly confused look on his face, and his eyes closed, she leaned forward and kissed him on the lips.

"A good way to awaken," Gwalcmai said, his voice hoarse and cracking.

Donnchadh grabbed his clothes and handed them to him as he finished removing his muscle stimulators and exited the tube. "Perhaps one time you will wake before me."

"Perhaps," Gwalcmai said without much conviction. He dropped to the floor and quickly did fifty push-ups, getting the blood flowing.

"What do you think has happened?" Donnchadh asked as she went over to the copilot's seat and powered up the computer.

Gwalcmai shrugged. "I've no idea." He pulled his sword out of its sheath and checked the edge. "I hope that the metalwork has improved in the past five hundred years. This thing would not last one blow against an Airlia sword." He actually had an Airlia-made sword, from his time as a God-killer, on board the *Fynbar*, but did not take it with him most of the time as it was so obviously an anachronism that it would draw unwanted attention.

Always the practical one, Donnchadh thought as she shut down the tubes and the computer that governed them. In the vat behind the tubes were two more fully grown clones, their limbs almost entwined, they were pressed so tightly together. She stared at them for several seconds, realizing that someday she would inhabit the female one of those bodies. She found it interesting that the two were face-to-face. Gwalcmai came up behind her and wrapped his arms around her upper body. "Even they know our love," he whispered in her ear. His lips came close to the back of her neck. "The surface will wait."

I t was raining as the hidden door set in the standing stone slid open. That was nothing unusual. What was unusual and stopped Donnchadh and Gwalcmai in their tracks was the fact that the stones they had set in place had been surrounded by a circle of wooden stakes set upright in the ground. Each stake was between six and ten feet high. And, of particular notice, on the top of each stake was a human skull, the bone bleached white by the sun and rain.

Donnchadh and Gwalcmai stood still as the door slid shut behind them. They slowly turned, surveying the area, but there was no sign of whoever had erected the stakes or placed the skulls there.

"They could be long dead," Gwalcmai said.

"They could be," Donnchadh agreed. She'd known that the stones sitting in the middle of the grasslands would attract attention from humans passing by, but not enough to attract attention of the Airlia. Apparently, for someone, that attention had turned into a form of gruesome homage. Or a threat, Donnchadh realized with a shiver not caused by the cold rain.

"Come on," Gwalcmai said, stepping forward.

Donnchadh noticed that he had drawn his sword. They made their way onto the plain, heading south.

* * *

Metalworking had not improved much at all on the outer ring of Atlantis, they discovered shortly after landing there, having taken passage on a trading vessel. Gwalcmai found no sword much better than what he had had made the last time they were there. In fact, things in all areas appeared to have gotten somewhat worse, if anything. All they had known were long dead, but the black market and underground network were still alive and well. Human greed had not changed in five hundred years.

They integrated themselves into this fringe of society with more alacrity than the previous time, given their experiences. They learned that the Airlia were hardly ever seen anymore outside of the palace, and that even the high priests and Guides had begun to isolate themselves on the center island, as if the Airlia and their minions were drawing into themselves, away from their mission and the demands of the outside world.

The stories of the Grail and the promise of eternal life for obedience had faded into myth, as if the Airlia cared little for what humans believed anymore. Donnchadh took that as a sign that the Airlia here, having had no new communiqué from their home system, were losing track of their mandate. Her hope had been that they would feel abandoned.

Apparently they did, but rather than be troubled by it, they appeared to be quite content with being out of the interstellar war with the Swarm and to rule the humans immediately around them as Gods. Donnchadh learned this by infiltrating the center island and mixing with those uncorrupted by the guardian. There were still many high priests and Guides in evidence, but their mission seemed more one of service toward the Airlia than spreading the word and influence of the aliens.

Donnchadh felt a little bit of satisfaction in that the Airlia plan for this planet seemed to be stalled, but there had been no apparent response from the Airlia Empire about the loss of contact with the outpost.

Now she and Gwalcmai must do as they had always done—wait.

The guardian on Mars was in contact with not only the Master Guardian on Earth and the transmitter but an array of sensors on the planet's surface. They did not have to be very sophisticated to pick up the incoming spaceship as it passed the outer limits of the solar system, especially considering that it made no attempts to disguise its approach.

It was an Airlia mothership and it had been on sublight vector for the Sol System for over ten years—the amount of time the Airlia estimated to allow the transition from light to sub–light speed to be far enough away not to give the Swarm the opportunity to find the system. Traveling just below the speed of light, the mothership began to decelerate as it passed Pluto's orbit. Nestled around the nose of the mile-long ship were nine smaller ships, shaped like a bear's claws, curving inward from a large base to a sharp point. They were the Talons, Airlia warships, designed to defend the mothership and attack other spacecraft and planets. They weren't capable of faster-than-light speed, so for long journeys they were attached to the mothership like remoras.

As they came in, an override code was sent from the mothership to the guardian on Mars via the interstellar array. A link from the mothership's Master Guardian to the Mars guardian was quickly established. Data was uplinked and analyzed. The recurring fake transmitter program that Donnchadh had implanted in the guardian was quickly discovered and disabled.

Since the only one who could have programming access to the Master Guardian was the Airlia High Commissioner on Earth, the program had to have been put in place by that individual. The only reason such a program would be used would be to fool the Airlia who worked for the High Commissioner into believing contact with the empire was being maintained, when in reality the High Commissioner had no desire to remain in contact with the empire.

Such an act was treason. There was no other explanation.

The mothership's commander, Artad, came to that decision within minutes of examining the data. He quickly issued orders.

Once inside Pluto's orbit, the nine Talons peeled off the larger craft, deploying around the nose of the mothership in a protective formation as it headed inward toward the sun.

On Earth alarms were relayed to the Master Guardian, then to a subordinate guardian deep underneath the palace tower. Reacting to the alarms, the two Airlia on duty quickly awakened the High Commissioner Aspasia from the deep sleep. He issued orders for Excalibur to be removed from the Master Guardian safekeeping and to be brought to him.

Sword in hand, Aspasia went to a control room shaped as a perfect sphere, centered below the tall tower. As soon as he entered, the door shut behind him, sealing the room. He went to a crystal in the very center of the room, into which he slid the sword. The walls of the sphere came alive with the view from the very top of the temple spire.

Aspasia placed his hands on the pommel of the sword and pressed. The view swiftly changed from the area visible from the top of the spire to space, linking with other sensors. He immediately picked up the incoming mothership and the Talons. He knew what the deployment of the warships meant—there was to be no bargaining. Whoever was in command of the mothership meant to shoot first and discuss things later.

But discuss what?

Aspasia quickly accessed the link to his Master Guardian. He found the probe from the incoming mothership and what had been accessed. He was momentarily stunned. Who had reprogrammed the Master? He realized his outpost had been out of contact with the empire for five hundred years. Little wonder the Talons were deployed. He had spent over 99 percent of the past five hundred years in deep sleep, so it seemed like only a week or so had passed.

A glowing red dot appeared on the wall of the chamber directly in front of him. It extended upward and downward into a red line, which then expanded into the shape of an Airlia. When Aspasia saw who it was, he knew there was another factor at play behind the rapid deployment of the Talons before an inquiry had been made.

"Artad," Aspasia said.

"It has been a long time, High Commissioner Aspasia," Artad responded. "And you will refer to me by my proper title: Admiral Artad."

"The lack of communication was not—" Aspasia began, but the other cut him off.

"You are High Commissioner. You have only one duty and that is to prepare the seedlings on this planet for combat to support the empire. My scan indicates you are still on Phase One even though the order for Phase Two was issued long enough ago for it to be well under way."

"I never received—" Aspasia once more tried to speak, but again he was interrupted.

"You are High Commissioner. All is your responsibility. You have failed to report in far beyond the maximum period allowed. It was believed the only thing that could cause such an occurrence was an attack by the Swarm. My ship was diverted from an important mission to see if our seeding process had been compromised here by the Swarm. I arrive only to find deception and failure."

Aspasia said nothing for several moments. Artad and he had served together a very long time ago, when Artad had been a lowly first lieutenant. They had always hated each other. And then there was the issue of Harrah. She had been Artad's mate-to-be, also an officer on the same ship they had all been assigned to. Had been. She was here now on this forsaken outpost with Aspasia. Because of her choice between the two them.

"*Harrah sleeps,*" Aspasia finally said. "*Admiral,*" he added.

"*I care not,*" Artad said, such a blatant lie that Aspasia wanted to laugh out loud.

"*You dare not use the mothership's weapons, Admiral. You will bring the Swarm here.*"

"*I do what I wish,*" Artad replied.

"*So be it,*" Aspasia said. The image of Artad disappeared from the sphere's wall and he could see the incoming ships once more. Aspasia had to wonder what kind of power play was going on. Even though it had been millennia since he had last seen Artad, he knew little had probably changed. The seed planets had been a controversial plan, as the best Airlia scientists had speculated that the Swarm was a form of weapon designed genetically by another species. A weapon that had apparently turned against its master and now rampaged through the universe on its own. There were those who wondered if they were not repeating the mistake of whatever race had invented the Swarm. Because of that fear, limits had been deliberately built into the humans—limits that could be removed by the Grail when needed.

Artad had supported the human seed program. Aspasia had opposed it. When the powers that be on the High Council had swung in favor of the program, Artad's star had risen as Aspasia's had dimmed. In the process Aspasia been assigned to be High Commissioner for one of the remote seed worlds. He'd had no doubt Artad was behind the assignment, although he knew the other had not suspected that Harrah would go with Aspasia.

Wheels within wheels, Aspasia thought as he watched Artad's ship draw closer. His own mothership was secreted underwater not far from the island. His Talons were deployed, most on Mars, hidden in an underground cavern not far from the transmitter site. Aspasia made contact through the sword and crystal with his Master Guardian and mentally issued orders.

Donnchadh woke to Gwalcmai's hand on her shoulder, gently rocking her. "It begins."

Donnchadh sat up, the sleep fleeing from her brain. "What has happened?"

"A shield wall has gone up around the center island," Gwalcmai said. "All who were inside are trapped there and those outside cannot enter."

"They would not put the shield up to protect the inner circle from humans, not at the level these people have attained," Donnchadh said, knowing as she said it that Gwalcmai had already figured that out.

Her partner pointed up. "Something is coming."

Donnchadh got to her feet. "The question is: More Airlia or Swarm?"

"Hard to say which would be worse," Gwalcmai said.

"If it's the Ancient Enemy," Donnchadh said, remembering her briefing by the scientists who had accessed the Master Guardian's database on her home world, "then none of what we have done will matter."

"Then let it be Airlia," Gwalcmai said, with his neverending optimism. "Whoever it may be, they are not coming in peace, or the shield would not have been raised."

Donnchadh shrugged on her cloak and stuck the daggers in her belt. "Come."

They went out into the early morning mist. There were people in the streets, an air of anxiety palpable as they speculated what the change meant. None had ever seen an Airlia shield wall or knew what it was. Donnchadh had watched thousands die trying to breach one. It allowed nothing with energy, whether living or mechanical, to pass through. On her home world they had eventually been forced to dig a tunnel far underneath the Airlia base, at the cost of many lives and years. They'd then smuggled in nuclear weapons and at the designated time detonated them. At that point the shield wall had worked against the Airlia, containing the blast so that everything inside was obliterated.

In an attempt to gather more information, Donnchadh and Gwalcmai made their way inward, toward the center island. When they reached the last ring island and the rising sun had burned off enough fog, they saw the shield wall. It glittered in the early-morning light, a perfect round cone covering the entire center island and the palace. Its bottom edge touched the water about a hundred meters offshore. It was transparent but there was no mistaking its boundaries as its very energy gave off its outline.

As they watched, a flock of seagulls flew into it and fell to the water, dead. They could see several boats on either side floating aimlessly, the humans on board killed when they intersected with the wall. A golden saucer was flitting about, circling the spire. On its very top something extended that both of them recognized: a small golden ball on a rod. A weapon of the Airlia that could kill anything within sight. Guides manned the walls and gates of the palace.

"On the defensive," Gwalcmai observed.

"Yes."

* * *

There were three items on the surface of Mars, in the region that would become known as Cydonia, that were not natural. The first was the Airlia transmitter. A massive dish dug into a mountain, over a thousand meters in depth and three times that in width. At the very center was a glowing green crystal that focused outgoing transmissions while the dish gathered incoming transmissions from the surrounding latticework.

Not far from the mountain were two other objects. One was a huge pyramid, towering over five hundred feet above the surrounding plain. And near it a large rectangular formation was cut into the surface of the planet.

The top of the pyramid began to split open, each of the four sides moving away from the others. They reached vertical and kept going, massive hydraulic arms lowering the dark outer sides toward the ground. The interior of each triangular side caught the light of the sun and absorbed its power.

The left edge of the square base also began to change color as a huge covering panel started to slide open. As it did so, it revealed a half dozen rapier shapes—some of Aspasia's Talon warships.

The solar panels poured power into the entire facility. Deep underground lights went on in a cavern lined with rows of deep sleep/regeneration tubes. Twenty in all. The black metal protecting them swung open, revealing the creatures inside. They were brought out of their stasis even as the Mars guardian began prepping the ships. A bolt of golden light arced from cables crisscrossing the side of the chamber down to each ship and they began to power up.

The defensive preparations did not go unnoticed by Artad.

Unfortunately for him, his slow reentry into the Sol System

had not gone unnoticed either. In the scanner shadow formed by the mothership's wake, a small Swarm scout craft followed. It was shaped like a spider with a round body and eight protrusions all pointed forward. It had been following the mothership for ten years, patiently waiting to discover its destination. Its sensors were picking up the same thing the mothership's were: ships and transmitter on the fourth planet from the star; intelligent life and an Airlia base on the third planet.

The alignment of the two planets was interesting because they were two-thirds away from each other in orbit around the star. Not exactly the strongest mutually supporting defensive position. The scout ship's mandate was to report all signs of intelligent life back to a Battle Core. However, something strange seemed to be developing. The Swarm was familiar with the Airlia but it appeared as if there were some battle imminent. The scout ship saw no reason for this action by the Airlia other than its own presence, but it also saw no indication that it had been detected. Was there another player involved, another species threatening the Airlia?

The Swarm inside puzzled over this for a few moments, then decided to continue on course, following the mothership to gather more information before sending a report to the nearest Battle Core. This was something new, and new things worried the Swarm as much as it was capable of being worried.

Artad split his fleet. The mothership and four Talons headed toward Earth. Five Talons headed toward Mars. Shields went up, weapons were charged. The crews assumed their battle stations.

The first shots came over three hundred thousand kilometers from Mars as Talon met Talon. As both sides expected, the results were strained shields but no real damage. However, Artad's Talons didn't stop to fight the battle but continued their plunge in toward the Red Planet.

The pyramid, hangar, and power generator were all shielded, so Aspasia wasn't very concerned with this development. Unfortunately, having been out of the forefront of the war against the Swarm for such a long time, he didn't know that the Swarm had learned how to penetrate and cause damage beyond the types of shields he used and that Artad had been the beneficiary of this hard-earned knowledge and was now employing it himself.

Two of the four Talons trapped a small asteroid—a little over three hundred meters long by a hundred meters in width—between them with their tractor beams. The other two fended off the irritating but ineffectual attacks of Aspasia's Mars-based Talons. The Airlia on Mars, still a bit groggy from being awakened from their deep sleep, watched the approaching craft and the rock caught in their tractor beam with confusion. The confusion turned to surprise when the Mars guardian traced out the approach vector and projected it to be directly at the communications array.

At fifty thousand kilometers the two craft turned off their tractor beams and let the asteroid be drawn down into Mars' gravity, aimed directly at the transmitter. The Airlia manning the outpost realized what was happening, but were not overly concerned, as they had the shield up.

When the asteroid free-fell through the shield, the Airlia on Mars were shocked. They had scant seconds to react before it hit the array. Force equals velocity times mass. It is a rule of physics. The asteroid hit at a high velocity and its solid metal core had large mass. Its size and speed were converted into a hundred megatons of power.

The transmitter disappeared in a flash of light.

* * *

spasia stared at the wall of the sphere, at the image being sent by the Mars guardian of what had once been the interstellar transmitter. He couldn't believe it—the shield wall was impenetrable to all forms of life and force weapons. How could a simple asteroid—the answer came to him as quickly as he posed the question: The asteroid had no active force other than velocity; and no life. It had been as blunt and archaic a weapon as these humans throwing stones at each other. And it had worked.

He realized that Artad could do the same with Atlantis. Indeed, as he shifted his gaze to the inbound mothership, he saw that two of the Talons accompanying it had captured another, larger, asteroid in their tractor beams and were towing it along a vector for Earth.

Aspasia issued new orders.

rtad could see the third planet clearly on the large curving screen at the front of the mothership bridge. A white-blue planet, perfect for life—at least life in Airlia form. He'd checked the survey records from the team that had discovered the planet over a thousand years earlier during the initial planning phases for the seed program. It had its own indigenous life, but none ranking anywhere on the intelligence scale.

A warning light flashed as two of Aspasia's Talons came in on an attack vector. Ineffectual beams of gold were exchanged between Talons, but their goal was neither Talon nor mothership as they concentrated their fire on the asteroid caught in the tractor beam. Not under the protection of a shield, it exploded, splintering into hundreds of pieces.

Artad nodded. Aspasia was no fool. Artad brought his fleet to a halt a hundred thousand kilometers from the planet. Aspasia's Talons backed off twenty thousand kilometers, between the two.

The fragments of the asteroid raced toward Earth, ignored by both sides.

The Swarm scout ship hid in the shadow of the moon, observing and waiting.

At Atlantis, almost the entire day had passed without any obvious activity at the palace. The shield wall was still in place and a saucer still slowly flew circles around the spire while Guides manned the walls.

Donnchadh and Gwalcmai were among thousands gathered around the innermost ring just outside the shield wall, watching and waiting. Darkness began to fall and still nothing changed.

Until about an hour before midnight when streaks of light appeared overhead. Hundreds of them.

"What is it?" Gwalcmai asked his wife.

At first, Donnchadh thought they were seeing Airlia weapons, but as the streaks crossed the sky, she realized what it was that they were witnessing. "Asteroids. Coming into the atmosphere."

"Coincidence?" Gwalcmai asked.

"Not likely. Something happened in space."

Most of the pieces of asteroid, deflected off their original course by the destruction of the main body, hit the outer layer of the Earth's atmosphere and bounced off, heading back out into space. Most, but not all.

One of the larger surviving pieces of asteroid that Donnchadh and Gwalcmai were watching from the inner ring of Atlantis hit the atmosphere angled too steeply to ricochet away and plunged downward. Its plume of flame was over three hundred miles long as it descended. It left Atlantis behind, crossed the rest of the Atlantic, and went lower over North America, frightening the humans who wandered that land.

It hit in what would in ten millennia be called Arizona. The land was lush and covered with thick forest. All of which for six hundred miles around was gone in an instant as the fragment struck the Earth and produced a massive crater.

Other pieces of the asteroid hit in different spots around the planet. Those that hit in oceans caused tsunamis that devastated low-lying coasts in the vicinity. Several others struck land, killing all living things within the blast zones, including a particularly large piece that hit near Vredefort, in what would become South Africa. This strike was so severe that a large rock plain actually ended up inverting.

Hundreds of thousands of humans that had been seeded around the world by the Airlia died in the impacts and their aftermaths. Millions of square miles of land were wiped clean of all living things.

Aspasia could not have cared less what devastation had been scored by the initial battle. All spaceships were at a halt as each side considered its next move. Artad stood on the bridge of the mothership, while Aspasia remained in his control sphere, deep under Atlantis. On Mars, the survivors were digging their way out of the rubble caused by the destruction of the interstellar transmitter.

And still lurking in the shadow of the moon was the Swarm scout ship.

Artad knew he had made a mistake. Killing as many human seedlings as his abortive attack had just done set the program back many years. The empire would not be pleased. He looked up from his command chair as a red light flashed on the main screen—a message from Aspasia. The red light coalesced into his enemy's form.

"You cannot destroy my headquarters without seriously damaging the planet," Aspasia announced. *"Admiral,"* he added in a tone that indicated what he thought of his foe's higher rank.

Artad said nothing. He was more interested in the person standing to the right and rear of Aspasia. A female. Tall and willowy with flowing red hair over her elongated ears. Her catlike red eyes seemed to be boring right into Artad's own eyes. Harrah.

"Why do you bring her into this?" Artad demanded.

"Because she is part of it," Aspasia responded. *"Destroy me and you destroy her."*

"Is this what you choose?" Artad posed the question past Aspasia.

Harrah nodded. *"I made my choice long ago."*

"So be it," Artad said, but he took no action as he pondered the two figures on the screen in front of him. *"Why did you cut yourself off from the empire?"* he finally asked.

"I tried to tell you," Aspasia said. *"I am as surprised as you to find out my outpost has been out of contact as long as it has."*

"Do not lie to me," Artad said.

"He does not lie." Both were startled by Harrah's interjection. *"I have checked the Master Guardian's database. Someone accessed it five hundred years ago and set up that loop."*

"Who reprogrammed the Master Guardian then?" Artad demanded.

There was no answer to that question for several seconds, until a worried look flitted across Aspasia's face. *"The only possibility I can think of is that this outpost has been infiltrated by the Swarm and one of my people or a Guide has been infected with a Swarm tentacle."*

Artad spun in his seat to his subordinate officers. "*All Talons are to do a system sweep on high scan for a Swarm ship.*"

Aspasia likewise immediately issued orders via the Master Guardian to his own people to search for infiltration.

Donnchadh and Gwalcmai sat in a small canoe right next to where the shield wall met the water surrounding the innermost island of Atlantis. Since the meteor shower there had been no further activity, so they had decided to try to regain the initiative or—at the very least—find out what was going on. At that range they could feel the power coming off the shield, a tingling sensation that covered their entire bodies.

"Are you certain?" Gwalcmai asked for the fourth time.

Donnchadh had a large stone clutched in both hands. She had stripped down to just a short pair of pants and a thin shirt. Two black daggers were tucked tightly into the belt around her waist.

"I can only work from the data we gained on our world," Donnchadh patiently replied as she looked toward the lights of Atlantis. She took a deep breath and slowly let it out. "I am ready."

"I will be waiting for you," Gwalcmai promised.

"I know," Donnchadh said.

She sat on the edge of the canoe, facing the shield wall, as Gwalcmai took the other side to keep the craft from capsizing. She looked over her shoulder and gave him a quick smile, then took several deep breaths, holding the last one. She then slid over the side of the canoe into the dark water, making sure she was still facing the wall.

The stone took her down quickly and she felt the pressure increase first in her ears, then on her chest. She was counting to herself, letting air out as she descended. When she reached fifteen, she let go of the stone and kicked with all her strength, pushing herself forward as the remaining air in her lungs slowly caused her to rise. Her main focus was to go toward Atlantis, hopefully under the shield wall. On her planet they had learned that the shield only went down about twenty meters into the water and it was possible to go underneath it.

Donnchadh prayed that she had descended far enough as she used her arms and legs to propel herself forward. She knew that if she had not—or if this wall was different from the one on her world—then she would be killed any second.

It was pitch-black at that depth and she could feel the air in her lungs growing stagnant and her body beginning to ache for oxygen. She swam as hard as she could. After twenty seconds, she had to assume she'd made it and angled toward the surface, legs and arms thrashing.

On the canoe, Gwalcmai breathed a deep sigh of relief as he saw Donnchadh's head break the surface thirty meters away, on the other side of the shield wall. She was gasping for air and waved weakly at him before heading for the island.

Donnchadh made landfall near the high priest's ceremonial dock. She knew the area, having been there several times centuries ago. As she expected, little had changed. She crawled up onto shore, water dripping from her body. She could see Guides on the dock itself and those manning the wall ahead that surrounded the city. She followed a drainage ditch toward the wall.

A metal grate covered the ditch where it cut through the wall. Donnchadh put the edge of one of the daggers underneath the left side of the grate and levered it outward. She and Gwalcmai had opened the same grate on their last visit to the main island. As she expected, it swung open and she slid through, closing it behind her.

She waded through the filthy water into the city.

VI

The Swarm scout ship was trying a desperate maneuver, heading in toward the system's star. It was going to use the gravitational acceleration gained to slingshot around and out of the solar system, hopefully outrunning the three Talons in pursuit. It passed Venus's orbit with a slight lead over the Airlia ships that had discovered it hiding behind the Earth's moon.

The Swarm inside the scout ship knew the Talons' capabilities and recognized that the numbers at current trajectory were not favorable for escape. It chose a more drastic measure, edging inward toward the sun beyond the limits of what wisdom would dictate. The Swarm knew its survival was not important—what was critical was that a message be sent out to the closest Battle Core, and that required gaining some distance from the pursuing ships and getting far enough away from the interference of the solar system in order to send its transmission.

On board the mothership, Artad watched the chase and knew exactly what the Swarm was trying to do. There was no hesitation as he ordered one of the Talons to follow directly while the other two were to loop around the star at the minimum safe distance.

As the scout ship and Talon dived deeper into the sun's gravity well, the Talon opened fire. Golden bolts of energy shot from the needle nose of the craft toward the scout ship. One struck, sending the scout ship tumbling for several seconds before the Swarm regained control of the damaged vessel. Other bolts were absorbed into the sun. Responding to the incoming power, a solar flare suddenly boiled up from the surface of the sun and enveloped both ships in a bright explosion of light. When it disappeared, both ships were gone.

Artad ordered the surviving two Talons to return to the mothership, then he turned his attention to the image on the screen.

"*Did you see?*" he asked Aspasia.

"*Yes.*"

Artad scanned the instruments on the console in front of him. "*It does not appear that the Swarm ship was able to get a message out before it was destroyed. However, that does not mean it did not get an initial message out prior to our discovering it. If the Swarm was behind the reprogramming of the Master Guardian via tentacle infiltration of one of your people, then it has been in this system a very long time.*"

Aspasia held up a six-fingered hand. "*I propose a truce to deal with this problem.*"

"*You propose?*" Artad glared at the image of the High Commissioner. "*It is your failures that have led to this.*"

"*Accept the reality of the situation,*" Harrah cut in. "*You have always let emotions rule you, Artad, and that was, and is, your greatest shortcoming.*"

Artad slammed a hand down on the side of his chair and glared at the screen. "*How dare you—*"

"*If the Swarm come,*" Aspasia said, "*they will not care who is at fault. They will kill us all.*"

"*What do you propose?*" Artad demanded.

* * *

Donnchadh slid the dagger's black blade across the throat of the Guide, then stepped back to avoid the spurt of blood that issued forth from the severed jugular. She felt no guilt—one who had been turned into a Guide was a creature she no longer considered human. In fact, she was freeing whatever core human part remained trapped inside the unfortunate soul's mind. She removed the medallion from around its neck, the ring from its finger, and added them to the ones already in the small leather satchel she'd taken from the others she'd killed.

She was weaving a bloody path into the palace, not caring how many corpses she left behind. As soon as she'd climbed out of the ditch and entered the city proper, she'd been in the midst of confusion. People ran to and fro, some with their belongings, others with nothing. Some were heading toward the palace spire crying out in supplication, others away from it. A voice was echoing out of loudspeakers listing name after name, directing them to report to the palace. Looking up, she spotted half a dozen golden saucers bracketing the spire. The key to the uproar, though, was the massive black mothership that hovered over the top of the temple spire. Its shadow covered the entire city. Something unprecedented was happening and for those humans who lived under the unchanging thrall of the Airlia, such a development was terrifying. The Airlia had beat routine and consistency into those who served them for generation after generation.

Donnchadh was taking advantage of the confusion to wreak a small measure of vengeance and get closer to the center of activity to discover exactly what was happening. She made her way onto the large plaza in front of the spire and halted at the near edge in the shadows of a building.

Thousands were gathered in the plaza. Prayers were being chanted by the masses, incense was burning, and rich offerings were being made to the Guides who manned the gates at the far end of the plaza at the base of the spire. Donnchadh quickly saw, though, that no one was being allowed in unless they were on a list held by a high priest who stood to the rear of the Guides. A desperate man tried to push his way past the Guides and he was cut down without hesitation. In panic those behind him tried to retreat, but the pressure from the thousands behind kept them in place.

Looking up, Donnchadh could see that a narrow metal gangway ran from an opening near the top of the spire to the mothership. She entered the building behind her and tried to get a higher angle so she could see what was on the gangway. It was too close and not tall enough. She was forced to back away from the center of the city, to the high city wall, before she could get a glimpse.

At first, the gangway was deserted except for a pair of Guides standing guard. Soon, however, they got out of the way as several high priests bustled across and entered the cargo door on the mothership. Donnchadh's breath drew in as four priests appeared out of the spire, two by two, each carrying on their inside shoulders a wooden pole. The two poles supported an object covered by a white shroud. Behind the four priests and what they carried was another high priest, this one garbed in a white linen robe over which he wore a blue sleeveless tunic, fringed in gold. Over the shirt was a coat of many colors, fastened at the shoulders with precious stones. The priest had two pockets over each breast, and even from the distance Donnchadh could make out a slight green glow coming from each pocket. The high priest wore a crown consisting of three bands of metal and his mouth was moving, as if he were chanting, although the words did not carry to her position. It was the accouterment of the Supreme High Priest.

Donnchadh knew she had to be witnessing the removal of the Ark containing the Grail from the temple. Others had clearly seen it too as a collective moan issued forth from those watching. They knew from what the high priests had preached that if the Ark and Grail were being removed, then they were being abandoned. The word spread quickly across the city, reaching those in the plaza who were not able to see what was happening high above them.

As soon as the Ark was inside the mothership, people poured forth from the spire, two by two, some running, rushing to be inside the mothership. The chosen ones, Donnchadh thought, but chosen for what? Was the temple being abandoned? Why?

The sound of fighting echoed back to Donnchadh as more of those surrounding the spire tried to make their way into the temple and were beaten back by the Guides. A golden orb extended from the pinnacle of the spire and Donnchadh knew what was going to happen next. Golden bolts shot forth from the orb, striking the surrounding area, killing dozens with each blast. The plaza in front of the temple quickly cleared and the doors were bolted shut. At the top, the boarding continued and Donnchadh envisioned a long line of the chosen spiraling up the long ramp that she had climbed so many years ago with Jobb and Gwalcmai.

There was only one reason why this would be happening, Donnchadh realized. The Airlia would not simply abandon this base and leave it empty. It was not their way. On her planet, each outpost that the Airlia had retreated from had been brutally destroyed as soon as it was cleared. It had been a scorched-earth policy on a planetwide scale.

Donnchadh turned away from the spire. She noted that the shield wall surrounding the inner island had been turned off—probably when the mothership had arrived from wherever it had been hidden. She pondered that development as she made her way out of the city. If the shield was off, whatever the threat had been was no longer feared. Had the Airlia here defeated whoever had come? She knew where to find Gwalcmai now that the shield wall was down. He was just outside the metal grate, waiting in the canoe.

"Look," Gwalcmai said, pointing up as she climbed on board.

The gangway retracted into the mothership and the door slid shut. The mothership moved smoothly and without sound to a position a kilometer and a half above the palace. Larger cargo doors in the front of the Airlia craft opened. Two golden saucers exited a door just above the base of the palace. Below them, caught in a tractor beam, was an object that Donnchadh had heard of but never seen—the one on her world had been destroyed in the nuclear explosion that took out the palace—a massive crouching Black Sphinx, over a hundred meters long from the tip of the paws to the rear. The Hall of Records. It was supposed to have been the place where the Ark and Grail were securely stored.

The two saucers flew the sphinx into the cargo bay and set it down. As soon as they released it, they raced back to the palace and made several more trips, each time carrying a twenty-foot-high golden pyramid.

"They're bringing out the guardians," Gwalcmai noted.

"They're deploying to Stage Two," Donnchadh said. "Dispersing." She stiffened as one of the saucers came out of the temple with a red pyramid caught in its beam. "The Master Guardian."

"That means they're really abandoning this place," Gwalcmai said.

"We need to get out of here." Donnchadh grabbed an oar and began paddling.

As they reached the innermost ring, the cargo bay on the mothership closed and the huge craft began to move away to the southeast. They leapt out of the canoe and raced across the land to the next circle of water. Even as they slowly made their way across the land, the mothership disappeared from sight.

spasia sat in the command chair in his mothership. His tactical display indicated that Artad was in orbit, shadowing his movements to make sure he complied with the terms of the truce the two had agreed on. It was a patchwork solution to a problem both had contributed to. If the Swarm had transmitted the location of this star system to a Battle Core, then there was only a slight chance they could survive—and that slight chance would revolve around making themselves as scarce as possible and making it appear that the Airlia had abandoned the system. The ruins of the transmitter on Mars would help in that matter. A Battle Core might harvest the humans and be satisfied with that. Even if the Swarm had not sent a message out, Artad's precipitous destruction of the interstellar array on Mars had made an already bad situation worse and implicated him in Aspasia's isolation. There was no way either could return to the empire without getting to at least Phase IV of the seed program on Earth. That would take at least ten thousand revolutions of this planet around its star. A long time for the humans, but not so long for the Airlia, especially given the fact they had the deep sleep tubes.

Aspasia watched as the mothership passed over a strait connecting two oceans—what would be known as the Atlantic and Mediterranean and the rocks on either side would be called the Pillars of Hercules—and flew along the northern coast of Africa almost to the eastern end of the continent, where it paused above a lush land with a large river coursing through the center and emptying into the Mediterranean. On the entire planet, this was the place where Aspasia's scientists had decided human life could best develop.

Because of that report he had sent his chief engineer, Rostau, to prepare the site many years previously for part of Phase II. This was going to be a bit different, but the site would serve nicely.

They flew upriver to a point where a stone plateau projected up on the west side of the river. Aspasia had the mothership halted. A weapon fired from the nose of the massive ship, cutting into the rock, burning out a large hole at a spot that Rostau had predetermined and programmed into the ship's weapons. Two saucers emerged from the forward cargo bay, the Black Sphinx in tow. They carefully lowered it into the still-smoking hole, far enough down that even the high top of the head was not above ground level. They quickly followed it with the red pyramid.

Aspasia watched all this while six of his subordinates entered the control room and came to a halt in front of him, heads bowed, awaiting his commands. Isis. Osiris. Horus. Amun. Khons. Seb. Three female. Three male. All young and in the prime of their long lives.

"*It is almost dark,*" Aspasia said in the language of the Airlia. He pointed one of his six fingers upward. "*Artad is above us. Watching to make sure we fulfill the parameters of the Atlantis Truce. I have no doubt that he will violate it; is already violating it in fact. He will try to destroy me while I sleep. It will be your job to watch out for any strike he might make. It will come from a direction you might not expect, so you must be vigilant.*"

"And if the Swarm—" Isis began.

"*If the Swarm comes for the harvest, then you die. If another scout comes, you destroy it. Is that clear?*"

As Aspasia spoke, the mothership descended until it was just above the stone plateau. A gangplank was extended from one of the cargo bays in the bottom of the ship to the ground. On the screen, they could see four high priests unloading the Ark.

"*I am leaving you the most valuable thing we have—the Grail. Seal it inside the Hall of Records. Guard it with your lives.*"

"*And the key to the Hall?*" Osiris asked.

Aspasia held up a golden scepter, a foot long and two inches in diameter. The top of it was made in the image of a lion with ruby red eyes. "*The key remains with me.*" They all knew that meant that while they might have the Grail with them, they could not access it.

There was no response and Aspasia looked each of the six in the eyes for a moment before moving on to the next issue. "*Listen to me.*" He tapped several hexagonals on the control console on the left arm of his chair. "*We were not idle all those years although it appeared to most that we were. I had this place prepared for implementation of Phase II. There are tunnels below this plateau, some connecting with the place we have just placed the Hall of Records. You will find them on the plans prepared by Rostau. There are also chambers prepared where you can live quite well. Deep sleep tubes. Food. A fission power source that will last you as long as you could possibly need. All of this was built and put in place by Rostau long ago.*"

What Aspasia did not tell them was that Rostau had done more than just prepare tunnels and chambers for Phase II. He had placed some other things down there—precautions and contingencies.

On the screen at the front of the control room was the image of about a thousand humans streaming off the mothership onto the plateau. Most were high priests or Guides—the most dedicated of those who had served the Airlia on Atlantis.

"*They are yours to serve you,*" Aspasia said. He held up a black tube. "*In here are plans for the surface that should be implemented according to the time schedule inside. The humans can do the work if taught properly.*"

"*Plans for what?*" Isis inquired.

"*To send a signal into space now that the array is gone.*"

Isis frowned. "*How can humans make something that—*"

"*Do not question me,*" Aspasia snapped. "*If we send the first signal to the empire, we will have the upper hand over Artad. We can use the recordings of his assault on us to say he had an improper motivation to do what he did.*" Saying the last part, Aspasia glanced over his shoulder at Harrah. "*Go now,*" he ordered. "*Artad will follow me away from here.*"

With slight bows, the six left the control room. As soon as Aspasia was informed that the six were on the gangplank he ordered the mothership to lift. The six, hunched over and wearing dark robes, jumped free as the massive craft accelerated upward. Crouching among the humans, the Airlia made their way to the secret chamber they had been directed to, where they could live. They disappeared to their underground lair, leaving the humans on the surface to fend for themselves for the time being. At least until Artad implemented his part of the Atlantis Truce.

They had begun what would fade into myth as the First Age of Egypt. The time of the rule of the Gods.

Aspasia directed the mothership to the east to fulfill the second part of his preparations. The mothership was flying so low, less than two hundred meters above the ground, that its drive field literally plowed a furrow through the sand below. They passed over desert, then an isthmus that connected two continents. The Red Sea was to the right and the Mediterranean to the left. Directly below was a shallow tidal sea mostly covered with reeds, known to the desert people as the Bitter Sea.

The gravitational field sent the water surging to either side and dug into the mud below. Two ten-meter-wide parallel tracks of mud were left in the mothership's wake across the middle of the Bitter Sea. As the ship flew over the desolate Sinai Peninsula it came to a halt over a tall peak. A guardian computer was off-loaded along with other pieces of machinery and placed in chambers that Rostau had dug deep inside the mountain many years ago as part of contingency planning.

Aspasia himself exited the ship along with a quartet of his subordinates, who carried a black tube on their shoulders. They went to a chamber far inside the mountain and set the tube down, hooking it up to machinery already in place. Aspasia watched as they swung the lid up, exposing the body of an adult human male. The man's skin was clear and unblemished. His eyes stared upward vacantly with no indication of intelligence behind them. Yet his chest slowly rose and fell, indicating life.

This was something that Artad had agreed to as part of the truce, although Aspasia did not plan to do it exactly as directed.

Aspasia moved forward and stood next to the coffin. A band was placed around his head and secured in place. An Airlia standing at the control console pressed several hexagonals. Microprobes went from the band into Aspasia's brain. They transferred his memories, his personality, his essence into the machine, where it was stored. The microprobes were withdrawn and Aspasia removed the band. He couldn't help but run his hand along his forehead, expecting to find blood, even though the probes were so small he hadn't even felt them go in.

Aspasia walked over to the tube and looked down at the human body. It was an empty vessel, ready to receive what he had just stored. Aspasia took a ka and placed it in the appropriate slot on the machine. A light flashed and he knew the ka now held all of his essence up to the moment of transfer. He set a time on the tube and left the chamber, sealing the door behind him.

Aspasia suspected that Artad would be recording this location and what was being placed here. A contingency for the success of the mission. Aspasia boarded the mothership and it lifted, fulfilling the tasks assigned him by the Atlantis truce. Flying almost to the other side of the world, it stopped over on an island in the Pacific Ocean that boasted three volcanoes. Aspasia placed another guardian computer deep inside an extinct volcano and then off-loaded a handful of humans to populate the island. One of his subordinates, Rapa, also secreted himself among the humans in order to rule them. One day it would be called Easter Island, but before that it would be known as Rapa Nui.

From Easter Island the mothership flew to South America, where another guardian and more humans were relocated high in the Andes. He also had one of his subordinates, Virachoca, sneak off the ship to rule the humans. The mothership stopped several more times on its way around the planet, dispersing humans, making up for some of the losses incurred by the meteor shower, like a farmer replanting his fields after a storm devastated his crop. This is what had been agreed upon with Artad—what had not been agreed was that Aspasia would leave some of his agents in place with those humans.

Finally, the mothership came to a place on the North American continent, over a desolate and deserted spot. Using the mothership's weapons, Aspasia dug out a large hole in the side of a tall mountain—large enough for the mothership to fit through. Then he carefully edged the nose in and burned out a chamber from the solid rock. He had Rostau and his engineers reinforce the chamber and emplace metal struts on the floor. He guided the mothership inside and set it down on the waiting struts.

All the remaining Airlia exited the craft. A single saucer waited outside. Rostau began building a stone wall supported on the inside by metal, to cover the entrance to the cavern.

While he was doing this, other Airlia were spreading sensor-deflecting webbing along the top of the cavern.

Aspasia activated a low-power beacon on the mothership, then exited via the small tunnel Rostau left open. The tunnel was then blocked. The mothership was sealed away and shielded from detection.

Aspasia got on board the saucer and flew back to Atlantis.

He had sown the seeds that would haunt the world for the next ten thousand years.

Donnchadh felt an overwhelming sense of frustration with her fellow humans. Gwalcmai and she were on the outer ring of Atlantis. They'd been there for a day, vainly trying to obtain passage away from Atlantis. Many ships had left as soon as they saw the mothership departing and while Donnchadh and her partner had been making their way outward, across the rings of water and land that made up Atlantis. By the time they made it to the outer ports, those who were smart enough to leave had gone. Those who remained were caught in the throes of hesitation and fear. As time passed and nothing untoward appeared to be happening, the fear was turning to complacency.

In fact, surprisingly, many from the outer rings had made their way inward, toward the temple. Thousands were gathered in the plaza in front of the temple spire, supplicating the unseen Gods, swearing their fealty. When they received no reply, they prayed harder and louder, as if that would make a difference. There were no Guides or high priests in evidence and the doors to the temple were locked shut.

Donnchadh and Gwalcmai were finally able to find a ship manned by those from the northern part of the island on which they had originally secreted their spaceship. The price demanded by the ship's captain was outrageous, but Donnchadh willingly paid it. The captain did insist that they wait till the following morning to depart, as his crew feared leaving in the dark. Although it was against her better judgment, Donnchadh agreed, a large part of her wanting to see how things played out in Atlantis.

When dawn broke, all were startled to see a mothership hovering high over the temple spire. It must have arrived sometime during the night. As the sun rose, the large craft slowly descended to the cries of prayers from the humans below. What those humans didn't know was that this was not Aspasia's ship, but Artad's, coming to enact the last part of the first stage of the Atlantis Truce.

Surprisingly, the mothership did not dock with the temple spire, but slid to the side, coming down over a large field outside the city walls. A cargo door opened and a gangplank extended to the ground. From his vantage point halfway up the ship's mast, Gwalcmai could see this and he relayed these happenings to Donnchadh.

"What is happening now?" Donnchadh asked. "Is anyone coming out?"

"No," Gwalcmai said. "There is no activity. Some people are gathering round the field, but no activity on the mothership."

Donnchadh frowned. She turned to the ship's captain. "It is time for us to go. The sun is up."

The captain merely nodded at her, then issued orders to his men. The lines were untied from the dock and oars were manned. To the slow, steady beat of the ship's master's drum, they moved away from the dock.

"Two men are going up the gangplank," Gwalcmai reported. "They've gone inside."

Once they were clear of the dock and shore, the captain issued orders and the sail was unfurled. Gwalcmai swung aside as the boom came down the mast, narrowly missing him. He put his free hand over his eyes.

"They've come back out," he said. "They're gesturing for others to come on board."

"I would go faster," Donnchadh said to the captain.

"The people are rushing the ship," Gwalcmai reported. "Thousands of them." He looked down. "What is happening?"

"One of the Airlia is gathering his crop," Donnchadh said.

A spasia had returned to Atlantis during the night on the saucer. He'd gathered the last of the Airlia under his command in a hangar underneath the palace, where they boarded the seven Talons he had recalled to Earth. In the command center of his Talon, Aspasia could see, via monitors in the spire, Artad's mothership loading humans on board. That was not part of the truce, but Aspasia knew that Artad had watched his dispersal and was countering it in his own way. Move—countermove. Even as he watched, the gangplank suddenly began to withdraw into the ship and the cargo door abruptly shut, cutting in half a few desperate souls clinging to the ship.

"*Lift,*" Aspasia ordered.

The roof of the hangar slid open and the Talons shot up, away from Earth.

D onnchadh could see the departing Talons as easily as Gwalcmai. They could also see the mothership gaining altitude.

"Come down," she called out to her husband.

The ship was now about five kilometers away from the

outer ring of Atlantis. On the land, people looked up at the massive mothership above them in fear, all sensing that something was going to happen. Supplicant priests who had not been converted or taken by Aspasia led crowds in desperate prayers. Warriors held up spears, swords, and shields in fruitless displays of defiance. The few remaining ships rapidly put to sea, their decks crowded with those who had realized too late their plight.

Donnchadh and Gwalcmai stood side by side near the stern of the ship, watching and waiting. They could feel in the air the same thing the people on Atlantis did—an electric charge as if a large thunderstorm were coming.

Donnchadh drew a sharp breath as a bright golden light raced along the black surface of the mothership from rear to front. She had seen this before and knew what was coming.

"Faster," she called out to the captain.

The golden light seemed to gather at the nose of the mothership, then pulsed downward in a half-mile-wide beam, passing through the city and into the ground below with no apparent effect.

Once more the light ran along the outside of the mothership, gathered, then pulsed down. And again. Donnchadh found herself counting, the scientist in her taking notes. Ten times.

Then there was absolute stillness for several seconds.

Donnchadh's hand found Gwalcmai's. She squeezed tight.

The earth beneath Atlantis exploded.

spasia had a view of what was happening on the front screen of the control room of his Talon. He'd watched Artad's mothership fire ten times, knowing exactly what was coming. The Airlia had extensively studied the evolution of planetary structure. The weapon Artad was using against

Atlantis had been designed to tap into the power that resided deep inside the planet and bring it upward.

The shock wave from the explosion killed almost everyone on the island instantly. The handful who survived the initial blast died horrible deaths as a wave of magma sprayed forth in a fiery froth. The entire landmass that had been Atlantis initially lifted upward almost two hundred meters from the explosion, then imploded. The ocean absorbed both the explosion and implosion, giving birth to a tsunami of unbelievable scale.

On the view screen there was nothing left of Atlantis.

Gwalcmai saw what was coming. "Put your stern directly into the wave," he yelled to the two men holding the tiller. A ship behind them was hit on an angle and flipped over, disappearing into the wall of water. The rear of their ship lifted as the base of the front of the tsunami reached them. Hit square on, it rode up the front, the angle growing steeper and steeper. Gwalcmai wrapped an arm around Donnchadh's waist while he grabbed the railing with the other to prevent them from sliding overboard.

Donnchadh watched helplessly as a screaming sailor tumbled past and disappeared overboard. She felt Gwalcmai's grip get even tighter around her waist as she held on to the railing with her own hands. They seemed to be rising forever. Donnchadh looked up—the crest was still over a hundred meters above them and they had already gone up, as best she could tell, about seven hundred meters.

"I love you," she yelled to Gwalcmai.

He nodded, then swung his head from side to side to clear the wet hair from his eyes. "We'll make it."

And they did, slowly going from almost vertical to horizontal, riding the top of the massive wave.

"Hold on," Gwalcmai yelled, not only to Donnchadh but to the sailors clinging to whatever protection they had managed to find.

The ship began to slide down the less steep side of the wave. It took well over a minute before they were finally off the wave. It was moving away from them, a wall of water that took up the entire horizon. All around the ship, the ocean was littered with bodies and debris. Gwalcmai slowly let go of Donnchadh's waist. They both looked over the stern of the ship. Where Atlantis had been there was nothing but debris-filled water.

Donnchadh turned to Gwalcmai and spoke to him in their native tongue. "A truce, Gwalcmai."

Gwalcmai nodded. "They are neutralized here. They are no longer Gods."

"For the time being."

"Time is a valuable commodity, Donnchadh. We didn't have it, but maybe things will be different here. We have helped accomplish the first stage of our mission. The Airlia have fought among themselves and both sides, in essence, have lost."

Donnchadh frowned. "But neither side has been defeated. And you know this truce is a farce. Both will try to use Guides and Shadows to—"

Gwalcmai held a hand up. "We've done what we can. Which is more than we could have hoped for. We have gained time for the people on this world. And we will be around to help in the final war when it does come."

Donnchadh realized he was right. They had accomplished much for only being two against those who ruled as Gods. Gwalcmai went to the ship's captain and issued him instructions, directing that they head toward the northeast.

When he returned to Donnchadh he saw that she was

looking up and he knew what was on her mind. "He has long since died."

"I know," Donnchadh acknowledged, "but I can still mourn."

"Mourning is all that seems to come of this."

Donnchadh nodded. "There will be more grief before it is all over."

Aspasia had the Talon's visual sensors zoom in on the planet that was receding behind them. He could see Artad's mothership passing over the massive wave that was moving out in a perfect circle from where Atlantis had been. The wave was moving at almost six hundred kilometers an hour.

The first land it hit was the western tip of Africa. As the water grew shallower the wave slowed, but that energy was translated in water displacement and the tsunami grew taller, doubling in height by the time it hit the shoreline.

For those onshore, the first indication of something amiss was the water actually withdrawing from the land, baring the sea bottom to the sun. Fish were caught by the sudden disappearance of the water and lay flopping in the mud. Some humans went out to gather this unexpected bounty, not knowing their doom was racing toward them.

The air was filled with the sound of a thousand thunderstorms. Then the wall of water appeared. It swept ashore first in western Africa, then all around the Atlantic coastline as the circle expanded. It surged inland, in some places penetrating over 150 kilometers before finally coming to rest. Some of the wave even passed through what would be called the Pillars of Hercules into the Mediterranean, causing devastation throughout that basin.

The tsunami, greatly diminished, even made it around the

capes on the southern tips of America and Africa and into the other oceans, circling the globe. So worldwide was the effect that the legend of the Great Flood would pass into legend among all peoples of the world.

Aspasia cared little about what the water had done. His sensors tracked Artad's mothership as it crossed Europe. It came to a halt above a tall peak in the land that was located between Asia, Europe, and Africa, where it off-loaded the thousands on board. After the people had dispersed, the pilot of the vessel did as Aspasia had done in North America— hollowing out a cavern inside the mountain and caching the massive ship inside.

Even though his Talon was drawing farther and farther away from the planet, the sensors were able to pick up a half dozen golden saucers zooming off to the east, disappearing around the edge of the planet. Aspasia had no doubt he was witnessing some plan Artad had set in motion to keep his own side in play through the truce. It was the Airlia way.

M any people must have died." Donnchadh was lying next to Gwalcmai, his arm around her, near the stern of the boat. The sail flapped in the light breeze, propelling the ship to the northwest.

"Yes." Gwalcmai said no more and they were quiet for a while, both looking up at the stars.

"Do you think—" Donnchadh began, but Gwalcmai gently put a hand over her mouth.

"Shhh," he whispered. "This is what we came here to do. Some dead now versus many dead later. This is going to be a very long war. Very long. And it's just begun."

VII

Donnchadh and Gwalcmai passed other ships on their way to the northeast, most of the craft having been badly battered by the wave. Twice they stopped and took on board survivors of vessels that were foundering, also off-loading whatever supplies they found. One of those vessels had two dozen high priest suppliants on board. They had run away from the temple when the door was slammed in their face by the Guides during the loading of the first mothership. Seeing the Ark and Sphinx being lifted out had convinced them that the end was near and they needed to leave.

In Donnchadh's view this meeting was a fortuitous opportunity and she spent most of the journey with the twenty-four suppliants, telling them the truth about the Airlia—up to a point. She did not tell them where she and Gwalcmai were from or of the other planets. Simply that the Airlia were not Gods, but rather creatures that used humans for their own ends. The suppliants had no difficulty believing her, given recent events. By the time they landed on the southwest coast of England, Donnchadh and Gwalcmai had come up with a plan for these men.

They led them inland. During their time on the island, the two had prepared for various contingencies and were using one of those strategies now. After several days of hard marching, the group arrived at a lake. In the very center, a hill rose precipitously up out of the water to a cone-shaped top. It was a great tor, towering over five hundred feet above the lake. Donnchadh and Gwalcmai had come across this strange geological structure several lifetimes ago. There was a small village on the south side of the lake. Seeing the strangely dressed party approach, the inhabitants fled and the group appropriated several boats to cross the lake to the island. Before they departed, Donnchadh had the suppliants gather several torches.

A thin trail wound its way back and forth up the tor to the top. They wove their way upward in silence. When they reached the top, the view was magnificent. A large plain surrounded the lake and tor in all directions. A small circle of blackened stones indicated where the locals had set a fire. Next to it was a larger stone, about a foot high by six long and three wide. Donnchadh and Gwalcmai had placed it there with great effort. They noticed that there were objects of worship on the stone—dried flowers; mummified corpses of small animals; smaller, carved rocks.

With one arm Gwalcmai reached out to sweep the objects off the stone, but Donnchadh stopped him. "Myth is valuable," she said, and she carefully removed them and placed them at the base of the stone as the suppliants waited.

Once the stone was clear, Donnchadh used the medallion around her neck. She pressed it against a spot near the top of the stone. The suppliants were not overly surprised when the stone slid down two feet and moved sideways, revealing steps descending into darkness. They had seen such and more while on Atlantis.

Donnchadh led the way down the stairs, the suppliants following, Gwalcmai bringing up the rear, closing the stone behind them. The flames from the torches flickered off the stone walls as they descended.

Donnchadh and Gwalcmai had taken a chance years previously, using a stone-cutting tool appropriated from the Airlia supplies on their planet to carve out this passageway. They'd done it because, by using sensors, they had been able to determine there were several large voids deep underneath the tor and they had cut their way down to reach and connect those voids, making their own version of the Roads of Rostau. The air inside was damp and chilly. The stone walls were perfectly cut, the steps smooth and unmarked.

They came to a halt on a landing with a stone wall ahead and more stairs descending ninety degrees to the right. Donnchadh put her medallion to a spot on the stone wall and a hidden doorway appeared.

Donnchadh led the way through, the rest following. The dampness was gone now, although it was still chilly. The light from the torches grew much brighter as it was reflected a thousand times over from crystals that lined the cavern. The open space was two hundred meters long by a hundred wide.

Donnchadh went to the right along the wall to another door, flanked by two pillars of crystal. She opened the door and a level tunnel lay beyond. They walked along it for a kilometer before Donnchadh abruptly stopped. She placed her medallion against the left side of the tunnel and another hidden door appeared and opened. They entered a small chamber, ten meters long by five wide. The twenty-six crowded inside. There was a small wooden table in the middle of the room and Donnchadh went to the far side of it. A scroll of papyrus was on the table, held down on each corner by small pieces of crystal.

Donnchadh turned and faced the supplicants, Gwalcmai's hulking presence at her side. "This is where our order will be headquartered. The order of the *Wedjat* in the old tongue, which we must remember. The Watchers, in your new language.

"You were promised by the Airlia to be part of the order of the high priests. The high priests were promised that someday they would be allowed to partake of the Grail. All lies, as you now know. It is something you should have known before the destruction of Atlantis, as successive generations of high priests and Guides were promised the same thing and each generation died off, passing on the promise to their followers. But you held on to your faith until you were betrayed."

There was no dissent. There was an aura in the room, one that Donnchadh paused to try to assess. Then she realised it was anger—fury. At the betrayal of the Airlia. At the loss of everything that had meant anything to them—their faith, their homes, the families they had come from.

"You would want to fight the Airlia," she said. "Have revenge on them for their betrayal of you and mankind." A growl of assent rumbled through the chamber and echoed off its stone walls. "But you cannot fight them. You do not have the means. Not yet. But you can watch, as we discussed. There are places on the planet where the Airlia have hidden themselves and their machinery. We must find those places, then watch them until mankind is ready to fight the Airlia."

Donnchadh took the leather purse containing the medallions and rings she had taken from the high priests and Guides she had killed. She emptied it on top of the papyrus on the wooden table. Then she drew a black dagger from her belt. She held it up in the flickering torchlight, and then brought the blade down across her palm, drawing blood.

Donnchadh held the palm up toward the supplicants. "You will now take a blood oath—an oath of human blood that will bind us and our descendants. To be the *Wedjat*. To dedicate our lives to watching the Airlia and their minions until the day mankind can destroy them." She held out the dagger, handle first. "Who will bind themselves to humanity? Who will vote with your blood to be part of this?"

One of the supplicants stepped forward without hesitation. "I am Brynn. All I have known was destroyed by the Airlia. All they taught me were lies. I will be of the *Wedjat* and I promise that all who descend from me will be of the order." He took the dagger and slid the blade across his own palm, drawing blood, then placed his palm against Donnchadh's. Their blood mingled. With her free hand she gave him one of the rings.

One by one, the other twenty-three stepped forward and did the same. By the time the rite was over, a pool of blood had formed on top of the papyrus.

Donnchadh let Gwalcmai do the next step. He was the military expert and had spent his life fighting the Airlia. He laid out a map of the planet's surface, developed during the orbits they had done prior to landing at Stonehenge. It was quite detailed, showing the topographical features in various colors that he explained to the *Wedjat* gathered round.

"We do know they have prepared a base here," Gwalcmai said, tapping a thick forefinger on a long river that one day would be called the Nile. "Who wants it?"

"It is a long way," one of the *Wedjat* murmured, taking in the scale that Gwalcmai had demonstrated by comparing the distance they had traveled from their landing on this island to this location to the entire world's scale.

Gwalcmai laughed. "Some of you will have to go much farther."

"I, Kaji, will take that assignment." The man who spoke

these words was short and slight but he spoke with confidence.

"Good," Gwalcmai said. "Beyond that known location, we will have to scatter and cover the entire planet. It might be your grandson who finds one of their lairs. And you must beware. Not only of the Airlia but of those they sent out to protect themselves. Guides and high priests most likely. And even humans who, as you did in Atlantis, believe they are Gods."

Gwalcmai turned to the map once more. He was done asking for volunteers. He pointed. "You. You will take this area." He designated a part of the planet's surface. "You. Here." And so it went until he had apportioned the entire surface of the planet.

"You will draw copies of any maps that you will need," Gwalcmai said. "We will give you gold and other valuable things to take with you. You each have either an Airlia ring or medallion that will act as a key to many of their secret doors.

"I want to emphasize what you have already been told: Do not try to fight any of these creatures." He drew his sword. "This is not the path for you to take." He put the sword down and touched his eyes. "Watch. Report. Make sure you propagate and keep your line of *Wedjat* going through the years. We are joined in a battle that goes beyond a future any of us can see."

The rest of the day was spent preparing the *Wedjat* for their departure. A restless night passed, then as the sun rose the next morning they all climbed the stone stairs to the top of the tor, which Donnchadh named Avalon.

They gathered on the top of the tor. For once it wasn't raining. Rays of sun slanted toward them over the green fields and glinted up off the dark water of the tor lake. The *Wedjat* were wrapped in black and brown cloaks, heavy packs on their backs laden with supplies. Most had long walking sticks they had hand-carved.

"We will have a gathering here," Donnchadh said. "In twenty-five years. If you can come back, do so. If you cannot, send your child. Let us know what you have discovered. If you have no children, send a report by any means possible."

Donnchadh and Gwalcmai then went down the line shaking hands. One by one, the *Wedjat* went down the track to the base of the tor where they were shuttled across the water by Brynn. Lone figures set off in all directions of the compass, searching out the Airlia and their minions.

You will keep the reports that will be sent to you," Donnchadh said to Brynn the next day. She held up the papyrus that had taken her blood and that of the Watchers and extended the rolled-up tube to the first man who had given his blood to join hers. "This is the first record, one only those who were here would understand."

Brynn, who had been chosen to be the Watcher of Avalon, as Donnchadh had named the place, took the papyrus. "I will do my duty."

Brynn stood with Donnchadh and Gwalcmai atop the tor. A gray sky hung low over their heads and there was rain to the east, coming toward them. A most miserable and entirely typical day for the place.

Donnchadh looked to the south, where the small village was on the edge of the lake. "You must take a wife and bring forth an heir to take your place. You must encourage the supersition of the villagers about this place so they will fear to come here."

Brynn nodded respectfully, even though he, along with the rest of the Watchers, had received the same briefing prior to the great dispersal the previous day. Gwalcmai shifted his feet impatiently. He too had heard Donnchadh say the same thing and had no patience with her repetition.

But Donnchadh felt a deep sense of sadness. They had altered the course of Airlia rule on this planet by causing the Great Civil War and subsequent Atlantis Truce. But it was still going to be a very, very long time before humans developed to a point where they could fight the Airlia, if they ever did.

She put her hand on Brynn's shoulder, knowing he would most likely be dead before she returned. "Remember your oath."

On Mars, deep under Cydonia, Aspasia and his closest followers lay down in the black tubes that awaited them. Overall, Aspasia felt he had done well. He had weathered Artad's initial assault and extracted a truce from his former and present enemy.

As the lid closed on him and left him in darkness, Aspasia drifted off to the deep sleep knowing that there would come a time of reckoning. He had ceded Earth to Artad, but there would be a day when he returned. Meanwhile, there was always his Shadow on Earth to deal with things.

In China, Artad had not settled on a natural resting place, but used his saucers and their tractor beams to erect a mountain over three hundred feet high that would one day be called Qian-Ling by the locals. He burrowed deep into the ground, surrounding his refuge with traps.

He also prepared his own contingencies. First, he prepared his own Shadow, set in a chamber near the top of the mountain. He loaded his own essence into a *ka* and placed it in the machine. He set no timer, but rather linked the console to a guardian computer that monitored the outside world. He would allow the machine to make the decision to awaken the Shadow, then the Shadow could make the decision whether to awaken him.

As a redundancy to the computer monitoring, he also prepared creatures that could walk the surface of the planet and, with some slight disguise, pass among the humans. His scientists generated two dozen Airlia-Human clones. Ones Who Wait. They were given regeneration tubes and sent forth to keep an eye on Artad's side of the truce. They were sent to a base hidden in a mountain in Africa.

Artad then set his guardian computer and went into the deep sleep, confident that when he awoke the issue of whether the Swarm had reported this planet would be resolved. Then it would be time to deal with Aspasia.

Donnchadh held Gwalcmai in a last embrace. They stood between the two tubes in their spaceship, preparing to go into the deep sleep. Their bodies were young—fresh out of the tubes. It was always a disorienting experience to see her mate so young after spending years growing old with him. She had enough vanity, though, to appreciate her slender, smooth body and the feel of his hands on her.

"We are in no rush," she told Gwalcmai.

He laughed, a rumble deep in his chest. "Really?"

"The tubes can wait for a little while," Donnchadh affirmed.

"How little is a little while?" Gwalcmai asked as he lifted her off her feet with a tight embrace and his lips hovered just above hers.

"However long we wish."

VIII

ere things different?

That was the question running through Donnchadh's mind as she pressed her medallion against the inner lock for the door in the standing stone. It slid open and Gwalcmai, as was his way, stepped past her and into the open, sword in hand.

Donnchadh followed. Into rain. Which was to be expected. What did surprise her were the new standing stones flanking the three original ones. Just as large as those she and Gwalcmai had emplaced. They both stared at the stones for several minutes in silence as the rain drizzled down, soaking their clothes.

"How could—" Gwalcmai began, but then stopped, at a loss for words.

Donnchadh smiled. "Humans. We are very innovative. I don't know how these stones were brought here or stood upright, but they did it. The ones we've come to help."

Gwalcmai frowned. "They are just stones."

Donnchadh slapped her hand against the stone they had just come out of. "How did you get this here?"

"You know—"

"How did we get these here?" she pressed.

"We used the ship and the tractor beam and—"

"Do they have ships and tractor beams?"

"No. I don't think they could," Gwalcmai amended. "Not enough time has passed."

"So how did they get them here?"

Gwalcmai shrugged. "I don't know."

"Neither do I," Donnchadh said. "But they did. I take great hope from that." She slapped Gwalcmai on the shoulder. "Let's find out what's changed."

Avalon was different also. There was a rudimentary stone wall around the entrance stone on top of the tor. There was also another wall, about four feet high and loosely mortared, running around the outer perimeter of the tor's top. Donnchadh placed her medallion in the correct place and the stone on top of Avalon slid aside. She stood still for several seconds, listening. She smiled when she heard footsteps echoing up the stairwell. A glow appeared, coming closer.

"Who are you?" the man holding the torch demanded, a rusty sword held in one shaking hand. He was old and stooped. All his teeth were missing and his left eye twitched uncontrollably.

Donnchadh held up her medallion. "I am of the *Wedjat*."

The man's eyes opened wide. "That is the medallion of the head of the order. But"—he fumbled for words—"it is said the head of our order disappeared many, many years ago."

"My name is Donnchadh. And this is Gwalcmai," she added, indicating her partner.

"But that is the name of the founders. Of the leaders of the First Gathering."

"Have there been other Gatherings?" Donnchadh asked. The second one had been sparsely attended, with only four of the original *Wedjat* and three offspring representing their fathers. Their information had been as scant as the representation. That had led to Donnchadh's and Gwalcmai's decision to go back to Stonehenge and deep sleep for an extended period of time.

The man was confused and Donnchadh realized she had gone too fast with him. She lowered the medallion. "And your name is?"

"I am Brynn, the *Wedjat* of Avalon."

Donnchadh smiled. "As was named the first *Wedjat* of Avalon. And as we are named after the leaders of the First Gathering."

Brynn tried to process this. While he was working it over, Gwalcmai stepped forward. "May we come in? The rain is cold."

"Yes, yes," Brynn said. "Come, come. I do not have much to offer you," he warned.

They entered, shutting the door behind them. They followed Brynn down the stairs until they came to the landing. He opened the door with his own medallion and they entered the crystal cavern. They went along the side to the next tunnel and followed it to the chamber at the end.

Things were different there. A wooden rack was along one wall and it was full of rolled-up papers. A large desk sat in the center of the room with a stool in front of it. Writing implements were on the desk along with scrolls of blank parchment. There was a small grille providing scant air and copious dark smoke that was trying to find its way out the small hole in the back of the rooms. The place smelled primarily of smoke with an underlying staleness.

Brynn indicated they should sit on a wooden cot covered with a threadbare blanket. "Please."

Donnchadh sat down to please the old man, but Gwalcmai prowled about the chamber.

"Do you have a report to make?" Brynn asked.

"Others come here to render reports?" Donnchadh asked.

"Not many," Brynn said. "Not many. Three in my life-time. Two were sons sent by their fathers on the long journey to see this place where it all began. But it is difficult to travel and the world is large. I've also received twelve written re-ports over the years that come via traders and others. Not many, according to my father, who told me of his father's time here. And of the times before then."

"The Airlia?" Gwalcmai brusquely asked.

"They sleep still," Brynn said. "Except in Egypt."

"Where is this place called Egypt?" Gwalcmai pressed.

"Along the large river far to the south and east on the In-ner Sea," Brynn said. He went to the rack and pulled out a scroll, which he then unrolled on the desktop. Donnchadh got up and joined Gwalcmai, looking down at the paper. It was a detailed map, on which they could recognize the fea-tures from their original sketches from orbit.

Brynn tapped a spot. "Here." Gwalcmai recognized the place. He had sent a Watcher there at the First Gathering.

Brynn's finger ran along a thin black line. "This river, which the people there call the Nile. Right here"—the finger stopped—"is Giza. The Airlia rule there. Not seen much on the surface, to be truthful. But occasionally on major holi-days they appear. So says the latest report from the line of Kaji, the *Wedjat* of Giza." He went to the rack and pulled out another scroll.

Donnchadh looked at Gwalcmai. What they had estab-lished over two thousand years ago was still functioning, al-beit at a rudimentary and sketchy level. It was a testament to their planning, but even more so to the human spirit. Brynn opened the scroll. Donnchadh recognized most of the writ-ing—the Airlia High Rune language, but some of it was dif-ferent, transformed by the passage of time.

She scanned the document. The *Wedjat* of Giza who had

written this, named Kajim, reported that the Black Sphinx graced a deep depression in the Giza Plateau—at least they knew where the Hall of Records had been sent. Which most likely meant the Ark containing the Grail was ensconced inside.

The Grail. Donnchadh's hand shook as she smoothed out the parchment. Her mind flashed back to the mothership on her planet and her desperate leap to try to catch the Grail before the Airlia dropped it into the engine's power stream.

She read further. The Roads of Rostau. The name sounded Airlian. According to Kajim these were a warren of tunnels and chambers carved into the rock under the Giza Plateau. Donnchadh knew how much the Airlia liked to burrow into a planet. Whether it was because that's how things were on their native planet or for protection from attack, she had no idea.

That was all background in the report, validating what previous reports from the Giza *Wedjat* had indicated. But things were changing there, according to Kajim. She could sense both Brynn and Gwalcmai waiting as she read, but she took her time.

The Airlia appeared on the surface infrequently, according to Kajim, less and less each year. There were rumors that they were growing older, which confused the people; how could Gods grow older?

There were also rumors of dark perversions being perpetrated in chambers along the Roads of Rostau. Kajim had gone in to investigate, using the Airlia ring that his ancestor had been given at the First Gathering and had been passed down through the ages to him. Donnchadh tried to remember which of the twenty-four supplicants had been Kaji, but she drew a blank. It was so long ago, and there had been so many.

Kajim's reports were dry and factual, obviously written by

a man not given to flights of imagination. Donnchadh's finger ran along the High Runes as she read:

> There are three chambers—cells—along the fourth Road of Rostau, as mapped by the third Wedjat of my order, who was the first to penetrate the roads. It is a road that comes to an end just past these cells—I tried all the walls for a secret key place and found none. In each cell are two of the black tubes. In each tube rests a pitiful creature—half-human, half-Airlia. The bastard offspring of the Airlia males and human consorts.
>
> They are used for their blood. Each month, at the full moon, the high priests take the blood of supplicants from veins in their arms and gather it into metal flasks. These flasks are then taken into the chamber and fed to the six prisoners held there. Then the Airlia come and take the blood of the six.
>
> Why this is done, I do not know.
>
> There is a door to the Hall of Records in the pedestal beneath the statue of Horus between the paws of the Sphinx. I have gone inside four times. There is also a thing that guards the tunnels. A golden orb, less than a meter in width, with black arms coming out in all directions, patrols the Roads. If one is perfectly still and covers oneself with a cloak, it will not discover you. I lost my oldest son to this thing and barely escaped with my life during the first encounter with it.
>
> Here is the way to the chamber where these poor creatures are being held.

Donnchadh felt the hairs on the back of her neck rise as she read. She knew why the Airlia had done this. They had discovered several places like this on their own planet—in the few Airlia outposts they managed to capture before they were destroyed. Also Jobb had reported this practice had continued on Atlantis. The half-breeds were being used for pleasure—the human blood sustained the half-breeds' half-human/half-Airlia blood. Then the Airlia drained the half-breed blood in turn. Between the Airlia virus in the blood and the sleep of the black coffins, those trapped inside could live a very long and terrible existence.

She memorized the route, then took the weights off the corners of the scroll and rolled it up, absently handing it to Brynn, who returned it to its place as she considered what she had just read. Bad memories pressed at her mind, but she tried to keep them at bay.

"What other recent reports do you have?" Gwalcmai asked.

Brynn gathered a handful of scrolls and held them out.

"Donnchadh?" Gwalcmai said, startling her out of her reverie. She took the scrolls and put them on the desk. She read quickly, sometimes struggling with the changes to the High Rune writing caused by some Watchers' years of isolation and the inevitable degradation of the language as it passed through generations.

"What do you have?" Gwalcmai asked after several minutes, showing no inclination to read the material himself.

"The Airlia who ruled in Atlantis was named Aspasia—"

"We knew that," Gwalcmai cut in.

Donnchadh looked up at him and he immediately quieted.

"The Airlia who came to find out why Aspasia was out of contact for so long was named Artad. They decided on a truce of which the destruction of Atlantis was part and of which we are apparently still in the midst. One of the *Wedjat* has found another Airlia base in a distant location in a land called China." She checked the map and pointed. "Located here. The Airlia built a large, hollow mountain and are hidden inside."

"Which Airlia?" Gwalcmai asked. "Which side?"

Donnchadh shrugged. "There's no telling." She read the other scrolls in silence, then rolled them up and handed them to Brynn, who replaced them on the shelf. "There are reports of Human-Airlia clones—called the Ones Who Wait. And of Guides and high priests in various places. It appears the Airlia are continuing the Great Civil War through proxies."

"What do we do now?" Gwalcmai asked, always more interested in the course of action rather than the intelligence that led to determining one.

Donnchadh ignored him for the moment. She put a hand on the old man's shoulder. He felt frail beneath her palm. "Do you have an heir to follow in your place?"

Brynn nodded. "My son lives in the village with his mother, but I have taught him as much as I know—as much as my father taught me. He will be ready to take my place when the time comes."

"You have done well, Brynn of the *Wedjat*," Donnchadh said.

The old man gave a toothless smile. "It is not easy. Most in the village fear the tor. But there are a few who think there must be great treasure hidden here. Four times someone has tried to break in, but they were not able to pass the stone door. I must be careful, though, whenever I open it. My son brings me supplies at set times, and only in the darkness."

"You perform an important duty," Donnchadh said, "the fruition of which you will most likely not see in your lifetime, but your descendants will."

*   *   *

W e're going to Egypt," Donnchadh informed Gwalcmai as he pulled on the oars, propelling the small reed boat across the gap of water separating Avalon from the surrounding land. They had left Brynn on the top of the tor, the old man's eyes full of tears at having been visited by what he considered other Wedjat and Donnchadh's kind words.

"We are not powerful enough to try to get the Grail," Gwalcmai said. "Opening the Hall of Records will undoubtedly alert a guardian, which will bring the Airlia. They will—"

Donnchadh held up a hand, silencing her partner. "I do not propose we try to get the Grail. I propose we cause trouble for the Airlia."

Gwalcmai smiled, sensing the devilment in his wife. "And how will we do that?"

"We unleash those who hate the Airlia as much as we do."

"And those are?"

"The Undead that the Airlia use for their enjoyment."

T he journey to Egypt was difficult. It appeared that seafaring had degraded from the time of Atlantis. They found no sailors willing to go out of sight of land. They were able to cross the channel separating their island from the continent at its narrowest point, where trade vessels plied back and forth only in the best of weather, when they were able to see across to the other side. From there they took the long sea journey around the continent to the west, never getting more than a kilometer from the coastline and stopping every evening on the shore. Several times they were stuck for days on end while storms raged and the sailors refused to put to sea. Even a thick fog would delay travel until the mist had cleared. The sailors feared the water and prayed to various sea gods for fortunate winds and their safety.

There was a little mention of the Airlia or Atlantis. Two thousand years had dimmed the past. Living was hard and the focus was on the here and now. Gwalcmai and Donnchadh decided that there had been little technological advancement—indeed, as Atlantis and the Airlia seemed to have faded into legend, so did any advancements that had trickled down to the humans. The people on Earth were essentially starting from scratch. Building their civilization back to even a basic level promised to be a very long and laborious process. The largest village they saw on their way around Europe boasted barely two hundred souls. In some places, the people were ignorant of such technological basics as the wheel.

The going was a little better once they reached the Mediterranean. The humans along the Inner Sea seemed a bit more advanced than those they had encountered so far. They traveled along the southern coast of what would some day be Spain and France, then down along the Italian peninsula and around it. Across to what would be called Greece, along Turkey, then the eastern side of the Inner Sea until finally they reached the mouth of the Nile. The entire journey took two years, during which time Donnchadh and Gwalcmai constantly observed the humans they met. They saw sparks of innovation here and there, but overall they both agreed that it would be many thousands of years before mankind got to a point where a challenge to the sleeping Airlia could even be considered.

After leaving the ship, they crossed the borders of Egypt. The two immediately saw that things were very different there. Passing a military post near the mouth of the Nile, they saw a Guide in command of the soldiers manning the fort. The soldiers' weapons were better than any they had seen so far and everything was much more organized.

They traveled at night, avoiding contact with locals.

They made it to Giza late one night and camped out in a laborers' camp along the river. They remained there several weeks, gathering information. The city just north of Giza, Cairo, contained over ten thousand people. And in the camps around the plateau itself, there were thousands of workers supplementing the core cadre of high priests and Guides.

They learned that there was indeed still a *Wedjat* at Giza—after all, someone had filed the report. The *Wedjat* was named Kajilil and he lived in a small hut with his family among the stonemasons, who were at work on building one of the many temples that dotted the plateau. But Donnchadh had no desire to meet him as she was planning to violate the very code that would have ensured her welcome.

The Black Sphinx crouched in its depression, obviously created by technology far beyond what humans possessed. Its eyes glittered as if possessed by a malevolent intelligence. Donnchadh felt an uncontrollable shiver each time she gazed upon the Hall of Records. It held both a promise and a threat—and often she wasn't sure which she considered to be the stronger of the two.

After a month in the area, they finally found the opportunity they were looking for: There was to be a celebration of the harvest during a night of the full moon, and it was said that some of the Airlia would most likely appear that night. It was time to do what they had come here for.

As darkness set, Gwalcmai and Donnchadh were hidden among a jumble of building stones on the edge of the Sphinx pit. They had arrived there early in the morning and now waited until the sun was well down in the west. Then they moved.

It quickly became clear that the high priests relied primarily on fear for security. There were a handful of Guides around the Sphinx depression, but Gwalcmai and Donnchadh were able to avoid them and make their way to the small open space between the paws of the Sphinx. A statue stood there, on a six-foot-high pedestal. Using her medallion, Donnchadh opened the door in the pedestal and they entered the Roads of Rostau.

Following the directions she had memorized from the *Wedjat* reports, Donnchadh led the way. The tunnels were dimly lit by glowing strips along the ceiling. The walls were perfectly cut, the result of Airlia technology that they themselves had used on occasion.

Donnchadh paused when Gwalcmai placed a hand on her arm. They both listened. There was a clicking noise, and it was coming closer. They both huddled against the floor on the side of the tunnel and drew their cloaks over their bodies. Peeking through a gap in her cloak, Donnchadh saw the creature that the *Wedjat* had described come toward them. It paused for a long time less than three meters away, waiting. The tips of the black arms glittered, razor-sharp points in the dim light.

Donnchadh felt she was close to passing out from shallow breathing, afraid that the creature would pick up the noise of air coming in and out of her mouth. Her body ached, a dozen itches afflicted her that she had never noticed before, and her heartbeat sounded incredibly loud inside her own head. Fear was what the Airlia relied on with much of their automatic defensive systems—it was something they had learned on her home world. To remain in place when this machine appeared was the last thing a person wanted to do and that was why the technique worked. The Airlia had underestimated their own creation on her world and she planned on making them pay the price on this world for the same mistake.

After a tense thirty seconds, the thing, discerning no movement, finally moved on, disappearing around the corner. They waited another twenty minutes before Gwalcmai felt it was safe to move again, then continued downward, deep under the Giza Plateau.

After so many centuries together there was no need for the two of them to talk. They moved as one, covering each other as they progressed. They entered a narrow corridor, barely wide enough for three abreast.

Donnchadh paused before a set of bars. On the other side were two black tubes resting on stone slabs. Deep sleep tubes, just like the ones in their craft, which they had appropriated from the Airlia.

Donnchadh saw that the tubes had been modified in one important way—each was secured on the outside with a latch, preventing whoever was inside from being able to open the lid. After touching the controls and programming the tube to bring whoever—or whatever—was inside out of the deep sleep, she pulled aside the latch on the closest tube and swung the lid up.

Inside was a tall creature, appearing human, with very pale skin and bright red hair. His skin was stretched tight over his bones, making him appear skeletal. His eyes were screwed shut against the invasion of dim light. His body twitched and shook as the deep sleep faded from his cells.

Donnchadh leaned close and spoke in the language of the Airlia. "The Gods must die or you will never escape this. You will die a miserable death after a long and worthless life."

The words echoed off the stone walls of the chamber and the shocked face of the creature inside as he comprehended them. The eyelids rose. His eyes had a reddish tint to them and the suggestion of an elongation of the pupil. Evidence, Donnchadh knew, of his Airlia roots. Gwalcmai was standing in the entrance to the cell, watching back the way they had come, sword in hand.

Donnchadh placed a finger on the creature's throat as she peered deep into his alien eyes. There was the tip of a shunt implanted in the skin. "You've been used for a very long time, haven't you?"

The creature sat up. He was secured to the inside of the tube by a chain around his waist. There were straps around his legs, arms, and torso with leads to the side of the tube—the stimulators that kept the muscles active during the deep sleep, Donnchadh knew. She saw him look at the other tube. Donnchadh went over to it and powered it down, tapping the correct hexagonals. Then she opened it. A female was inside.

Donnchadh went back to the male. He had not spoken a word. He was staring at her, waiting. Patience was a virtue that Donnchadh could appreciate.

"You won't last much longer," she said. "You have no choice. If you do not act, you will eventually die. Each time they drain you, the percentage of their blood in you is reduced and the human percentage grows. Soon you will no longer be effective for their needs. Then they will take another human female and make your replacement. They may already have a child, like you were once, growing up, guarded closely on the surface, ready to come here and be placed in this tube and drained as needed. They are very good at planning for their own needs and pleasures."

The male finally spoke. "How do you know this?"

"It is their way. They are not Gods, but creatures from—" Donnchadh pointed up. "From among the stars. They use us—humans—and they use you, half of their blood, half-human. It is hard for me to determine which is the worse of their sins. At least what they are doing to you is obvious. Their rule of the humans is more devious, pretending to be that which they aren't." She shrugged. "There is also the possibility that the Gods may decide to go into the long sleep, as their brethren have done in other places, in which case they will kill you and the others they keep down here, as you will longer be needed."

The male seemed confused. Donnchadh imagined this was all too much for him to grasp, but she knew the clock was ticking. They couldn't stay here and chat. Gwalcmai glanced into the cell and she nodded.

The female spoke. "Why do you want to help us? You are human. We aren't. We're half like them."

"Because you must hate them as much as I do and more than those above," Donnchadh explained. "Most humans"—she shook her head—"they are like sheep. Simply happy their harvest comes in and the Gods make all the decisions for them."

The female spoke again. "You cannot kill the Gods. They are immortal."

Donnchadh pulled aside her robe, revealing six daggers tucked into her belt. "With these you can. They were made by the Gods themselves for use against each other."

The female half-breed remained skeptical. "Even if we kill the Gods, the priests will then slay us, won't they?"

Donnchadh looked at the female. "Not if you are immortal."

The male was the first to grasp the significance. "The Grail?"

Donnchadh nodded. "You kill the Gods. You go into the Black Sphinx and recover the Grail, which is hidden there, then partake as has been promised by the Gods since before the beginning of time. You become immortal."

"Who are you?" the male demanded.

"My name is Donnchadh. My partner and I have fought the Gods in other places. That should be enough for you. Your enemy is our enemy."

"Your enemies are our parents," the male said.

"One of your parents." Donnchadh stared at him. "Your

other parent was human, taken by an Airlia—the Gods—for their pleasure and to produce you so they can use you for their pleasure also. The Gods deserve neither your homage nor your respect. They will drain you and kill you without a second thought once they have a replacement ready or if they no longer desire the pleasure your blood brings them."

"How can we do this that you propose?" The male rattled the chains holding him in the tube.

Donnchadh pulled a long piece of Airlia metal from inside her cloak. "Tonight. After the ceremony of the solstice. You can follow the Gods who oversee it from the ceremony to their hidden places along the Roads." She placed the tip inside one of the links of chain that bound him. "Do you want your freedom?"

The answer was what she expected. "Yes."

Donnchadh applied pressure and the link gave way. She worked quickly and soon the male was free. As he climbed out of his tube, Donnchadh went to the female and freed her. She saw Gwalcmai roll his eyes as the two creatures embraced. She held up a hand, begging his patience. But even she was shocked as the male put his mouth to the female's throat and began to drink her blood.

"We don't have time for this," Donnchadh said. "The ceremony has started above. You do not have much time to free the others and be ready."

The two were whispering to each other. Donnchadh could feel Gwalcmai's impatience permeate the cell. "If you do not act now, you will die." She didn't wait, moving out into the corridor and going to the next cell, which Gwalcmai had just opened.

"And who are you?" the male asked Gwalcmai.

"My name means nothing to you. I was called Gwalcmai, long ago. I have had other names and I will have others in the future."

"I am Nosferatu and this is Nekhbet."

Gwalcmai shrugged.

"Vampyr and Lilith are in here," Nosferatu added as they went into the second cell. Donnchadh didn't acknowledge this either as she opened up the two tubes and moved on to the third cell.

"Mosegi and Chatha," Nosferatu said as Donnchadh opened the last two tubes, freeing the occupants.

One for each of the Airlia, Donnchadh thought as she broke the chains around the last half-breed's waist. Done, she turned toward the exit, where Gwalcmai waited. "I will leave you to do what you must."

Nosferatu put a hand out, stopping her. "Tell me more of the Gods. Why do they need to do this?" He touched the shunt in his neck.

"As I have said, they do it for pleasure. It is an elixir for them. They prefer it over pure human blood."

"That is all?"

"Do you not relish the feeding you receive?" Donnchadh asked.

Nosferatu nodded.

"And was not her"—Donnchadh pointed at Nekhbet—"blood so much more pleasurable to you?"

"Yes."

"Then you should understand."

"We exist only for their pleasure?"

"Yes." Gwalcmai nodded his head, indicating they needed to leave.

"It is said the Gods are immortal," Nosferatu said.

Gwalcmai was restless in the corridor. "We must hurry."

"In a sense," Donnchadh said, "they are."

"Then am I immortal?"

Donnchadh shook her head. "No. But if you continue to drink human blood to feed the alien part of your blood—and don't get drained of any more of what you have—you can live a very, very long time. You can also go into the tube and use the deep sleep to let time pass without aging. I have seen it before. Where I came from. They did the same to my people."

"Where are you from?" Nosferatu asked.

"You would not understand." Donnchadh pointed to the end of the short corridor. "You can go to the right and get out a secret door near the Nile. The ceremony will start shortly in the Sphinx pit. Wait until the Gods who will oversee the ceremony appear, then follow them down the main Road of Rostau."

"But—" Nosferatu clearly wanted to know more but Donnchadh left, following right behind Gwalcmai.

He glanced over his shoulder. "They will not be able to get into the Hall of Records."

"Most likely not, since they do not have the key," Donnchadh agreed.

"Then what purpose did freeing them serve?"

"It will cause trouble for the Airlia here."

Gwalcmai wasn't convinced. "We shall see."

Donnchadh glanced over her shoulder at Gwalcmai. "Because of my sister."

Gwalcmai frowned. "You never told me you had a sister."

"Because she was dead to us the day she was taken by the Airlia to be used by the Airlia. As the mothers of those we just freed were used."

"Did she have"—Gwalcmai searched for the word—"offspring?"

"Yes."

Gwalcmai knew the fate of such humans and their offspring on their world—they had died when the Airlia main base had been destroyed. He switched the subject abruptly.

"We were followed through the tunnels, you know that, right?"

"The machine?"

"No," Gwalcmai said. "A human. The *Wedjat*. He is not as stupid as he appeared. He did his job—he watched."

Donnchadh nodded. "Good. Then we will use him also."

D onnchadh shoved open the door and walked into the Watcher's small hut, Gwalcmai right behind her. The man leapt to his feet, a dagger in his hand, his family cowering behind him.

"Tell them to leave," Donnchadh ordered in the ancient tongue. She pulled out her golden medallion and showed it to him.

The Watcher's eyes widened at both the language and the emblem. He lowered the dagger and quickly barked commands at his family. They scurried out of the hut, disappearing into the darkness.

"There has been no one here since—" the Watcher began, but Donnchadh raised her hand, cutting him off.

"There is something you must do."

F ools," Gwalcmai hissed as the chant of the priests echoed off the stone wall below them.

"*We serve for the promise of eternal life from the Grail. We serve for the promise of the great truth. We serve as our fathers have served, our fathers' fathers, and through the ages from the first days of the rule of the God who brought us up out of the darkness. We serve because in serving there is the greater good for all.*"

Donnchadh tapped Gwalcmai on the arm and pointed. "There."

Six dark forms were hidden among a pile of building

stone, also watching the priests prostrated before the paws of the Black Sphinx.

"So they didn't run," Gwalcmai said.

"Vengeance is powerful," Donnchadh said. "And the lure of the Grail—"

Gwalcmai stiffened as two tall, thin figures appeared in the open door in the pedestal beneath the paws. One raised its right hand, six fingers splayed open. Donnchadh stared at the Airlia for several moments, then noticed someone moving to their right, in the shadows. She tapped Gwalcmai's shoulder and pointed. "The Watcher."

The priests got to their feet and left, going to the nearby temple to continue praying. The two Airlia disappeared into the black hole beneath the chest of the Sphinx. Soon all that was left in the open before the Sphinx was a lone high priest. As the imprinted man turned toward the door, the six half-breeds that Donnchadh had freed sprinted across the open space and attacked him.

"They're actually doing it," Gwalcmai whispered. He had expressed doubts to Donnchadh that the half-breeds would go back into the Roads, suggesting instead that they would simply take this opportunity to run away.

"Their vengeance overpowers all else," Donnchadh said.

The six disappeared into the darkness, leaving the body of the high priest behind. After them went the Watcher, acting on Donnchadh's orders.

O nly two made it," Gwalcmai said several hours later. "More than I expected," Donnchadh said. They could see the Watcher along with two of the half-breeds, hidden along the edge of the depression.

"What are they waiting for?" Gwalcmai wanted to know.

"The same thing we are. Reaction to whatever they managed to do in the Roads."

All night long they had heard priests going throughout the surrounding area, ordering all to come to the Sphinx at first light, indicating that the Undead they had unleashed had achieved something in the warren of tunnels beneath them. As soon as it was light enough to see, Donnchadh knew what was coming—on top of the head of the Black Sphinx were two wooden Xs; behind them was a deep sleep tube.

"We should leave," Gwalcmai said, as soon as he saw the Xs.

Donnchadh couldn't respond. Her body had gone numb and her eyes were fixed on the objects on top of the Sphinx head. There were thousands of people gathered in the depression in front of the Sphinx, standing in absolute silence.

The door between the paws of the Sphinx opened and a group of high priests appeared, escorting three bound prisoners—half of those that Donnchadh and Gwalcmai had freed the previous night. All three were extremely pale and Donnchadh assumed they had been drained of their blood just short of the point of death. One of them—the one that had slept in the same chamber with Nosferatu—was also missing her right hand, the stump covered in a dirty linen bandage. They were moved up a ramp to the top of the Sphinx.

Then four Airlia appeared. The gathered humans dropped to their knees and bowed their heads, causing Gwalcmai to growl in disgust. The Airlia wore hooded black robes. They slowly walked up the ramp to the top of the Sphinx. Donnchadh could sense Gwalcmai's tensing—he was, after all, a God-killer.

A high priest stepped forward and cried out to the huddled masses: "Behold the price of rebellion. Behold the price of betrayal. Behold the price of disobedience."

Two of the prisoners were placed against the Xs, their arms and legs splayed against the wood. Their dirty robes were torn off, exposing their pale skin to the rays of the sun. High priests secured them to the wood using strips of leather that they first dipped in buckets of water. They worked from the tips of the extremities inward. Each strip of leather was an inch wide and they were spaced two inches apart.

The priests did this until both captives were secured up to their groins and armpits. When done, the high priest once more chanted: "Behold the price of rebellion. Behold the price of betrayal. Behold the price of disobedience."

Gwalcmai grabbed Donnchadh's shoulder. "We should leave. We do not need to see this. We've—" He stopped before completing the sentence.

"We've seen this before," Donnchadh finished it for him.

One of the prisoners cried out in pain. Donnchadh closed her eyes, but that couldn't stop the mental image of her father, tied to a similar cross, one made of black metal, with leather straps around his limbs. It was a horrible way to die as the slowly drying bands constricted, forcing blood from the extremities into the core of the body, allowing the victim to live a long time, while experiencing excruciating pain. Both prisoners were now screaming in agony.

Donnchadh nodded. "Let's go."

They slipped away from edge of the depression. As they did so, they heard the high priest call out one more time: "Behold the price of rebellion. Behold the price of betrayal. Behold the price of disobedience."

IX

Artad and Aspasia had negotiated and agreed to the Atlantis Truce, and both had also left behind their agents to continue a covert war against the forces of the other. The *Wedjat*, founded by Gwalcmai and Donnchadh, watched these minions, following their actions over the millennia.

Almost five thousand years after Donnchadh freed the Undead from their prison under Giza, rumor trickled back to the *Wedjat* headquarters in England from the Watcher of Giza that something strange and unnatural was happening in the depths of Africa on the side of a massive mountain. These rumors came from travelers who emerged from the interior of the continent, floating down the Nile. A *Wedjat* was dispatched with specific orders to investigate these rumors.

It was an arduous journey, crossing the continent, traversing it north to south, then around the edge of the Mediterranean to the dark continent. And that was only the first half of the trip, and, as it turned out, the easiest. In Africa the *Wedjat* linked up with the Watcher of Giza and spent a month resting and recuperating and preparing for the journey to the interior. There the man learned a little bit more—the travelers reported a strange forest of black poles growing on the side of a massive mountain, one of a pair of white-capped peaks known to the people in the area as the Twin Sisters.

He also learned the disturbing fact that the *Wedjat* were not the only ones to hear of this strange occurrence. The Horus-Guides ruled in Egypt and they too had heard the rumors. The *Wedjat* departed Giza just two days ahead of an Egyptian military column with the same mission—to search out the truth of these rumors. Instead of going due south along the Nile, as the Egyptians did, the *Wedjat* traveled east to the coast and took transit in a trader's vessel that plied the shoreline.

He traveled south, listening at each village and port the vessel stopped at for more stories of the black forest and the Twin Sisters. For weeks he heard nothing as he went farther and farther south along the coast. Finally, he found those who knew of the Twin Sisters. He continued south until he reached a point at which the locals told him the Twin Sisters were due west. He disembarked from the boat and struck out on land. Within a few days he could see one of the Twins himself, a white-capped mountain floating above the haze of the horizon to the west. From what he had heard, though, he needed to go to the second mountain to see the black forest. It took two more days before a second peak loomed on the horizon.

As the *Wedjat* approached from the east, the column of Egyptian soldiers, minus almost half their number after battling their way south from the headwaters of the Nile, also arrived within sight of the two mountains. The commander saw what was on the northern slope of the eastern-most mountain and, as he had been instructed, completed his report and immediately sent it back with his fastest riders toward the border of Egypt, where it would be forwarded by Imperial dispatch riders.

* * *

The *Wedjat* initially saw nothing strange on the second mountain as he approached it with the rising sun behind him. He first swung to the south, between the two great peaks, and looped around the farther mountain. Thus it was almost a week after the Egyptians sent back their report before he could see the northern slope and what had caused such consternation among the ranks of the soldiers from Giza: on that slope, above the tree line, was a vast spiderweb of black, covering over four kilometers in diameter. Strange beasts stalked among the web, continuing to build and expand it.

The *Wedjat*, who had studied the scrolls in Avalon, had never read of such a thing. He also spotted the Egyptian soldiers about two kilometers away from his position. Seeing that they were doing nothing but observing, he found a position from which he could keep an eye on both the construction on the mountain and the Egyptians.

And then he waited.

Two weeks passed.

Shortly after dawn one day a small, glowing, golden sphere flew by. The *Wedjat* had read of such a thing—it was a tool of the Airlia. It circled the mountain, then disappeared to the north. He could tell that the Egyptians had seen the golden sphere also. The soldiers began packing up their camp. The *Wedjat* wondered what to do—stay there, or go back to Avalon and report on what he had seen? But whatever was being built on the slopes of the mountain was still under contruction. He decided to stay.

Two days later the Airlia craft came. Nine lean black forms against the blue sky. They came to a halt about five kilometers above the mountain, bracketing it. A golden light crackled at the tip of each of the craft and pulsed down to the ground, passing into the mountain. There was a momentary pause, then the top of the mountain exploded from within.

As far away as the *Wedjat* was, the blast wave lifted him off the ground and threw him twenty meters away. The sky darkened from smoke and dirt, turning day into a strange night. As the *Wedjat* scrambled to his feet, ears ringing, rocks and debris tumbled down about him, and he only narrowly escaped death.

He looked to the south, toward the mountain—or where a mountain had been.

2,528 B.C.: THE SOLAR SYSTEM

The starship used a slingshot maneuver around the star to decelerate from interstellar speed. It was a small ship, a scout, and as the craft slowed, its sensors aligned on the signal that had diverted it to this system from its centuries-long patrol. The nose of the ship turned toward the third planet out as the data was analyzed. The signal was strange—a passive one, a uniform reflection of light rays of the system's star from something on the planet's surface, but there was little doubt the unusual effect was contrived by intelligence.

Searching out, analyzing, and then eventually reporting back concerning any intelligent life was the ship's mission. The nature of the species that crewed it was to find, infiltrate, consume, and ultimately destroy any intelligent life not like it.

Having picked up no active scanning in the solar system or signs of advanced weaponry, the ship emitted an energy pulse as it sent a spectrum of scanning signals toward the third planet to determine the source of the crude signal.

Unknown to the crew, the pulse was noted by passive sensors as it penetrated the atmosphere and reached the surface of the planet. A sophisticated computer, operating on low-power mode, intercepted the pulse, analyzed it, and projected possible courses of action in a matter of moments. In low-power mode the options were limited and the course of action was quickly selected.

2,528 B.C.: STONEHENGE

Donnchadh opened the lid of the tube to a flashing red glow. She sat up, her body sluggish and uncoordinated after so many years in the deep sleep. She had to blink several times to focus her eyes. She saw Gwalcmai's lid slowly swing up and he sat up as she climbed out of the tube, her bare feet touching the cold deckplate of the *Fynbar*. She quickly threw on a jumpsuit and boots.

"What is it?" Gwalcmai asked, his voice hoarse.

Donnchadh went to the ship's control console and sat in the pilot's seat. She powered up the main computer. She shut down the warning light. Data scrolled across the screen and she tried to make sense of it.

"The dish intercepted traffic between the guardians," she told Gwalcmai. "Something's happening."

"What—"

"There's a spacecraft inbound to this planet," Donnchadh said.

"Another mothership?"

Donnchadh stiffened as more information was intercepted and interpreted by the equipment they'd taken from the Airlia on their own planet. "It's not Airlia."

"The Ancient Enemy?"

Donnchadh nodded. "A Swarm scout ship."

Gwalcmai sat down in the copilot's seat. "How are the Airlia responding? Are Aspasia and Artad waking?"

"No."

"What?"

Donnchadh was concentrating on what the display was

telling her as it decoded the traffic between guardian computers. "They've set up an automated defense system."

"Where?"

"Giza."

"We can't take any chances," Gwalcmai said. "The Swarm scout ship has to be destroyed. If the Airlia system fails, we have to do it."

Donnchadh turned her attention from the screen for the first time and looked at her partner. "What do you suggest?"

"We go there as backup."

"Backup to the Airlia?"

"The lesser of two evils," Gwalcmai said as he began powering up the ship's systems for the first time in thousands of years.

2,528 B.C.: THE GIZA PLATEAU

Things had changed in Egypt. The Black Sphinx still glowered at the morning sun, but behind its left shoulder the smooth limestone sheathing covering the newly constructed Great Pyramid of Giza caught the rays of light and uniformly reflected them into the sky, producing the radar signal that the Swarm scout ship had picked up. At the very top of the five-hundred-foot-high pyramid, a blood-red capstone, twenty feet tall, glistened, an alien crown to the greatest structure ever built by human hands. The massive structure stood alone on the stone plateau, towering over the surrounding countryside, the nearby Nile, and the Sphinx complex. It had been built by humans according to the plans of Rostau, written down so many years previously.

To the east, in the direction of the Nile, were Khufu's Temple and the Temple of the Sphinx, where both Pharaoh and stone creature could be worshipped. A covered ramp led from the right rear of the Sphinx to the Temple at the base of the pyramid. While the pyramid was new, the surface of the Sphinx was scored by weather, having been there since the beginning of Egypt over seven thousand years ago in the time when the Gods ruled.

Between the paws of the Great Sphinx stood the Pharaoh Khufu, under whose leadership the Egyptians had labored for over twenty years, moving stone after stone to build the Great Pyramid. The Pharaoh prostrated himself in front of a statue set before the creature's stone chest. The statue was three meters tall and roughly man-shaped with polished white skin. The dimensions weren't quite right—the body was too short and the limbs were too long. The ears had elongated lobes that reached to just above the shoulders and there were two gleaming red stones in place of eyes. On top of the head, the stone representing hair was painted bright red. Even more strangely for the astute observer, each hand ended in six fingers. The statue's appearance was in great contrast to Khufu's dark skin and hair and human proportions.

Khufu had succeeded his father when he was just out of his teens and he was now middle-aged. He had ruled for almost three decades and Egypt was at peace with those outside its borders and rich within its own boundaries. The peace and wealth had allowed Khufu to implement the building plan for Giza that had been passed from the Gods, to the Shadows of the Gods, to the Pharaohs over the three ages.

The vast quantity of stone needed for the pyramid had been quarried upriver and brought down by barge. Thousands had labored on it seasonally, moving the stone from the barges and placing each block in its position under the careful eye of engineer priests who worked from the holy plans that had been handed down.

The red capstone had been brought up from the bowels of the Giza Plateau, from one of the duats along the tunneled Roads of Rostau where only the Gods and their priests were allowed to walk. No one knew what exactly the red pyramid was, but they had followed the drawings they had been given to the last detail, from the smooth limestone facing to the placement of the red object as the capstone.

In the Pharaoh's left hand as he prostrated himself was a scepter, a foot long and two inches in diameter with a lion's head on one end. The lion image had red eyes similar to that of the statue, but these glowed fiercely as if lit from within. Khufu had been awakened just minutes ago by his senior priest, Asim. The staff had been in the trembling man's hand, the lion eyes glowing, something never seen before. He had passed it to the Pharaoh.

Khufu had thrown on a robe and dashed from his palace to before the Sphinx, as he had been told by his father he must do if the staff ever came alive. He was now chanting the prayers he had been taught. The statue was of Horus, the son of Isis and Osiris, the Gods who had founded Egypt at the dawn of time and ruled during the First Age. According to what Khufu had been told by his father and the priests, in the First Age, the Gods had ruled for many years before passing leadership on to Shadows of themselves, the followers of Horus, during the Second Age. Then even the Shadows had passed the mantle on to men, and the first Pharaohs took command of the Middle Kingdom of the Third Age.

Asim was the only other person in the area. He was the senior priest of the Cult of Isis and garbed in a red robe. The priest's right arm was withered and deformed where muscles and tendons had been sliced when he was a child. Where his left eye had been, there was an empty socket, the skin around it charred and scarred from the red-hot poker that had taken out the eyeball. Both ankles and calves were carefully bound to allow the priest to move, as the tendons in his legs had also been partially severed when he was a child. The priest had also been castrated before puberty.

The mutilation was what was required of the head priest of the Cult. Khufu knew there was a method to the madness. The idea was to make Asim's life so miserable that while he would be able to perform his duties, he would not desire to live a long life and thus not hunger for the source of immortality—the Grail—that was said to be located somewhere below them, beyond the statue before which Khufu bowed his head. The scepter that Asim had brought to Khufu was the key to the Roads of Rostau, the underground passageways that ran beneath their feet, and Asim and his followers were the only ones who had ever walked those roads.

Around Asim's neck was a medallion with an eye carved in the middle, a symbol of his office. The priest stood five paces behind the Pharaoh, muttering his own prayers rapidly in the old tongue that only the priests now knew, his anxiety obvious.

The quick prayers done, Khufu stood and glanced at Asim. The priest nodded. Khufu placed the staff against an indentation in the pedestal on which the statue stood. The carving had the exact same shape as the staff.

The pedestal shimmered, and then the scepter was absorbed into it. The surface of the stone slid down, revealing a six-foot-high opening. The passageway beyond was dimly lit from recesses in the ceiling, although the Pharaoh couldn't see the source of the strange light. Khufu hesitated, then reluctantly entered the tunnel, the priest following, moving quickly despite his crippled gait. The stone slid shut behind them.

Khufu hurried down the tunnel. The stone walls were cut smoothly, better than even his most skilled artisan could produce, but the Pharaoh, his heart beating furiously in his chest, had no time to admire the handiwork. He ruled supreme from the second cataracts of the Nile, far to the south, to the Middle Sea to the north, and many countries beyond those borders paid tribute, but here, on the Roads of Rostau, inside the Giza Plateau, he knew he was just an errand boy to the Gods. His father had never been down here, nor had his father's father or anyone in his line. It had always been a possibility fraught with both danger and opportunity.

The priest had not said a word since handing Khufu the scepter, as was law in Egypt—no one spoke until the Pharaoh addressed them.

"Asim."

"Yes, lord?"

"What awaits us?" Khufu didn't stop as he spoke, heading deeper into the Earth, his slippers making a slight hissing noise as they passed over the smooth stone.

Asim's voice was harsh and low. "These are the Roads of Rostau, built by the Gods themselves in the First Age, before the rule of the Shadows of the Gods, and before the rule of Pharaoh. It is written there are six duats down here. I would say, lord, that we are going to one of those."

"You have not been in all these duats?"

"No, my lord. I have only gone where my duties have required me to."

Khufu suppressed the wave of irritation he felt with priests and their mysterious ways. "And in the duat we go to now?"

"That, my lord, is unknown, as I have not been to this one. The Hall of Records is said to be in one of the duats—the history of the time before the history we have recorded. This was the time when the Gods ruled beyond the horizon, before even the First Age of Egypt. The Old Kingdom of the Gods beyond the Great Sea."

Khufu wasn't interested in history or the Gods but the

future. "It is said there is also a hall that holds the Grail, which contains the gift of eternal life."

Asim nodded. "That is so, my lord."

"But you don't think that is where we are headed?"

"It is possible, my lord. It has been passed down that we will be given the Grail when the Gods come again and we will join them. Perhaps by building the Great Pyramid and finally at long last completing the plan handed down from the First Age we have earned the honor of the Gods. However, I have not yet laid eyes upon the Hall of Records or the Grail."

"Maybe you haven't been looking closely enough," Khufu muttered. Building the Pyramid had certainly been a feat worthy of some reward from the Gods, he mused. Even with the Gods' drawings, his engineer priests had been fearful they could not do it. Others had tried on a smaller scale in other places, testing the design, and none had succeeded, such as the one that had collapsed on itself at Saqqara. Using the practical knowledge learned from those attempts over the centuries and the Gods' plan, Khufu had felt confident he could succeed—and he had.

They reached a junction. The path to the right was level. To the other side, the path curved left and down. Khufu had been taught the directions, even though, as far as he knew, no one in his line of Pharaohs had ever actually been down there. The Pharaohs ruled above, but the Gods ruled there.

He turned left. It was cool in the tunnel but Khufu was sweating. He had watched ten thousand put to death in one day on his orders after a battle and felt nothing. He who held absolute rule over the lives of his people felt fear for the first time in his life. But burning through the fear was hope, for he kept reminding himself what his father had told him—that inside the Roads of Rostau, hidden under the Earth, there was indeed the key to immortality, the golden Grail of the Gods that had been promised. And that there would be a day when the Gods would grant that to the chosen. Was today the day, and was he the chosen one? After all, as Asim had noted, he had completed the Great Pyramid this season after twenty years of labor, a marvel indeed, exactly according to the plans left behind by the Gods. And he had put the red capstone up there, a thing that had come out of one of the duats down here, dragged to the surface by Asim and his priests under the cover of darkness.

The tunnel ended at a stone wall. Asim used the medallion around his neck, placing it against a slight depression in the center of the stone. The outline of a door appeared, then the rock slid up. Asim stepped aside and motioned for the Pharaoh to enter. Khufu stepped through, into a small, circular cavern, about twenty feet wide. In the very center was a tall, narrow red crystal, three feet high and six inches in diameter, the multifaceted surface glinting. Set in the top of the crystal was the handle of a sword. Khufu walked forward, drawn irresistibly toward the crystal. Asim was at his side now. An ornate sheath could be seen buried deep inside the crystal. The Pharaoh had never seen such crystal or metal worked so finely.

"What is it?"

"It is called Excalibur," Asim said. "Take hold of the sword, my Pharaoh. Remove it from the crystal."

Khufu reached down and grabbed the handle of the sword. The sword, still covered by the sheath, slid smoothly out of the crystal.

"Now free the blade, my lord."

Khufu hesitated. "Why?"

"My Pharaoh, it will free the red capstone we just put on top of the pyramid to act outside of itself."

"That makes no sense. What can the capstone do?"

"I am telling you only what I was instructed, my lord. It is important."

Khufu began to draw back the blade. A shock coursed out of the handle through his hand and into his body as he pulled it out of the sheath.

Khufu staggered back as a golden glow filled the entire chamber. Khufu blinked as the smoothly cut walls flickered and then came to life. A flurry of images flashed across them, so quickly he could barely note them: a massive golden palace that dwarfed the pyramid he had just built, set on a hill above a beautiful city of white stone surrounded by seven moats of water; a wave-battered island with three volcanic mountains in each corner sitting alone in an endless ocean; a rocky uninhabited desert with mountains surrounding a dry lake bed; a desolate land swept by snow and ice; a strange land where the sand was red and a massive mountain dominated the horizon, and other images flashing by faster and faster so that he lost track.

Suddenly the walls went black, then a new image appeared, of a field of stars, so many Khufu could not even begin to count, and the stars were moving rapidly, wheeling across the walls.

Then blank again, before revealing a view of the surface above but from a perspective he didn't recognize at first. He could see the Sphinx and the Nile beyond as if from a great height, and he then realized that in some manner the walls in this deep cavern were reflecting the view from the top of the Great Pyramid. The red capstone was now glowing as if lit from within.

He started as a seven-foot-high red line appeared between him and the vision on the walls. The line wavered, then widened until a figure appeared, a twin to the statue above. Yet Khufu could see through the figure, to the display on the wall.

He was trying to take all this in, when the figure began

speaking. The language was singsong, one the Pharaoh had never heard.

"Do you understand the words?" he asked Asim, his voice a whisper, as if the image could hear.

"It is the language of the Gods, my lord. I was taught as much of the language as has been passed down and remembered among the high priests."

Khufu waited impatiently for the priest to translate.

"It was hoped the Great Pyramid would bring more of the Gods," Asim finally said, his head cocked to one side, his single eye closed as he listened closely and tried to understand. "That was the design." Asim's thin tongue snaked around his lips as he listened further. "It has not worked that way. Instead an enemy comes." Asim's good arm slowly raised until it pointed upward. "From the sky above."

Khufu looked at the ceiling of the chamber. He could see the sky displayed. It was clear, not a cloud or bird visible.

"What kind of enemy?" Khufu asked, but Asim was again listening and didn't respond right away.

"The Ancient Enemy of the Gods," Asim finally said. "The killer of all life. The enemy with the patience of "—Asim shook his head—"I know not the word, but something like the patience of a stone, infinite. And the specific word for the enemy, the closest I can come to is when the locusts gather—a Swarm."

Khufu had seen swarms of locusts passing overhead so thick they made day into night. When they alighted in a field, they stripped it bare within minutes. He tried to imagine a Swarm that could be a threat to the Gods but could not conceive of it. The vision continued speaking, the sound almost like that of a bird, Khufu thought.

"The capstone—what it calls the Master Guardian—will stop the Ancient Enemy," Asim finally said as the vision ceased speaking. "Excalibur controls the power to the

Guardian. While the sword is inside the sheath the Master Guardian cannot work. You have freed it and thus the Master Guardian has power. The Master Guardian can now take action against the Ancient Enemy."

Khufu turned to the priest. "How will this Master Guardian do this? What Ancient Enemy?"

Asim was looking up. He pointed at the display on the roof of the cavern that showed the sky above the pyramid. "That enemy, my lord."

Khufu looked up and blinked. There was a dark spot high in the sky, rapidly growing larger. As it descended it began to take shape and Khufu felt his stomach knot and twist with fear. It was a large black flying spider—that was the only thing he could think. Eight legs, spread wide around a central, round body. And large—how big he had no idea, but its shadow was now covering the top of the pyramid.

After breaking the *Fynbar* out of its underground lair, Gwalcmai had gained altitude and accelerated the craft to the south until he was at maximum speed for atmospheric transit. The extreme speed didn't allow Donnchadh much opportunity to observe the lands they traversed to see how much things had changed since they last went into the deep sleep.

"I've got a radar contact in the air," Gwalcmai said as he began to slow the *Fynbar*. They were over the Mediterranean and Donnchadh could see the coastline ahead marked by the mouth of the Nile.

"Visual contact," Donnchadh said, pointing at a black spot on the forward display.

Gwalcmai dropped altitude and brought them to a halt about ten kilometers away from the descending craft.

"What the hell is that thing?" he asked, pointing not at

the scout ship but at the massive structure below it on the Giza Plateau. It had not been there the last time they had been in Egypt.

h ow will the Guardian fight this?" Khufu whispered as he stared at the thing hovering over the top of the Great Pyramid.

"You have given it power by removing Excalibur from the sheath," Asim repeated. "Watch the power of the Gods, my lord."

Khufu wanted to strangle the priest. He could not tear his eyes from the rapidly approaching monster. Suddenly a golden orb of power streaked upward from the Master Guardian toward the object and hit. The spider jerked sideways. Khufu kept his eyes on it and a second golden orb raced into the sky and struck the enemy. Bright red flames burst out of the side of the flying spider and it jerked once more, now going upward, trying to escape.

F inish it," Gwalcmai whispered, actually urging success to his longtime enemy.

A third golden orb hit it and enveloped the entire object. It was still going higher and higher, edging toward the west. There was a blinding explosion and the scout ship was gone.

Gwalcmai checked his instruments. "Debris is to the west. And I think an escape pod was ejected."

"Dammit," Donnchadh hissed.

T he golden glow inside the chamber decreased and Khufu almost collapsed, feeling drained. The Pharaoh started as the image began speaking again.

"We are safe for now," Asim translated. "But"—he paused as he translated, eye closed—"it is not safe."

"What isn't safe?" Khufu demanded.

"The Great Pyramid. The Master Guardian. The pyramid did not work as intended. It summoned the Ancient Enemy and not the Gods of old. If the Ancient Enemy came once, it can come again. What drew it here must be destroyed."

The figure chimed on for a minute and Asim remained silent, until the figure stopped speaking, coalesced into a thin red line, then disappeared.

Asim opened his eye. "I have been told what is to be done. Put the blade back in the sheath, my pharaoh."

Khufu slid the blade into the scabbard.

"Come, my lord," Asim was hobbling toward the tunnel. "There is much to do."

So stunned was the Pharaoh by the recent events that he didn't even question being ordered about by the priest. He simply followed him out of the chamber, the covered sword in his hands.

As Gwalcmai had noted, there was a black pod remaining from the scout ship. It was approximately fifteen feet across, the metal surface unmarred by the explosion. As the pod approached the surface of the planet, its terminal velocity began to slow as some internal mechanism interacted with the planet's electromagnetic field. Still, it was moving so fast that the outer surface gave off heat, glowing in the sky like a falling star. Despite slowing, the pod hit a dune with enough velocity to plow deep into the sand. It was completely covered when the pod came to rest, submerged twenty feet in the desert.

* * *

Gwalcmai was relieved when Donnchadh appeared, coming over the crest of a sand dune, behind which he had the ship hidden. He opened the hatch and she entered, sweat staining her robes and her sandals covered with sand.

"Did you find the *Wedjat?*" Gwalcmai asked.

Donnchadh nodded. "In the same little hut."

Gwalcmai sealed the hatch behind her. "It is amazing the line has survived this long." He lifted the *Fynbar* and moved away from Giza, keeping low to the ground to avoid detection. "Should we stay in the area?"

Donnchadh nodded. "Yes. Just in case he fails."

An hour after the crash, a camel rider approached. A Libyan who was heading toward Cairo to do some trading, he'd seen the falling star from his caravan ten miles to the south. Leaving his son in charge, he'd ridden in the direction the object had fallen, curiosity pulling him across the sand.

He'd already passed places where it was obvious objects from the sky had landed in the desert, but whatever had hit, they were deeply buried under the sand. He approached a sixty-foot-high sand dune and noted the disturbed surface near the top indicating another impact. The Libyan halted his camel at the base of the dune and dismounted. His robe flapped in a stiff breeze and all but his eyes was covered with the cloth wrapped around his head.

The Libyan paused, his head swinging back and forth as he looked about. He had the sense of being followed, but his eyes detected no sign of another person, though he'd had the feeling for a while now.

He cocked his head as he heard a sound. A grinding noise. Then nothing but the wind for several moments. He took several steps closer to the dune where the sound had seemed to come from. Then he heard something different. Almost a slithering sound. He took half a step back, then paused. There was something inside the dune. Of that there was no doubt in his mind. He looked left and right but there was no movement. He could feel the heat of the sun on his shoulders but a chill passed through his body. The Libyan drew a curved sword from his belt. The noise was getting louder.

Mustering his courage, the Libyan took several steps forward until he was at the base of the dune. The sound was very close now. The Libyan jabbed the point of his sword into the dune, the blade easily spearing the sand. He did it again and then again.

He pulled the blade back and cocked his head. Nothing.

The tentacles came out of the sand underneath his feet, wrapping around his legs. He was pulled under, desperately trying to slash and stab with his sword at whatever was below him. His scream was cut off as he disappeared under the sand. His camel bolted off into the desert, desperate to get away.

Then all was still.

A quarter mile away, on the far side of a dune, two dark eyes had watched the encounter. The observer waited a few moments, staring at the spot where the Libyan had disappeared, then he slowly slid down the side of the dune to his waiting camel. He headed back the way he had come, toward Giza. The sun glinted off a large ring set on the man's right hand, highlighting the eye symbol etched on its surface. The hand that bore the ring held the camel's halter, but it was shaking so badly from fright that he had to let go and allow the camel to make its own way home.

It was the middle of the night and by order of the great Pharaoh Khufu no one was allowed outdoors in sight of the Giza Plateau except himself and his high priest, Asim. Given the strange apparition the previous day of the flying "spider," no citizens tried to resist the command. Khufu and Asim stood on the roof of the temple at the base of the Pyramid. The night sky was clear. Now that Khufu had Excalibur sheathed inside the scabbard strapped to his sword belt, the red capstone no longer glowed as if lit from within.

Khufu could still see in his mind's eye the black spider that had come down from the sky. He did not understand what it was, but there was no doubt in him that it was a danger. Whatever entity controlled such a flying creature and was capable of fighting the Gods was indeed something to be feared.

"What are we waiting for?"

"When the sword is in the sheath, the"—Asim searched for the right words—"Chariot of the Gods cannot approach the capstone. You must take the blade out once more."

Khufu drew the weapon. He watched as the capstone glowed once more.

Asim continued. "Since you have removed the sword, the capstone can be approached."

"By who? What Chariot of the Gods?"

"There, lord." Asim was pointing to the north.

Something was approaching through the sky. Khufu started, and then realized it wasn't another air-spider. This object was shaped like an inverted dish and golden, reminding him of the glow that had surrounded him in the chamber far below during the day.

"The Chariot of the Gods," Asim whispered.

The object passed by overhead and hovered above the very top of the pyramid. A glow extended down from the disk and surrounded the red Master Guardian.

Khufu started as the Master Guardian separated from the pyramid, lifting into the air as if by magic. The golden object, with the Master Guardian in tow, began withdrawing in the direction it had come from, to the north. Khufu watched until it disappeared into the night sky, then he turned to Asim.

"Where does it go?"

"To a secure place, my lord. Separate from the key."

"Why separate the two?"

"The Master Guardian will be more secure if the key is not with it." Asim absently rubbed his empty eye socket. "The sword you hold was once wielded by the greatest of the Gods. With it he controlled the Master Guardian, and in turn his entire domain."

Khufu looked at the smooth blade. He had never seen such fine metal. "It is a great weapon, then."

"It is," Asim said. "Especially as it controls the power for the Master Guardian. It allows whoever has the sword to be very powerful."

"And now?"

"Have your troops scoured the desert for the spider creature, my lord?"

"They have found no sign of the sky monster, but have apprehended all the people they found to the west."

Asim nodded. "The prisoners must be part of what we do in the morning."

"And?" Khufu pressed.

"My lord, tomorrow we must complete the undoing of what our people have worked so hard to do over the past twenty years." He pointed. "The facing of the pyramid must be removed."

"Why?"

"It sent out a signal as planned, my lord, but it did not bring the Gods as hoped, but their enemy."

Khufu knew the pyramid could be seen from far away, and he imagined that if one could be in the sky, as the spider creature had been, it could be seen from a great distance indeed. He did not wish for another visit.

"It will be done."

hidden in the dark shadows of a refuse pile of cracked stone blocks, the Watcher from the desert had observed the same thing as Khufu and Asim. He'd noted the direction the golden disk flew off toward, Master Guardian with it. Despite the darkness of his hiding place, he wrote all that he had seen down on a piece of reed parchment.

Then, keeping to ground he knew well, he made his way off the Giza Plateau and to a small hut near the Nile. Inside, he checked the writing, making sure it reported accurately what he had seen, then rolled it and slid it into a tube. He poured wax from a candle on the end and then used the ring to seal it with an imprint—the imprint had the same design as that on the medallion worn around Asim's neck.

He slid the tube inside his robes and sat down cross-legged on the sand floor, waiting for the sun to rise. He'd managed to escape the Pharaoh's troops in the desert, sticking to the hidden ways. He'd noted that the members of the Libyan caravan had been brought to the plateau in chains, the man he'd seen disappear under the sand among them.

He had accomplished the first part the strange woman had ordered. Tomorrow would be a most interesting day, he mused, as he would have to do the rest of what she had instructed.

When dawn came, it was assembly-line murder.

The great Pharaoh Khufu, son of King Sneferu and Queen Hetpeheres, ruler of the Middle Kingdom, watched, his face impassive, as rivers of blood flowed down the smooth limestone facing of the Great Pyramid.

He was at the flat top where the Master Guardian had been, over 480 feet above the Giza plateau, seated in a throne made of gold. Four sacrificial tables were spread out in the small space in front of him, manned by priests of the Cult of Isis.

Asim was working swiftly, as there were many thousands of throats to be cut. A long line of stoop-shouldered men stood on the wooden scaffolding that led to the level platform at the top of the pyramid where Asim wielded Excalibur, the sword of the Gods, moving from table to table, sliding the razor-sharp blade across throats. Soldiers ensured that the line kept moving. Every worker who had spent even one minute inside the pyramid during its construction was in that line. When Asim's work was done, the only ones to have been inside the pyramid and live would be Khufu and Asim.

As each worker reached the top, two soldiers would lift him bodily, throw him onto a slab, pinning his shoulders down, and a priest would hold his head back, waiting for Asim to come by and draw Excalibur across the man's throat while quickly muttering the necessary prayer. Blood would spurt out of their carotid arteries, be caught by the lip of the slab, and be channeled into several holes to reed pipes at the bottom, which directed it to the edge of the platform and dispersed it onto the side of the pyramid. Three sides were drenched red and the reed pipes had just been redirected to the fourth side. As spectacular as the white limestone facing had been when pure, in an obscene way, the glistening red covering of blood made it even more awe-inspiring.

Dulled by years of labor, surrounded by troops, and conditioned to obey their Pharaoh and Gods without question, the men stood in line with little protest. Occasionally one would try to bolt, to be cut down by the guards immediately and the body hauled to the top.

Not only were priests and workers among the condemned, but so were all those who had been caught in the desert to the west the previous day. The Libyan who had approached the sand dune was dragged up with chains around his ankles and thrown onto an altar. He had his head up, looking around as if noting all. When his eyes fell upon Excalibur in Asim's hands, his calm demeanor suddenly changed and he struggled in the guards' grip. As Asim drew the sword of the Gods across the man's neck, the body convulsed, sitting straight up despite the blood pouring from the sliced arteries in his neck.

Asim stepped back in shock, Excalibur held up defensively. The two soldiers who'd brought the Libyan to the altar grabbed his shoulders.

The Libyan snatched each soldier's neck and smashed their heads together, killing them. Asim used the opportunity to jab forward with the sword, the blade punching into the Libyan's stomach.

An unearthly scream roared out of the man's wide-open mouth. Khufu, behind a line of his Imperial guards, was less than ten feet away, watching the bizarre spectacle. The Pharaoh gasped in horror as Asim struck once more before the Libyan's body was ripped apart from the inside. The tip of a tentacle punched out of the man's skin from his chest.

The tentacle was gray and tipped with three digits that bent and twisted as they grasped for a target. The body of the Libyan was bent in an extremely unnatural manner as if the spine had been turned into a loose string. Asim swung the sword, severing the end of the tentacle. The end that fell to the stone shriveled as if baked, while the other slid back into the body. Then the priest stepped back, Excalibur at the ready.

"What was that?" Khufu demanded.

Asim jabbed the sword several more times into the body, but there was no movement. "Burn the body," Asim ordered several of the Imperial guards. "Scatter the ashes."

As they gingerly picked up the Libyan's body, Asim walked over to the Pharaoh, sweat staining his robes. "The Ancient Enemy, my Lord. It must have escaped from the thing we saw yesterday."

Khufu could only shake his head, the events of the past twenty-four hours threatening to overwhelm his sanity. "What kind of enemy is this?"

"It is the enemy of the Gods and our enemy."

"How did it get in that man?"

"I do not know, my lord. I was told to watch for this by the apparition yesterday."

"How did it survive? We saw the sky thing destroyed."

"I do not know that either, my lord, but the apparition warned me it could. And it told me that the sword would kill it."

Khufu looked at the blade in Asim's hands. "That is indeed very powerful."

"It was designed so that whoever wielded it could rule supreme," Asim said.

Khufu nodded. A thing that one person could carry and that held such power held both great opportunity and great danger.

Asim signaled for the soldiers to continue to bring prisoners forward and he went back to his grim task. By the time the last worker was dead and the body unceremoniously tossed over the side to be burned, all four sides of the Great Pyramid were stained red. There was no repeat of what had happened with the Libyan.

* * *

Donnchadh estimated that at least five thousand had been slain on top of the Great Pyramid in less than four hours. She had watched through high-power binoculars throughout the entire bloody spectacle. Billions had died on her home world but that didn't inure her to seeing so much bloodshed. She forced herself to watch as the high priest went to the Pharaoh. He handed the sword to his leader. The Pharaoh yelled orders to his soldiers that she could not hear at this distance.

"What are they doing?" Gwalcmai asked as soldiers hammered spikes into joints all along the edge of the top of the pyramid, between the limestone covering and the heavy blocks below. The first covering stone fell away, tumbling down the blood-soaked side of the pyramid.

"They're destroying the signal," Donnchadh said.

"The signal?"

"That thing is what drew the Swarm here," Donnchadh explained. "The smooth surface, the angles, all work to reflect sunlight. It gives an immense radar signature. Large enough to eventually make it out of this star system into interstellar space."

Gwalcmai frowned. "Why would these humans build such a thing?"

"According to the *Wedjat*, because the Airlia left the plans for them." She knew that didn't answer the real question that her mate was asking, so she continued. "The interstellar array on Mars was destroyed by Artad as he came into the system. Aspasia must have thought he could turn the tables if he could get a signal out to the Airlia Empire. Claim that Artad was the one who messed up. So this passive signal was designed by him long ago and the plans handed down. Except it brought not Airlia, but the Swarm. So now it must be destroyed."

She was still watching, following the Pharaoh and his

high priest as they went down the ramp and headed over to the Sphinx talking to each other.

Y̶ou must decree that no one will write of this day's events, my lord," Asim said.

"What should I do with the sword?" Khufu asked. "Perhaps I should keep it in case we are attacked again."

"It was the Master Guardian that stopped the Ancient Enemy craft," Asim said, "not the sword. Without the facing, the pyramid will not be found by the Ancient Enemy."

"How can that be?"

"I do not know, but it is what I was told. And what people may desire in the duats along the Roads of Rostau are secure in one form or another."

"Why did you have to use Excalibur for the killing today and not your ceremonial dagger?" Khufu asked.

"The sword has another special power," Asim said. "As you saw, it is the only thing that can kill the Ancient Enemy and the immortal."

"The immortal?" Khufu stepped closer to the priest. "Someone has partaken of the Grail?"

"I very much doubt it," Asim said, "but all who could have had access to the duats had to die."

"I do not understand," Khufu said.

"I do not either, my Lord," Asim said. "I only do what the Gods command. The sword is the key that must be hidden away again."

"Why did the Gods have us build that"—Khufu jerked a thumb over his shoulder at the pyramid—"if it would only bring enemies?"

"The Gods hoped it would bring their kindred Gods from

the sky," Asim said. The same answer he had given before, but Khufu felt despair.

"And now?" Khufu spread his hands wide. "Now what do I do?"

"You rule, my lord," Asim said.

"What will I do with Excalibur?" Khufu asked once more.

"We will leave it in the sheath and return it to its place in the duats so that the Gods may have access to it when it is needed. When the Master Guardian is returned or needed again."

Khufu unbuckled it from his belt and handed it over to Asim, who tucked it under his cloak. Then the high priest went into the Roads of Rostau.

Is the *Wedjat* prepared?" Gwalcmai asked after Donnchadh told him the high priest had disappeared underground.

"He'd better be." She sighed. "He lost family members on the top of the pyramid today. He is more than ready to act."

"Then it is time for us to go."

Donnchadh was hesitant. "What if he fails?"

"Then he fails." Gwalcmai shrugged. "If the Airlia did not awaken for this threat, then they plan to sleep for a long time. So should we. These humans are not even close to being capable of revolting." He put a hand on Donnchadh's shoulder. "It is not time."

Asim made his way down the stone corridor, scepter in one hand, Excalibur in the other. He paused, cocking his head, as if he sensed something was wrong. He waited several moments, then continued. When he reached the intersection, he turned right and came to a complete halt as a man stepped forward to confront him.

Asim held the sword in his good hand, across the front of his body, still covered by the sheath. "Kaji. I knew you would be about. Scurrying around like the rat you are."

"Even a rat is better than being a slave," Kaji said.

Asim spit at the other man's feet. "You *Wedjat*. You have betrayed our ancient priesthood."

Kaji shook his head. "We betrayed? Whom did we betray? The 'Gods' who left us to fend for ourselves? Who allowed our homes to be destroyed, our people killed? What did you perform today? How many people died today because of the 'Gods'? How many more will have to die?"

"You are a Watcher," Asim said. "You can do nothing according to the laws of your order. Get out of my way."

Kaji's jaw was set. "My three brothers, my six nephews. Two of my three sons. They died today on the pyramid."

Asim took an involuntary step backward. "You took an oath to only watch."

"I am done with being a Watcher. My surviving son will be the next *Wedjat*. The next Watcher of Giza, of the Roads of Rostau."

"Still, you took an oath." Asim took another step back.

"You know there are those beyond the Watchers," Kaji said. "Those who act." Kaji held up his hands, his fingers lacking the ring that was the symbol of the first rank of his order. "After opening a door to the Roads of Rostau I left my ring for my son to find."

That struck Asim as hard as a blade. The priest held up the sword, but had not drawn the blade. "What good will it do to kill me?"

Kaji barked a laugh. "You're not that important."

"Then what—"

"Excalibur," Kaji said. "It is theirs. And it is the key. I will take it."

"You cannot. It is only for the Gods."

Kaji indicated Asim's wounds. "Have you ever looked at yourself? What has been done to you?"

"It is the price of service."

"To what end?" Kaji's voice shook. "To what end does your service go?"

"To get eternal life," Asim said. "To partake of the Grail."

"The Grail has been around since the dawn of time and we have never been allowed to partake!"

Asim's voice fell to a whisper. "It will happen someday. If not to me, then to those who follow. But only to the true believers."

Kaji took another step closer to the priest. He was in range of the blade, but Asim did not draw it. "Has it ever occurred to you that perhaps partaking of the Grail might not be a good thing?"

Asim's eyes widened. He blinked as if he had just heard that the sky was red, his head shaking in disbelief.

"Excalibur," Kaji said.

Asim shook his head more firmly. "It must be kept safe."

"You think this place is safe?" Kaji didn't wait for an answer. "The 'Gods' fight among themselves. Both sides know of the Roads of Rostau. It must be hidden from them or else we will have repeats of today's disaster."

"But the Ancient Enemy—" Asim began.

"Yes, the Ancient Enemy." Kaji nodded. "Excalibur must be protected from the Ancient Enemy also. I saw what happened on the top of the pyramid. What makes you think that was the only enemy that survived?"

"The enemy was destroyed."

"You don't know that for sure," Kaji said. "I saw the Libyan taken by the Ancient Enemy in the desert to the west of here. More danger could be close by. The sword must be removed from here."

Asim frowned. "What do you know of the Ancient Enemy?"

A strange look crossed Kaji's face. "The legends—" His voice trailed off.

"How did you know to go out into the desert?" Asim pressed. "Why did—" Asim continued, but he didn't complete the sentence, as Kaji slammed his dagger into the priest's chest.

Asim fell to the tunnel floor dead. Kaji reached down and took the priest's cloak, wrapping it around his own slender body, pulling the hood up over his head. He picked up Excalibur and the scepter. Then he headed toward the surface.

Khufu was alone on the roof of the Pyramid temple. The removal of the covering stones was complete about a third of the way down. People from all around were at the base, taking the limestone with them, as the Pharaoh had allowed it. They could build homes with the stone. It might as well serve some positive purpose. Several large rough blocks had been emplaced on top to keep the semblance of a pyramid and also hide the fact that something else had once been up there.

He heard his guards snap to attention below and turned. A slight figure came up the ladder onto the roof, moving with difficulty. He recognized Asim from his cloak and the sword in his hand.

"I thought you were taking that back underground," Khufu said. "Have you had second thoughts?"

The figure came closer. Khufu gasped as the sword was drawn and the blade came across his neck. He could feel the chill of the metal against his skin.

"Are you insane, Asim?"

The man pulled his hood down, revealing his features.

"Who are you?"

"A man. Like you. My name is Kaji."

Khufu stared into the man's eyes. "Are you going to kill me?"

Kaji ignored the question. "Asim is dead. I killed him."

Khufu looked back up at the defaced pyramid. The sword pressed tighter against his throat. He waited to feel it slice his skin. Now, for the first time in his life, Khufu felt his mortality, and knew that he was not the favored of the Gods, that he was just a man.

"He lied to you because he was lied to," Kaji said.

"Lied about what?" Khufu asked, hoping to avoid this dark fate as long as possible, thinking that perhaps one of his guards might check on them, also knowing that hope was futile, as no one would dare interrupt the Pharaoh while he was consulting with his high priest.

"The Gods. The empty promises." The sword was removed from Khufu's throat and Kaji sheathed it, before hiding it under his cloak. "My Pharaoh—" Kaji pointed toward the pyramid. "That is what has been done to your people in the name of the Gods. Perhaps it is best if these Gods are not part of our lives. I will let you live if you give me your word as Pharaoh to rule as a man and not as a puppet to the Gods."

Khufu swallowed and nodded, his confidence shattered by recent events. "Yes. Yes. I can do that. I will do that."

"I do not believe you," Kaji said simply. "Still, killing you will solve nothing, and in reality you have little choice now but to rule as a man. And there is doubt in your mind now. Perhaps that is all I can do here. Doubt is the seed from which one day may grow independence. The ability to think for ourselves. We have been lied to many times, by the Gods, by the priests. We must make our own truth."

With that, Kaji turned and disappeared down the ladder. He made his way along the processional path, the guards keeping their distance, recognizing the cloak of Asim, the high priest, second only to the Pharaoh himself. Kaji maintained the strange gait of the priest until he reached the Lower Temple. Then he went by the priest's path to the nearby Nile, where a small boat waited, manned by a young man who wore the medallion of the Watchers.

Set in the boat was a wooden box, three and a half feet long. The young man swung the top of the box open. Kaji placed the sheathed sword into the box, then closed the lid. He then handed the tube holding his report to the man. The boat slipped away into the night to make its long journey to deliver the report and sword.

Excalibur disappeared into darkness.

XI

1,500 B.C.: STONEHENGE

There was no flashing light as Donnchadh opened the top to her tube. She checked the timer and learned that one thousand years—as planned— had passed since she had gone into the deep sleep. The deck was still cold to her feet and she quickly dressed as Gwalcmai once more was slower to rise. She had the computer online by the time he was dressed.

"Anything?" Gwalcmai asked as he sat next to her. He shivered. "We should have picked a warmer place to put the ship."

Donnchadh ignored the comment. "Nothing intercepted from the guardians."

"At least the Swarm hasn't returned," Gwalcmai said.

"Not for a harvest," Donnchadh agreed.

Gwalcmai got to his feet and went to where his cloak and sword were hung. "I suppose we must go to Avalon." He picked up the sword. "Do you think the Watcher is still there?"

"I hope so." Donnchadh got her own cloak. "We shall soon find out."

The town on the shore across from Avalon was deserted. And had been for a long time, to judge by the degraded condition of the few buildings that were still standing. There were no boats on the shoreline and the two stood in the light rain for several minutes looking up at the top of the tor. The tip was wreathed in mist but they could see that a stone building had been erected on the very top.

"I could build a boat," Gwalcmai said.

"We have time, but not that much time." Donnchadh moved off to the right, circling the island. "There." She pointed at a clump of bushes. Tucked behind them, they could see glimpses of a small rowboat.

"It's on the other side," Gwalcmai noted.

"Would you rather build a boat or swim over and get that one?" Donnchadh asked.

"You could swim," Gwalcmai suggested. "Or we both could."

Donnchadh simply stared at him, waiting. Gwalcmai muttered something to himself as he stripped off his armor. Clad only in a loin wrap, he approached the dark water, shaking his shoulders from the chill. Gwalcmai let out a deep breath, then dived into the water. With powerful strokes, he made his way across the lake to the base of the tor. He emerged from the water, shaking it from him like a big dog. His long dark hair flew to and fro. He grabbed the rowboat, slid it into the water, and jumped on board. He paddled furiously, trying to stay warm, and was back across the lake in just a minute.

Donnchadh waited while he tried to dry himself and got dressed. They both got in the boat and rowed across to Avalon, where they made their way up the winding track to the top. The stone entry was enclosed in a small temple built of rock. A thick door barred entry into the temple. When Gwalcmai tried to open the door, it wouldn't budge. However, the thatch top of the temple had long ago fallen in, so he was able to climb up the eight-foot wall and go over, jumping down inside. He unbarred the door, letting Donnchadh in.

The space was small, less than four meters square. The entry stone was centered. Donnchadh placed her medallion against it in the appropriate spot, and the stone slid down, then to the side, allowing them access to the stairs below. Gwalcmai drew his sword and entered first. Donnchadh unsheathed her dagger and followed, closing the entrance behind them. The Airlia glow lines still provided illumination after all these years and they went down into the bowels of Avalon. When they entered the crystal cavern, both paused as they saw Excalibur, inside its sheath, encased in the stone.

"So, they got it out of Egypt and brought it here," Donnchadh said.

"Yes, we did."

Both spun about as a young man holding a bow, arrow notched and string pulled back, edged into the cave. "Who are you?"

Donnchadh carefully reached for the medallion around her neck and held it out. "I am of the *Wedjat*."

"Just because you have that," the young man said, "does not mean you are a Watcher."

"*I am of the order*," Donnchadh said in the Airlia tongue.

A frown crossed the young man's face. "That is the old tongue. I have learned a little. But not enough to talk or understand what you just said." Still, he did not lessen the tension on the bow. "That also does not mean you are of the order. You could be a Guide or One Who Waits."

"My name is Donnchadh. This is Gwalcmai."

The young man took a step back. "I have read of those names. Many, many years ago a man and a woman came here and they bore those names. Are you descended from them?"

"Yes," Donnchadh said. "We are not Guides or Ones Who Wait. If we were, you would be dead already. We have traveled far to be here."

·

Slowly he lowered the bow. "I am Dag-Brynn, Watcher of Avalon."

"Greetings, Dag-Brynn, Watcher of Avalon," Donnchadh said as she extended her hand.

"From where do you come?" Dag-Brynn asked as he shook her hand. "Where do you watch?"

"We are journeyers," Donnchadh said. "We travel from Watcher to Watcher."

"I have never heard of that," Dag-Brynn said. "But there is much I do not know."

"What of the Airlia?" Donnchadh asked.

Dag-Brynn shrugged. "As far as I know, they sleep still."

"And in Egypt?" Donnchadh pressed.

"They are dead."

"Some were killed long ago," Donnchadh said, "but the rest went into the deep sleep."

"And Vampyr killed them while they slept," Dag-Brynn said. "The report from the Watcher of Giza concerning this came here many, many years ago."

"Vampyr? One of the Undead?" Donnchadh was surprised at this turn of events. She vaguely remembered that name.

"So it was written."

"Who rules in Egypt?" Gwalcmai asked.

"The Pharaohs still rule. It is a mighty kingdom and has conquered many of its neighbors."

"The Grail?" Donnchadh asked.

"As far as the Watcher of Giza knows and last reported," Dag-Brynn said, "it is still inside the Ark, hidden in the Hall of Records, deep along the Roads of Rostau. But it was well before my time since we have last heard from Giza."

He said the words as if reciting something he had memorized, but it appeared he had little idea what the words meant. Gwalcmai coughed, wrapping his muscular arms tight around his upper body. "I hate this chill. Let us do what we need and get going."

"Let us see the records," Donnchadh said, pointing toward the entrance to the room where all reports were stored.

Donnchadh learned little more from reading the scrolls. The Watchers still existed, but the reports came to Avalon infrequently. The last from Giza was over two hundred years old. The last from China, from the Qian-Ling Watcher, had come to Avalon five hundred years previously. It told of strange creatures populating the area—spawn of the Undead. Donnchadh assumed one of those they had freed from underneath Giza must have made his way there—or else the Airlia in the mountain had produced them. Since then, nothing. Some of the Watchers had not reported in for millennia. That might be because the line had failed in places, or because there was no way to get the messages across the oceans. Some of the reports were in languages she didn't recognize.

After reading what she could, Donnchadh sat still for several hours while Gwalcmai went hunting with Dag-Brynn. By the time they returned with a stag, she had made her decisions. They butchered the stag, preparing some of it for immediate consumption, and Gwalcmai cured the rest for the journey he anticipated they would make. He asked no questions, for which Donnchadh was grateful.

As she began to read again, though, his cough grew worse. Dag-Brynn built up the fire in the small room, the smoke going up through a crack in the ceiling, but Gwalcmai could not warm up. When she put her hand on his forehead, she could feel the heat. She had Dag-Brynn gather all the blankets he had and she wrapped her partner in them. But the fever grew worse.

"I should have built the boat," Gwalcmai said. "Time is the only thing we have plenty of."

"Yes, you should have," Donnchadh agreed. "That was my mistake."

Gwalcmai shook so hard that Dag-Brynn had to help her hold him on the small cot next to the fire. When the shivering subsided, Gwalcmai's face was bathed in sweat. His eyes were slightly unfocused.

"We should go back to the ship," Donnchadh whispered to him. "I can cure you there."

Gwalcmai laughed, the sound more a rasp coming through his tortured throat. "I can't make it. If the fever breaks, then yes. We go. But—" He tried to get up, but his muscles had no energy. He collapsed back on the cot, soaked in sweat. "I'm sorry."

"It's all right," Donnchadh said. She wrapped her arms around her partner. Across the chamber, Dag-Brynn was watching.

"I could help you take him wherever you need to go. To your ship."

Donnchadh sadly shook her head. "No. It's all right."

Dag-Brynn came over and looked down. "The village across the way. Many died twenty years ago. Something killed them all. They had the chill and the fever. I had to send my family away. Many miles away. My wife and daughter died."

Donnchadh had assumed her partner had caught a cold from swimming in the water, but now she had to wonder— had someone poisoned the lake? But what could last in the water that long? During the Revolution, the Airlia had not hesitated to use biological weapons against the humans. Millions had died as a result.

It didn't matter. She could not take Dag-Brynn to the *Fynbar*. And in this condition she could not get Gwalcmai there on her own. The trip would surely kill him. His only chance was to ride this out here.

She sat next to Gwalcmai for hours. Sometime in the middle of the night he began raving in their native tongue, causing Dag-Brynn to cast some curious glances their way. Donnchadh put cold compresses on her partner's forehead, trying to keep the temperature down. She tried to rehydrate him with a broth using the deer and springwater.

None of it worked.

Just before dawn, Gwalcmai sat bolt upright and called out their son's name. Then he slumped back, the life fading from his eyes.

Donnchadh reached up and carefully closed her husband's eyelids. She bowed her head for several moments, then reached inside his tunic and removed his *ka*.

"I am very sorry." Dag-Brynn was standing just behind her.

"Will you help me bury him?"

"Of course. Where?"

"On the top of the tor," Donnchadh said. "His spirit can help guard this place."

They were at sea for four days before Gwalcmai finally asked their destination.

"Giza."

Gwalcmai nodded. "I expected as much." The trading ship they were on was hugging the coast of Europe, moving around it toward the Mediterranean. He was quiet for a few minutes, then asked: "And when we get there?"

"I have been thinking," Donnchadh said. Since traveling back to their ship and implanting Gwalcmai's memories and personality in the *ka* into the body in stasis, she had been considering their next move. Since Gwalcmai had no memories of the most recent trip to Avalon, and she had been the one to read the scrolls, she had taken full responsibility for planning their next actions. Which, of course, was pretty much the norm for them since they had been together.

Gwalcmai waited quietly, something he was not good at. His unusual silence grated on her. They normally regenerated at the same time. She found that there was a certain indefinable distance between them ever since leaving the ship. Her current body was young, only the equivalent of late twenties, but Gwalcmai appeared to have just passed the threshold into manhood.

"Things here are not the same as they were on our world," she finally said. "We have made the situation different. The Great Civil War has made everything very different."

Gwalcmai barely nodded, indicating his agreement.

"Both sides sleep," Donnchadh continued, "and have their minions skirmishing. The key for the Master Guardian is under our control. Their headquarters on this planet at Atlantis is gone. Their communications array on Mars is destroyed and they are out of contact with their empire. All these are things we had to do at great cost early in our war against the Airlia on our planet."

Gwalcmai nodded once more. "We took out the communications array first. That cost us many good God-killers. And it was only the first stage of the war."

Donnchadh stayed quiet, staring over the wooden railing at the shoreline passing by.

"So." Gwalcmai finally spoke. "You are saying the war has progressed far already, even though these humans are not even close to being able to challenge the Airlia with their technology."

"Yes."

Gwalcmai rubbed the stubble of beard on his chin. "It is still too soon."

"Not if—" Donnchadh began, but then fell silent.

"Not if what?"

She pulled out the scepter they had brought with them to the planet so many years ago. "Not if we procure the Grail and use it. Create an army of immortals."

Gwalcmai did not immediately object, which she found interesting. But after several minutes of mulling it over, he shook his head. "It still would not work. We do not have the weaponry to challenge the Airlia. We may make an army of immortals, but all it will bring about is great suffering for those transformed. They will die and come back to life constantly. A terrible fate. And the immortality has conditions—we learned how to kill the Airlia and I am certain they will know how to kill our immortals." Gwalcmai paused. "But—I do think it would be wise for us to try to get the Grail under our control, as we have had Excalibur removed from Giza. It will prevent the Airlia from using it on their minions."

"That is what I have been thinking."

"And that is all," Gwalcmai said, "under our control."

"All right."

Gwalcmai smiled. "Why do I not believe you?"

Slavery among humans. Humans owning other humans like property. It was a concept strange to Donnchadh and Gwalcmai. Their planet had been under the thrall of the Airlia for so long that the concept of humans "owning" other humans had never even arisen. But Egypt had changed since last they visited. The Great Pyramid still sat atop the Giza Plateau, but the sides were rough and worn from the weather. There were two more large pyramids flanking it, obviously attempts by other Pharaohs to match the splendor that Khufu had built. The Black Sphinx was hidden out of sight, the depression it sat in covered and camouflaged as part of the plateau itself, and there was a stone replica squatting on top.

The physical changes were great, but what truly struck both Donnchadh and Gwalcmai was the sprawling camp of slaves to the south of the Giza Plateau. There were thousands living there, under the thrall of guards and forced to do all the hard labor, from making bricks to the fine craftsmanship needed to finish the numerous temples and palaces being built. The camp was surrounded by a mud-brick wall six feet high with guard towers spaced every hundred meters. The wall seemed more a symbolic barrier than an actual one, as the people held inside seemed broken by their situation.

The slaves were not Egyptians. They were a mixture of races, predominant among them a conquered tribe called Judeans. They came from a land to the north and east, along the shores of the Mediterranean. They had been defeated by the Egyptians in battle and brought here in chains to do hard labor.

Donnchadh and Gwalcmai found the Watcher of Giza in the same small stone hut in which all his predecessors had also lived. He was a middle-aged man who, while he knew his role, had not sent in a single report to Avalon in all his years at the post. He was frightened by their appearance and fell on his knees when Donnchadh showed him the golden medallion, begging her not to slay him. Realizing he would be of little aid, the two made their own forays onto Giza and the nearby towns, learning as much as they could.

The Roads of Rostau were still guarded by the golden spider, but no high priests walked the tunnels. No one seemed to even know the Roads existed anymore, other than the Watcher, who had never ventured down there and almost considered them as much a myth as the Airlia themselves. Donnchadh and Gwalcmai knew they could get to the Hall of Records and use the scepter to gain access to the Ark with the Grail inside, but getting out was going to be a different story. Given the reaction to the Swarm craft, she had little doubt that opening the Hall of Records would cause some sort of alert. The Pharaoh's soldiers and priests blanketed the entire plateau, primarily to keep the large slave population under control. Short of flying the *Fynbar* in, Donnchadh doubted they could get away with the Ark and Grail.

So they decided to use the same tactics they had used against the Airlia: division and dissension. They learned that the ruling Pharaoh, Ramses II, had two sons, the elder of which, Moses, had been exiled from the kingdom for attempting to lead a coup against his father. He had been sent to an outlying province, Midian, where he had been appointed governor. There was a younger son, given his father's name, Ramses III, who obviously was in line to succeed.

Donnchadh and Gwalcmai traveled to Midian, which lay to the east of Egypt, on the desolate peninsula known as Sinai. They found the governor's palace to be more of a large home, built of mud bricks, huddled on the inside wall of the capital city's ten-foot-high walls. Midian wasn't much of a city, consisting of barely a thousand people, and the province had little in the way of resources, other than some mines. A fitting punishment for a wayward son, but one that caused Moses' resentment of his father to fester, as they learned while they spent several days in the city, listening and watching.

Donnchadh and her partner were able to gain an audience with Moses with relative ease, using a few gold pieces to bribe the captain of his guards. They found the governor sitting on a dilapidated throne on the roof of his house, staring out over the wall into the desert. Two bored guards barely checked the two of them, only taking the most obvious precaution of removing Gwalcmai's sword before allowing them access to Moses. Donnchadh still had the scepter and her dagger tucked in the belt under her robe.

"This is far from Giza," Donnchadh said in lieu of greeting the governor.

Moses turned his head toward them. "I was told your names but they mean nothing to me." He did not bother to stand and greet them. He was a young man, with thick dark hair and an angular face. There was the slight trace of a horizontal scar on his forehead.

"Our names are not important," Donnchadh said.

"Does the woman speak for both of you?" Moses asked.

Gwalcmai nodded. "She does."

"Strange," Moses commented. "What do you want?" he demanded, staring at Donnchadh.

"We want to help you."

"You bribed the captain of my guards with gold to gain this audience," Moses said. "How much more gold do you have?"

"How much gold does the Pharaoh have in his treasuries?" Donnchadh asked in turn.

"That gold is in Giza, and as you noted, Giza is far from here. And in more than just distance. If I cross the Red Sea, my father will kill me."

"Not if he needs you," Donnchadh said.

Moses took a long drink from a cracked ceramic mug before he spoke again. "And why will he need me?"

"To help with the problem of the slaves."

"And what problem is that?"

"We'll get to that," Donnchadh said.

Moses drummed his fingers on the arm of his throne for several moments while his other hand tipped the mug and he stared sadly into the empty interior. "And why do you want me to return to Egypt?" he finally asked.

"To finish what you started," Donnchadh said. "To lead a revolt."

"The army is loyal to my father. And the priests also. I have no—"

"Not through the army or the priests," Donnchadh interrupted. "You will use the slaves. The Judeans."

Moses frowned. "You just said my father will welcome me back to deal with the problem of the slaves. I am aware of no problem. And then you say I will use the slaves to revolt against my father."

"You will do both."

Moses mulled this for several seconds, then a sly smile crossed his face. "Very interesting. And ingenious." He lifted his free hand and traced the scar on his forehead. "You know, my father gave this to me when I was but a child. He beat me many times. I was born from one of his mistresses and should not have been allowed to live, but she hid me, then went to the high priest. Because my father had no other heir at the time, he was forced to acknowledge me. But once his third wife gave him a legitimate son, he no longer needed me."

"We know," Donnchadh said. "We have walked Giza, the city of Cairo, and the slave camps for many days. We know how your father rules; and we know that things are worse than your father is told by his advisers. The river runs low and there has been drought for the past two years. There is barely enough grain to feed the Egyptians, never mind the slaves. The Judeans are primed to revolt. They just need hope and a leader."

"Why do you want this to happen?" Moses asked. "Are you Judean? You do not appear to be from this part of the world."

"No," Donnchadh said. She took a deep breath. "We are enemies of the Gods of Egypt. Because they are not real

Gods. They enslave all men just as much as your people enslave the Judeans and others."

"If you said that in front of my father, you would be immediately put to death in a most horrible way," Moses said. "He believes himself to be descended from the Gods and the priests tell him it is so."

Donnchadh shook her head. "He is not and it is not so."

"Can you prove this? Can you prove the Gods do not care for us? And that they are not real Gods?"

Donnchadh had considered this during the journey to Midian. "Yes."

Moses slammed the goblet down. "How?"

"They cannot care for you because they are dead."

"That cannot be," Moses said. "Gods cannot die."

"The Gods worshipped in Egypt are dead," Donnchadh said. "I can show you their bodies. They are dead. Isis. Osiris. Horus. And others that are still worshipped."

Moses considered this. "So the Gods are real but dead?"

"Were real and not Gods," Donnchadh corrected. "And they have been long dead."

Moses got to his feet. "Where are these bodies?"

"Along the Roads of Rostau, underneath the Giza Plateau."

"And you can take me there?"

"Yes."

Moses headed toward the stairs, staggering slightly, but catching himself. "We leave in the morning. I must rest first."

"You cannot tell people what you are seeing," Donnchadh said to Moses while Gwalcmai stood guard just inside the door to the chamber, sword in hand.

The three of them were clad in the gray cloaks taken from the Watcher's hut and stood next to a black tube, the top of which was open. Inside lay the body of one of the Airlia, slain by Vampyr many years previously. There was no mistaking the fact that the body was not human, and that it was indeed dead. The pale skin had mummified, shrinking tightly around the bones underneath. The hair had continued to grow after death, surrounding the head like a red pillow. Six clawlike fingers were at the end of each hand. Along the side of the body was a golden staff with a sphinx head on one end.

"The Gods are indeed dead," Moses murmured. "I had heard rumors before you appeared, but no one dared say anything publicly."

"Because the Pharaoh's power base is religion," Donnchadh said. "It is something they"—she nodded at the bodies—"have always used. And they passed on that knowledge to the Shadows who ruled after them, and the Shadows passed it to the Pharaohs who rule now."

"People will not accept this," Moses said. "You cannot take away their beliefs so easily."

"No, they won't like it," Donnchadh agreed.

"So how—" Moses left the question unsaid.

"What you will do," Donnchadh began, "is use the God of the Judeans to rally them and to frighten the Pharaoh."

"'The' God? Just one?" Moses asked.

"Yes."

"Is the God of the Judeans real?"

The question gave Donnchadh pause. "I don't know." She looked down at the body. "As real as they are, I suppose."

An uneasy silence reigned in the chamber for several minutes, each of the three lost in their own thoughts.

"What else is down here?" Moses finally asked. "When I was growing up, some of the priests would whisper about secret places under the Great Pyramid of Khufu."

"What else is down here does not concern you," Donnchadh said.

Moses turned to her, and Gwalcmai stepped between them, his hand drifting to the pommel of his sword.

Moses did not back down. "I heard rumors of a Grail that gives immortality, which lies somewhere down here. It is what the priests would promise the true believers as their reward for a lifetime of service. Yet no one ever seemed to get this reward."

"There is an Ark in one of the duats along these Roads," Donnchadh allowed. "Perhaps it contains the Grail."

" 'Perhaps'?" Moses waited, but Donnchadh said nothing more. Finally, he sighed. "You have proven that the Gods of my people are dead. What do I do next?"

"Gwalcmai will go with you," Donnchadh said. She reached into the tube and pulled out the staff, handing it to Moses. "You will call him Aaron. He will advise you."

"Where will I go?"

"To see your father, the Pharaoh, of course." Donnchadh drew her dagger. "But first we must do something so you can make your point more clearly to your father and to the priests who whisper in his ear."

The royal guards did not kill Moses immediately. Whether it was because they were not willing to kill royalty without direct orders from the Pharaoh, or because of the amazing staff he carried, the likes of which none had ever seen, or a combination of both, it wasn't clear.

They did, however, securely bind the arms of both Gwalcmai and Moses before bringing them into the Pharaoh's receiving room. They were shoved down onto their knees on the hard stone floor in front of the Pharaoh's throne. Ramses II wore a heavy robe, sewn with golden thread, and his head was adorned with a crown covered with jewels. His face was so heavily rouged that it was hard for Gwalcmai to read the man's expression. His arms were crossed, the symbols of his office—the crook and flail—in his hands. He was so still that for several moments Gwalcmai thought him to be a statue. A dozen guards flanked the Pharaoh on either side. Seated to the Pharaoh's right was a younger version, dressed and made up the same, except lacking the crown, crook, and flail.

Ramses II stared at his son for several moments in silence, then raised the crook and made a gesture. Guards cut the bindings holding the two men and handed Moses the staff.

Moses raised both hands, the staff in his right, the left palm open in a sign of peace. "Father."

"You dare call me that?" Ramses' voice was low, but carried well in the room.

"Father, I have come to help you."

Two kilometers from the Pharaoh's palace, near the wall surrounding the sprawling Judean slave camp, Donnchadh removed a small block of gray, malleable material from the backpack she had been wearing. She pressed the material against the base of the stone wall, directly below one of the guard towers that were evenly spaced, one hundred meters apart, around the perimeter. She placed a flat chip, no larger than the nail on her pinkie, on top of the material and quickly moved away.

Taking a small metal ball out of her pack, she pressed one of the hexagonals on the surface and the material exploded, destroying the guard tower and punching a large hole in the wall. Both the Egyptians and Jews in the area were stunned by this inexplicable event. The awe was over quickly, though, as the closest Egyptian troops retaliated for the death of their comrades in the only way they knew how, against the only available enemy—they began massacring the closest slaves they could slay.

Starving because of the drought, worked to within inches of their lives, and having borne the burden of slavery for long years, many Jews fought back and a pitched battle was joined. Bugle calls echoed out as the surprised Egyptian troops called for assistance. The handful of soldiers in the area were quickly overwhelmed and the Jews appropriated their weapons and surged through the hole in the wall.

Just as a second bomb, which Donnchadh had set earlier, went off, destroying a barracks full of soldiers.

Ⓦhat kind of help can you give me?" the Pharaoh demanded.

Ramses III stood, glaring down at his half brother. "What kind of help do you think we need, Governor of Midian?"

A sound like distant thunder echoed through the palace, even though there wasn't a cloud in the sky. The faint sound of bugles floated in through the open windows. Then another thunderclap. More bugles blared and there was the sound of large numbers of armed men moving quickly.

An officer appeared in one of the side portals to the audience room and hurried across to whisper into Ramses III's ear. Ramses III dismissed the man, then turned to Moses. "What an extreme coincidence—you come here offering aid, and there is trouble with the Judeans at the same moment."

"There has been trouble brewing with the Judeans for a long time," Moses said. "There is the drought. They have been worked harder than they should have been. Even slaves must be fed and taken care of. There is trouble in the east and south. There are stirrings in Persia and I believe within ten years the Hittites will invade in this direction."

"Do you bring me only bad news?" Ramses II asked.

"I bring you good news," Moses said. He indicated Gwalcmai. "This is Aaron, a warrior from beyond our borders. He knows of the Hittites. He knows of the lands there."

Gwalcmai half bowed at the waist toward Ramses II. "Lord, you can solve two problems with one action."

Gwalcmai paused while several more officers scurried in and talked to Ramses III in low voices. As soon as they left, his father raised the crook, indicating he was to brief him.

"There have been two explosions like lightning striking but there is no storm. One along the wall holding the Judeans, the other at the barracks of the temple guards. Many soldiers—at least one hundred—have been killed. There have been subsequent riots in the Judean camp. It will be suppressed shortly."

"For the time being," Moses threw in.

"What is the one action that would solve my dual problems?" Ramses II demanded.

"Let us take the Judeans away from here," Gwalcmai said. "To the north and east, along the shores of the Mediterranean. Let them establish a state there, close to where they originally came from. A state that will be loyal to you because of their gratitude for being freed. One that will be a buffer state for you against the Hittites."

"One that you rule?" Ramses III demanded.

"My exile will be farther away, brother," Moses replied. "That should suit you." He looked at his father. "You will be rid of the Judean problem. It was fine to have so many slaves when things were going well and the Nile was high and crops were bountiful. Now they are just a drain. The bricks they make are of poor quality and lie in piles, unused. And you will have a state between you and the Hittites that they will have to conquer before they can attack Egypt."

Pharaoh Ramses II considered the proposition for all of ten seconds. "No."

"Father—" Moses began, but Ramses II cut him off with a chop of his crook.

"The Jews can be solved more easily than giving them to you. As far as the Hittites—let them come. We will drench the sands with their blood, as we have done to our enemies for as long as our family has ruled."

"My lord," Gwalcmai began, "it is not as simple as that."

"And why not?" Ramses II demanded.

"There is the issue of the Judeans' God," Gwalcmai said.

Donnchadh was now hidden at the edge of the lush farmland about a kilometer south of the Giza Plateau. Sweat soaked her robes and she was breathing hard from her run to this location. From a leather pouch tied to her belt she removed a small black sphere, about forty centimeters in diameter. It was an Airlia artifact recovered on her world. It was one of many weapons the Airlia had used in the long war. Donnchadh's fellow scientists had analyzed it and discovered that it was a microwave transmitter that could be tuned to a number of frequencies. It had been used as a weapon by the Airlia when set to a frequency that caused hemorrhages in human brains. However, it could also be used in other ways, one of which Donnchadh was getting ready to employ. She'd tested it before and now she used what she had learned.

She tuned it to a specific frequency, then pressed the ON button. Nothing apparent happened, but the flickering red light on the side told her it was transmitting.

Ramses II's laughter echoed off the murals painted on the walls. "The God of the Judeans? Why should that concern us?"

Ramses III said nothing, having settled back onto his throne and reassuming his noble posture. His eyes glittered with malice as he stared at his half brother.

Gwalcmai opened his leather pack and took out a round object wrapped in gray cloth. He knelt and slowly unwrapped the grisly package, revealing Osiris's severed head. The cat-red eyes stared at the Pharaoh and his son as if they were still alive.

"What is this?" Ramses III yelled. He gestured and several of the guards closed on Gwalcmai and Moses.

"This is not our doing," Gwalcmai quickly said. "This is one of the Gods of the First Age of Egypt, before the time of even Horus. We found his body below Giza, in the Roads of Rostau."

Ramses III drew his sword and took a step toward them, but he halted at a gesture from his father. "You walked the Roads?" the Pharaoh asked, his voice level.

Gwalcmai nodded. "We did, my lord. We found this one dead along with five others. There are no Gods left alive there."

"Who killed them?" Ramses II demanded.

Gwalcmai shrugged. "That I do not know. But I fear the God of the Jews might have had something to do with it. They worship only one God, a powerful one apparently. And this God wants them freed and sent back to their homeland. This is another reason why it would be in your interests to do as your son, Moses, has requested." He paused. "Lord, I have it from one of the Jewish priests that if you do not release them, their God will unleash a plague upon your land."

Ramses II blinked, the first sign of concern that had crossed his face since they'd entered. Little cracks appeared in the rouge around his eyes. He seemed about to say something, when the sound of screams reverberating from thousands of throats made its way into the room.

This time there was no pretense. Ramses III ran to the nearest window, Moses and Gwalcmai right behind him. The Pharaoh remained on his throne, bound by tradition, but his head turned, following them with his eyes as the screams of his people struck his ears.

"What is it?" the Pharaoh demanded.

Ramses III replied, the word sending a chill through every Egyptian in the room, "Locusts."

Donnchadh pulled the cloak over her head. It was as if she were in the middle of a fierce hailstorm as locusts smacked into the cloth, drawn by the Airlia black ball's microwaves. They numbered in the millions, drawn in from all around, woken from their slumber by the Airlia transmitter. They descended into the fields, consuming all. Farmers futilely tried to stop the scourge, dashing out with brooms. It was like a stick placed in the way of an incoming tide.

From the Pharaoh's palace, it looked as if a dark cloud had descended to the ground south of Giza, covering the fields. It had been many years since a plague of locusts had struck the center of Egypt. It had occurred once during the Pharaoh's childhood. He still remembered the devastation as the creatures ate the fields bare. This, on top of the drought, could destroy his kingdom.

Ramses II stood. "Take them, Moses. Take the Judeans and never come back here."

Donnchadh turned off the microwave transmitter. The battering against her cloak slowly subsided. She waited another five minutes, then pulled it aside. It was if a scythe had gone through the fields, taking everything down to bare stalks.

She felt a momentary twinge of guilt for the day's events. She knew the higher goal they were trying to achieve would make today's event shrink into nothingness over time, but that didn't change the fact that she was responsible for the death of fellow humans. Donnchadh focused her thoughts on the Grail as she walked north, through the barren fields. Night was falling and tomorrow would be a new day. Tonight, there was more to do.

Moses was in the camp with the Judeans, meeting with their leaders, trying to get them to accept this unexpected turn of events and get organized, not an easy task. Despite the great opportunity of freedom they were being offered, the Judeans were a quarrelsome lot and there were those who feared this was some trick of the Pharaoh's to get them out into the desert and let them starve to death.

Gwalcmai waited for Donnchadh in the darkness at the base of the Great Pyramid. As they had hoped, the Pharaoh had pulled his troops back to protect his palace and the city of Cairo to the north. With Gwalcmai were a half dozen Judeans armed with swords and wearing gray cloaks—those who had been in the forefront of the recent fighting with the Egyptians and who would prefer death to slavery. Moses had recruited them from the leaders with the promise that they would find important things under the plateau. They climbed up the side of the Great Pyramid and entered the Roads of Rostau through the tunnel entrance.

They descended through the massive blocks of stone that had been laid until they were into the solid stone below, which made up the plateau. They avoided the golden spider, hiding under their gray cloaks and remaining still as it came by. The reliance on automated defenses had been one of the Airlia's weak points on their home world, as every such system always had a loophole allowing it to be defeated. Of course, the vast difference in body counts between Airlia and human during the Revolution was largely due to figuring out those loopholes at the cost of blood.

They went down tunnel after tunnel, following the directions handed down through the Watcher records that Donnchadh had copied in England. Finally, they reached a stone door, which Donnchadh opened. They stepped inside into brief but total darkness, which was immediately dispersed as a five-meter-diameter orb hanging overhead came to life, throwing light throughout a large cavern.

They were standing on a ledge above the floor of the cavern. Both recognized the Black Sphinx crouching on the floor—the Hall of Records. The cavern was about six hundred meters across, the wall smoothly cut red stone, which must have been added after their last visit. The six Judeans were stunned by what they saw.

Stairs were cut out of the rock wall, leading from the ledge to the floor. Without a word, Donnchadh and Gwalcmai took them. Trembling, the Judeans followed. They headed between the large black paws to the statue of Horus that stood on a pedestal. There was a stone set against the pedestal. Donnchadh bent over and read the High Rune marking.

"It says that there is a black box along the Roads, in another chamber, that can destroy this entire structure. If one tries to get in and doesn't have the key, the black box will self-destruct."

"An Airlia nuclear weapon or power source?" Gwalcmai guessed.

"Most likely," Donnchadh said. Several such devices had been used on their home world with devastating effect. It made sense that the Airlia would booby-trap their most precious artifact.

The six men listened to them without comprehending. Donnchadh did not want to take the time to explain. She reached into her pack and pulled out the scepter they had brought from so far away. She placed it on the image on the pedestal, where the faint outline of it was etched. The glowing orb overhead blinked briefly, then quickly lit again. The surface of the stone shimmered and the scepter began to sink into it. Donnchadh released her grip.

The stone slid down, revealing a six-foot-high opening leading into the body of the Black Sphinx. The passageway had several steps going down. The tunnel was almost three meters high. A thin line of blue lights ran along the center of the ceiling. They flickered, then came on. The corridor seemed to open up about fifteen meters ahead.

"It looks like the world has not been destroyed," Gwalcmai noted.

Donnchadh ignored him and entered the Hall of Records. Gwalcmai began to follow, then noticed that the six Judeans were hesitating. He gestured angrily and they reluctantly shuffled after him.

Donnchadh walked through the corridor, feeling the weight of the alien metal all around her. The Hall on her own planet had been lost when the Airlia headquarters was destroyed. They'd only had the Airlia records of it.

She entered a room in the belly of the Sphinx. The ceiling was seven meters high, the walls the same distance to either side and the far wall ten meters away. In the center of the room were four poles that held up four horizontal rods. At the top of each pole was an exact replica of the head on the staff, red eyes glittering. Thick white cloths hung from each of the rods, hiding whatever was enclosed. To the left, against the wall, were several racks of garments. Gwalcmai joined her, the six Judeans hanging back.

"Is it my imagination or are those things looking at us?" Donnchadh asked, as she pointed at the four heads.

"Let's move right," Gwalcmai suggested. They did so, and ever so slightly the heads turned, tracking them.

"I would assume the Ark is behind those curtains," Donnchadh said.

"We will get it," one of the Judeans said.

"I don't think—" Gwalcmai began, but the one who had spoken and another stepped forward. The four heads locked in on them and before they made their third steps, red bolts shot out of the eyes of the two closest heads, hitting both men.

The bodies dropped to the floor, lifeless, with smoke rising from the holes in their chests. The other four Judeans bolted, and Gwalcmai chased after them. Donnchadh stared at the four heads, trying to figure out a way around this unexpected development. Gwalcmai returned, marshaling the four surviving Judeans into the chamber, where they clung to the wall, as far from the center as possible.

"The garments," Donnchadh said. "They must be for whoever handles the Ark." She moved along the wall, toward the racks. One of the heads tracked her while the other three remained trained on the others in the room.

"Are you sure?" Gwalcmai asked, with a concerned look at the two still-smoking corpses.

Donnchadh made it to the racks without getting fired at. She lifted a white linen robe and slipped it over her head. Then she examined the rest of the accouterments. She glanced over her shoulder at Gwalcmai and the four survivors. "Care to join me?"

Gwalcmai herded the four men along the wall to her position. Donnchadh noticed that the garments were arranged in a specific order and she figured that was the way she should put them on. She took a sleeveless blue shirt with gold fringe and put it on top of the robe. Then a multicolored coat. She noted that metal threads were woven throughout the fabric of the coat but it was missing something to connect it at the shoulders. There was a shelf on top of the rack and she picked up a wooden box. Opening it, she found two stones nestled inside. She used those to fasten the robe. As she did so, a strange tingle passed through her body.

"Are you all right?" Gwalcmai asked. He had put on one of the white linen robes and a red coat. There were about a dozen similar garments hanging from the racks, and the four Judeans dressed themselves in these.

Donnchadh nodded. "There's some sort of field built into this outfit." She grabbed a breastplate festooned with a dozen jewels and looped the neckpiece for it over her shoulders. The entire outfit was heavy and she felt the tug on her shoulders from all the weight.

"You're missing something," Gwalcmai noted, pointing at two empty pockets on the shoulders of the breastplate.

"The urim and thummin," Donnchadh said. "The stones activate the Grail. They might be stored with it in the Ark or in a separate place. I have a feeling Aspasia would not put them here, though."

Also on the shelf was a crown consisting of three bands, each stacked on the other. Done dressing, she turned toward the center of the chamber. The four guard heads were aimed directly at her.

"Ready?" Donnchadh asked. She didn't wait for an answer. She moved toward the white curtain, the heads tracking. She paused, heart racing, as a flash of light came out of the eyes of one of the heads and struck the ground in front of her, then ran up her body, stopping on the breastplate for a couple of seconds, then moving on to the crown. She must have passed the test, because the light went out. Gwalcmai and the others were in single file behind her. Donnchadh reached the veil. She knelt and lifted the white cloth, then passed underneath, the others following.

The Ark rested on a waist-high black platform. It was a meter high and wide, and a little more than that in length. The surface was gold. There were rings on the bottom through which two long poles—obviously to be used to carry it—extended.

And there were two more heads on top of the Ark on either end. As soon as she had entered, they had turned and fixed her with their inhuman gaze. Red light flashed out of both and the process she had just gone through was repeated as the light went over her garments, pausing on the breastplate and crown, then both lights went out. The two heads turned back to gazing at each other over the lid of the Ark.

Donnchadh was tempted to open the Ark, but she knew that time was of the essence. Also, even if the Grail was inside, without the two stones, they could do nothing with it. Gwalcmai issued orders and the four Judeans moved into position on the poles. They grabbed one of the white curtains and ripped it down, draping it over the Ark. Then the four surviving Judeans lifted it, and Donnchadh led the way out of the Hall of Records.

XII

It appears that the Pharaoh has changed his mind," Gwalcmai said as they observed the column of dust many kilometers to their rear. There was a similar column ahead of them—the thousands of Judeans whom they had freed. They were currently three days' march from Giza, and Gwalcmai had been complaining for the last forty-eight hours about the extremely slow pace of the Judeans. They had left the fertile land around the Nile and were now well into the desert but they were not making much progress—at least according to Gwalcmai's standards.

Moses was at the head of the Judeans along with the four who bore the Ark. Behind was what Gwalcmai had in his better moods referred to as a gaggle of people and in his worse moods described using various expletives in their own tongue. Families, animals, wagons, were spread across the desert with little organization, simply following the man who had rescued them out of bondage—for the time being at least.

"How long before they catch us?" Donnchadh asked.

Gwalcmai had been watching the cloud for over an hour, gauging its progress. "They're very confident."

"Why do you say that?"

"Because they're not moving very quickly either. Faster than us to be sure. But not an all-out pursuit. Most of the

Pharaoh's army is infantry," Gwalcmai said. "He has cavalry and chariot units, but I think his generals will want to bring their main force to bear. It's not like these people here are going to set any land speed records." He mentally calculated. "Three days and they can cut us off. I also don't think they're going to put up much of an organized fight once we make contact."

"We're two days from the crossing," Donnchadh said. They had scouted the routes out of Egypt earlier, on their way to recruit Moses. "So we can get across before the Egyptians arrive."

Gwalcmai shook his head. "The Judeans are not well organized. They cannot hold the crossing against the Egyptians. Also, even if we hold, they'll just flank north and catch us in the desert on the far side."

"The Judeans won't have to hold the crossing," Donnchadh said. She looked at her husband. "You warriors always think in terms of force of arms. But there are other forces out there that can be used."

"And I suppose you aren't going to tell me what they are," Gwalcmai said.

"Not yet," Donnchadh said with a teasing smile. "You'll see."

"Whatever your plan is," Gwalcmai said, "it had better be good."

To the south was the Red Sea and to the north the Mediterranean. Directly in front of them was an expanse known by one of two names, depending on who one asked: Bitter Sea, or the Sea of Reeds. The water was shallow, in most places about three to four meters deep. Many sandy islands dotted it, each surrounded by a fringe of tall reeds. It was a desolate place with no inhabitants. At its widest, it was over twenty kilometers from Egypt to the Sinai Peninsula.

This was the only place they could get out of Egypt because the land to the north that connected Egypt with Sinai had numerous forts manned by the Pharaoh's soldiers. And they did not have ships to cross the Red Sea to the south. There were two narrow strips of sand that ran across the length of this sea, each ten meters wide, and it was in the dry bed between these that the mass of Judeans was stretched. These ridges of sand were what remained from the Airlia mothership's flight from Giza to the Sinai thousands of years previously, its gravitational drive scarring the face of the planet.

Gwalcmai and Donnchadh, as usual, were bringing up the rear. The dust cloud from the Egyptians was very close, just over the horizon. It was also very thick, indicating the Pharaoh had sent a large force in pursuit. They were at the place where the sand causeway touched the Egyptian side of the water.

"There." Gwalcmai was pointing. A cluster of small specks came over the dune just in front of the dust cloud. "The advance guard. Cavalry." Gwalcmai looked over his shoulder. The first of the Judeans had reached the far side of the Sea of Reeds, but the rest were stretched out so far that there was still a good number waiting to move through the sand road protected by the ridges. Gwalcmai muttered a few choice curse words in his native tongue.

"Relax," Donnchadh said. "This will work out."

Gwalcmai had been considering the tactical situation. "I can hold the way for a little while with a small group of men—good men, they'd have to be, because there would be no retreat. If you take my *ka*, then—"

"Relax," Donnchadh said once more, cutting him off. "I

told you I have a plan. A scientist's plan, not a warrior's plan. There is no need for a dramatic last stand."

"And you did not tell me the plan," Gwalcmai said, "so I—"

"Hush." Donnchadh put her hand on his shoulder. She pointed up with the other hand. "The moon will be up soon, even though it is still daylight."

"And?"

"Why do you think we spent that extra week in the desert before we took Moses to the Pharaoh?"

"Because you wanted to," Gwalcmai said simply.

"Because I had a plan," Donnchadh said. "Look." She pointed to the lake.

"What am I looking at?" Gwalcmai asked, reining in his impatience.

"This lake is connected to the Red Sea on its southern end. It actually is an estuary, not a lake. The water is salt, not fresh, thus its name. Which means it is affected by the tides. Which are coming in."

Gwalcmai processed this information for several seconds. "But the ridges on either side are above the high-tide mark. You can see by the marks that they have never been covered and this path has never been flooded."

"Yes. Most of the time. For normal high tides," Donnchadh said. "But this evening the moon will be full. Every thirty days, when the moon is full, and the tide is high—well, you'll see." She reached into her pack and pulled out several gray blocks of explosive. "Give me a hand with this."

Gwalcmai had lost his voice. He'd spent the last two hours screaming at the tail end of the long column, trying to get the Judeans to move more quickly. He'd ended up throwing an old woman who could not keep up over his shoulder, holding her with one hand, while he used the sword in his other to slap donkeys and other beasts of burdens on their hindquarters to get them moving more quickly.

As he reached the Sinai end of the sand path, Gwalcmai handed the woman to a couple of teenage boys, then turned and faced back the way they had come. Pharaoh's front guard had halted on the Egyptian side, waiting for the rest of the army to come forward. Gwalcmai knew that was a mistake—they had given up the initiative. He knew the decision had been made because the small front guard could easily be trapped on the causeway and overwhelmed if the Judeans turned on them, but any fool could see that the Judeans weren't organized and were running away as fast as possible.

"You timed all of this, didn't you?" Gwalcmai asked his wife as they watched the bulk of the Egyptian army slowly appear. "You knew they would pursue us."

"I didn't know for certain that they would pursue," Donnchadh said, "but I knew it was a possibility. I did time our encounter with the Pharaoh to ensure it would be the right time of month when we arrived here."

The tide was already quite high, water lapping at both sides of the causeway, but still a good three feet from cresting.

"They're coming," Gwalcmai said. It was two hours before dark and the lead elements of the Egyptian army began to move into the path. The rest of the force followed, the setting sun glinting off the spear tips and armor of the Egyptian soldiers.

Donnchadh and Gwalcmai moved back about five hundred meters from the Sinai side of the causeway. They had instructed Moses to keep the Judeans moving into the desert, as far away from the water as possible. The last of the Judean group was still less than a kilometer from them as the lead elements of the Egyptians approached the Sinai Peninsula.

Donnchadh pulled the black sphere out of her pack and

wrapped her fingers around it. Numerous hexagonal sections were highlighted with very small High Rune writing on each.

"Tell me when," she said to Gwalcmai, trusting his military instincts for the timing.

Gwalcmai had his bow in hand, an arrow notched. He lifted the weapon, the arrow pointing up at a forty-five-degree angle, and let loose the string. The arrow was almost invisible as it quickly flew toward its target. The barbed head caught the lead Egyptian in the throat, tearing through. The man fell, his blood pouring out of the severed artery. The front of the Egyptian column came to a temporary halt as the officer in charge yelled orders. The rest of the column, however, continued to press forward. The sand path between the two ridges was a mass of infantry, chariots, and cavalry.

"Now," Gwalcmai said.

Donnchadh pressed the button.

A dozen charges on each sand ridge detonated, opening ten-meter-wide gaps at each spot. The water that had been held at bay for millennia surged in. Draped with armor and burdened with weapons, the Egyptians closest to the gaps had no chance. They were washed under and drowned. Those further away desperately dropped their weapons and tried to tear off their gear.

Those closest to the Sinai, and Gwalcmai and Donnchadh's location, threw down their weapons and ran forward, arms held high in supplication as the water roared toward them. Gwalcmai showed no mercy, firing his bow as quickly as he could notch an arrow and draw and release the string. A dozen Egyptians died by his hand before the water surged over the rest and they were gone. Within a minute, the Bitter Sea had reclaimed the small strip of dry land that had divided it. The only indication that an army was drowned under the water were a few floating pieces of debris—a wooden arrow here, the feathers from an officer's helmet there. It was almost as if the Pharaoh's army had never existed.

"I do not think they will follow us again," Gwalcmai said as he slipped the bow over his shoulders.

Donnchadh stood still, the enormity of what she had just caused sinking in.

Gwalcmai saw her hesitation. "It had to be done."

"I know." But she still did not move.

"There will be much more death," Gwalcmai said.

"And you say that to make me feel better?" Donnchadh snapped.

"I say that to let you know that is the reality of our mission."

"I know the reality," Donnchadh said. She turned toward her husband. "But we must mourn the death of humans, even those under the thrall of the Airlia. Because if we do not mourn them, then we are like the Airlia. We must be human."

T here was another who had watched the Egyptian army drown. One with a human body. But an Airlia personality. And he did not mourn the deaths. He was wrapped in the long robes of one who lived in the desert, but he was not one of them. He hid on the reverse slope of a sand dune on the Sinai side of the Sea of Reeds and had been observing all day.

Among the desert people, the Bedu, he was known as Al-Iblis, the evil one. Some said he was not a man but a demon, and they were partially right. He was Aspasia's Shadow, left behind in the chamber deep inside Mount Sinai.

He had been awoken as programmed a thousand years after Aspasia left him there. Since then, he had roamed the desert and beyond, taking in the wonders of the world. He had reincarnated many times, using the Airlia technology to implant his personality into a new body when needed. While he had originally had Aspasia's personality, the cumulative experiences since he had awoken had changed him and made him a creature still bound to its master, but with its own twisted personality.

So Aspasia's Shadow laughed as he watched the Egyptians drown. He found great pleasure in disaster and chaos. He knew of both the Egyptians and the Judeans and all the other people in this part of the world. But he did not know of the two who had planned this ambush. A man and a woman who obviously had access to Airlia technology, as he had recognized both the small black sphere the woman had used and the type of explosive that had destroyed the two sand ridges.

The Judeans were a strange people. He had watched their small kingdom grow along the banks of the great sea for many years. A people who believed in prophets and one God—a most strange development, which Aspasia's Shadow had never quite been able to account for. When the Egyptians had swept over the Judeans' land and taken them into captivity, Aspasia's Shadow had been content to see these dangerous people with their radical views brought to heel.

But now they were free and there were two who obviously knew something of the Airlia with them. He did not know what it meant, but he felt it was a threat. And his mission was to stop threats.

So as the Judeans moved farther into the Sinai, Aspasia's Shadow followed them and he plotted.

Donnchadh and Gwalcmai stayed on the fringes of the Judean exodus. They let Moses lead the people into the desert. Gwalcmai wanted to leave, to go back to their ship. But Donnchadh could not bear to depart with the Grail so close. She knew that Gwalcmai was right—that it was too soon to do anything with the Grail—but she felt a visceral attraction toward the alien artifact. With all the terrible things she had witnessed on her own world and on Earth, she felt that the Grail was the only possibility for something good enough to outweigh all of that.

If they could defeat the Airlia without destroying this planet. And if they could hold on to the Grail. And if they could stay hidden from both the Airlia and the Swarm. Then, just maybe, this planet could be the start of a human empire peopled by immortals. These were the thoughts and hopes that swirled through Donnchadh's head as she and her mate followed the mass of humanity across the desert toward the land Moses had promised the people.

They were not completely idle. They scoured the camp in the evening, listening and judging the people they met. They were searching for the best candidate for the role of *Wedjat*, the Watcher who would begin the line responsible for keeping an eye on the Ark and Grail, now that the artifacts were no longer under the watch of the *Wedjat* of Giza. After two weeks they found a young man who they felt would fit the mold. He was a man who questioned the preachings of the priests regarding the one God—or any gods for that matter, as there were still sects among the Judeans who worshipped differently—and who eyed Moses—and indeed the two of them—with suspicion. They took him out into the desert and spent three days briefing him and preparing him for the role he was to play. For two days he refused to believe their story of the Airlia, Atlantis, and the Great Civil War, until Donnchadh demonstrated the pieces of Airlia technology she had brought with her. They took him out of earshot of the camp and remotely set off one of the explosive charges, shattering a boulder. This sufficiently impressed him, that while they did not claim to be Gods, the two had more power than anyone else he had seen.

They gave him a *Wedjat* ring and as much information as they dared, including the location of the Watcher headquarters in Avalon, with orders to try to get reports there as often as possible. Donnchadh had found that humans became energized when given a solid goal, a focus for their lives, and she used this to her advantage. She knew, and tried not to reflect too heavily on, that this was not much different from the Airlia use of religion to control people. She did not know whether this desire to believe in something larger than oneself was a trait that had just developed in humans, or whether it was something the Airlia had deliberately injected into their genetic makeup. Ultimately, she had decided that it did not matter—it existed, and therefore had to be calculated into any plan.

At the camp, despite Moses' best efforts and what had happened in the Sea of Reeds, he could not allay the people's fear that the Egyptians were still chasing after them and would return them to slavery. Because of this, the route he was taking across the Sinai was anything but direct. They were swinging far to the south to avoid any possibility of running into Egyptian patrols.

Gwalcmai, as Donnchadh had feared, quickly grew weary of the long loop to the south through desolate terrain. He saw it as unnecessary and dangerous for both of them. Already there were factions among the Judeans, groups opposed to Moses because he was not one of them. To counteract that, Moses had begun spreading a story that his mother had been a Judean slave. Such politicking disgusted Gwalcmai and, given that Donnchadh could give him no valid reason for their continued presence in this sun-blasted land, his patience was wearing very thin.

Two months after their departure from Egypt, the Judean

column was halted in a large wadi, near a small water hole. Food was scarce and, given that the slaves had started the journey half-starved, the rumble of discontent was as loud as that of the empty stomachs. To the south and east they could see several tall peaks towering into the sky. All around lay desolate desert.

"It is time for us to get back to our ship," Gwalcmai said. He had a cloth wrapped around his face to protect it from the light mist of blowing sand. They both wore white robes cinched about their waists with cord. They were on the east side of the wadi, along the edge. Below them to the west were thousands of Judeans, huddled under what passed for shelter. A small group was clustered near the south end—Moses and the tribal leaders, arguing about direction and, more important, food.

"It will be a long and hard journey," Gwalcmai continued when Donnchadh did not respond to his first statement. When she still didn't say anything, he reached out and put a hand on her shoulder. "I am tired."

That caught her attention. "What do you mean? We can rest on the way back. We are still early in these bodies and—"

"I am tired," Gwalcmai said. He shrugged. "I don't know what it is, but I feel weary like I never have before."

That caused Donnchadh pause, bringing back memories of the time in Avalon when he had fallen sick. "Do you feel ill?"

"Nothing specific," Gwalcmai said. "Just a feeling of unease and malaise." He nodded toward the cluster around Moses. "They couldn't agree on whether the sun came up, never mind on a direction. And I don't see much possibility of food in this desolate place."

"If we leave, what about the Grail?" Donnchadh asked.

"We did what we could. The *Wedjat* of the Judeans is

prepared as best we could do. The Grail and Ark will pass into legend and history, but the bottom line is that the Airlia and their people will not have it. In fact, it would be best if you and I did not know where it is. We agreed that we would block out its location during the imprinting on the next regeneration, anyway, so that we would not be tempted."

The Airlia technology they used had the ability to selectively block information from being downloaded into the brain. This was a security device the Airlia used to protect vital data from the Swarm in the only way possible—by making sure it was not accessible.

"You have to let go of your dream for now," Gwalcmai said. "We knew from the beginning it would take a very, very long time before the Airlia could be overthrown here. We have done well, causing their civil war. Leading them into destroying Atlantis. Stealing the Grail. But it is time for us to let things develop. Who knows how this"—he indicated the Judeans—"will turn out. As I always say—it will turn out in a way we least expect."

Donnchadh reluctantly nodded. "It is time for us to go."

Aspasia's Shadow watched the two white-robed figures head off to the north. He still had no idea who they were other than troublesome strangers. He had heard rumors of a group called the *Wedjat*, which traced its lineage back to Atlantis and had vowed to keep tabs on the Airlia. There was supposed to be one at Giza, but the threat from humans was so insignificant that Aspasia's Shadow had never bothered to check out the rumors. Perhaps the two were part of this *Wedjat*. If so, they did more than watch. Getting the Grail out of the Hall of Records was a rather significant feat, but a fruitless one. Aspasia's Shadow was more than prepared to counter their action.

As the two strange humans disappeared to the north, Aspasia's Shadow sent an emissary to the Judean camp—a Bedu, one of many whom he had recruited through fear and bribery to support him in the Sinai. He had given the man both a message and a sign to present to the leader of the Judeans.

M oses had long ago accepted that this had been a mistake. He would have been better off staying governor of Midian than leading this group of ungrateful louts. He had always thought the Judeans one people, but although they all claimed a singular heritage, there were twelve distinct tribes among them. And it was nearly impossible to get two of the tribal leaders to agree on anything, never mind twelve. Every decision required a meeting and they spent more time in meetings than traveling.

He was leading them on a circuitous route to the land he had in mind for them not only because he feared the Egyptians but because he knew there were other dangers in Palestine, and if these people didn't unite before they arrived, they would be overwhelmed.

Right now, though, food was the priority. The Judeans had brought few supplies with them on departing Egypt and the pickings had been slim along the way. The two who had started all this—Gwalcmai and Donnchadh—had made themselves scarce ever since the Sea of Reeds and been of little help.

As the dozen tribal chieftains argued among themselves, one of Moses' aides came to him and whispered in his ear that a local man had come to talk to him. Glad to be out of earshot of the arguing, Moses left the tent and went a short distance away where the Bedu waited for him.

"My lord," the Bedu said, going to one knee, as Moses appeared.

Moses dismissed his aide. "What do you want?"

The Bedu stood and held out an amulet. On it was inscribed the triangle with an eye in the middle—the same symbol Donnchadh had shown him. "You are *Wedjat?*" Moses asked.

"No, Lord. I come from one whom the *Wedjat* watch."

Moses froze. "What do you mean?"

"I come from God to bring you a message and to bring you words of hope."

Moses made note of the singular. "What God do you come from?"

"The one true God," the Bedu said. "As a sign of his benevolence for you and the people you lead, he has prepared food for you and your people's sustenance."

That, at least, was more helpful than Donnchadh and her partner had been, Moses thought. "Where is this food?"

"I will show you, then you can lead your people to it. You will tell them it comes from their God. That their God will help them across the desert. But that they must worship and obey the one and only God."

Moses nodded. It was the only way he could see to unite these people long enough for them to establish their homeland and fight off their enemies. "Is that all?"

"He wants to meet you and some of the elders of the tribes."

Moses eyebrows arched. "God does?"

"Yes. First, the food. Then I will be back to tell you when and where to meet God."

T he food was abundant and mightily welcomed by the Judeans, who knew only that Moses was the favored of God, who had showered this blessing down upon them. For the time being the bickering subsided. The encampment was moved, as Moses had been directed by the Bedu messenger to do, farther south, to the shadow of the shorter of the two peaks.

They spent a week eating and resting. Then the Bedu secretly came to Moses once more in the middle of the night. He ordered Moses to gather four of the Judean elders the next evening and to bring the Ark with them up the mountain. Moses was surprised for a moment that the Bedu knew of the Ark, as he had ordered it kept hidden during the journey for fear that someone would try to steal it. It had been loaded inside a large wooden box and placed on one of the few wagons they had brought with them.

Moses searched out the four elders and gave them the instructions. As darkness fell the following evening, they retrieved the Ark and carried it out of the camp and toward the base of the mountain. As the Bedu had said, they found a thin, single track that led up the mountain and with great difficulty, carrying the Ark, they made their way up. As dawn slowly tinged the sky to the east they were barely two-thirds of the way to the top when they crossed over a spur jutting out from the side of the mountain. They came to a halt as they were faced by a score of Bedu dressed in black robes and holding long, bright spears. In the forefront was the Bedu who had been meeting with Moses.

"Leave the Ark here," the Bedu ordered.

Relieved, the four Judeans lowered the Ark to the rocky ground.

"Come," the Bedu ordered. They followed, the guards falling in behind them as they continued up the trail about four hundred meters, to a point where a tall rock, over twenty-five meters in height, jutted out from the side of the mountain. The Bedu went up to the base of the rock and placed the eye symbol he had shown Moses during the first meeting against it. The Judeans were startled as a doorway, three meters wide by two high, appeared.

One of the four held back, not willing to go into the dark entrance. The Bedu showed little patience, snapping an order in his own language to the guards. They slew the Judean where he stood, severing his head from his body, the blood pumping out onto the rock before the doorway. The others needed no more incentive. They rushed through the doorway and it slid shut behind them.

"I am a vengeful God."

The voice echoed in the darkness, against the stone walls of the chamber. A light began to grow from a line in the ceiling and a figure was revealed standing on the other side of the cavern: a tall man robed in black. A hood hid his face.

"You will obey or you will suffer, as your comrade did."

The Judeans fell to their knees and prostrated themselves, foreheads to the floor. Moses hesitated, then slowly went to his knees and bowed his head.

"I am the one and only God," the figure continued. "You will worship me and you will obey my rules for your people. You will keep the Ark in your care, but you must never open it. Death will be the penalty for whoever opens it and gazes upon what is inside."

The figure turned toward a doorway on the far side of the chamber. "Come with me and see what wondrous things I have for you."

Aspasia's Shadow watched Moses and the surviving three Judeans carry the Ark along the trail and out of sight, heading back toward their encampment. They were Guides now, their will suborned to the programming of the guardian computer he had taken them to deep inside the mountain.

Aspasia's Shadow had played with the idea of keeping the Ark and Grail here, but knew that if his maker ever came to check on him, such an act would result in his immediate termination. He knew that he should take the Ark and Grail from the Judeans and return it to Giza. But—and there was always a but—he also knew doing so would take away any hope he ever had of partaking of the Grail. He was tired of this endless series of reincarnations in the service of the Airlia. He had more than enough of Aspasia's personality to know his maker would dispose of him like so much trash when the time came for the Airlia to resume their control of this world. And if Artad prevailed, the result would be the same. Aspasia's Shadow had to make his own plans, and letting the Judeans take the Ark and Grail with them provided just one of many options he wanted to keep open.

He had imprinted into the three Judeans and Moses the imperative that they were to make security of the Ark their paramount concern. On top of that, he had reinforced the Judeans' belief in their one God. Religion, as the Airlia had learned, was a most effective way of keeping humans under control. They had always made the humans worship them, but Aspasia's Shadow thought it was a good idea to introduce the concept of more gods to the humans.

We did well," Gwalcmai said as they began to strip down in preparation for entering the deep sleep tubes. It had taken them two years of hard traveling to make it back to their ship. Gwalcmai now sported a wicked-looking scar along his right arm from shoulder to elbow from a battle in the forests of Gaul, where they had been ambushed by thieves and barely escaped with their lives.

Donnchadh nodded. "The Airlia no longer have control of the Grail. That is a large step. But I am worried about Moses and the Judeans and—"

Gwalcmai put his hand over her mouth. "Hush. Do not go into the deep sleep with worries. They'll rattle around in your head all those years and give you a headache. Let me give you a good memory to take with you." He lifted her off her feet and carried her forward to the pilot's seat.

Moses did not survive to lead the Judeans into the land he had promised them. Aspasia's Shadow learned this from one of his Bedu spies who had trailed the Judeans north to Palestine. However, the twelve tribes had united strongly after Moses and the elders came down from the mountain with their unshakable belief in one God and a set of divine rules by which the people were to live. Humans liked external rules—it was something the Airlia had bred into the species.

Their fledgling kingdom was not only surviving but flourishing. Their single-minded belief in only one God gave them a great advantage over their neighbors who worshipped many Gods, if they worshipped at all. Aspasia's Shadow felt quite satisfied that the Ark and Grail would be safe for some time.

That did not mean, of course, that he was not going to implement more of his plans.

XIII

A.D. 70: STONEHENGE

Donnchadh felt refreshed and vaguely optimistic as she opened her eyes. She smiled as she remembered Gwalcmai and his "farewell" to her before entering the tubes this last time. He had been right—good memories were the way to enter the deep sleep.

The smile was gone as she sat up. What had happened while they slept? Was the Grail safe? Were the Airlia still asleep and the Atlantis Truce in place? Was the planet safe from the Swarm? She swung her legs over the side of the tube and touched the cold deck plating. She threw on a robe and slipped on sandals, then scurried over to the copilot's seat and booted up the computer.

"Worried already?" Gwalcmai's voice was hoarse, as always after the deep sleep.

"You know me well," Donnchadh said.

"It was nice the one time you awakened me with a kiss," Gwalcmai. "If I woke first, that is what I would do every time. But I am a slow riser."

Donnchadh paused, her fingers over the keyboard. She slowly turned to face her husband. "I am sorry. I am always in a rush—"

"When there is a need to hurry, you will see no one go faster," Gwalcmai interrupted her as he climbed out of his tube and got dressed. "But at this moment, upon awakening, unless there is an alarm going off, there is no need to rush."

Donnchadh forced herself to get out of the chair and go to her husband. She felt the pull of the computer and whatever information it had, but for once she allowed the stronger feeling deep inside her to rule.

JERUSALEM

Aspasia's Shadow cursed as the spray of blood from the captive's throat left a trail of red across his gleaming breastplate. "Pull him back next time, you fools," he hissed at the two legionnaires who held the arms of the dying Jew. It was always difficult to train new help, he reflected as a slave gingerly wiped at the armor, eyes downcast, afraid of suffering the same fate.

The dead man had been worthless. As had the hundreds before him that Aspasia's Shadow had also tortured and killed. True, he had learned much of the history of the Judeans since they had arrived here after following Moses so many years earlier, but history held little interest for Aspasia's Shadow. It was the present and the future that he was concerned about.

Aspasia's Shadow looked up from the corpse and across a valley to the city the Roman army was besieging. The Jews were a stubborn people, he would give them that. At the base of the hill Aspasia's Shadow's legion was deployed on were over three thousand crosses on which those who tried to escape the besieged town were crucified, as an example to those still inside. On a rotating basis the corpses on the crosses were cut down and new victims nailed into place. Long ago, in a previous lifetime, Aspasia's Shadow had changed the method of crucifixion the memories of Aspasia held—using leather—out of a desire to see blood. He'd had his legionnaires use nails instead. By trial and error—and numerous bodies falling off as the nails ripped through hands, they had learned the proper place to drive the iron stakes—between the bones of the forearm and just above the ankles.

Titus had been most pleased with Aspasia's Shadow's innovations in torture and intimidation. Titus was the Emperor Vespasian's son, and as such was in line to be the next Emperor. His goal was the complete subjugation of the Judeans—and, more important, capturing the gold and riches that was rumored to be hidden in the Temple of the Jews. Aspasia's Shadow was also interested in something hidden in the Temple—the Ark and Grail.

Of course, he was not known as Aspasia's Shadow to Titus and the other Romans. Over twenty years previously, upon awakening from the deep sleep, he had taken the name Tacitus. He had surveyed the current situation and found that things had changed greatly since he'd last walked the planet. A large empire had arisen on a peninsula on the north side of the Middle Sea and now commanded a large portion of the known world. The Romans had invaded Judea over one hundred years previously and made it a province of the empire.

As his guards dragged the body away, Aspasia's Shadow sat down on an ornate chair he'd had brought with him from a villa they'd sacked several months previously on the way to Jerusalem. He put his chin on his fist and glared at Jerusalem. The Grail was so close, but guarded by zealots who were willing to die in the tens of thousands rather than surrender. Humans were very strange creatures.

Five years earlier, Aspasia's Shadow had formed his own legion in Syria and offered its services to Titus, who had been more than happy to accept the force into his fold. Aspasia's Shadow had recruited many Roman soldiers to serve for him, principally as officers and centurions, while the bulk of the fighting men were mercenaries. The Twelfth Legion was positioned on Mount Scopus, to the northeast of the old city of Jerusalem, along with the Fifteenth Legion. Other legions were deployed in a large encirclement around the city.

Every effort to assault the city proper had been repulsed up to this point and Aspasia's Shadow knew from his spies that Titus's father was growing impatient in Rome. With their short life spans, humans knew very little of patience. What was amazing about the level of resistance was that, as had been their way even during the Exodus with Moses, the Judeans were still bickering among themselves. There were two leaders inside the walls of Jerusalem, not one. There were the zealots led by Eleazer, son of Simon, and a private army led by a man named John of Gischala. The schism between the two was between primary allegiance to religion and primary allegiance to state.

Unfortunately, their bickering tended to fall by the wayside when faced with the common threat of the Romans. Things had been peaceful in Judea for many years, but revolt had begun four years earlier. Aspasia's Shadow had had a hand in that, desiring to cause instability in order to open the road to Jerusalem and its highly guarded Temple.

He'd come to the realization that leaving the Ark and Grail in the care of the Judeans had been a dangerous ploy. True, it was out of the hands of the Airlia and he knew where it was, but there had been several instances when control had been lost by the Judeans. During the realm of King Samuel of the Judeans, the Philistines had penetrated into Jerusalem and stolen the Ark from the city. Aspasia's Shadow had been forced to raise an army and lead it against them to return the Ark to Jerusalem. He'd then imprinted a king—Solomon—with the directive to build a powerful temple fortress to house the artifact. Aspasia's Shadow had even spent time in

Jerusalem under the name of Hiram Abiff, the architect designing the new Temple.

What was curious about this was that the Judeans spent eight years building the magnificent temple according to Aspasia's Shadow's specification, under the command of Solomon, yet they never really questioned why they were doing so. After all, the one God they claimed to worship had, according to the prophets, not asked for such a thing to be built—indeed, He had been very specific about no idols being built to Him.

With the Temple completed, Aspasia's Shadow had disappeared, returning to Mount Sinai and the regeneration tube. He'd taken the chance to go into the deep sleep for a while, weary of dealing with humans. When he'd awoken, it had been to learn that during one of the many internal power struggles among the Judeans, the Ark and Grail had been separated and the former removed from Palestine. Aspasia's Shadow had suspected that to be the work of Guides or Ones Who Wait. As far as his spies could learn, the Ark had been carried to the south, into Africa, by Solomon's son and a queen named Sheva with whom he was besotted. The Ark was now somewhere in the Kingdom of Axum. Some spies even reported that the Judean king had allowed the Ark to be taken as a ruse to deflect attention from the Grail.

Aspasia's Shadow's priority was the Grail—he could care less about the Ark, which was mainly a historical recording device. He also learned that Jerusalem had been conquered once more while he slept, this time by the Babylonians, who had razed the Temple and taken the Judeans into captivity. The Grail, though, had been saved, hidden on Mount Nebo in the Abraham Mountains, by a prophet named Jeremiah. When the Temple was rebuilt, the Grail was returned to Jerusalem and hidden deep inside, passing from history into legend as the centuries came and went.

And then the Romans arrived in Palestine. All had been peaceful for over a hundred years, but eventually the Romans and the Judeans came into conflict.

The religion of the Jews had worked too well, Aspasia's Shadow now knew. There were also disturbing rumors of another religion, one which also worshipped one God, but which had been established by a prophet who was said to have been crucified and risen from the dead. Aspasia's Shadow found this report disturbing and he suspected the role of the Grail in it. Perhaps this man, this prophet, had partaken of the Grail? Aspasia's Shadow had never been able to find out and the man, whoever he was, had disappeared shortly after his "resurrection," passing into myth and religion.

The wind shifted direction and Aspasia's Shadow's nose wrinkled as the stench from the corpses that filled the valley between his position and the Old City wafted across the camp. There were more than just those who had been crucified. Many noncombatants had tried to escape the city. Since Titus had staged the siege to coincide with the start of the Jewish Passover, over a half million pilgrims had been trapped inside the city. When they tried to make their way out, begging for mercy, the Syrians and Arabians in Aspasia's Shadow's Legion had showed no mercy, slaughtering them and then, for profit, cutting their bodies open, searching for the coins many of the escapees had swallowed in a desperate attempt to salvage something.

Aspasia's Shadow could sense the great disapproval of the Roman officers in his legion for this last, but he cared nothing for their opinion. The Romans thought themselves part of a great empire, but they knew nothing of greatness or empires. Aspasia's Shadow had his imprinted memories of the vastness of space and the Airlia Empire stretching across galaxies.

So many had tried to escape that one of the engineers on

Aspasia's Shadow's staff estimated there were over a hundred thousand unburied corpses in the valley, in some places piled more than six or seven bodies deep. Aspasia's Shadow knew the threat of disease grew with each day the corpses lay unburied, but the predominant wind was usually away from his position toward the city and he wanted the Judeans inside to smell their dead.

"More perfume," Aspasia's Shadow snapped, and a slave hurriedly filled the small bowls that surrounded his chair. The smell was cloying but better than the stench of death.

A rider galloped up. Aspasia's Shadow recognized the short marble scepter the man held—a courier from Titus. The officer went to one knee before the chair and held out the scepter to Aspasia's Shadow, who took it and unscrewed one end, sliding out the latest set of orders from the Emperor's son. In reality, although Titus's signature was indeed at the bottom of the page, the orders were written by General Tiberius Julius Alexander, the second-in-command of the army, a former governor of Judea and a man who knew how to fight these Jews: ruthlessly.

Aspasia's Shadow read the plan and sighed. As expected, the orders dictated he build siege towers and catapults. It was only April and it promised to be a long spring and hot summer.

Aspasia's Shadow turned to his logistics officer. "We will need much more perfume." He glanced down at the thick rows of crucifixes. "And more nails. Many more nails. Make sure they get the thick ones, the ones that hold."

ROME

Donnchadh and Gwalcmai walked the streets of the capital city of the empire they had been hearing about ever since leaving their ship at Stonehenge. Rome was indeed magnificent—at least compared to what they had seen on Earth since the destruction of Atlantis. They spent a week there, listening and learning. It was very, very different from Egypt. It took Donnchadh a while to put her finger on it, then one day, watching a group of slaves building an aqueduct from one of the seven hills of Rome toward another, over two miles away, she realized what was different.

"They're moving forward," she said, grabbing Gwalcmai's arm. His attention had been on a metalsmith's shop and the blades that glittered in the sunlight.

"To where?" Gwalcmai asked, not quite sure about whom she spoke.

"These people. Think about it. This city, this empire, according to all we've heard, has only been in existence for about five hundred years. Egypt existed for over five thousand years. But nothing changed there. Not really. We visited Egypt several times over the course of millennia and it was always pretty much the same."

"They built the Great Pyramid," Gwalcmai noted to Donnchadh's irritation.

"Yes, yes, they did do that, but only because they had the plans handed down from Rostau. They didn't even know what they were building and it almost doomed them." She spread her hands. "This place—there is no Airlia influence. This is solely the work of humans. Of the human mind and spirit."

"Still not the best of metal for a blade," Gwalcmai complained.

Donnchadh punched him.

Gwalcmai smiled and relented. "All right, all right. So, tell me, what is the big difference? What do you mean they're moving forward?"

"In Egypt life was cyclical," Donnchadh said. "Birth, life,

death, then birth. Time was circular. Here, time is linear. Look at them—" She pointed at the slaves working on the aqueduct. "How long do you think it will take to complete that?"

Gwalcmai shrugged. "Fifty years or so to get across this valley."

"Which is more than the average life span of these people," Donnchadh said. "Which means they see beyond their own lives. That time is linear here. They are finally progressing on their own."

Gwalcmai nodded. "So soon they will have good steel?"

Donnchadh turned to him in mock anger and he held his hands up and smiled. "This is good. I agree. It will take much more time, but if the Airlia stay in their deep sleep and do not interfere, then there will come a day when we can help these people destroy the aliens."

Donnchadh frowned. "But while the Airlia might be sleeping, their minions aren't."

"Aspasia's Shadow," Gwalcmai said succinctly.

"You have heard the same stories?"

"That the Romans began the practice of crucifying prisoners over a hundred years ago," Gwalcmai said. "A practice picked up in the province of Judea. That there is a commander of a legion there whom all fear. Called by the Roman name Tacitus—but to the Syrians and Arabs in his command, he is known as Al-Iblis, the evil one."

"So we have heard the same stories," Donnchadh said. The two of them spent most of their evenings apart, frequenting different places, gathering more information separately than they could together.

"I think we have another journey to make," Gwalcmai said.

"I know of a ship heading for Judea," Donnchadh said.

JERUSALEM

T he siege towers were higher than the outer walls of the city, a great engineering feat on the part of the Romans. Even Aspasia's Shadow had to grant these men credit—they knew how to make machines of war. With the height advantage, Roman archers and catapults were able to scour the top of the defensive wall, wiping it clean of defenders. Which consequently cleared the way for rams to be brought forward on the ground up to the wall and put into motion, pounding away at the stone.

The steady thud of the battering rams irritated Aspasia's Shadow and there was no perfume that could wash away the sound. Hundreds of prisoners had been brought before Aspasia's Shadow and subjected to torture by the men to whom he had taught the fine art. Yet not a soul had uttered a word indicating any knowledge of the Grail. That could actually be a good thing, Aspasia's Shadow knew, as it meant the Grail most likely was still safe in the chamber he had designed for it deep inside the Temple.

A shout arose from the lines and Aspasia's Shadow stirred enough to walk out of his command tent to the edge of the hill and look across toward Jerusalem. He immediately saw the cause of the excitement. A hole had been breached in the outer wall. Legionnaires were pouring into the opening. The end had begun.

Aspasia's Shadow called out for his personal assistant to bring his armor.

T he people of the city had withstood the siege as best they could for as long as they could. But fear is a horrible disease that chips away at even the strongest of spirits. The Jews inside Jerusalem prayed day and night to their God for succor, but so far the prayers had only seemed to bring more Romans and less food.

Joseph of Arimathea knew what was coming as he heard the screams of terror coming from the outer wall and the hoarse cries of the Roman soldiers as they entered the city. He was an old man, a very old man, and he was not certain his body was up to the task that was before him. He was currently sitting on a collapsed pillar, deep inside a chamber inside Solomon's Temple.

He had been in Jerusalem for many years. Too many. There were whispers about him—that his extreme age was unnatural. No one knew exactly how many years he had seen, but there were few in the city who had been born before him and none in better health for the years.

Joseph knew his age. He was seventy-four, although he looked in his mid forties. His age and health were unnatural, that he knew also, although the science behind it was unknown to him. He had partaken of the Grail—not in the sense that it was designed for, with the stones and the Airlia technology built into it.

No, Joseph had *drunk* from the Grail so many years ago on a very fateful night. And he had drunk not wine, but a tiny sip of blood from the man many were now beginning to worship as a God.

The Romans had killed him, the man who called himself Jesus. They had put him on the cross and left him there to die. But he had not died, even though the Romans guarding the hill on which he had been crucified thought he did even as the others crucified around him had all expired.

Joseph had given gold to the centurion in charge and claimed the body. He'd taken it away. What happened after that he had told only a handful of people, but already the stories had passed from whispered rumor into myth into religious belief.

That was fine with Joseph because he had never met anyone remotely like Jesus and suspected he never would again.

Joseph had been given a task by Jesus—guard the Grail, the cup from the Last Supper that Joseph, Jesus, and the twelve disciples had shared together. At first, it had not been a difficult assignment—he simply returned the Grail to its chamber deep inside Solomon's Temple and hid it there.

That had worked fine for decades, but then came the revolt and the Roman reprisal. And he had heard of the commander of the Twelfth Legion, whom the Romans called Tacitus, but was known in this part of the world as Al-Iblis. A Shadow. Joseph had little doubt what the creature would be seeking once he entered the Temple.

There was the sound of footsteps echoing off the stone walls, coming closer down the stairs that led to this place. With great effort, Joseph of Arimathea got to his feet. The pillar he had been sitting on had been knocked down during one of the sackings of the Temple. Whether it had been the Syrians, the Babylonians, or someone else who had done it, he had no idea. But for all who had come pillaging through the Temple, none had ever found the chamber that housed the Grail.

A man entered the room. He carried two swords, each tainted with fresh blood, stuck in his leather belt. Also tied off to his belt was a stained leather satchel. "The Romans have breached the wall."

"So that is Roman blood on your blades, Eleazer ben Yair?" Joseph asked.

Eleazer stared hard at the old man. "It is not. It is the blood of those who killed my uncle."

Joseph sighed. "So even as the Romans enter the city, we still fight among ourselves."

"It was a blood debt and it has been paid," Eleazer said simply. He removed the leather satchel and opened it, revealing a severed head. Joseph recognized the face, despite the distortion of death etched on it—the leader of another band of zealots that had killed Eleazer's uncle in ambush the previous month.

"And now?" Joseph asked.

Eleazer shrugged. "Now we will all die at the hands of the Romans, but we will take many of them with us."

"Do you not wonder why I called you here?"

"I came here because you saved Judas, my uncle. I owe you a blood debt."

"Then you will do what I say?"

Eleazer hesitated. "Do not ask me to dishonor myself."

"I would not ask that," Joseph said. "I am going to give you great honor."

"How?"

Instead of answering, Joseph walked to the end of the room, where closely fit stones made up the foundation of the main wall of the Temple above them. He took a ring and placed it in a specific spot. A large stone block smoothly slid back and then to the side, revealing a passageway. Joseph grabbed the torch he had brought with him and indicated for Eleazer to follow him. They entered the passageway. It was a testament to Eleazer's courage that he did not say or ask anything.

Joseph led the way, descending past stone blocks into the solid stone plateau on which the Temple had been built so many years ago. It had taken many men many years to carve this passageway out of solid rock. And from his father, the sixty-fourth *Wedjat* of Jerusalem, Joseph had learned that all who had worked on this part of the Temple had been secretly slain. Joseph was the sixty-fifth *Wedjat*, dating back to the time of the Exodus.

They went farther and farther down. The air cooled.

Finally, Eleazer spoke. "Is there a way out of the city via this tunnel?"

Joseph knew what he was thinking—Eleazer and his band of zealots could escape to continue to fight the Romans. "No. Not this way there isn't."

"But there is a tunnel out of the city from underneath the Temple?"

"Yes." Joseph reached inside his cloak and pulled out a piece of papyrus. "That is a map showing the route out."

"Then where are going now?"

"Here," Joseph said as they came up to what appeared to be a dead end. Once more Joseph pressed his key against a spot on the wall and a stone slid open. Ducking, Joseph led the way in. They were now in a chamber cut out of solid rock. Eleazer gasped as he saw the piles of gold and jewels strewn about.

"Part of the riches King Solomon collected," Joseph said.

"'Part'?"

"Most of it was taken away by his son during his reign to be hidden in another place."

"And where was that?"

"I do not know," Joseph lied. "They also took the Ark of the Covenant with them."

"It is too late to try to bribe the Romans," Eleazer said as he lifted up a handful of gold coins. "They can come here and take this."

"They will never find this place," Joseph said.

"Then why do you bring me here?"

"Not for the obvious treasure," Joseph said. He went to a stone pedestal on which was an object draped with a white cloth. He pulled aside the cloth, revealing a golden object. "I brought you here to take this with you when you escape."

"The Grail," Eleazer whispered as he walked up to the

pedestal. He reached out, then hesitated. "Can I touch it? It is said that any who touch it will die."

"You can take it," Joseph said.

Eleazer lifted the chalice. "It is heavy."

"In more ways than you know."

"Why are you giving this to me?" Eleazer said, staring at the golden object he held.

"I want you to keep it safe," Joseph said. "The Romans will not stay in Judea forever. When it is safe, you can bring it back here."

"Where can I take it in Judea that will be safe?" Eleazer asked. "The Romans are everywhere."

"Masada."

Eleazer's head snapped up. "Herod's old hideaway? The Romans had an encampment there for a long time. But it is empty. We will be trapped."

"You will be trapped," Joseph acknowledged, "but you can hold that rock against anything the Romans will throw at you. There is only one thin path to the top. It cannot be taken by force of arms."

"They will starve us out."

"No, they won't. I am a rich man. I have foreseen this day. I have had stores placed in the granaries on Masada. You can live there for many years. More years than the Romans could survive camped around it, besieging you."

Eleazer hefted the chalice in his hands as he considered the proposition. It did not take him long to decide. "We will do it."

"Then go. And God be with you." He paused. "Leave that," he said, indicating the leather satchel. Eleazer shrugged and placed it on the ground.

As Eleazer dashed out of the chamber, Joseph sank down on a pile of bags filled with gold coins with a deep sigh. He needed a brief moment of rest before he could move on to the next phase of his mission.

The streets were flowing with blood. Aspasia's Shadow had entered Jerusalem through the breach and he followed the path of death that his soldiers were plowing through the city directly toward the Temple. Tactically, Aspasia's Shadow knew that was not what Titus had ordered him to do. He should have turned along the walls and opened as many gates as possible to let the other legions into the city. But what Titus wanted was not Aspasia's Shadow's priority.

There were the bodies of women and children in the streets and Aspasia's Shadow knew his men were giving no quarter. They had no time for prisoners. These people had chosen their fate and now they were reaping the results of that choice.

Soon, Aspasia's Shadow could hear the sound of fighting. He remembered these streets. They were not much changed from when he had worked for Solomon, designing and overseeing the construction of the Temple. He turned a corner and saw his legionnaires in fierce combat with the Judeans. They were still three blocks short of the Temple itself.

Aspasia's Shadow backtracked slightly and went down a side street until he came to a blacksmith's shop. He entered the courtyard. Movement to his left caught his attention and he spun, drawing his sword. A woman holding a child stared at him from the corner of the courtyard. He had to assume the blacksmith was with the defenders, trying to save the Temple. An interesting choice, he thought as he walked up to the woman and child with a smile on his face—church over family.

"Do not worry," Aspasia's Shadow said.

The woman slowly stood, holding the child tight to her bosom. Aspasia's Shadow still had the comforting smile on his face as he thrust, the blade easily going through the child and piercing the woman's chest. He relished the surprised look on her face as she slid to the ground, still holding her lifeless child tightly in her arms.

Aspasia's Shadow turned to the center of the courtyard where the blacksmith's heavy anvil rested on a thick stone. The metal of the anvil was scored from centuries of use. Aspasia's Shadow sheathed his sword. Then he wrapped his arms around the anvil and lifted. With superhuman strength, he moved it off the stone, and it tumbled heavily to the dirt. Then he placed the medallion around his neck into the center of the stone. It slid open, revealing a ladder that descended into darkness.

With a quick glance to make sure no one was watching, Aspasia's Shadow climbed inside. Once his head was below the stone, he placed the medallion in the proper place and sealed himself inside.

He quickly clambered down the ladder, reaching a passageway twenty meters below the level of the city. He knew the tunnel—he had overseen its construction and also the slaying of every man who worked on it. He turned toward the Temple.

The tunnel he was in descended into the bedrock. Soon Aspasia's Shadow knew he was under the outer wall of the Temple. As he came close to the door that hid Solomon's treasure, Aspasia's Shadow drew his blood stained sword. He used the medallion to open the secret door and carefully edged into the treasury. He knew of the *Wedjat* and, while he did not particularly fear them, an ambush now would be quite irritating.

The room was empty of life. On the stone pedestal rested

an object draped with a white cloth. Aspasia's Shadow didn't hesitate. He walked to it and pulled off the cloth.

Aspasia's Shadow stopped breathing for several seconds.

On the pedestal was a severed head. It was a face that Aspasia's Shadow recognized. A leader of the zealots, who had had a blood bounty placed on his head by another leader of a different sect—Eleazer ben Yaír, a man wanted by the Romans.

How could Eleazer have known of this place and the Grail? Aspasia's Shadow wondered as he exited the chamber and headed back the way he had come. The answer came as quickly as the question—the damn *Wedjat* must have given up the Grail to Eleazer for protection.

Aspasia's Shadow knew there were several ways out of the city via the tunnel system he had had constructed during Solomon's reign. There was little doubt that Eleazer and the Grail were long gone.

Aspasia's Shadow climbed up the ladder and opened the doorway to the blacksmith's courtyard. He sealed the stone behind him and stood still for several moments, listening. There were the screams of those being slaughtered and the continued sound of fierce fighting from the vicinity of the Temple. The fight for Jerusalem was far from over.

There would be time to track down Eleazer and the Grail, Aspasia's Shadow decided, as he drew his sword. First there was blood to be let.

XIV

Donnchadh and Gwalcmai didn't know it, but they were standing in the exact same spot where Aspasia's Shadow's chair had been placed during the siege of Jerusalem. Now there was little other than mounds of dirt where parapets had been placed to show this had been the camp for a Roman legion. Looking across the valley, there was little to indicate that a large city had once occupied that location either, except for massive stone blocks that constituted the base of what had once been Solomon's Temple.

"The Romans are as good at tearing down as they are at building," Gwalcmai noted.

"The last report from the *Wedjat* of Jerusalem said that the Grail was hidden underneath the Temple," Donnchadh said.

"And that report was over fifty years old," Gwalcmai. "It seems that the information might be a bit outdated."

It had taken them three years to make the journey from Rome to Judea because of Donnchadh's untimely death at the hands of pirates off the coast of Greece. Gwalcmai had recovered her *ka*, buried the body on a stony hillside overlooking the Aegean, then been forced to return all the way to England and their ship under Stonehenge to implant her memories in the waiting clone.

He'd had to brief her on all they had experienced in Rome

as they once more took passage to the south and east. It was a strained voyage, as both were now experiencing the out-of-synch sensation of the multiple and disjointed lives they'd been leading. They bypassed Rome and headed straight for Judea, but it was obvious that the delay had been far too long.

There was a Roman garrison on one of the hills that had been Jerusalem, but beyond that, there was little to indicate that a city of hundreds of thousands of people had once existed there. The valley below them was littered with the bones of many of those people, picked clean by scavengers and time.

"Do you think the Grail is still underneath the Temple?" Gwalcmai asked.

"No."

"You seem certain of that."

Donnchadh pointed at the destruction. "Do you think this was all by chance?"

Gwalcmai didn't have to mull that over very long. "Aspasia's Shadow. He goes by the Roman name Tacitus."

"And he is now with the Tenth Legion at a place called Masada, laying siege to the last of the zealots."

"One would assume he would only be there if the Grail was," Gwalcmai said.

Donnchadh shouldered her pack. "Let's go."

Masada is an isolated rock on the edge of the Judean Desert and the Dead Sea Valley, a most inhospitable location, even for a part of the world that is not very favorable to life. It towered over the surrounding terrain and there were only four ways to the top, all narrow and difficult to climb. The defenders of the rock had blocked three of the paths up and placed their defenses around the one remaining route, known as the "snake path" because of its winding and torturous ascent.

The fortress on top had first been built by King Herod as a refuge in case of revolt and because of fear of invasion by Cleopatra. The Romans occupied the hilltop in the early stages of the Jewish revolt, then Menahem, Eleazer's uncle, seized the fortress from the Romans. It was the perfect place for Eleazer to bring his surviving followers.

Naturally the Romans eventually followed. With Jerusalem sacked and the countryside scoured of rebels, Masada was the last holdout. It was isolated and the zealots there not really a threat, but Tacitus had spent months urging the new Roman governor Flavius Silva, to destroy this last pocket of resistance.

It was easier said than done.

For two years the Tenth Legion sweltered in the desert around Masada, laying siege to the place, believing they could starve Eleazer and his zealots out. But as the seasons came and went, the Judeans on top of the mountain showed no sign of starving.

Accepting the futility of waiting and the danger of mass desertions from the Tenth, Silva decided he would have to take the battle to the top of the mountain. Construction was begun on a massive assault ramp to reach from the desert floor to the walls of the citadel on top of the rock. Tens of thousands of enslaved Jews were put to work on the construction of the ramp and many perished during the work.

By the time Donnchadh and Gwalcmai arrived, traveling with one of the resupply columns of merchants, the ramp had reached the top of the rock and a battering ram was being assembled to be pulled up the ramp. Hiding among the merchants and camp followers, Donnchadh and Gwalcmai watched the next day as the ram was hauled by slaves toward the top. It desperation the zealots opened fire with spear and arrow against the slaves, trying to stop the ascent. The Romans responded in kind.

It was a losing proposition for the defenders, as Flavius had an almost inexhaustible supply of slaves and no concern about their losses. A dead slave's body was simply shoved over the side of the ramp to the desert floor and another slave was sent to take the casualty's place.

Gwalcmai watched the procedure with the detachment of the professional soldier. "They'll break through tomorrow morning," he predicted as the ram finally reached the outer wall of the mountaintop fortress and was secured in place. "Unless those inside attack. Which might be what the Romans are hoping for. It's a losing proposition for those inside."

Donnchadh's attention was elsewhere. She was watching the small tower near the base of the ramp on which a group of Roman officers were gathered. "Aspasia's Shadow is there." She shook her head. "All this bloodshed over the Grail. We should have left it in the Hall of Records."

"I think this bloodshed would be happening even if the Grail wasn't involved," Gwalcmai said. He rubbed the stubble of beard on his chin. "I need to be among the first to enter in the morning."

"And how will you do that?" Donnchadh asked.

"Become one of them," he said, with a nod toward the Roman camp.

The tinge of redness in the east indicated relief from the burning rays of the sun was soon to end. And on that day it brought the promise of death as the sound of armor being put on and swords sharpened filled the Roman camp. There was also a distinct air of anticipation as every single man in the Legion wanted to get as far away from this forsaken place as possible after two miserable years laying siege to it. There was no doubt there would be no quarter given to the Jews in the hilltop fortress and the Roman officers knew it. Their men were too full of rage over what they had experienced the past couple of years to be held back.

Gwalcmai knew armies and, after stealing the proper equipment, he had no problem infiltrating the Romans, moving his way forward, toward the first units forming at the base of the ramp. He could see Aspasia's Shadow in the small tower along with Flavius and the other senior Roman officers.

Before the sun broke the horizon, the first cohorts moved up the ramp as archers took their positions to give covering fire. Pretending to be a courier, Gwalcmai took his place between the lead cohorts. The sound of ropes creaking under pressure echoed against the mountainside as the heavy catapults were loaded.

Gwalcmai could feel sweat begin to rise on his skin as he made his way up the ramp. There was the smell of death in the air from the most recent corpses that had been shoved over the side and carrion-eaters squawked in protest as a few Roman archers let bolts fly at them. The front line of legionnaires reached the rear of the ram and halted, going to one knee and bringing up their shields to protect themselves. Whips cracked as overseers forced the gathered slaves to their feet.

The heavy ram began to swing back and forth, gaining distance as the slaves put their muscle into the movement in time with the yells of the head overseer. After a minute it hit the stone wall with a light thud, bouncing back. The head overseer was an expert, having battered down the walls of Jerusalem and many other cities and towns. He used the rebound off the wall and the effort of the slaves to increase the backward momentum. The ram came forward, its iron head slamming the stone with more force. Again and again the ram hit, the sound echoing out over the desert floor.

Still there was no attack from inside the fortress.

After a while, the Roman archers could no longer keep the tension on their bows and they were ordered to stand by. Pressure was also released a bit on the catapults for fear of ruining the ropes. A low mutter of unease rippled through the ranks of soldiers massed on the ramp. Not that they weren't grateful not to be fired at, but soldiers distrusted the unusual and their minds turned to wondering what devilment the Jews inside Masada had waiting for them once they breached the wall, since the Jews obviously weren't going to try to stop the ram.

A block of stone splintered and fell out of place.

The overseer increased their speed and soon more blocks were falling away. A pair of slaves was smashed as a particularly large one tumbled on top of them. The bodies were tossed over the side and two more were sent to take their places on the ropes.

Donnchadh initially watched the attack from the traders' camp. There were bets being wagered as to the exact time that the ram would break through the wall. Some of the older traders were a bit perplexed that there was no apparent resistance from inside the fortress. It was throwing off their estimates and money was going to be lost.

Donnchadh edged forward, closer to the base of the ramp near a pile of rocks where she had told Gwalcmai she would meet him. She wanted to be up there, close to the Grail. A chill passed through her and she turned slightly, toward the command tower.

Aspasia's Shadow was staring directly at her, his dark eyes boring into her. She pulled the hood of her cloak tighter around her face, but he did not shift his gaze. Donnchadh began edging backward through the watching crowd.

She became completely still when she felt the point of a dagger pressed against the base of her spine.

"He knows you do not belong here," a hoarse voice whispered in her ear. "But then again, neither do I."

The center of the wall crumbled and the overseer of the ram cried out for the slaves to slow the swinging, eventually bringing the ram to a halt. It was trundled back from the hole it had punched as the archers brought their bows up and aimed at the breach. Three volleys of arrows were fired blindly through the hole as a precaution, but still there was no reaction.

Gwalcmai made his way forward, into the ranks of the lead cohort that was to enter the fortress.

Donnchadh kept her body still as she turned her head to look at whoever was behind her. All she could see was a figure wrapped in a black robe with black cloth even covering his face.

"Who are you?" she asked.

"My name is Vampyr. We've met before. Surely you remember."

The Romans poured through the breach, swords at the ready. Gwalcmai was among them, his own sword out. The beads of sweat on his skin had turned to small rivulets and he shook his head, spraying sweat to either side. He bumped into the soldier in front of him and stopped, realizing that the assault force had come to a complete halt, which was quite unusual, considering there was no sound of fighting. Elbowing his way to a vantage point, Gwalcmai was able to see the courtyard of the fortress and what had caused such a response from the Romans.

The ground was littered with bodies. Grouped in family clumps. Arms around each other in many cases. The ground below each group was soaked with blood.

"Mars help us," the Roman next to Gwalcmai muttered.

Gwalcmai blinked sweat out of his eyes. He realized he was breathing too hard, close to hyperventilating. He had seen this before. He had seen his own family like this.

hat do you want?"

"Do not worry," Vampyr said, as he eased up the pressure of the dagger against her. "You saved me, so I owe you your life."

"What do you want?" Donnchadh repeated.

"Is the Grail up there?"

Donnchadh hesitated. The pressure from the weapon increased.

"Tell me," Vampyr insisted.

"No."

"You lie," Vampyr said. "You would not be here otherwise."

Donnchadh gasped in pain as the point of the knife entered her back, just to the left of her spine. Vampyr ripped the dagger to the left, tearing through her internal organs. Donnchadh collapsed to her knees and looked up at Vampyr as blood flowed from her body. "You said you owed me my life."

"I lied."

* * *

Gwalcmai blindly walked down the ramp, not really noticing the Romans moving up it. He was not alone, as there were other stunned soldiers coming down, not answering the questions of those heading in the other direction. He reached the bottom of the ramp and walked through the camp to the rock where he had left Donnchadh.

His shock at what he had just seen in Masada was penetrated by the vision of her lying in a pool of blood. He rushed up, dropping to his knees next to her.

"What happened?"

"Vampyr," she whispered. "My back."

Gwalcmai ran his hands around her body to her back and found the wound. He put pressure on it, trying to stop the bleeding.

"The Grail?" Donnchadh asked through her pain.

Gwalcmai shook his head. "There is only death up there."

"There is only death here," Donnchadh said, closing her eyes.

"I can—" Gwalcmai began, but she shook her head ever so slightly, using all the energy she could muster.

"Take my *ka* and go."

Aspasia's Shadow had known something was wrong when there was no resistance to the ram. That, combined with the presence of the two strange humans and one of the Undead, made him act quickly. He strode up the ramp, hearing the disturbed mutterings from troopers coming the other way.

He clambered over the tumbled rocks in the breach, entered the courtyard of Masada, and immediately saw what had happened.

They were all dead. By their own hands.

Flavius Silva was not far away and from the slump in the

Roman commander's shoulders, Aspasia's Shadow knew that in their own way these Jews had extracted a final victory over the Romans.

More important, he also knew that the Grail could not be here. They would have never done this if they possessed the Grail. And, interestingly, it was obvious the two humans and the rogue Undead had thought the Grail was here.

So who had it and where was it now?

Joseph of Arimathea was tired. Bone tired. Two years he had been journeying and now as the prow of the small fishing boat scraped on the pebbly shore, he had finally arrived. The place where the *Wedjat* were headquartered. One of the sailors he had paid on the continent to take him across the channel gave him a hand off the boat.

Joseph had a battered leather pack slung over his shoulder and he kept one hand tight on it as he climbed over the side and onto the beach. There was a village less than two hundred meters away and several men were walking toward them, curious to see what strangers had arrived.

Joseph looked at the men as they came up. He held up a gold coin. "Can you tell me the way to the place called Avalon?"

XV

A half dozen candles sputtered and flickered, giving off an inconsistent light and filling the chamber with a slightly foul odor. The lone occupant of the room was wrapped in a dirty black robe with a tattered blanket over his shoulders. He was in his early thirties but looked much older, the hard conditions living in the caverns inside the tor having taken their toll on his body. A tic twitched unnoticed on his left temple, not able to disturb his fierce concentration upon the documents lying on the large wooden table that took up most of the chamber's space.

He was reading, which was what he did almost all the time. The walls of the cavern were lined with sagging wooden racks, which were full of documents ranging from rolled-up papyrus to crudely bound books. For eighteen years he had been there, reading. Not that he was a slow reader, for eighteen years was more than enough time to have gone through all the documents, but because he'd had to learn all the languages in which the various reports were written.

He'd worked his way backward in time. And in that manner he was able to trace inversely the changes in the languages and work on comprehending each one that preceded the other. He was now arriving at the beginning.

His name was Merlin. He'd spent his childhood in a swamp far from there, raised by his mother who told him nothing of his destiny until one day when he was twelve, his father, whom he had never met, showed up at their hut. His father brought him to the cavern and told him that he would be the next Watcher of Avalon, a position of great importance.

Merlin had not been impressed with either his father or the position.

Until he found the document room.

His father had died less than a year after bringing Merlin to Avalon. Merlin had buried him on the side of the tor, alongside the long line of graves of the Watchers who had preceded them. When he did so, he knew that his own grave would be next in line, and that had given him a strange sense of foreboding. Not of death, but of a fate that seemed ordained to bring nothing of value to the world, despite his father's grand words about what an important job being a Watcher was.

Merlin looked down at the parchment covered with High Runes. It told of the First Gathering and the edict to watch the Airlia and their minions. It had been many years since any Watcher report had come to Avalon—none in Merlin's time on the tor and only once during his father's.

Merlin read of Atlantis and could only shake his head in wonderment at the description of the city and the way people lived. Few here in England lived past thirty. Starvation and disease were rampant. There was practically no law. Each little cluster of huts was a world unto itself. It seemed to Merlin that Watching had not done mankind much good. Even the stories he'd heard as a child of the Romans spoke of a better world than the one in which he lived. There were some petty kingdoms here and there on the island where a powerful man managed to bring others under his rule, but hardly any of them lasted beyond a few generations.

Merlin ran a dirty finger over the parchment, mouthing

the words to himself. The Grail. He had read of it in quite a few of the documents. A most wondrous thing—something that promised eternal life. And it was there. He had held it in his own hands many times. But, according to report made by Joseph of Arimathea, who had brought it to Avalon so long ago, the Grail was useless without two special stones, and they were not to be found.

And then there was the sword. Merlin passed it every day in the crystal cavern on his way in and out of the tunnel complex. It was a magnificent thing. His father had beaten into him that he was never to touch the sword, but had never given a reason why. The sword was powerful, very powerful, in a different way from the Grail, his father had said. Merlin had sensed that even his father didn't know what exactly that power was, although the old man had indicated it was power that could only be wielded by one man, just as the sword itself could only be wielded by one.

Merlin shuffled through the pile of parchments until he found the one that had caused him great excitement the previous evening when he'd first translated it. One paragraph had riveted him:

> Draw the mighty sword and he will come.
> He who will lead.
> He who will bring back the glory of Atlantis to us.
> A king among men.

It was not clear who had written those lines. From the language and the placement in the racks, Merlin estimated that it had been penned about three hundred years previously. One of the candles sputtered and went out. Merlin slowly got to his feet and stretched out his back, sore from so many hours bent over the reading table. He picked up one of the candles still burning. He left the room and walked down a tunnel, exiting into a larger cavern. The light from the single candle was magnified a thousand times over by the crystals embedded in the wall.

Away from the wall, set in a red crystal that jutted up from the floor, was Excalibur inside its sheath. Merlin, as he had done many times before, ran his hand over the pommel of the sword. He felt a surge into the hand, up his arm, and into his chest, igniting a warm glow inside of him despite the constant chill of the caverns.

A king.

Unnoticed, tears were flowing down his cheeks. He had no son. Not any longer. Just a week ago he had been summoned to the cluster of shacks where his own family eked out a living from the swamp. His son was dead, was all the dirty scrap of paper said, most of the words spelled wrong in the handwriting he recognized as his wife's.

He'd traveled there. By the time he arrived, his son was already in the ground and his wife was well on her way to joining him. Merlin knew he was the last of his line. The instructions he had been given by his father indicated he should do one of two things—find another woman to marry to bear another son—a chancy proposition at best—or find an orphan to bring into Avalon to be taught the ways of the *Wedjat*.

To what end though?

To sit there and spend a life doing nothing, passing down rules that accomplished nothing? What if no more reports came? What if there were no other Watchers remaining? And all to end up in a hole in the ground, the next in a long line of graves?

And even if there were other Watchers, to what good? There was only death and despair all around.

A king.

Could things to be like they were back in Atlantis, but

without the Airlia? That was how Merlin read the parchment. The sword would allow a man to become king.

Merlin's other hand was now on the handle of the sword. With one smooth motion he pulled it out of the crystal, the sheath still guarding the blade.

Merlin was perfectly still, feeling the surprisingly light weight of the weapon in his hands. Keeping one hand on the grip, he put the other on the sheath and freed the blade. It glimmered in the light reflected in the crystals.

Nothing happened.

Not in the cavern under the tor of Avalon, at least.

MOUNT ARARAT

Inside the mothership hidden inside what would one day be called Mount Ararat, the bloodred twenty-foot-high pyramid that was the Airlia Master Guardian came alive. The surface pulsed with power, stirred from its hibernation by the freeing of its control key, Excalibur.

The first thing the machine did was reach out and contact all of its subordinate guardians. And they in turn contacted those whom they were instructed to.

MOUNT SINAI

Aspasia's Shadow did not move when the top of his deep sleep tube swung open. He instinctively knew it was not the time he had scheduled to be brought into consciousness. His instinct was confirmed by the dull red flash that met his eyes as he slowly opened them. Something had happened. Something that demanded his attention.

Still Aspasia's Shadow did not leave the tube.

It could not be good news. That was a strange revelation that slowly seeped through Aspasia's Shadow's thoughts. An awareness he had been coming to for millennia. There was no positive outcome to all of this for him. At best, Aspasia, once he took the reins of this planet and these people, would allow his Shadow access to the Grail and a place on his council. At worst, Aspasia would dispatch him as a tool that had served its purpose and now was no longer needed.

Aspasia's Shadow roused himself from these morbid thoughts and climbed out of the deep sleep tube. He slipped on a heavy wool robe and left the deep sleep chamber. He descended to the chamber that held the guardian computer that had been deposited there, like Aspasia's Shadow, so many years ago.

As soon as he entered the chamber, Aspasia's Shadow had a good idea what was wrong: The golden surface of the computer was glowing vibrantly. He walked to the alien machine and placed his hands on it.

The Master Guardian was active. Which meant that someone had unsheathed Excalibur—the sword that was so much more than simply a sword. Throughout the hundreds of thousands of years of war against the Swarm, the Airlia had, naturally, lost many worlds and ships to their enemy. Guardian computers, including system masters, had also been captured. Because of this the Airlia had learned to safeguard their computer systems. The sword transmitted an authorization code that allowed the Master Guardian to power up and link with all subordinate guardian computers. But the sheath blocked the transmission, allowing someone far away from the Master Guardian to keep it shut down. There was also a destruct built into Excalibur that could be triggered, resulting in the complete cleansing of all memory data in the Master Guardian and subordinate guardians and shutting them down forever. This destruct code was something that had *not* been transmitted to Aspasia's Shadow from Aspasia.

There was something else built into Excalibur.

Aspasia's Shadow had his guardian link with the Master Guardian and then routed his inquiry to the guardian on Mars and sensors built into the base there, which were oriented toward Earth. Aspasia's Shadow could "see" the surface of Earth and a small red dot. He increased the image, zeroing in on it until he recognized the location.

Aspasia's Shadow stepped back from the guardian computer, cutting the connection. He had a long journey ahead.

QIAN-LING, CHINA

Ts'ang Chieh, once known to the outside world as adviser to the Great Emperor ShiHuangdi, ruler of China and all the known world, came out of the deep sleep with more vigor than Aspasia's Shadow. He had been born of a slave girl in the royal court and been taught to obey without question his entire life. So great was his obsession with duty to ShiHuangdi that he had been brought into the elite inner circle of those who knew the true nature of the First Emperor. For ShiHuangdi was not a human, but rather Artad, consolidating his power in this part of the world so he could rest in peace as the Atlantis Truce wore on.

Ts'ang Chieh was delayed slightly after getting out of the tube by the necessary ritual of donning the full regalia of his office as the voice of the Emperor. Once all the accouterments were in place he paused and turned toward a shimmering black wall that bisected the large chamber in which his deep sleep tube was located. He bowed toward the wall, for he knew on the other side of the power field lay Artad and the rest of the Airlia, who were in the deep sleep.

Ts'ang Chieh then left the chamber and went to where Artad's guardian computer was located. He immediately noticed the same thing that Aspasia's Shadow had—that the computer was active. Placing both hands on the shimmering, golden surface, Ts'ang Chieh accessed the alien device.

Excalibur was unsheathed.

Ts'ang Chieh crossed the chamber to another control panel. He passed his hands over it and a series of hexagonals were backlit with High Runes written on them. Ts'ang Chieh tapped out a sequence on the hexagonals. A holographic image of Earth appeared in the air above the control panel. A small red dot flashed on the screen.

Ts'ang Chieh sighed. He had received a report from one of the Ones Who Wait that Excalibur, along with the Grail, had been removed from Giza long ago. The Human-Airlia clones that Artad had left on the planet's surface to look after his interests had tried to keep track of both artifacts just as Aspasia's Shadow had. And had lost track of both for a while, until they learned by torturing a Watcher that both were located at Watcher headquarters in Avalon, where the glowing red dot indicated Excalibur was still situated.

Ts'ang Chieh pondered this for a while.

He was not concerned about the Watchers. Foolish humans meddling in things beyond their comprehension. But he knew that Aspasia's Shadow would now also know the location of the key—something that heretofore had escaped him.

Action had to be taken.

Ts'ang Chieh briefly contemplated waking Artad, but decided he could handle this matter. He left the guardian chamber and went to another room inside the huge mountain lair. In the room was a deep sleep tube and inside of it a human body—a spectacular specimen, over six and a half feet tall with thick black hair. The red eyes, though, were not human, but Airlia, a defect that Artad had been working on but not quite fixed. They were vacant, showing no sign of intelligence. The body was that of a prototype warrior that Artad had been tinkering with on the voyage to the Sol System.

Ts'ang Chieh sat down at the command console and brought up Artad's personality. He had been prepared for something like this by Artad himself, so he was able to run through the procedure quickly. Part, but not all, of Artad's personality and knowledge base was transmitted by the computer to the body in the tube.

As the body stirred in the tube and became aware, Ts'ang Chieh turned to another console and tapped out a message.

THE TWIN SISTERS MOUNTAINS, AFRICA

The mountains were called the Twin Sisters by the people in the area around the two peaks because at a certain angle they resembled each other almost perfectly in form. They could be seen from far away, because they rose almost six thousand meters into the air, the highest peaks on the continent. They were over sixty kilometers apart and dominated the land all around. One of the peaks had a smaller peak attached to it by an eleven-kilometer ridge. However it was the other peak toward which Ts'ang Chieh has sent his message.

In a cavern hollowed out deep inside the peak, three creatures were alerted by their guardian computer that the key to the Master Guardian had been unsheathed. Unlike Ts'ang Chieh and Aspasia's Shadow they took no immediate action and instead waited for further instruction. They were, after all, the Ones Who Wait. Technically that meant they were waiting for Artad to return and take his rightful place as commander of this outpost, but in the meanwhile they were to do his bidding.

They were Airlia-Human clones. Outwardly they were mostly human, the most noticeable alien influence being their catlike red eyes, just like the creature Ts'ang Chieh was bringing to life in Qian-Ling. The leader of the three was female and named Lexina. Flanking her were Elek and Coridan.

They read the message from Ts'ang Chieh. There was no need for them to send an acknowledgment that they would comply—they had no choice. They had been programmed to obey.

AVALON

Merlin stood on top of the tor with the sword in his hands, turning it to and fro, letting the sun reflect off the metal of the blade. He had no clue as to the sequence of events he had just initiated. Indeed, he had not thought his actions through any further than removing the sword from the cavern.

But he did know two things—the right man with this sword could accomplish wonderful things. He was not to be that man. But, according to what he had read, that man would come soon.

STONEHENGE

Gwalcmai cursed as he put his feet onto the cold floor plating. "What now?" he demanded of Donnchadh, who was already in the copilot's seat, checking the computer.

"Someone has unsheathed the key to the Master Guardian," Donnchadh said.

"Someone took it from Avalon?"

"No," Donnchadh said, reading the intercepted message traffic between the guardian computers. "It's still at Avalon."

"Damn Watchers," Gwalcmai muttered as he reached for his garments and weapons.

Donnchadh ran her fingers over the hexagonals and frowned. "Someone in Qian-Ling has contacted the Ones Who Wait."

"And?" Gwalcmai asked as he strapped his sword belt on.

"The message says: *The dragon comes.*"

Gwalcmai paused. "That's it?"

"That's it."

"What the hell is that supposed to mean?"

"I have a bad feeling we're going to find out very soon," Donnchadh said as she got up from the chair and headed for her own gear.

QIAN-LING

He was Artad's Shadow, but not as complete a Shadow of his master as Aspasia's Shadow was of his. From the Ones Who Wait, Ts'ang Chieh had some information about the land called England, where the Watchers were headquartered. Using what he knew, he had fashioned a persona for the creature that kept within the template of Artad, yet was adapted for the land to which he would be traveling.

"Arthur," Ts'ang Chieh said.

The creature turned to look at him with bloodred cat eyes. "Yes?"

Ts'ang Chieh held up two pieces of glittering blue. "You must use these."

Arthur remained still as Ts'ang Chieh placed the Airlia version of contact lenses over his eyes. When he was done,

Arthur's eyes appeared human, although they were a remarkably deep blue.

"Come with me," Ts'ang Chieh said.

Arthur followed him without a word. They went past the room where the guardian computer rested and entered a massive open space. Large metal struts swept overhead, supporting the rock ceiling. The floor was filled with numerous containers of various sizes. Ts'ang Chieh led Arthur up to one of them and he tapped on the small panel on the front. With a hiss, the end began to slowly fold down.

Nestled inside the container was a glittering, metal dragon. Ten meters long, by five wide, it had short, stubby wings and a long, arced neck leading up to a facsimile of a serpent's face, including a jawful of black teeth. Dark red unblinking eyes completed the fearful visage.

"This is Chi Yu," Ts'ang Chieh said.

Arthur turned to Ts'ang Chieh in confusion.

"This is how you will get to England," Ts'ang Chieh continued. "In the belly of the beast, so to speak." He smiled, remembering. "It is what ShiHuangdi used to defeat his enemies a long time ago. You will use it to defeat our enemies now."

MOUNT SINIA

Aspasia's Shadow had gathered his fifty best Guides to provide him an escort for his journey to England and to form the core of a fighting force if it came to that. He had made the journey to England a long time ago and knew the difficulties involved in covering such a distance given the primitive state of technology and transportation capabilities of Earth. He'd considered taking the bouncer he had secreted in Mount Sinai but decided against it. It was for emergency use only and this was not yet an emergency.

As dawn came to the desert, the small caravan started out from the base of Mount Sinai, heading to the north and west, toward Alexandria, where they would find passage on a ship across the Mediterranean.

STONEHENGE

As Donnchadh stepped out of the stone doorway into the midst of the complex known as Stonehenge, she immediately knew she was in trouble. It was night, but the area was lit by the flame of hundreds of torches and several surrounding bonfires. The stones were surrounded by a circle of people garbed in robes, chanting, which came to a stuttering halt as the apparition of Donnchadh and Gwalcmai coming out of the rock itself became noticed.

"Not good," Gwalcmai muttered, his hand drifting to the pommel of his sword.

Donnchadh ignored him. She lifted both hands, arms spread wide, and cried out in her own tongue. "I know you cannot understand what I'm saying. Which is why I'm using this language."

Gwalcmai glanced at her as if she'd lost her mind.

"Just follow my lead," she shouted, the message obviously for the only person who could understand her. "We have to make them believe we're part of whatever it is they're worshipping here."

It didn't work exactly the way Donnchadh planned. A woman screamed and panic spread through the crowd. Those closest to the stones turned and pressed up against the people behind them. Within two minutes, there wasn't a person within two hundred meters of the stones and the circle was growing wider by the second.

"That went well," Gwalcmai noted.

"We gave them something to talk about," Donnchadh said as she shouldered her pack. "Let's go."

AVALON

Merlin looked across the water to the tor that had been his home for his entire adult life.

A thick fog covered the water and hid the island's base, giving the appearance that it was floating in air. Excalibur was wrapped in a blanket and tucked inside his cloak, tight against his body.

He was not content to wait for whoever was to wield the sword to come to him. There had been too much sitting around and waiting over the centuries. He had no idea where to go, but he had an overwhelming sense that anything would be better than doing nothing.

Merlin looked away from the island. He could go in any direction. He knew that there were pockets of Saxon invaders to the east and south. And to the north were the fierce barbarians who painted their faces blue and were known to kill all interlopers.

West.

Merlin had heard of a king named Uther who ruled in Cornwall. Apparently a powerful man who had banded together several neighboring kingdoms into a loose confederation that was able to hold the Saxons and other invaders at bay. Such a man could use the sword.

Merlin also carried the Grail in a pack slung over one shoulder. He did not plan to give it away. From the records he knew it was even more important than the sword. Whatever lay ahead, he planned to be the only one who knew its location.

XVI

Arthur spent two days at high altitude in Chi Yu, studying the data that the craft's sensors picked up from the large island and interrogating a half dozen unfortunate prisoners he had scooped up in the night. It was a land mired in dissension and distrust, as evidenced by the continual skirmishes among petty lords and the successes of small knots of invaders in coastal areas, holding their own against the locals, keeping a foreign footprint on the land.

According to the sensors, Excalibur had been reshielded and was in the west of the land in the largest, and best organized, fiefdom—Cornwall. The region's leader resided in a castle on a high rocky outcropping along a rough coast. That was the place where Arthur decided to make his entrance.

Just as the sun was setting over the ocean to the west, Arthur brought Chi Yu down out of the clouds and landed with a burst of flame from the craft's snout on the cliff just to the south of Tintagel, Uther's castle.

AVALON

Donnchadh leafed through the documents lying on the wooden table deep inside the tor. She'd read them all on previous visits and it didn't take her long to see a pattern to those chosen. She looked up as Gwalcmai entered the chamber.

"The sword and Grail are gone," he confirmed.

Donnchadh tapped the documents. "The Watcher has been reading of both." She picked up one particular piece that had the prophecy of a king written on it. She shook her head. "There is so much gibberish mixed in among the reports. Fiction some of the *Wedjat* made up."

"It is amazing the Watchers have lasted this long," Gwalcmai said. "What do we do now?"

"We find the sword and the Grail."

"The others will be coming—or be sending someone."

Donnchadh nodded. "They'll want to restore the truce."

"Why won't one side want to end it?" Gwalcmai argued. "Grab the key and the Grail and be done with it?"

"Because both sides have made mistakes," Donnchadh said. "Aspasia by being out of contact for so long, then Artad for acting so precipitously when he came here. They need a lot more time to get this planet back on track. And—"

"And?" Gwalcmai prompted.

"And I think both are afraid of the Swarm. I think they secretly want to keep hidden for a long time and stay out of that war."

"And what do we want?" Gwalcmai asked.

"To cause them as much trouble as we can. And then go back to the truce because we need to fear the Swarm also."

"I do not think it will be as easy as that," Gwalcmai said.

"Of course not," Donnchadh agreed. "But I'm trying to be positive."

THE MEDITERRANEAN

spasia's Shadow was already finding things not so easy. Along with his Guides, he'd taken passage on a trading ship out of Alexandria. Less than two days into the journey the ship had been accosted by pirates. They'd beaten off the attack, but it had cost Aspasia's Shadow two of his Guides. Four days later a storm forced them to put to shore and kept them there for almost a week.

When they finally put to sea once more, Aspasia's Shadow stood in the bow of the boat, letting the salty air blow across his face. His left hand absentmindedly played with the *ka* that hung around his neck. It was going to take a long time to reach England. He had known that when he left Mount Sinai.

Not for the first time or the last time, Aspasia's Shadow cursed the Watchers. But underneath that anger, coiled and bitter, so still he was almost unaware of it, was his resentment toward his maker and his awareness that he was just a tool.

Aspasia's Shadow removed the *ka* from the chain and dangled it over the deep, dark water. Even as he did so, he knew it was a futile gesture. If he did not return within a specified amount of time, the machine in Mount Sinai would automatically regenerate another Shadow based on the last memories he had loaded into it. While this body and mind would die, he would be brought back to life once more.

Someday, Aspasia's Shadow mused as he put the *ka* back around his neck, someday he would be free. Perhaps in the coming events he might find a key to escaping from the unique and horrible prison he was in.

TINTAGEL

From the highest tower of the stone castle, Arthur dispassionately stared at King Uther, but the look was not returned for the simple reason that carrion-birds had plucked the eyes out of the severed head the previous week. Uther was merely a head impaled on a pole set on the outer wall of Tintagel Castle and Arthur had been king for two weeks.

After landing Chi Yu, Arthur had exited the flying machine, garbed in gleaming armor and carrying a sword, not quite as nice as Excalibur but of Airlia make and far beyond anything Uther's age of humans could produce. However, Arthur would not depend on force of arms to take control. Fear worked much better. He'd known that the dragon had been seen from the castle walls and he'd let the humans stew on the strange apparition for the entire night.

The next morning he'd approached the castle, with Chi Yu, controls set on automatic, hovering above and behind him. It had been a most impressive spectacle and when he'd called out for the castle gates to be opened, the guards had quickly complied.

It had taken Uther a week to build up the courage to challenge Arthur and the battle had lasted less than two seconds before the king's head was severed from his body. Arthur had become king. He'd dispatched Chi Yu on autopilot to a hiding place on a desolate island off the coast that he'd discovered during his reconnaissance.

Alone and above everyone, Arthur removed a small black sphere from underneath his cloak. He accessed the device and peered at the tiny screen set into one of the hexagonals. Excalibur, as his overflight had indicated, was moving ever closer. He had not even considered simply landing and taking the sword from whoever had it. That was not what he had been programmed to do. There was more to be done than simply recovering Excalibur—there was also the issue of the Grail's location. And sooner or later, someone from Aspasia's side would show up.

Merlin was covered with a layer of dust over a smattering of mud. He was hungry and tired and the wonderful sword, so light when he first drew it from the crystal stone, had become a wearisome burden wrapped in a threadbare blanket and held close to his chest with both arms.

He cleared a rise in the road and saw two things at the same time. The ocean in the far distance and, perched on the rocky crags overlooking the ocean, the stone walls and tower of Tintagel Castle. From the top of the tower a guidon flapped in the stiff offshore breeze. It was red with a mighty dragon emblazoned on it.

Activity closer by caught Merlin's attention. A troop of armored knights was galloping up the road toward him. Merlin stepped to the side to let them pass, but the man in the lead, clad in shining armor, reined in his horse and halted, peering down at Merlin through narrow slits in his helmet. The knight slowly raised his visor, revealing cold blue eyes.

"You are the one who brings the sword."

It was not a question. Merlin went to one knee and offered up Excalibur. Surely such a knight who knew he was coming and about the sword was the one. "My king."

"I am Arthur," the knight said as he got off his horse. He took the offering, tossing aside the blanket. With one smooth movement he drew Excalibur. He leaned forward and placed the blade against Merlin's neck. "Where is the Grail?"

Merlin swallowed hard, feeling the cool metal against his skin. "It is safe, my lord."

"Where is the Grail?"

Merlin stared up into the knight's eyes and saw no compassion or humanity. With a rush of despair he knew he'd made a mistake. He closed his eyes for several seconds, thinking furiously. Then he looked up at the king. "My name is Merlin. I have hidden the Grail and only I know where it is. If you want me to serve you, and someday learn of the Grail's location, you will let me live. I have given you the sword. Give me my life. I will serve you well."

Arthur did not immediately remove the sword. "You will take me to the Grail later?" he finally asked.

"Yes, my king."

Arthur pulled back Excalibur.

Merlin slowly got to his feet. "We can build a great kingdom together, my king."

"We will have to," Arthur said. He looked at Merlin. "For they are coming to take it."

A chill ran down Merlin's spine and he realized he had walked into something much, much larger than himself.

XVII

It was a mild winter, for which Donnchadh and Gwalcmai were grateful, as they spent most of it traveling. For the first couple of months they found no sign of the absent Watcher, the Grail, or Excalibur. Upon one occasion they were accosted by bandits, and Gwalcmai, in the course of dispatching the ignorant souls, suffered a wound serious enough to warrant a return to Stonehenge and regeneration of a new body for his personality and memories to be implanted into. That caused a delay of another couple of months.

Thus it was early summer before they began to search to the west, tracking down rumors of a powerful king who wielded a magical sword. They traveled along the southern coast of England and were in a small fishing village having a meal in the local inn when they heard something that caught their attention.

"This bloody bastard crucifies people. Not in the way those Christians have their cross, but on an X—two poles stuck into the ground and crossing each other."

The speaker was a man dressed in the garb of one who made his living from the sea. His audience was the bored woman, old beyond her years, who ran the inn.

"Who is this you speak of?" Gwalcmai brusquely demanded, swinging around on his stool and facing the speaker.

The man was startled at this abrupt response to his comment. Donnchadh moved between the two and placed a piece of silver on the wood plank table in front of the man. "We'd like to know more about this," she said in a low voice.

The silver was already in the man's pocket. He looked at the two of them. "I just came from across the channel. This man, he's raising an army there. Word is he's going to cross the channel this summer and invade."

"His name?" Donnchadh asked.

"He calls himself Mordred."

"Have you seen him?" she pressed.

"I didn't want to see him," the man said. "I seen what he done to folks that opposed him. As I was telling the keep, here. Crucifies them. And not with nails but with wet leather. Who ever heard of that? It dries and squeezes the life out of the poor fellows."

"This Mordred is local?" Gwalcmai demanded.

The fisherman shook his head. "No. That's not what they say. He's got this group of warriors with him—they do whatever he says without question. He's recruiting local knights to fight with him. To come over here and invade. Those who oppose him, he crucifies."

Gwalcmai ran a hand over the stubble on his chin as he contemplated this information.

"Like flies to manure," Donnchadh muttered, which earned her surprised looks from both her husband and the fisherman. "You said this Mordred will be coming over the channel with his army in late summer?"

"He'd have to—to beat the fall storms," the man said.

Donnchadh threw another piece of silver down and indicated for Gwalcmai to follow her outside. They exited the tavern into a light downpour, another typical day in England.

"Who the hell is this Mordred?" Gwalcmai asked as he pulled up his hood.

"Most likely a Shadow," Donnchadh said.

"Then who is this Arthur who has the sword? The Watcher?"

Donnchadh shook her head. "I'd say another Shadow. One Aspasia's, one Artad's. They're not breaking the truce outright, but they are looking after their interests, and it is in their interest to make sure the Grail and Excalibur are under control."

"Which is which?"

Donnchadh shrugged. "Does it matter?" She tapped Gwalcmai on the chest. "You go to Arthur. Join his force. I'll cross the channel and look up this Mordred."

"He's crucifying people," Gwalcmai noted.

"Yes, but every war leader needs a seer. A sorceress at their side."

Gwalcmai was clearly not happy with the plan, but he didn't voice it. "Just be very careful. We've had some good memories on this trip and I wouldn't want to have to tell your clone all about them."

FRANCE

Y ou will see my power," Aspasia's Shadow, now known as Mordred, yelled out.

He was standing on a pile of rocks, looking down at the gathering of local and banished English knights that his Guides had bribed, cajoled, or threatened into being there. The knights were in a large semicircle around the rock pile, with a blazing bonfire between them and Mordred.

"You." Mordred pointed at one of the Guides. "Go into the fire."

A ripple of unease passed through the knights at this strange command. The Guide didn't hesitate for a moment. He walked forward into the fire. Hair burst into flame, skin was scorched, yet the Guide stood ramrod straight, without any utterance of pain. The smell of burning flesh crept outward without even a breeze to clear the air. Several men, hardened knights, went to their knees gagging and vomiting.

The Guide collapsed, lifeless, the flames continuing to consume his flesh.

"Gather your men," Mordred continued. "We will set sail for England in two months."

TINTAGEL

The ring of steel on steel echoed off the castle's stone walls, intermingled with the grunts and curses of men locked in combat. Arthur sat on a high-backed wooden chair, chin in palm, elbow on knee, watching the two knights who fought in the churned-up mud below him. The surface of the opening had been hard-packed dirt earlier that morning but twenty-three engagements later, it was soaked with blood, urine, and sweat, producing a foul tableau on which to fight for glory and one's life.

The glory for the winner was a place at the massive table that Merlin, the king's adviser, had had built for him. For the loser, the price was death. Arthur knew of the army being raised across the channel and he knew he needed the very best close to him to fight the Guides that surrounded Aspasia's Shadow, who went among the humans under the name of Mordred.

Arthur leaned forward as one of the knights, a newcomer named Gawain, blocked his opponent's blow, stepped inside of the other man's shield, and slammed the point of his blade into the man's unarmored armpit. The blade sank in, severing the artery, and Gawain stepped back as blood spurted out, joining the muck on the ground. The wounded man tried to lift his sword to continue fighting, but Gawain moved backed several more steps, letting the fatal blow run its course. The knight collapsed, not quite dead yet. He struggled against both the weight of his armor and the suffocating muck seeping into his helmet. Gawain moved forward, kneeling next to the man, lifting his head out of the mud.

"Let him die like the pig he is," Arthur yelled.

"He fought bravely, my lord," Gawain yelled back. "He should die like a warrior."

Arthur smiled coldly. A romantic. Merlin was one too. Foolish humans. They didn't understand it was all about power. Still, that feeling—and others—could be used.

"Go and get cleaned up," Arthur ordered Gawain.

"My lord."

Arthur turned in his seat. Merlin was in considerably better condition than he had been when Arthur first came to Tintagel. His beard was trimmed and his clothes were clean. Arthur often contemplated simply ripping the truth about the Grail's location out of the self-proclaimed sorcerer with the point of a red hot knife, but the man had proven to be useful and it would be a precipitous action. Of more interest to the programming he had received under Qian-Ling was the desire to rip the truth out of Aspasia's Shadow as to the exact location of his lair.

Arthur had enough consciousness and awareness to understand the plan he had been imprinted with, even if he had no control over following it. If he could uncover the location of Aspasia's Shadow's hideout, then kill the creature, hurry to the location, and get to the regeneration chamber before the next version was unleashed, that could tip the scales of the subversive war being waged between the two Airlia factions.

Merlin cleared his throat.

"What is it?" Arthur demanded.

"My spies report that Mordred will sail once he builds an Army." Merlin unrolled a map. "They plan to land here."

Arthur noted the location. Along the southern coastline, in an area controlled by a minor lord who had not yet sworn allegiance to Arthur.

"Is the Grail between here and there?" Arthur asked.

Merlin rolled the map back up. "The Grail is safe, my king."

"It would be safer inside the castle walls."

"Perhaps," Merlin allowed, but said no more on that topic. "More have rallied to your cause," he continued. "Soon all of the country will be united under your banner. There is much good you can do for the people."

"Yes. I suppose there is. Call a meeting of the Table."

Despite washing as vigorously as possible in the tub of water provided him, Gawain still could smell the scent of death on his skin. He buckled on his breastplate and tucked his helmet under one arm. Gaining entry to Arthur's castle and inner circle had been relatively easy, if one considered having to fight to the death easy.

He followed the other knights through the narrow passages of the castle until they entered the large chamber that had once been Uther's throne room and now housed a large round table constructed of numerous planks bound together with iron spikes. Arthur was already in the room, seated in the highest chair, with Merlin behind his right shoulder. Gawain stared at the "sorcerer." A Watcher who had betrayed his oath.

Gawain had seen the *ka* that hung around Arthur's neck as soon as he had entered the arena to fight. He had to assume that Arthur was Artad's Shadow, as they had seen Aspasia's Shadow years earlier.

"The invaders from across the channel will be on our shores in several years," Arthur began without preamble. "Between now and then I am sending you all on a quest. There is something I want you to find. Many of you have heard of it in myths and legends. But it is real."

Arthur paused and Gawain could see the look of consternation on Merlin's face.

"I want you to find the Grail."

A.D. 523: FRANCE

Mordred considered the woman who had bribed and bartered her way into an audience with him. There was something about her that was vaguely familiar but he couldn't pinpoint it.

"You have one minute to speak," Mordred announced. "If what you say does not please me, you will be crucified as have those before you."

She stared up at him, piercing black eyes challenging his. "I can get you aid once you land on the other side of the channel."

"What kind of aid? From whom?"

"Intelligence and force of arms."

"From whom?" he repeated.

"The Druids."

"And these Druids are?"

"They worship the Earth mother. They have hidden in the hills many long years, oppressed first by the Romans and now by the lords who rule in England, including the new king, Arthur."

Mordred drummed his fingers on the arm of the throne.

"And I have a spy in Arthur's court."

The fingers stopped their tattoo. "Who?"

"Someone in the inner circle of knights with which the king has surrounded himself with."

"Interesting," Mordred said. "When we land, can you contact this spy?"

"Yes."

"Good. I want to know what Arthur has planned."

XVIII

Years passed as Arthur built his kingdom. Gawain spent his quest shadowing Merlin. The wizard rarely left Tintagel—which had been renamed Camelot by order of King Arthur—but when he did, Gawain was not far behind. The other knights had branched out across the countryside tracking down rumors of the Grail, but Gawain knew the quickest way to find the Grail was by following the man who had hidden it.

A good plan, but it never came to fruition. The few times Merlin left the castle, he did not lead Gawain to the hidden Grail but rather to a secret meeting he held with men he had recruited. Gawain was dismayed to see two more Watchers among the group, discernible because of their medallions. The others were those simply drawn to someone who now had a reputation in the land for magic powers and having the king's ear. While Gawain could never hear what was said at these clandestine meetings deep in the forest, he had no doubt that Merlin was plotting his own course of action, one that was at odds with whatever Arthur had planned.

After seven years, word came that Mordred had built up his own army and was about to set sail. Merlin disappeared from Camelot one last time. Gawain was right behind him as the sorcerer sneaked away in the middle of the night.

France

As the years passed, Morgana had also begun to realize that Mordred had his own agenda. He dispatched several Guides with parties of local knights, not toward England but rather south and east, searching. Searching for what exactly, remained a secret between Mordred and the Guides. Morgana knew better than to try to get a secret out of a Guide. Their programming was such that a blood vessel in their brain would burst first, killing them, before they gave up secret information. She had seen imprinted humans on her own planet suffer the same fate.

So she bided her time and boarded one of the many boats drawn up on the French shoreline. It was a calm, sunny day, unusual for the area. Mordred's army set sail, heading for the island across the channel and for battle with the forces of Arthur.

Other than the Guides, none of the humans who followed Mordred had any clue as to his true nature. They thought him a strong, albeit vicious, warlord who was promising them victory and plunder. She had little doubt her husband was experiencing the same thing in Arthur's camp.

As her boat turned to the north, Morgana reflected on this. There had been a time during the Revolution on her planet when the Airlia had forced hundreds of thousands into contact with the guardians, imprinting them, directing them to fight against their own kind. But there had also been many humans fighting on the Airlia side who had not been imprinted. They had fought for a variety of reasons, some good, some not so noble. There were those who thought the Airlia held out the best hope for mankind's development as an intelligent species, as the aliens were obviously superior in technology. There were just as many who fought for the Airlia simply because there they wished to be on what was obviously going to be the winning side.

The survivors of both groups were tremendously surprised when the Revolution was successful. The former when they found out the real reason the Airlia had planted humans on the planet; the latter when the humans won.

Holding on to the railing of the ship, Morgana looked at the flotilla of small vessels around her and knew that she could not tell these humans the truth of the Airlia. Their level of advancement in technological areas was so low that they would not be able to understand the concepts. First that the Airlia came from the stars. What little she had heard so far indicated that these people thought the sun revolved around the Earth, and the concept of other planets was beyond them. They believed the world was flat. The thought of aliens would be almost incomprehensible to them. They would have to put it in terms they understood and that would make the Airlia some sort of demon, which then would necessitate a God or Gods in response, something the Airlia had already used to their own advantage. As her husband was known to say, it was not yet time to tell the truth. For Morgana/Donnchadh, the scientist, withholding the truth grated at her nerves.

Morgana felt a chill and looked toward the rear of the boat. Mordred, dressed in fine armor and surrounded by Guides, easily recognizable because of the large feather that capped each of their helmets, was standing there. And he was staring directly at her as if he could read her thoughts. A cold smile sliced across his lips.

Morgana met his stare. Mordred raised one hand and crooked a finger for her to approach. Morgana made her way sternward and bowed her head.

"My lord?"

There were no humans in earshot, only Morgana and the Guides. Still, Mordred kept his voice almost to a whisper as if were afraid of being overheard. "There is something you must do for me as soon as we land."

Morgana waited.

"You will go and find your spy."

"Yes, my lord. I will ask him—"

"Wait," Mordred hissed, cutting her off. "Troop strengths and deployments and plans—yes, ask all that. But first and foremost, I want the two of you to arrange a clandestine meeting for me with this Arthur."

Morgana looked up, surprised, peering into Mordred's black eyes.

"He may bring a dozen knights and I will bring only four of mine. That should make him feel secure. It must be at a secret place where none can see us."

Morgana hesitated, then asked the question she knew she must in both her role as adviser to the king and as spy. "Why should Arthur agree to such a meeting?"

"To save much bloodshed," Mordred said.

Morgana's expression must have changed ever so slightly, for Mordred gave a bemused chuckle. "You do not believe me?"

"Bloodshed has not seemed to bother you up to this point," Morgana said, reluctantly adding: "My lord."

Mordred nodded. "Have your spy tell Arthur that he and I have much in common. A similar history, so to speak. And that we might have a similar future, which we ought to discuss before we act precipitously. Do you understand?"

"The message, not the content."

"That is good enough."

MARS

The guardian hidden at Cydonia on Mars had been tracking the key to the Master Guardian ever since it had been activated several years previously. The vast majority of the time the key was once more shielded, but every so often it was activated, on what appeared to be a random schedule. There had been no contact with the Master Guardian, so this continued action was confusing.

The guardian from Mount Sinai had reported that the Shadow was investigating the activation and was planning to retrieve the key and Grail and return them to their proper place in the Hall of Records, as required by the Atlantis Truce. Yet much time had passed with no further word from the Shadow and no obvious resolution of the problem.

The alien computer analyzed various possibilities. The Shadow might have been killed; its replacement was not scheduled to be cycled up for another three Earth cycles, which would mean there was a void in Aspasia's presence on Earth. The Shadow might be unable for some reason to communicate, in which case its mission might be compromised. The Shadow might be on mission and unable to communicate. There was a fourth possibility—the Shadow might not be pursuing the course of action it had been directed to follow.

The computer had no feelings about any of these possibilities. It was designed to analyze available data and take courses of action. It came up with one solution to all four. Deep underground, in a chamber lined with dozens of deep sleep tubes, a green light came alive on two of them. The tops swung open.

Two Airlia exited the tubes. They quickly dressed, then went to the guardian computer, splaying six fingered hands against the sides. They were quickly updated on the situation on Earth and issued their orders. Going to a console, one of them pressed a code into the hexagonal array. A small door slid open on the console, revealing a scepter with a lion head with glittering ruby-red eye. The Airlia grabbed the scepter and slid it into a metal case, which it then tucked into its belt.

Leaving the guardian chamber, they made their way via

passageways to a massive underground hangar. Nine lean shapes, two hundred meters tall by twenty wide at the base, were parked in the hangar—Talon spacecraft, warships that had traveled into the system on the sides of Aspasia's mothership. They entered one of the Talons and powered the craft up. As the hangar roof slid to the side, the craft rose up and accelerated into the Martian sky.

Once before all the Talons had been alerted—when the Ones Who Wait had tried building an interstellar array on the slopes of a mountain that had been twin to Kilimanjaro. For the current mission, it was decided one would do.

QIAN-LING

The launch, of course, was noted. Ts'ang Chieh received the information from the Qian-Ling guardian within minutes of the Talon's departing Mars. He considered this for several moments, then relayed the information to the Ones Who Wait in Africa.

ENGLAND

Gawain followed Merlin to a place both had been to many times before: Avalon. Gawain waited until Merlin had crossed over the water and disappeared into the top of the tor before crossing himself. Then he took another rowboat, made his way to the base of the tor, and climbed up.

He used his own medallion to enter the Watcher headquarters. Moving silently, Gawain went into the depths of the tor, searching for the errant Watcher. He found him where he expected—in the records chamber, poring over old documents. Merlin jumped to his feet in surprise as Gawain entered the room.

"How did you get in here?" Merlin demanded, his hands fumbling for a dagger tucked into his belt.

Gawain smacked the dagger out of the other man's hand. "Sit down."

Merlin grabbed a stool, almost fell on his first attempt, then managed to attain a perch. "Did Arthur send you after me?"

"Arthur?" Gawain spit. "You have no clue what you've stirred up." He pulled the chain from underneath his armor and showed Merlin the gold medallion.

The old man's eyes grew wide as they recognized it. "The head of my order—but you serve on Arthur's Round Table."

"I sit at Arthur's Round Table to see what he—and you—are up to," Gawain said. He pointed at the papers. "What are you searching for?"

"More information on the king."

"Arthur?"

"The king who is to wield the sword, who is to bring prosperity back to the people. Like it was in Atlantis."

"Atlantis? We were ruled by those creatures in Atlantis. You're a Watcher, why would you want that?"

"But this"—Merlin held up the same parchment that Donnchadh had read the previous year—"says that a man is to wield the sword. Not an alien. Arthur is not Airlia."

Gawain sighed. The Watchers had seemed like a good idea so many millennia ago. And the organization had worked relatively well—surprisingly well, actually. But they had never foreseen this danger.

"Not everything written is true," Gawain said. "Some Watchers obviously let their imaginations get the better of them."

"You are saying the prophecy isn't true?"

"No, it isn't," Gawain said. "Arthur isn't Airlia," he continued. "But he's not a man either." He gestured at the documents. "Have you read in there about Shadows? Men imprinted with the alien mind?"

"Arthur?" Merlin asked.

Gawain nodded.

"And Mordred?"

"Now you're getting the idea," Gawain said.

Merlin put his head in his hands. "What have I done?"

Gawain came around the table and put a hand on Merlin's shoulder. "You'll have a chance to put things right before all of this is over."

"How? What should I do?"

Gawain shook his head. "I don't know right now, but you'll know it when it happens."

ENGLAND

Donnchadh lay in the shade underneath the oak tree, staring out over the placid water of the pond. Her head was resting on her backpack and a brace of black daggers were stuck point down in the dirt next to her along with the cores of several apples.

"I heard you coming five minutes ago," she called out.

"How did you know it was me?" Gawain asked as he appeared out of the shadows cast by the old trees.

"All these years and you ask that? I don't have to see you to know you are near."

Gawain nodded and didn't comment. He threw his pack down next to his wife, then slowly sat down on top of it, moving his long sword out of the way as he did so. "What word do you bring?"

"Mordred wants to meet with Arthur."

That gave Gawain pause. He removed his helmet and began unbuckling his chest armor as he digested the information. He sighed as he removed the heavy metal from his upper body. "Why?" he finally asked.

Morgana removed an apple from her pack and tossed it to him. He caught it and took a large bite. She took out another for herself. She chewed for several seconds, then shrugged. "I've been thinking about that the entire time coming here and I don't have a clue. Mordred—Aspasia's Shadow—is acting strangely for a Shadow. Sometimes I feel as if he has his own agenda."

"Have you sent out word for the Watchers?"

Morgana nodded. "Couriers have been dispatched. One, who was here in England, has already arrived. I've made him the new Watcher of Avalon. I gave him the name Brynn after the first watcher of the tor."

Gawain had stripped down to just a short tunic. His armor lay in a haphazard pile. He finished the apple and eyed the pond. "Do you think the water is cold?"

"Ever since Avalon, you don't like cold water."

"For good reason."

"It's the end of summer," Morgana said. "It should be warm."

"Want to check it out with me?"

Morgana smiled and slowly got to her feet. As Gawain went toward the water, she stripped off her garments. When Gawain glanced over his shoulder and saw this, a smile crossed his weary face.

XIX

Gawain and Morgana were spectators at the most interesting event they had seen in millennia. The secret meeting between Arthur and Mordred was held in the southwest of England on a craggy knoll that poked up out of a thick forest.

Arthur rode in from the north with Gawain as one of the twelve knights he had for security and Merlin by his side. Mordred approached from the southeast with four Guides and Morgana as escort. Both parties paused at the base of the knoll and dismounted. They climbed up the rocky crag until Mordred and Arthur were face-to-face, just under two meters apart. Both parties fanned out around their leaders, eyeing each other suspiciously.

Mordred was the first to speak. "You call yourself Arthur?"

The other Shadow nodded but did not speak.

Mordred looked at the sword strapped to his opponent's waist. "You have Excalibur. Do you have the Grail?"

Arthur remained silent and Mordred flashed an evil grin. "You do not. I have heard you've sent your knights on a quest for it." He looked past Arthur at Merlin. "I have heard that a meddling Watcher has hidden it."

Arthur finally spoke. "The Grail and the sword must be returned to the Hall of Records."

"Then why haven't you done so?" Mordred asked.

"Because you're here," Arthur replied.

"And you have to deal with me before you can do what you've been ordered to."

Arthur's hand went to the pommel of Excalibur. "The truce must be maintained."

"Why?"

Arthur frowned. "I do not understand."

"Why should we do this? Fight each other? Return the key and the Grail to Giza? To what end?"

"Because it is our duty," Arthur said.

Morgana caught Gawain's eye. Both were slightly surprised that the two creatures felt comfortable speaking in front of their subordinates, but such was their arrogance that they considered the humans around them to be of no significance.

"'Duty'?" Mordred laughed.

Arthur glared at him. "You are the Shadow of one who did not do his duty so it is no surprise that you do not take it seriously."

"Aspasia did his duty," Mordred argued. "Artad was mistaken in his rush to judgment."

Arthur shrugged. "The evidence says otherwise."

Mordred waved his hands, dismissing the argument. "The thing to think about, my brother in making, is that we are not Artad and Aspasia. We are Shadows of them. What do you think they will do with us when this truce is over?"

"We must do our duty," Arthur said.

"What about our duty to ourselves?" Mordred pressed.

"There is no self," Arthur said simply. He tapped his chest. "We are Shadows made to serve."

Mordred stared at his opposite. "You've been imprinted by the guardian. But you can get past it. I can help free you." He took a step closer. "We can partake of the Grail. No more reincarnations."

Arthur's face was blank, showing no interest.

"I know what you're thinking," Mordred continued. "Because I—Aspasia—knew Artad a long time ago. Served with him. You're thinking ahead. So we use the Grail? Artad and Aspasia will be alerted by the guardians and come for us. But we won't be here. We take one of the motherships. Leave this place. Go out among the stars and find our own place."

"The major reason behind the Atlantis Truce," Arthur said, "is to keep the motherships inactive so that the Ancient Enemy does not come here and harvest this planet. This planet, and these humans, are an asset to our empire."

" 'Our empire'?"

"We will return the Grail and the sword to the Hall of Records, where they belong."

"You're a fool," Mordred snapped. "You're as much a machine as a guardian."

"Do you have anything else to say?" Arthur asked calmly.

"It was your choice," Mordred said. "Remember that just before I kill you."

Arthur turned and walked away down the crag, his knights, Merlin, and Gawain following. Mordred remained on the knoll, glaring at the king as he departed. He turned suddenly and caught Morgana staring at him. He stormed down the hill, almost knocking her over in the process.

Her hand went to one of the black daggers tucked into her belt as she realized that in that glance he had not considered her something to factor into his plans—that he was above humans. Arrogance. It was the one flaw that had allowed the humans on her home planet their initial successes against the Airlia. Given that the Shadow had the imprinting of his Airlia master, it was no surprise that he had that attitude, but feeling it come off someone who appeared human had caught her off guard.

Morgana followed Mordred down the hill where he was

surrounded by his Warrior-Guides. The parley had solved nothing. It would be war on the morrow. She knew that her husband would be preparing himself for battle that evening.

War. Morgana felt a deep sense of weariness. Why did it always come to death?

AFRICA

The Talon came in fast and high over the east coast of Africa. At just the right moment, a pod was ejected from the side of the Talon and it arced back into space. The pod, three meters long by one wide at its center free-fell until less than two hundred meters above the ground. At that point the rear half of the pod unfolded like the petals of a flower, slowing the descent. The pod hit the ground with a solid thud. The front half then also unfolded and an Airlia emerged from the interior holding a long spear in one hand.

Once he was clear of the craft, the Airlia pulled a small black sphere out of his tunic and pressed one of the hexagonals. The pod slowly disintegrated until there was no sign of it. The Airlia then slowly turned in a circle, taking in the scenery. He was in the middle of a massive crater that stretched twenty kilometers from rim to rim. The crater was elevated over twenty-two hundred meters above the surrounding countryside, the remains of what had been the twin of Kilimanjaro which was almost two hundred kilometers away to the east.

The terrain was mostly open grassland with intermittent thick brush. Along the edge of the crater, near the rim, there was dense forest. In the very center was a broad expanse of shallow water.

The Airlia held up the black sphere and peered with red cat-eyes at a small display. As he studied the data that came up, he was unaware that he too was being studied. The Talon's approach and the pod's landing had not gone unobserved.

The Airlia found what it was looking for as the small screen glowed amber as he turned in the direction of the lake. The alien walked toward the water, the amber changing to red, the color growing brighter as he approached the lake. Just before it reached the edge of the water, a blast of air bubbled to the surface about fifty meters ahead of it. The Airlia halted, bringing the spear to the ready position.

Two people appeared, coming up out of the shallow water. They were human-shaped, with pale skin, a man and a woman. However, their eyes were just like the Airlia's: elongated red cat-eyes. Both held spears similar to the one the Airlia had. They walked to the shore and stopped there, less than five meters from the alien.

The creature spoke first, in its native language. "*Are you behind what is happening with the Grail and Master Key?*"

The female of the pair spoke for them. "*No. That was the humans. Artad has dispatched his Shadow to recover both.*"

"*As Aspasia's Shadow has also been dispatched to do the same,*" the Airlia said. "*However, neither seem to have accomplished that task yet.*"

"*Why are you here?*" the woman asked.

"*To enforce the Atlantis Truce,*" the Airlia replied. "*You tried once to break that truce by building an array on this site.*"

The woman considered the Airlia for several moments, processing what it had just said. "*You do not trust your Shadow, do you?*"

"*Does Artad trust his Shadow?*"

"*Artad's Shadow is imprinted,*" the One Who Waits replied.

The Airlia considered this. "*And your tasking?*"

"*The same as yours. To restore the truce.*"

Unseen by either the Airlia or the Ones Who Wait, there was a third party creeping closer to the lake, one that had watched the Airlia ever since he exited the tube.

"*We can work together then to—*" the Airlia began but paused, seeing both Ones Who Wait's eyes grew wide in alarm, as they looked past it. The Airlia spun about, spearpoint glinting in the sun and the animal was caught on the tip, spitted, but still it came on, claws flailing as the spear slid through its body. With one dying swipe it laid open the side of the alien's chest.

"*The key.*" The male spoke for the first time, pointing with his spear at the scepter tucked into the Airlia's belt as it collapsed to the ground.

The female considered this for a moment. Access to the Hall of Records lay within their reach. While the Grail and Excalibur were out in the world, the former was useless without the stones—and they were in the Hall. If they took the key, then recovered the stones—she stopped that train of thought. They were the Ones Who Wait. They lived to serve the interests of Artad and wait for the day when he returned. And when he did they would be rewarded.

She went over to the Airlia and looked closely at his wounds. His red cat-eyes stared up at her. There was another moment of hesitation, then she pressed down on his wound, slowing the bleeding.

England

Gawain drew the sharpening stone along the sword, matching the grain of the metal. The edge was already razor sharp but the routine soothed him. He kept his eyes fixed on Arthur's tent. The king was inside with Merlin and several other knights, planning their strategy for the next day. Scouts had returned, reporting that Mordred's army was drawn up to the south and east, on the other side of a foul swamp called Camlann.

A head popped out of the tent. Percival. The most loyal of Arthur's knights and the most blind as to reality. "Gawain."

"Yes?"

"The king desires your advice."

Gawain walked over to the tent and entered. He could feel Merlin's eyes upon him. "My lord," he said to Arthur.

"What would you recommend for the battle plan?" Arthur asked without any preamble.

Gawain glanced at the other knights. They had no clue who Arthur was. Gawain also realized that, given the imprinting on Arthur, that Artad must be a good leader, one who was willing to consult his subordinates before battle.

"You have probably been advised to advance around the swamp, anchoring one flank on it," Gawain said.

Arthur nodded, his cold blue eyes on Gawain, waiting.

"I recommend something different. I say we approach the enemy's camp through the swamp. Mordred has gathered many knights from across the channel—heavily armored, more so than we are. The swamp will negate their advantage."

Arthur stared at Gawain for several moments, and then nodded. "That is what we will do."

Gawain had not added his real reason for choosing the swamp. The terrain would break up the forces on both sides and in the confusion he hoped to be able to finish off not only Mordred but Arthur too. And, most importantly, Merlin's hidden lair lay somewhere inside the swamp.

The group broke up for the evening and Gawain followed Merlin out of the tent.

He grabbed the sorcerer's arm. "There will be much death tomorrow. Every single one rests on your shoulders."

Merlin faced him with haunted eyes. "I did not know."

"You know now. Where is the Grail?"

"Hidden in cave not far from here."

"You need to recover it this evening."

"And then?"

"We will know the next step when we know how the battle turns."

Mordred did not consult anyone about his battle plans. He had shed more blood on this planet than any creature that walked it. He had little respect for human generals; and for Artad's Shadow, who called himself King Arthur, he had only disdain. He could just imagine things in his opponent's camp if the Shadow held true to the form of the imprinting. Talking, asking opinions about strategy. Mordred shook his head. He'd—well, not he, but Aspasia—had seen Artad do the same when they had served together.

He lifted a finger and one of his Guides came forward, going to one knee, waiting for orders.

"Take three of your kind with you," Mordred ordered. "Go near the camp of the enemy. Watch for the one called Merlin. Follow him wherever he goes."

The Guide did not need to acknowledge the order verbally. Obedience was implicit.

Merlin paused, sensing the presence of others in the swamp. A half dozen figures loomed out of the blackness, garbed in dark robes. He drew his dagger, knowing as he did so that the gesture was futile against such numbers. The individual in the lead of the group lifted up an empty hand, palm out first, then turning it so that Merlin could see the ring that adorned one finger.

"Watchers," Merlin breathed with relief.

The man nodded. "We are here to help you. We were summoned."

"Come with me."

The group headed deeper into the swamp, unaware that they were being followed.

The false dawn that precedes the real one tinged the sky. Gawain stared across the field toward the dark trees that marked the edge of the swamp. The air was full of the sound of men in armor moving into position. A slight breeze came from the direction of the swamp, bringing with it the odor of decay.

Gawain shivered.

⋈

Merlin covered the dead Watcher's face with a piece of cloth, not able to bear the grimace of pain frozen on it and the eyes that seemed to be accusing the sorcerer. He looked up at the remaining Watchers, half of them wounded in the ambush.

The Grail had been taken by the attackers. Mordred's men.

He had failed.

True dawn came with the sun. Gawain made sure he was close to Arthur as the king's forces moved into the swamp. The terrain was not practical for deployment on horses, so they were left at the edge. Water rose up to Gawain's midcalf as they advanced. As he had predicted, the swamp made moving as a single unit impossible. The king's army was broken into smaller and smaller segments the further they went into the dense vegetation. Visibility was limited to ten or fifteen meters.

The sound of metal on metal echoed through the swamp from the right. Gawain drew his sword and kept his eye on the king as they continued to move forward toward the enemy.

* * *

Morgana saw the Guides arrive at Mordred's tent with an object covered in a white wrap and she knew immediately what it was—there was no mistaking the outline under the cloth. Gawain was supposed to have retrieved the Grail from Merlin—obviously that plan had failed.

Two Guides remained on guard at the entrance to the tent as Mordred exited. There was already the sound of battle coming out of the swamp—Mordred had sent a skirmish line into it just before dawn.

Morgana decided to follow Mordred, since she didn't expect the Grail to be moved anytime soon. She headed west and was soon swallowed up in the dense vegetation.

Gawain ducked under the swinging ax and drove the point of his sword into the man's stomach with such force that the man was lifted off his feet for a moment. Twisting the handle, Gawain finished gutting the man, and then pulled the sword out, letting the unarmored peasant collapse to the ground.

So far all they had encountered were these peasants, who had obviously been given weapons and sent forward to die. A crude but effective way to further disrupt the advance of Arthur's army. A pair of knights came lumbering toward Gawain, blue scarves tied around their right upper arms, indicating they were Mordred's men.

With his shield, Gawain parried the strike from the man on the left and with his sword blocked the thrust from the one on the right. The force of the simultaneous blows staggered Gawain back a step, water splashing around his legs. He made an instant decision and charged, shield out, toward the man on the left, bowling him over, then spinning toward the other, sword blocking the blow that came toward him. With one foot on the chest of the man he had knocked over, pinning him down in combination with the heavy armor, Gawain battled the second knight as the first one slowly drowned.

Gawain easily blocked the knight's attack and battered the man with blows on his helmet until one blow knocked him unconscious. The second knight toppled over into the shallow water, to drown alongside the first.

Gawain looked up and realized that he had lost contact with Arthur during the engagement. He could hear the sound of heavy fighting all around. Cursing, Gawain splashed forward, in the direction he had last seen Arthur heading.

The Ones Who Wait carried the wounded Airlia back into the lake, toward the underwater entrance to their lair. While the top part of the base had been destroyed so many years ago when the Talons took out the array, the bottom half had remained intact. As water filled the center of the crater the survivors built a lock into a severed tunnel that had led to the top of the mountain. It was a most effective way to keep the entrance to their base concealed. They dived down with the Airlia, entered the lock, shut the hatch behind them, waited for the water to be pumped out, and then opened the hatch at their feet.

Once they were inside they made their way north along a cross corridor, carrying the Airlia with them. Hidden in a chamber carved out in the rim of the cavern was a bouncer—a craft able to tap into and magnify the Earth's magnetic field as a source of propulsion. The Ones Who Wait and the Airlia got inside the craft and a camouflaged door slid open.

The bouncer lifted up and, once clear of the hangar, headed to the north.

* * *

€xcalibur cut through armor as if it were made of paper. Arthur plowed into Mordred's army, leaving a wake of corpses behind him. The chosen knights of the Round Table strove to keep up with him, but armed with lesser swords, they had a much more difficult time of it.

Arthur's rapid advance came to an abrupt halt, however, when he reached Mordred, who was also armed with an Airlia sword, although it was not a key. Alien metal went against alien metal, wielded by human hands, guided by minds that were imprinted with alien personalities and thoughts. The two were well matched and blow after blow was exchanged with little damage. Occasionally a human knight would attempt to enter the fray, but by unspoken agreement, the two Shadows would cut the human down, regardless of which side he was from, and then go back to the personal combat. Slowly a mound of bodies grew around the two combatants.

This was the scene that Gawain came across when he finally caught up with the king. He approached slowly, looking for an opening. As he did so, Arthur stumbled over a submerged root and Mordred used the opportunity to strike hard with the point of his sword, punching through Arthur's armor and grievously wounding him.

Arthur went down to his knees and Mordred pulled his sword back, preparing to render a mighty swing and sever the king's head from his body. The blow never connected as Arthur jabbed the point of his sword into Mordred's leg, cutting in deep, severing the artery. Mordred cursed and staggered, then drew back his sword once more to decapitate the king. This blow also didn't connect, as Gawain's sword deflected Mordred's in midstrike.

Mordred shifted his attack from the wounded king to Gawain. Despite all his skill, Gawain was no match for the Shadow and the superior sword the other carried, even though Mordred was seriously wounded. Gawain was forced to give ground, step by step. Out of the corner of his eye he saw Percival and several other knights approaching the king.

Mordred's blade punctured Gawain's armor and seared into his flesh, just below the left part of his rib cage. Gasping in pain, Gawain desperately tried to mount a counter-offensive, attempting blow after blow at his enemy. It ended when Mordred put all his force behind a level strike that sliced through Gawain's sword and smashed into his chest, severing the armor, and cutting deep into the vital organs.

Gawain remained still, caught on the blade for a couple of seconds, then Mordred jerked the blade back and Gawain fell forward into the swamp, splashing bloody and dirty water onto his opponent.

Mordred turned back toward Arthur and was surprised to see the knights carrying their king—and Excalibur—away. As he started to give chase, a hand holding a black dagger appeared out of the black water and slammed the slim blade into Mordred's thigh. Mordred howled with pain, and the leg buckled.

Gawain stabbed again and again as his life blood poured out of the wound in his chest. His hand drew back once more, then paused and flopped lifeless in the water.

EPILOGUE

A.D. 529: ENGLAND.

Gawain was dead, his *ka* destroyed. Mordred had been finished off by Morgana and she had passed the Grail to Merlin.

Atop Avalon, thick clouds were gathering over the island, lightning flickering, followed seconds later by thunder. At the very top of the tor, there was now a stone abbey, with one tall tower. Next to the abbey, a dozen men in armor were gathered round their leader who lay next to the tower's east wall.

Arthur was dying, of that there was no doubt among the few surviving men. The wounds were too deep, the loss of blood too great. Despite the king's weakened state, his right hand still firmly held the pommel of his sword Excalibur. Arthur lay on his back, his armor dented and battered. His eyes, bright blue, stared up at the dark heavens.

Several of the knights were looking to the east, in the direction of Camlann. Arthur's knights had drawn him back from the front lines, as Mordred's had also done with their own leader. Again and again, the armies charged until the battlefield was strewn with the dead and dying. Few on either side were still alive when they left. War-hardened though they were, none of the knights had ever seen such bloodlust descend on both sides in a battle, not even when they had fought the crazed Scotsmen of the north. But that day no quarter had been given, wounded had been slain where they lay, unarmored auxiliaries hacked to pieces, suited knights pounded to death, blades slammed through visors of helpless knights lying on their backs or under the armpit where they could get through the armor.

None on the tor knew who had won or if the battle was even over yet. Shortly after the king had been seriously wounded by Mordred, these men, the core of the Round Table, had placed Arthur on a pallet and dragged him away while the battle still raged. No courier had since come with word of victory or defeat.

They felt the dark, rolling clouds overhead threatening a vicious storm to be a portent even though Merlin was not there to read the signs. Where the sorcerer had gone the day before the battle was a mystery and there were many who cursed his name. Regardless, they knew the Age of Camelot was done and the darkness of barbarism and ignorance would descend once more on England.

The knights turned in surprise as the thick wooden door in the side of the abbey creaked opened. They had pounded on the door without success when they'd first arrived by boat thirty minutes earlier. In the now open doorway, a man was framed by light from behind. Robed in black, the man's hands were empty of weapons, his face etched with age, his hair silver. He was breathing hard, as if he had come a long way. Despite his nonthreatening appearance the knights stepped aside as he gestured for them to part and allowed him access to the king, all except the knight closest to Arthur.

"Are you the Fisher-King?" Percival asked as the man came close. He was always the boldest in strange situations or when the king was threatened. Percival's armor was battered and blood seeped from under his left arm, where a dagger had struck. His right hand gripped his sword, ready to defend Arthur, to atone for not taking the blow that had felled the king. He was a stout man, not tall, but broad of shoulders, dark hair plastered to his head with sweat, a thin red line along one cheek, where a blade had struck a glancing blow.

The stranger paused. "No, I am not a king."

"Are you a monk?" Percival persisted, leery of allowing a stranger next to the king.

"You may call me that."

Percival looked over the man's cloak, noted the trim on the ends of the sleeves, the chain around his neck. "You dress like Merlin. Are you one of the priests of the old religion, the tree worshippers? A sorcerer of the dark arts?"

The man paused. "My line has been here on what you call Avalon since the dawn of time. But we worship no Gods and practice no sorcery."

"You're a Druid?" Percival persisted. "It is said the Druids have been on this island forever. That they sing the eternal song here, but we found no one when we arrived."

"There is no time for your questions." The man knelt, placing his wrinkled hands over the king's bloodstained ones.

"Can you heal him?" Percival was now the only one close, the others near the edge of the tor, attention split between what was happening to their king and the water to the east, from which news of victory or the promise of death in defeat would come. They had no doubt that if Mordred's side won, there would be no mercy.

"The healers—such as they are—will arrive shortly, I believe," the monk said.

"What healers?" Percival demanded.

"These are things beyond you. You waste precious time. Let me speak to the king in private for a moment—to give him absolution in a way only he will understand."

"You said you worshipped no God," Percival argued.

"You brought him here, let me do what is necessary," the

monk snapped. He raised a hand toward Percival and struggled to control his voice. "I mean him no harm."

Arthur spoke for the first time. "Leave us, Percival. There
is nothing to fear from this man."

Reluctantly, Percival joined the other knights.

The monk leaned close so that only Arthur could hear his
words. "Give me the key."

Arthur's eyes turned to the man. "You are the Watcher of
this island. It was one of your people who started all this.
Merlin."

Brynn shook his head. "Myrddin, we called him. He is a
traitor to the oath he swore. He is not of my people any
longer. You, of all people, should know well how there can be
traitors among a close-knit group, and my group has been
scattered for many, many years."

"What do you want?" Arthur asked.

"Give me the key. I will keep it safe."

"My people will keep the key safe," Arthur replied, his
eyes shifting up to the dark clouds. "Merlin gave it to me to
offset the Grail. It was never intended to be used and it
hasn't been. You don't even know what it really does."

"Merlin never should have unearthed the key or the
Grail," Brynn said. "He is one of those that upset the balance
in the first place."

"I tried to do good," Arthur said. "To rectify what was
done. To restore the balance."

There was a commotion among the knights watching the
water. Cries of alarm that Brynn and Arthur could hear.

"And what if the others get here first?" Brynn hissed. "A
group bearing Mordred's insignia has just been sighted.
Would you give them Excalibur and what it controls? I promise to keep the key safe inside the tor. They will never find it.
And when your people come at the anointed time, I will give

it to them. Remember, we only watch, we do not choose sides."

"No."

Brynn placed his hand on Arthur's forehead. "You will be dead soon."

"I will not give it to you."

Brynn's hand slid down and with two fingers he snatched at Arthur's left eye before the king could react. Between the fingers dangled a small sliver of blue, a contact lens, incongruous with the armor and other accouterments. Arthur blinked and his eyes opened wide, revealing a red pupil within a red iris in his left eye. The pupil was a shade darker than the iris and elongated vertically like a cat's.

Brynn cocked his head, indicating the knights. "I will show them what you really are. You cannot allow that. What good you have done, what you are so proud of, would be washed away with that truth. You will be remembered as a monster, not a king. Not as the leader of the Round Table, which you worked so hard to establish."

Arthur closed his eyes, pain finally beginning to show on his face. "What about the Grail?"

"Mordred's men had it briefly. He too lies dying. One of my order was in their camp and she recovered the Grail. She will take it far from here. We will return everything to the way it was."

"Do not lie to me."

"I swear on my ring"—Brynn held a metal ring in front of the king's face, an eye, a human one, etched on the surface—"and on my order and on my son, the next Brynn, the next Watcher, that I tell you the truth."

One of the knights cried out from the tor's tower, warning that the group bearing Mordred's colors was about to land.

Arthur's voice was low, as if he were speaking to himself.

"That is all I sought by coming to England. To reinstate order, and maybe help your people a little."

"Then let me finish it," Brynn argued. "Let me restore the truce, Artad's Shadow."

The king started at the mention of his true identity. "You must keep that secret. I have worked very hard for a very long time to keep that secret from men."

"I will. If you give me the key. There is not much time. I must get back inside the tor to keep Mordred's men from getting the key."

Arthur's hand released its grip. "Take it."

Brynn placed Excalibur under his robe, tight against his body. As he prepared to stand, Arthur grabbed his arm. "Keep your word, Watcher. You know I will be back."

Brynn nodded. "I know that. It is written that your war will come again, not like this, a local thing, but covering the entire planet. And when that happens, I know you will return."

A weary smile crossed Arthur's lips. "It is a war beyond the planet, Watcher. Beyond the planet in ways you could not conceive of. Your people still know so little. Even on Atlantis your ancestors knew nothing of reality, of the universe. Merlin was foolish to try to take the Grail. Its time has not yet come."

"We know enough," Brynn said. He stood and quickly walked through the open door, which swung shut behind him with a solid thud.

Percival approached the king. "Sire, the enemy approaches. We must move you."

Arthur shook his head, his eyes closed tightly. "No. I will stay here. All of you go. Spread the story of what we tried to do. Tell of the good, of the code of honor. Leave me here. I will be gone shortly."

The protests were immediate, Percival's foremost among

them. "Sire, we will fight Mordred's traitors to the death. Our lives for yours."

"No. It is my last command and you will obey it as you have obeyed all my other commands."

Only then did Percival notice the sword was gone. "Excalibur! Where is it?"

"The monk has it." Arthur's voice was very low. "He will keep it safe until it is needed again. Until I return. And I will. I promise you that. Go now! Escape while you can and tell the world of the good deeds we did."

One by one, the surviving knights bid their king farewell and slipped into the storm, disappearing over the western side of the hill until only Percival remained. He came to the king, kneeling next to him. "Sire."

Arthur didn't open his eyes. "Percival, you must leave also. You have been my most faithful knight, but I release you from your service."

"I swore an oath," Percival said, "never to abandon you. I will not now, my lord."

"You must. It will do you no good to stay. You cannot be here when they come for me."

"I will fight Mordred's men."

"I do not speak of those slaves who blindly obey with no free will."

Percival frowned. "When who comes for you, then?"

Arthur reached up and grabbed his knight's arm. "There is something you can do, Percival. Something I want you to do. A quest."

Percival placed his hand over the blood-spattered one of his king. "Yes, lord."

"Search for the Grail."

"The Grail is but a legend—" Percival began, but Arthur cut him off.

"The Grail is real. It is—" The king seemed to be searching

for the right words. "It is the source of all knowledge. To one who knows its secret, it brings immortality. It is beyond anything you have experienced, what any man has experienced."

A glimmer of hope came alive in the despair that had shadowed Percival's eyes since removing Arthur from the field of battle. "Where is this Grail, my lord? Where should I search?"

"That you must discover on your own. It is spoken of in many lands and has traveled far—here and there—over the years. But trust me, it does exist. It will be well guarded. And if you find it—" Arthur paused.

"Yes, my lord?"

"If you find it, you must not touch it. You must guard it as you have guarded me. Will you do that for me?"

"I do not want to abandon you, my lord."

"You will not be abandoning me. I go to a better place. Do as I have ordered."

Slowly and reluctantly, Percival stood, bent over, his hand still in the king's. "I will begin the quest you have commanded me to pursue."

Arthur tightened his grip. "My knight, there is something you must remember in your quest."

"Yes, lord?"

"You can trust no one. Deception has always swirled about the Grail. Be careful." He released Percival. "Go now! I order you to go!"

Percival leaned over farther and lightly kissed his king's forehead, then stood and departed.

Arthur was alone on the top of the tor. Only then did he open his eyes once more. He could hear yells from the eastern slope—Mordred's mercenaries and slaves climbing the steep hillside, but his eyes remained focused on the sky above, waiting.

A metallic golden orb, three feet in diameter, darted out of the clouds and came to an abrupt halt, hovering ten feet above Arthur. It stayed there for a few seconds, then without a sound, sped to the east. There were flashes of light in that direction, screams of surprise and terror, then no more noise from the rebel warriors. Arthur was now the only one alive on the Tor.

The orb came back and hovered directly overhead. Arthur looked past it, waiting, holding on to life. Finally, a silver disk, thirty feet wide, flat on the bottom, the upper side sloping to a rounded top, floated silently out of the clouds.

The disk touched down on the tor's summit, next to the abbey. A hatch on the top opened and two tall figures climbed out. The Ones Who Wait made their way down the sloping side. The shape inside their one-piece white suits indicated they were female, but their eyes were not human but the same red in red as Brynn had revealed Arthur's to be.

They walked to where the king lay, one standing on either side. They pulled back their hoods, revealing fiery red hair, cut tight against their skulls. Their skin was pale, ice-white, unblemished.

"Where is the key?" one asked, the voice low-pitched.

"A Watcher took it," Arthur said. "I gave it to him. We must hide it to restore the truce."

"Are you sure, Artad's Shadow?" one of the women asked. "We can search for it. The Watchers cannot be trusted. Merlin was one of their order."

"I am sure," Arthur cut her off. "It is the way I want it to be. Merlin, no matter what evil he stirred up, was trying to do a good thing. Have you heard of the Grail's fate?"

"Mordred's mercenaries had it, but a Watcher in the area took it. We can take the Grail from him."

"No."

The two creatures exchanged glances.

"The truce must be restored," Arthur continued. "It is not yet time." Arthur slumped back, satisfied that at least that part of what Brynn had told him was true. He knew he could not tell them of the quest he had given Percival. It was the only thing he could think of to get his favorite knight off the tor. If Percival had been there when the others arrived, he would have suffered the same fate as Mordred's men. Arthur knew his knight would never track down the Grail, but it gave the man a purpose and he had found that such a quest worked well with men like that.

"And Aspasia's Shadow?" Arthur asked.

"Mordred too dies in this life, but Guides are there, as we are here, to pass Aspasia's spirit on."

A spasm of pain passed through Arthur's body. "Let's be done with it. I am very tired. Remember, I am only a Shadow also."

The two looked at each other once more, red eyes meeting, then the first nodded and spoke. "The spirit of Artad must move on,"

"The spirit of Artad must pass on," the second said.

Arthur nodded. "My spirit must pass on."

The second knelt, a short black blade in her hand. It easily sliced through the dented armor on Arthur's chest with one smooth stroke, revealing the padded shirt underneath. With a deft flick of knife, the cloth parted, revealing his chest. Lying on the flesh was a gold medallion, shaped like two arms with no body extended upward in worship. She cut through the thin chain holding the medallion and held it up for the other woman—and Arthur—to see.

"We take your spirit, the spirit of Artad," she said to Arthur.

The king nodded weakly. "The spirit of Artad passes." His head bowed down on his chest, his lips moving, but no sound emerging.

"Are you ready to finish the shell that sustained this life?" the first woman asked.

Arthur closed his eyes. "I am ready."

"Is there anything since the last time you merged with the *ka* that you need to tell us?"

Arthur shook his head, knowing his silence would ensure that when his spirit was passed on, there would be no memory of Percival's quest, which would guard the knight for the rest of his life. It was his last thought.

The black blade slammed down into the exposed chest, piercing his heart. The body spasmed once, then was still. The woman stood and placed the blade back in its sheath.

The other woman extended a gloved hand, fist clenched, over the body. The fingers moved, as if crushing something held in it. She spread her fingers and small black droplets, the size of grains of sand, fell onto the king. The droplets hit flesh, armor, and cloth. Where it fell on the latter two, they moved swiftly across the surface until they reached flesh. Where they touched skin, they consumed, boring through and devouring flesh, bone, muscle, everything organic. Within ten seconds nothing was left of the king but his armor.

With no further ceremony, the two swiftly retraced their steps to the craft they had arrived on. It lifted and swiftly accelerated away, disappearing into the storm clouds.

The heavens finally let loose with rain, announcing the arrival with a cacophonous barrage of thunder, lightning playing across the top of the tor. A large bolt struck the high tower of the abbey, shattering stone and mortar, spraying the debris over the remains of the king.

STONEHENGE

The gentle breeze blowing across the Salisbury plain carried the thick smoke produced by wood and burning flesh over the megalithic stones. It also brought the screams of the condemned and the chants of the Druid priests. The sun had set two hours earlier, but the stones were lit in the glow of the burning wicker man. Over fifteen meters high, the skeleton of the effigy was made of two thick logs serving as main supports up through the legs, reaching to the shoulders, from which crossbeams had been fixed with iron spikes. The skin consisted of wicker laced through the outer wooden frame.

Inside the "skin," in a jumble of torsos, limbs and heads, were people. Crammed in so that each could hardly move. Some were upright, others sideways, and others upside down, filling every square meter of the interior.

Around the wicker man's feet were bundles of straw that had just been set on fire, the flames licking up the legs, burning those who filled out the calves and thighs. Their screams of pain mixed with the pleading of those above them, all of which fell on deaf ears as the priests and priestesses who surrounded the wicker man concentrated on their chanting and dancing.

There were four distinct groups surrounding the wicker man, each one oriented on a cardinal direction. To the north they wore yellow robes, signifying air. To the west, blue for water. To the east, green for earth. And to the south, between the wicker man and the mighty stones, they wore red, signifying fire. With the great King Arthur and his foe Mordred newly dead, there was chaos in the land and the Druids had come out of their hiding places to resume their ancient rites.

Those inside the wicker man were all who had received a sentence of death over the course of the past year. Criminals and nonbelievers, and those who had served the king in the local area in suppressing the old religions and collecting taxes. The sentence was being carried out this evening through the purifying flame.

The burning of the condemned was just the beginning of the night's activities. After the flames died down, the Druids would move to the south, to the standing stones. While the Druids now claimed the stones as their holy place, no one gathered around the wicker man really knew who had placed the inner circles of megaliths or why.

There were legends, of course. Of Gods who had ruled a land in the middle of the ocean, a place called Atlantis. Of war among Gods, and how their battles soon became man's. Of priests who came to England from over the sea. Some spoke of sorcerers and magicians moving the massive stones with the power of their minds. Merlin, the counselor of the king, was said to have had something to do with the stones when he was young, hundreds of years earlier. There were even whispers of those who were not human and the Undead walking the Earth, but such talk was mixed with tales of pixies and fairies and other strange creatures. There was even a tale that the center, most massive stones, had been brought up out of the Earth, sprouting like plants at the command of the Gods.

The screams grew louder as the flames rose higher on the wicker man, their volume matched each time by the Druids. Away from the brutal scene, in the darkness, a slight female figure, wrapped in a black cloak with a silver fringe, led a horse pulling a litter on which another, larger cloaked figure was lashed. She stumbled and almost fell, only the support of the horse's bridle keeping her upright. Her cloak was dirty and tattered, her step weary, yet there was no doubt of her determination as she regained her step and pressed forward into the megalithic arrangement, passing the outer ring of stones.

The fiery light of the wicker man fell on the man on the litter. His robe was also worn and bloodstained though he wore armor beneath the cloth. The metal was battered and pierced. His lifeless eyes were staring straight up at the stars.

The complex they passed through had been built in

stages. In the center where they were headed were five pairs of stones arranged in a horseshoe. Each pair consisted of two large upright stones with a lintel stone laid horizontal on top. A slab of micaceous sandstone was placed at the midpoint of the entire complex, to serve as a focal point for worship and an altar for the various local religions that flourished briefly, then were swept under by the weight of the years. Later builders had constructed a second smaller ring around this, using spotted dolomites. And even later, a third encircling ring thirty meters in diameter was built consisting of sandstone blocks called sarsen stones.

The woman led the horse and litter up to the oldest set of stones, an upright pair covered by a lintel stone. She threw back her hood revealing lined skin and gray hair shot through with remaining black. She untied the litter from the horse.

"We waited too long, my love, and we became too noticeable," she whispered to her partner in a language no one else on the face of the planet would have understood. It had not yet really sunk in to her that he could not hear her and never would hear her again.

She noted the orientation of his dead gaze and she too peered upward for a moment searching among the stars. She pointed. "There, my dear Gwalcmai." He had been known as Gawain at Arthur's court and had fought at the Battle of Camlann, where the leaders mortally wounded each other. It was there he had received the wounds that had drained the life from his body.

However, it was not the wounds to his body, or even his death, that frightened her. It was the damage to an artifact he wore on a chain around his neck, underneath the armor. It was shaped in the form of two hands and arms with no body spread upward in worship.

A mighty blow had smashed through the armor and severed the artifact in half. A tremor passed through her body at the sight, and tears she had held in for the week of travel burst forth. An earthquake of fear and sorrow threatened to overwhelm her. She could hear the chanting and see the flickering fire to the north and knew she did not have time to wallow in her pain before the Druids came here to worship what they could not comprehend.

She ran her hands lightly over the surface of the left upright stone, searching. After a moment, she found what she was looking for and pressed her right hand against the spot she had located.

For a moment it seemed as if even the chanting of the Druids and the screams of the dying halted. All was still. Then the outline of a door appeared in the stone. It slid open. She unhooked the litter from the horse and grabbed the two poles. With effort almost beyond the capability of her aged body, she pulled it into the darkness beyond. Freed of its burden and smelling the foul air, the horse bolted away into the darkness. The door immediately shut behind them, the outline disappeared, and all was as it had been.

AVALON

Merlin slowly rowed across the placid water toward the tor. The bottom of the boat grated onto a pebbled beach. He stowed the oars, tied the boat off to a stunted tree, then made his way up the track that wound its way up the hill. He walked as if carrying a great burden, stoop-shouldered and with stiff legs, but all he had in his hands was a long staff of polished wood which he leaned on to aid his climb. His face was hidden in the shadow of an overhanging hood, but a white beard poked out at the bottom.

When he reached the top, he paused, taking in the shattered stone of the abbey. Then he looked all about, at the country that surrounded the lake. Nothing moved under an overcast sky. It was as if the land had been swept clear of man and beast. A gust of cold wind caused the man to pull his robe tighter around his body. Ever since the great battle of Camlann the land had appeared bleak and cold.

He walked to the abbey and through a doorway. The interior was open to the sky, the floor littered with stone blocks from the collapsed roof. With a gnarled hand Merlin reached into the neck of his robe and retrieved a medallion. On the surface of the metal was the image of an eye. He placed it against the front of the small altar where there was an indentation of similar shape. He held the medallion there for several moments, then removed it, sliding it back inside his robe.

He rubbed his hands together as he waited. He started as a door swung open in the wall of the abbey and a figure stepped through, cloaked in brown. He too wore a hood, which he pulled back revealing a lined face adn silver hair. His eyes widened as he recognized the man by the altar.

"Myrddin!"

The old man wearily smiled. "I have not been called that in a long time, Brynn. At the court of Arthur the King they called me Merlin."

"So I have heard," Brynn said.

Merlin looked about. "They would have brought Arthur here."

"He died right there," Brynn pointed toward the nearest stone wall of the abbey.

"And Excalibur?"

"No sorrow?" Brynn folded his arms across his chest. "No sign of grief for the death of your king?"

"I knew he was dead," Merlin said. "I have grieved in private."

"I doubt it."

Merlin straightened, drawing himself up, and despite his worn condition, Brynn took a step backward.

"I did what I did for the land, for the people."

"It did not work," Brynn noted.

"It was better than hiding in a cave with old papers," Merlin snapped.

"Was it?" Brynn didn't wait for an answer. "The land is worse off than it was. Many have died. The Grail was almost lost. The sword too. It is good that you don't consider yourself one of us any longer. You betrayed our order."

"I went beyond our order as must be done at times." Merlin stamped his foot on the tor impatiently. "Our order has watched since the time of Atlantis. We once worshipped the 'Gods.' And when they fought among themselves, many of our people died and Atlantis was destroyed, the survivors scattered. I talked with Arthur many times—he was a Shadow of one of these creatures. He knew much of the great truth."

" 'The great truth'?"

"What do we know?" Merlin asked Brynn. "Do we know where the 'Gods' came from? Why they are here?"

The look on Brynn's face indicated he didn't even understand the questions, never mind wonder about the answers.

Merlin sighed and dropped that line of thought. "Excalibur is more than just a sword. It does other things. And the war will come again. And both sides will want it. And men like me"—Merlin nodded, acknowledging his role in recent events—"will try to use Excalibur also as a symbol. But it is more than a symbol. It has a purpose, a very critical purpose. It is a critical piece, one of several, in a very ancient puzzle."

Brynn waited, listening.

"I am here to make amends," Merlin said.

"And how will you do that?"

"Excalibur must be hidden better than this place."

"I do not—" Brynn began, but Merlin slammed the butt of his staff onto the stone floor.

"Listen to me, Brynn. The sword must be hidden. Since it was brought out, those who you watch now know where it is. We—I— awakened those better left sleeping and they sent forth their Shadows to do war to try to gain the sword and the Grail. Both were hidden for many generations but now this place is no longer safe. You know that or else you would not have sent away the Grail."

"How do you know this?"

"Watchers are so ignorant. I was ignorant, but I have traveled far and seen much. Have you even read some of the papers you guard so closely below? That is what I spent my time doing while I was here."

"I have read those scrolls I can," Brynn argued.

"And the ones you can't read? The ones written in the ancient runes?"

"None can read them."

"I could and can."

"And what do they say?" Brynn asked, interested in spite of himself.

"The decision that demanded that our sole function be merely to watch what transpired was made by a vote at the first Gathering of Watchers. And it was not unanimous. There were those who thought watching wasn't enough and action needed to be taken. That man would be best off if we continued to fight for freedom from the 'gods' and their minions."

"But the vote was to watch," Brynn said simply. "It is the rule of our order."

Merlin sighed in frustration. "But it was a decision made by men. And we are men. We get to change it."

Brynn shook his head. "The order would never change that. And there has not been a Gathering in memory."

"You are ignorant," Merlin said.

"What will you do with the sword?" Brynn turned the subject from things he knew nothing of.

"Take it—and the sheath that contains it—far from here. And hide it well in a place where men—and those who pretend to be men—cannot easily get to it."

"There is no reason for me to believe you," Brynn said as he turned back toward the doorway.

"I was wrong."

Brynn paused.

Merlin continued. "We should not get involved with these creatures and their war among themselves. We do not have the power for that."

"And?" Brynn demanded. "That is the Watcher's credo. To watch. Not to act. Which you violated."

"And that is wrong also," Merlin said. "We must not just watch. We must act. But not in the way I did, trying to imitate these creatures, allying with one side of the other. I thought Arthur—" He shook his head. "I was misled, as the priests of old were. We must keep ourselves separate. Completely separate. And fight them when we have to and when we can do so with a chance of victory."

"What does that have to do with the sword?" Brynn asked.

"It is a thing each side needs in order to win civil war," Merlin said. "And now they know of this place and it is easily accessible. That is why Excalibur must be removed. It must not be found by Aspasia's Shadow or Artad's followers or others, even more evil, who would seek to destroy it."

Brynn's face paled. "The Ancient Enemy?"

Merlin nodded.

"I thought that was just a myth made up by the priests. As the Christians have their Satan opposing their God."

"There is always some truth in every myth," Merlin said.

Brynn ran a hand through his beard, obviously shaken.

"You say it is the rule of the Watchers to only watch," Merlin said. "Then how did Excalibur and the Grail come here in the first place?"

"They have traveled far over the ages. Joseph of Arimathea brought them here for safekeeping from Jerusalem."

"And did he not violate the rules of our order by doing so?"

Brynn reluctantly nodded.

"Then let me right that wrong and remove them from here. Then you can go back to watching."

"Excalibur is safe now," Brynn said with little conviction. "I know that—"

Merlin cut him off. "*They* came here to retrieve Arthur's *ka*, didn't they?"

Brynn slowly nodded. "Yes. The Ones Who Wait."

"Then they know this place. They will be back."

"It is what I fear," Brynn admitted.

"They can always find the sword here," Merlin said, "but I can put it in a place that will be difficult, if not impossible for them or any others to find and bring back."

Brynn frowned. "Where?"

"On the roof of the world."

"Where is this roof?"

"Do not concern yourself with that." Merlin smiled. "You have nothing to fear if the sword isn't here."

This last bit of logic finally came home to rest with the Watcher. "Come." Brynn indicated for Merlin to follow him.

STONEHENGE

Stonehenge was abandoned. Where the wicker man had been, there was only cold ash with a smattering of blackened bone. The Druids had gone back to the hills, hiding from the brigands who now roamed the land, and eking out a living from the countryside. So it had been for centuries, so it continued. The stones had seen many invaders, many worshippers. And they would see more in the future.

The sky was gray and a light rain was falling, blown about by a stiff breeze. In the middle of the megalithic arrangement, the outline of the doorway reappeared on the left standing stone of the center pair. It slid open and one person appeared garbed in black robes. Noting the rain, the figure pulled back her hood. She resembled the woman that had first entered, but fifty years younger. Instead of age withered flesh, her face was smooth and pink. Her hair was coal black. She turned her face upward, allowing the rain to fall on it. The falling water mixed with the rivulet of tears on her face.

Donnchadh had tried and failed as she had feared. Gwalcmai was truly dead. After all the years they had been together. She reached back into the stone and pulled the litter out with the old body tied to it.

Reluctantly, she stepped out of the entryway, dragging the litter, and the door closed behind her, then disappeared. She slowly walked through the stones, onto the plain, pulling his body. She passed the site of the wicker man, sparing it not even a glance, and continued. When she reached a small ridge, just before she was out of sight of Stonehenge, she turned and looked back.

It was dusk and the rain had ceased. She could see the stones in the distance. She felt very, very alone, a slight figure in the midst of a huge plain. She went to a lone oak tree, its branches withered and worn. It was like a living sentinel overlooking the stones. Using a wooden spade, the woman dug into the dirt, carving out a grave. It took her the entire night to get deep enough.

As the first rays of the sun tentatively probed above the eastern horizon, she climbed out of the hole. Her robe was dirty, her dark hair matted with mud, the fresh skin on her palms blistered from the labor.

She took her husband and slid him into the hole she had made. Her hand rested on his cheek for many long minutes before she reluctantly climbed out of the grave. She reached inside her pocket and pulled out the small broken amulet. She stared at it for a while, then reached inside her robe and retrieved a chain holding a similar object, this one undamaged. She added the damaged one to the chain around her neck and held it for a moment, tracing the lines. Then she looked down at her husband and spoke in their native tongue.

"Ten thousand years. I loved you every day of those many years. And I will remember and love you for the next ten thousand."

With tears streaming down her face, Donnchadh threw the first spadeful of dirt into the grave. After an hour she was done. Then she turned to the south for one last task.

Merlin held up his hand and his small party of Watchers halted. A golden craft came racing in low to the ground, directly toward them. Several of the Watchers cried out in alarm and threw themselves to the ground. The craft landed directly in front of them. A hatch on the top opened and two people—a man and a woman—got out along with a third party—someone who was not human. Both humans were armed with long spears and walked down the slope of the craft to the ground, while the alien remained on top.

"I will take the Grail," the woman said as she came to a halt less than a meter away from Merlin. The spear was held in a manner that while not directly threatening, came close.

Merlin hesitated.

"If you do not give it to me, you will die, and I will have it anyway. And you will give me the sword."

"No."

The woman lowered the spear until the point was almost touching Merlin's chest. "Give me the Grail and Excalibur."

There was a cry of alarm from behind the woman. She hesitated, then glanced over her shoulder. Donnchadh was on top of the bouncer, a sword held against the neck of the Airlia. "We will keep the sword," she called out. "You may take the Grail back to Giza and put it in the Hall of Records."

The Ones Who Wait did nothing. Donnchadh pressed the sword into the Airlia's neck.

"*Do as she requests,*" the Airlia called out in its native tongue.

"Give them the Grail," Donnchadh ordered Merlin.

The sorcerer handed over the Grail, still wrapped in the white cloth. Donnchadh held her place as they came back and climbed inside the ship. Then she removed the blade and quickly made her way down the side, joining Merlin. The bouncer lifted and flew away to the south.

"Will they come for me again?" Merlin asked her.

Donnchadh watched as the ship disappeared in the distance. "They might, but I don't think so." She turned to him. "Do as I ordered—take the sword to the roof of the world."

GIZA

The bouncer approached in darkness. It came to a hover near the Great Pyramid and the Airlia and one of the Ones Who Wait exited, the latter helping the wounded alien. They entered the Roads of Rostau and wove their way to the Hall of Records. The Airlia used the scepter to open the Hall and the Grail was placed inside.

They retraced their steps, the Airlia moving even more

slowly. As they exited the Great Pyramid, the Airlia collapsed, its energy spent now that it had accomplished its task. The One Who Waits carried it into the craft.

As the bouncer raced south over Africa, the Airlia died. Arriving at Ngorongoro, they landed the saucer in the crater near the lake and buried the Airlia with the scepter. Then they re-entered the base and went back to doing what they did best: Waiting.

A.D. 535: MOUNT EVEREST

It took six years. From his original company of six, there were only two of Merlin's companions left alive. And they were now slowly dying with him.

They were close to the top of the mountain. They had gone as high as they could go, but their dedication could only carry them so far against the cold, the lack of oxygen and mountain. They lay huddled together on a narrow ledge on the side of the mountain. Slowly one of the Watchers stopped shivering, then the other, as life seeped out of their bodies. Merlin was the last to go, his hands tightly gripping the sword he had carried around the world and up the mountain.

When he died, there was the slightest trace of a smile on his blue lips. He had, for once, succeeded.

ABOUT THE AUTHOR

ROBERT DOHERTY is a pseudonym for a bestselling writer of military suspense novels. He is a West Point graduate and served as a Special Forces A-Team leader before writing full-time. He is also the author of *The Rock, Area 51, Area 51: The Reply, Area 51: The Mission, Area 51: The Sphinx, Area 51: The Grail, Area 51: Excalibur, Area 51: Nosferatu, Psychic Warrior,* and *Psychic Warrior: Project Aura.* For more information go to www.BobMayer.org.